Praise for Cathy Gohlke

Ladies of the Lake

"*Ladies of the Lake* touched my heart as it chronicled the enduring power of lifelong friendships. Her characters came alive on the pages, sharing joys and sorrows, war and tragedy, betrayal, love, and forgiveness. Their deeply forged bonds were beautifully portrayed, reminding me to treasure my own dear friends."

LYNN AUSTIN, bestselling author of *Long Way Home*

"Reading *Ladies of the Lake* is like unwrapping a beautiful present. I savored every page until, with sweet tears, I discovered the most wonderful surprise near the end. Thank you, Cathy Gohlke, for this treasured gift—another redemption story crafted from your heart."

MELANIE DOBSON, award-winning author of *The Winter Rose*

Night Bird Calling

"*Night Bird Calling* . . . interlaces themes of redemption, friendship, and grace, and its depiction of a small Southern town is reminiscent of writings by Lisa Wingate."

Booklist

"A gripping story. . . . Gohlke creates a cast readers will love, and the strong themes of the bonds of family forged outside one's kin resonate. [Her] fans will love this."

Publishers Weekly

The Medallion

"A riveting read from cover to cover, *The Medallion* is one of those extraordinary novels that will linger in the mind and memory long after the book itself is finished."

Midwest Book Reviews

"This is a thought-provoking novel of courage, survival, and unselfish assistance during the Holocaust."

Historical Novel Society

"Cathy Gohlke skillfully weaves true stories of heroism and sacrifice into her novel to create a realistic portrayal of Poland during WWII. *The Medallion* is a stunning story of impossible choices and the enduring power of faith and love."

LYNN AUSTIN, bestselling author of *Long Way Home*

"A master storyteller, Cathy Gohlke has created unforgettable characters in unthinkable circumstances. This story completely undid me, then stitched me back together with hope. A novel that has grabbed my heart—and won't let go—for what I'm sure will be a very long time."

HEIDI CHIAVAROLI, Carol Award–winning author of *The Hidden Side*

Until We Find Home

"Gohlke's powerful historical novel features a suspenseful and heart-wrenching plot and unforgettable characters."

Library Journal, starred review

"Gohlke's latest takes place in England's lush Lake District during the early days of World War II. Readers will likely smile at appearances from various literary icons, such as Beatrix Potter and C. S. Lewis, among others. The story is well researched and well written."

"Splendid at every turn! *Until We Find Home* is a lushly penned novel about a courageous young woman whose definition of love—and trust—is challenged in every way. A must for fans of WWII and British front history. Not to be missed!"

"*Until We Find Home* is a deeply moving war story. . . . Gohlke's well-developed characters, vivid descriptions, and lush setting details immerse readers into the story. All the way to the very last page, readers will be rooting for the unlikely family forged through the hardships of war."

Secrets She Kept

"Cathy Gohlke's *Secrets She Kept* is a page-turner with great pacing and style. She's a terrific writer."

"This well-researched epic depicts life under the Nazi regime with passionate attention. While the Sterling family story serves as a warning about digging into the past, it is also a touching example of the healing power of forgiveness and the rejuvenating power of faith."

"Gripping . . . emotional . . . masterfully told, this is an unforgettable tale of finding family, faith, and love."

Radiant Lit

Saving Amelie

"Moving. . . . At times both emotional and suspenseful, this is a fantastic novel for those who love both historical fiction and human-interest stories."

Romantic Times

"In this compelling and tense novel, Gohlke tells a haunting story of the courageous few who worked tirelessly and at great risk to themselves to save people they did not know. . . . Reminiscent of Tatiana de Rosnay's stirring stories of human compassion and hope, this should appeal to fans of both authors as well as to historical fiction readers."

Library Journal

LADIES OF THE LAKE

ALSO BY CATHY GOHLKE

Ladies of the Lake

a novel

of the

CATHY GOHLKE

Tyndale House Publishers
Carol Stream, Illinois

Visit Tyndale online at tyndale.com.

Visit Cathy Gohlke's website at cathygohlke.com.

Tyndale and Tyndale's quill logo are registered trademarks of Tyndale House Ministries.

Ladies of the Lake

Edited by Sarah Mason Rische

Cover designed by Jacqueline L. Nuñez

Published in association with the literary agency of Natasha Kern Literary Agency, Inc., P.O. Box 1069, White Salmon, WA 98672.

Scripture quotations are taken from the *Holy Bible*, King James Version.

Ladies of the Lake is a work of fiction. Where real people, events, establishments, organizations, or locales appear, they are used fictitiously. All other elements of the novel are drawn from the author's imagination.

For information about special discounts for bulk purchases, please contact Tyndale House Publishers at csresponse@tyndale.com, or call 1-855-277-9400.

Library of Congress Cataloging-in-Publication Data

A catalog record for this book is available from the Library of Congress.

ISBN 978-1-4964-5353-2 (HC)

ISBN 978-1-4964-5354-9 (SC)

Printed in the United States of America

29	28	27	26	25	24	23
7	6	5	4	3	2	1

Prologue

We—Susannah Eudora Calhoun, Ruth Mason Hennessey, Dorothy Marie Belding, and Adelaide Rose MacNeill, hereafter known as the Ladies of the Lake—do solemnly swear this day of our graduation from Lakeside Ladies Academy, July 9 in the year of our Lord 1910, that we shall stick by one another through thick and thin, maintain a healthy correspondence from wherever in the world our paths might wander, and be always at the ready to come to the aid of any sister among us in need. To the best of our ability, we vow to meet here, in this hallowed gazebo, every two years to reclaim and celebrate our sisterhood. Nothing but death will free us from these vows.

Signed, and sealed with pinpricks of our blood,

Susannah Eudora Calhoun
Ruth Mason Hennessey
Dorothy Marie Belding
Adelaide Rose MacNeill

Farmington, Connecticut, July 9, 1910

Chapter One

MAY 1935

It had been easy to set aside the engraved invitation to the July graduation for Lakeside Ladies Academy, less easy to ignore persistent letters from my beloved Bernadette with her daughterly pleas to attend
the "most important event" of her life. Still, I never expected a call
from the United States when Portia summoned me to the phone in
the downstairs hallway.

"Mrs. Murray?"

I recognized the voice on the other end of the line immediately.
My heart leapt to my throat. Seventeen years and nearly eight hundred miles were stripped away. Pulling a lace and linen handkerchief
from my pocket, I wrapped it round the mouthpiece, intent on dis-
guising my voice. Some part of my being thought how clever I was
to consider that in such a moment.

"Mrs. Murray, are you there?"

"Yes."

"Good morning. This is Mrs. Meyer—Headmistress Dorothy Meyer, calling from Connecticut, from Lakeside Ladies Academy."

Mrs. Meyer. Dorothy. Dot—my Dot. I could not respond.

"I—I'm calling on behalf of your daughter, Bernadette."

And then it struck me that the headmistress wouldn't place a long-distance call across the border for anything less than life threatened. "Is Bernadette unwell?"

"No, no, nothing like that. I don't mean to alarm you. Bernadette has asked me to personally invite you to our upcoming graduation. Your daughter has worked diligently these five years and wants so much to share this momentous day with her mother."

"No, Mrs.—" I couldn't say her name.

"Meyer." She paused, as if she thought I'd forgotten. "Mrs. Murray, I realize that it's not my place to pry or push, but Bernadette has expressed that your unwillingness to come into public may be for fear—"

"No, it is not your place." I could barely control the tremor in my voice.

A moment of silence.

"Mrs. Murray, Bernadette carries her own scars, and yet she's worked so hard to override her shyness, to achieve scholastically. She's come out of her shell exponentially and formed close friendships among the girls. They no longer see her scars. They love her spirit, her vitality and caring heart. They love *her*. We all do. She's to be named valedictorian. Please know that we will embrace you as the mother of such a wonderful girl. She's a daughter to be so very proud of."

I loved hearing of Bernadette's accomplishments and friendships. It was why I'd sent her there, what I wanted—needed—for her that I could not give her. Dot's voice sounded unchanged after so many years. If she only knew . . . but she must never know.

"My love to Bernadette, Mrs.—goodbye." While Dot still spoke, I fumbled the receiver toward its cradle, missed, and finally set it into place. Pulling my handkerchief away, I twisted it into knots.

"Is Bernadette all right?" Portia, my longtime housemaid—more friend than maid—stood on the landing, waiting and listening.

I swallowed, pushing away the past, summoning the present, though it sat askew in my brain. "Yes, fine."

"That woman, she wants you to come to the graduation, doesn't she? That's why she called?"

"I'm not going."

"You owe it to Bernadette."

Portia might be my friend, my only friend, but she pushed too hard, and it was at such times I wanted to remind her of her place. Though she would scoff at the notion of "place" as much as I.

I ignored her and walked into the library.

She followed me. "You sent her to that school so she'd come out of herself, grow a life she couldn't grow inside these prison walls. Now she's done it, you should be proud."

"I've always been proud of Bernadette. And our home is not a prison."

"You can wear a veil if you're worried about—"

"Leave off, Portia. This is not your concern."

"Not my concern after looking after the both of you all these years? You've gotten to be like that Miss Haversham woman in that Dickens book you've been reading aloud. You'll keep on till you die like—"

"Portia, please. And it's Havisham."

Portia stopped. I'd insulted her and I was immediately sorry. After a long moment she walked back toward the kitchen, mumbling, "Seems to me you ought to show some of that gumption you're always preaching—and maybe a little respect." The kitchen door swung closed behind her, but I could still hear indecipherable grumbles, pots slammed onto the stove, and dishes dropped, likely chipped, into the sink.

I closed the library door, pressing my back against it, and gritted my teeth. If only I could so easily shut out the memories.

I pulled aside the draperies and threw open every window in the room, determined to usher in the sun.

Spring had finally bloomed in Halifax. The heady scent of lilacs and the tantalizing fragrance of early roses, sweet peas, lilies of the valley, and ivory peonies pierced with scarlet centers poured through open windows. Still chilly enough to warrant a fire once the sun set, but by day I filled the house with the outdoors.

Wrapping a second cardigan over my shoulders, I sat behind my desk and straightened the stack of manuscript pages to edit. I pulled my typewriter front and center. There was work to do this day, and I would not be put off by Dorothy's phone call.

My breath caught.

Dorothy. Dot. Dottie. My dearest friend. Once. Long ago. What would you say if you knew it was really me on the other end of that telephone line, that I wasn't Rosaline Murray after all? That Bernadette is actually . . . No. I wouldn't finish that thought, not even in my mind. But to remember Dot, and with her Ruth and Susannah, the Ladies of the Lake, my years at Lakeside Ladies Academy . . . and all the rest . . . I didn't want to remember, but how could I forget?

~

AUTUMN 1905

Never would I have gone away to school, never would I have met the girls if the storm had not come—that sudden, violent storm between the mainland and Prince Edward Island.

It was only meant to be a day's shopping trip by ferry to Halifax. My parents had intended to return home by nightfall. Wind, rain, and dark came, but they did not. Almost as one life they perished together, just as they'd lived each day.

I was eleven years old and in school the day of the storm. That's what we called it. There was life before the day of the storm, and life after. I attended a two-room school for all the grades in our small community, which meant twenty-three students. Teacher sent us home early when the sky darkened. Looking back, I believe that was irresponsible. We should have remained in the schoolhouse and ridden out the storm together. But the teacher was young and I think not so very bright.

Drenched when I reached home, I built a fire, made myself a spare evening tea, wrote in my journal, and got myself to bed that night. The storm raged until dawn broke. In eleven years, nearly twelve, I'd lived through much foul weather that swept the island. Most times I would not have been afraid. I'd have believed that when the sky darkened, my parents and indeed the ferry would have remained docked in Halifax, determined to wait out the storm, and that ferry and parents would arrive early the next morning. But something in the dark of night told me they wouldn't, that they would never return, that by morning I would be most truly orphaned, and I wondered, *What will I do then?*

Bodies washed up onto the shore of PEI—Prince Edward Island— one at a time, and in twos and threes. I was told a local fisherman identified my parents' bodies before I reached the docks. I never knew who. I still remember finding my mother's red heeled pump washed ashore two days after the storm. She'd been so proud of those shoes. I only ever found the one.

Funerals for victims stretched throughout the week. My half brother, Lemuel, Dad's son born of a first wife who'd died with the baby in birthing their second child, came from Halifax to attend the burials, settle our parents' estate, and sell the house.

The upheaval, the packing of Mother's and Dad's books and the selling and carting away of Mother's pump organ, nearly did me in— so much so that I couldn't even pen the words in my journal, though from the time I learned to write I'd written everything there, each and every night. I remained stoic on the outside, refusing to cry in front of this half brother I little knew, who'd left home ages ago, thirteen years older than I.

Looking back, my imagining that I'd stay on PEI seems naive. I'd believed Lemuel would agree to let me live with my best friend, Eliza Billings, and her family. We'd been inseparable since we were toddlers at church, at school, through summer holidays spent on the shore. To

Eliza's and my astonishment, her parents did not offer, and Lemuel scoffed at my notion of charity.

That was when I first feared he meant for me to leave the island with its craggy hills and dales, its wild winds and rambling woods, its millions of wildflowers in summer and rocky red-sandstone shore that rushed down to the sea. I didn't know if I could live without those things, or without the morning breath of the sea. They were part of all my life, part of me.

I feared then that he meant for me to go and live with him and his wife and infant son in Halifax. I hated the city and I'd only met any of them twice in my life—but the thought had not seemed to enter his mind.

"You'll begin term next week at Lakeside Ladies Academy in Connecticut. It's a good ladies' school with a fine reputation. You should get along well enough."

"Leave Prince Edward Island?" Saying the words aloud brought a rock, more coarse than any that could be found along the shore, to my throat.

"Well, you certainly can't stay here. We've no family left on the island."

"What about the Macneills that run the post office? They're clan."

"They're old," he scoffed, "and they're not Father's MacNeills. They've no obligation."

"But—"

"One small trunk, Adelaide. Rules of dress are strict, and you won't need more. If there is a uniform, I'll arrange with the headmistress to see you're supplied. You'll leave in the morning."

"In the morning? Leave all my things?" *Leave my home—home of my body and home of my heart, my spirit?*

He glanced over the row of dolls on my shelf, the stacks of books beside my bed and baskets of rocks and pine cones in my room, then shook his head in near disgust.

"At least, I must say goodbye to—"

"No one expects that from a girl your age after such an event. I must get back to business in Halifax, and the sooner you're enrolled, the better, the less you'll find yourself behind, though I imagine you may need to repeat a grade to catch up with the other students. PEI doesn't offer much in education." If he'd snorted, he couldn't have sounded more derisive.

Everyone will expect a goodbye and a thank-you for all they've done, all they are to me, and I need to beg them, to plead, please, oh, please write me in faraway Connecticut. A girl my age knows all of that.

But, of course, I never said those things. I walked to my room, my last night in the old house, the home where I was born, where short weeks before my parents had hugged me and kissed me and told me how dearly I was loved. I closed my bedroom door, leaned my back against it, and wept.

Little did I know at that tender age that Lakeside Ladies Academy would be the saving of me—from Lemuel and his coldness, from becoming a ward of the Crown, shunted from family to family, place to place. Little did I know that I would find a home and family there, or that I would one day so violently lose it.

Chapter Two

My twelfth birthday came the day we stepped onto the remaining ferry bound for Halifax. Lemuel never mentioned my special day. I wondered if he knew, or if he knew but didn't care. I watched the red shore until I could see it no more, until the red and white lighthouse faded from view in my swim of tears. Salt tears came to many from the wind, for it was up that day, so I didn't worry what Lemuel thought.

Once we reached Halifax, I dragged my trunk, too heavy to carry, ashore. I'd packed as tightly as possible my few leather-bound treasures—*The Complete Poems of Robert Burns* and novels from the pens of dearest friends whom of course I'd never met. Charles Dickens, Louisa May Alcott, Robert Louis Stevenson. Beside them rested the journals Dad had given me over the years, and fewer clothes. So much was left behind. I wondered if some new girl would live there, would sleep in my cozy quilted bed in my dear old room. I wondered if she'd

9

discover my pine cones and rocks, the feathers of grebes and nightjars and blue jays that I'd collected, and if she'd treasure them, or if her mother would throw them out as so much trash.

Lemuel hoofed from the ferry's dock to the shipping office, carrying one end of my trunk as I carried the other—so fast I could barely keep up. My brother orchestrated arrangements inside while I stood outdoors soaking in the warm September sun, eyes closed, hoping it might thaw my numbness and draw any remaining tears from my body before they shed.

Half an hour later and twice as exasperated, Lemuel pushed through the door, grabbed and shouldered my trunk, and shouted over his shoulder, "Come, Adelaide. There's a ship leaving on the hour. You can still catch it if we run."

A ship? Already? I hadn't set eyes on my sister-in-law or nephew. The plan had been for me to spend the night in their home at the very least. I hurried after Lemuel. Running was nothing new to me, but he fairly flew.

We reached the gangplank shortly before it was taken up. Lemuel carried my trunk to the top, showed the officer my ticket, dropped my trunk, and turned toward me, not quite looking me in the eye. "You'll be fine. Once you reach Boston, you'll take a train to Hartford. From there, someone from the school will meet you. Your train ticket will be waiting at the station under my name. I'll wire ahead."

My head swam, it was all happening so fast. "How will I get from the ship to the train station?"

"Take a cab, for pity's sake!"

As if I'd traveled all my life, as if I had any idea what that meant.

He must have felt my panic for he reached into his breast pocket and pulled out an envelope. "This should cover your needs until I set up an allowance account for you." Still, he did not meet my eyes.

The officer coughed.

"Now go. You're holding up everyone."

"Lemuel!" He wasn't gentle but he was all of Mother and Dad left to me in the world.

"Adelaide." He looked at me then. "You'll be fine. I—I'll write." It pained him to say it. I wondered if he would or if, once rid of me, that would be the end. And then he was gone.

"This way, miss." A too-cheerful porter hefted my trunk. A rope was hooked across the gangway. I don't know what happened outside the ship, if Lemuel waited to see me off, to witness the ship's leaving the harbor—my leaving Nova Scotia perhaps forever. I followed the porter down a darkened hallway, my eyes squinting to adjust themselves to the shock of losing the sun.

The porter opened a cabin door, stowed my trunk at the foot of one of the narrow berths, and waited a moment, his hand in front of him. I didn't understand why. After staring a few moments, he grimaced, as if I'd failed him, too, somehow, then closed the door, leaving me alone.

Lemuel had booked my ticket second class. There were two berths and apparently one had already been taken.

I sat on the edge of my bed, my throat thick for want of water or tea. Or perhaps it was the unshed tears for need of someone's arms around me, those arms now resting in the little cemetery outside the clapboard church on the island. At last, I lay down, drew up my knees, and pulled my coat close.

~

My eyes opened to find an older woman standing over me, frowning, gray tendrils escaping her tightly pulled bun.

I started, not sure if I was dreaming.

"Oh!" she gasped. "I never meant to frighten you, my dear. I'm Mrs. Simmons, Mildred Simmons. We're cabinmates, apparently. And you are?"

I struggled to sit up and moistened my lips. "Adelaide. Adelaide MacNeill."

"What a pretty name for a lovely girl!" She looked as if she meant it. "The last call for second class dining has just gone, and I'm on my way to the dining room. Would you like to join me? I wasn't certain if you'd rather sleep, but it is the last call until breakfast."

I hadn't eaten since morning. Even then, I'd scarcely kept down tea and half a slice of dry toast. Uncertain I could eat, the rumble in my stomach said I might. "Yes, thank you." I slipped my feet to the floor and pushed hair from my eyes. I must have looked a fright, windblown, rumpled, sleepy. Mrs. Simmons didn't seem to mind. "Must I change for dinner? Is this a grand ship?" Mother had once told me that on grand ships people changed their clothing for dinner.

Mrs. Simmons smiled. "There's no need for us to change, but a brush and comb wouldn't come amiss."

I blinked back tears—tears that came too easily since the day of the storm—and fished through my bag. I pulled the ties from my braids and fumbled with knots.

"May I?" Mrs. Simmons offered, palm held out for my hairbrush.

I sniffed, handed it to her, and turned my back so she could brush. I was nearly as tall as she, so it couldn't have been easy for her.

"Your parents must think you a very responsible and grown young lady to send you traveling alone." She brushed so gently.

I shuddered, doing my best to hold back. If only she wouldn't say anything kind!

"Why, you're trembling, child. Are you quite all right?"

"Yes. Yes."

She finished brushing and braided my hair down the middle of my back. "There, now. So much better. Shall we?" She led the way. Never was I so grateful for someone to take charge. Mrs. Simmons wound us through a maze of corridors, up onto one of the decks and through another set of doors to a dining room. I'd never seen a room so big or so many places laid. "Here's the table for our cabin. Two seats left together, how nice."

I listened for sarcasm or condescension in her voice as I'd heard in Lemuel's, but there was none. Thankfully, she asked me nothing more during the meal, other than *Can you feel the ship roll? Do you like the soup? Wasn't that tart lovely?* The others at our table kept to themselves, which suited me.

After dinner we strolled the deck, drinking in the balm of cold night and wind—the breath of the sea. A welcome gift. Mrs. Simmons didn't rush me, though looking back, I think she must have been cold.

We took turns readying ourselves for bed, giving one another privacy. When lights were extinguished and a few moments had passed, she whispered into the dark from across the cabin, "Do you want to talk, my dear?"

Her sympathetic voice opened my floodgates. I told her through choked sobs of the violent storm, of my parents swept overboard in roiling waves, of the recovering of their bodies, of Mother's lone red shoe, their burial, the coming of Lemuel and the selling of our home, the rush to Halifax with no time to say goodbye to my friends or my parents' graves or even one of my old fairy haunts, nor the copse of trees in the glen or the cliff that stood sentinel over the shore. Now I was on my way to the States to a school with people I'd never met, and Lemuel had assured me I'd be found wanting, too stupid from my island upbringing to sit with girls my age.

Mrs. Simmons listened, occasionally sniffing, exclaiming, or whispering "oh" in sympathy, just enough to keep me going. I talked until I was spent, until tears and shudders stopped, and I lay still. Only then did Mrs. Simmons begin to pray aloud.

"Dear God and Father of us all, we come to You tonight heartbroken, grieving the sudden and terrible loss of Adelaide's beloved mother and father. We grieve for the loss of their strong arms about her, for the loss of the home she dearly loved—the home where she was born, felt safe, and had expected to grow to womanhood.

"Now she's on a journey, Lord, into the unknown. Be with her, Father. Let her know Your love and care. Bring others into her life to help her. Remind her daily in tangible ways that she does not travel this life alone. Hold her, guide her, protect her, Father, assuring her often that she is Your precious daughter.

"Thank You for going ahead of us, for assigning our berths in this cabin together on this voyage, Lord. Only You could have orchestrated such a gift for us both. Bless Adelaide with sweet rest this night, and wake her in the morning with the courage and peace only You can give.

"Thank You, Father, for placing this dear girl, my new friend, in my path. Through Jesus Christ our Lord, amen."

"Amen," I whispered so quietly I hoped God heard.

"Good night, my dear."

"Good night, Mrs. Simmons."

❧

I hadn't expected to sleep, but I did, and I didn't dream, at least not that I could remember.

By the time we docked in Boston, Mrs. Simmons had truly taken charge, insisting that she would see me safely onto the train to Hartford. I had no mind to turn her down.

As good as her word, she waited until I'd retrieved my ticket at the window of the New York, New Haven and Hartford Railroad and boarded the train. She explained so many details about travel, writing each one down on a sheet of stationery she retrieved from her bag, for which I was grateful, green as I was and sure to forget with all the newness of everything. Before waving me off she wrote her address on the bottom of the page.

"Now, when you've settled, you must write and tell me all about your new school. I'll want to know what subjects you like best and the names of your new friends. You will make friends quickly. No one can resist wanting to be your friend, Adelaide, and you're sure to find a sympathetic spirit or two if you keep your eyes and heart open and your smile at the ready. Just you mind that."

If I'd had a grandmother or a guardian angel, I would've wanted her to be just like Mrs. Simmons . . . I would have wanted her to *be* Mrs. Simmons.

Leaning out the window, I waved goodbye until the train rounded the bend and I could no longer see her. Sitting by myself felt awkward, so I stared out the window, watching the fields and countryside fly by, then studied the paper in my hand.

With the list Mrs. Simmons had written out, I no longer felt so alone, not so entirely at sea. I leaned my head against the backrest of my seat, sighed, and closed my eyes. Mother's face swam before me with Dad's behind her. I could see Mother's sparkling eyes and dimpled smile, the worry lines in Dad's brow, the graying streaks among the dark of his hair. How I wanted to reach out for them. I knew if I opened my eyes, they'd be gone, so I kept them closed until I must have fallen asleep.

A blast of the whistle woke me as the train lurched to a stop. New passengers boarded, and a man sat opposite me. I turned slightly to stare out the window, not wanting to make conversation, hoping he wouldn't.

I forced myself to imagine Lakeside Ladies Academy. Would there really be a lake? A lake was not the sea, but as Mrs. Simmons had suggested, it might prove something quite wonderful in its own right, magical even. *Magic.* Once I'd believed in magic, in fairies and the wee folk in tales from the old country, but Mother's and Dad's deaths knocked the believing right out of me. I wondered if, as Mrs. Simmons expected, I might find a friend at school—not just any friend, but a best friend. Oh, I hoped so.

—

The train pulled into Hartford Station with a jerk, a sudden stop, and another jerk so that my coat flew from the overhead compartment. The gentleman seated across the aisle caught it before it hit the floor. "Yours, I believe?" He smiled.

"Thank you, sir." Surely I blushed, busying myself collecting my purse and coat.

Compartment doors opened and we all filed down the steps onto the platform.

Lemuel had said someone from the school would meet me at

the station, but I'd no idea who that might be or what they'd look like or where to wait. That old green feeling came back. I refused to cry and thought of Mrs. Simmons and what she'd said to do when uncertain. *"Straighten your shoulders, breathe deeply, say a prayer, and think through your options."*

She'd said to look for someone with a railroad uniform and show them the ticket for my trunk, then ask them to deliver it to the ladies' waiting room, where anyone coming to meet me would surely search for me. Once the porter had my ticket and tipped his hat, I followed a group of ladies who walked purposefully, as if they knew where they were going. Sure enough, they entered a ladies' waiting room.

I found a seat on the far end of a bench. Within a few minutes my trunk was set at my feet by a porter. Half an hour passed, and then an hour. Daylight waned and I began to wonder what I'd do if the waiting room closed, if the train station was locked and I was left alone on the platform.

A few moments later the door blew open and a girl, no older than I, bounded in—a girl with flaming ginger hair all atangle, sparkling green eyes, and a spray of freckles splashed over her nose. She scanned the faces in the room. I sat up straight. When our eyes caught, she grinned something like the Cheshire cat from *Alice's Adventures in Wonderland* and headed straight for me. "MacNeill? Adelaide MacNeill?"

"Yes, yes." I stood, relieved.

She grabbed my hand and shook it heartily. "Dorothy Belding. Call me Dot. Welcome to Lakeside—or Hartford, for now. I'm your Old Girl—at least until tomorrow when as a New Girl, you'll get your official Old Girl."

I'd no notion what she was talking about.

"Is that all you brought?" She glanced at the trunk at my feet.

I nodded, too flummoxed to speak.

"Travel light, do you? Just as well. We're taking Young Clem and he's slow as molasses with a load. We'll make good time." She grabbed one end of my trunk, eyebrows rising at its heft. "Well, come on! If we get going, we'll just make dinner. Beef stew tonight. Mrs. Potts's biscuits rise light as your granny's feather pillow!"

I picked up the other end and hurried after her, thinking that I had no granny now, nor ever that I knew of, except back in Scotland. It hit me then that I'd have to explain to every new girl I met about my parents and their violent end. I shuddered and stumbled on. Dorothy—Dot—walked and talked apace.

Following her down the platform and around the side of the building was one thing, but her accent was new to me, and I wasn't sure I caught every word or its meaning. I'd have understood more if she spoke in French or Gaelic, though Dad rarely spoke the old tongue at home anymore. *Dad, oh, Dad, where are you now when I need you so?*

But there was not a moment to wonder. Dot counted, "One, two, three," and together we swung my trunk up and into the back of a wagon loaded with produce. The driver jumped down and tipped his hat with an "Afternoon, miss. Welcome to Lakeside. Jeremiah Potts, I am. Shoulda let me do that. Looks heavy."

"Not a bit!" Dorothy exclaimed, leaving me no need to answer. But Mr. Potts had a kindly face and a courtly, rustic manner, reminding me of some of the fishermen back home.

He gave me his strong hand to climb aboard behind Dot, who'd scrambled ahead and made a place for us both on an upturned wooden box set against the buckboard's seat and covered with a patchwork quilt.

I'd barely gotten myself situated when the wagon creaked and the horse snorted, plodding forward. *Young Clem. What a funny name for an old horse!* He was chestnut with a crooked cream blaze down his forehead, a black nose, and cream forelock and mane, a friendly-looking sort that didn't appear up to a trot.

Dot hadn't stopped talking. Finally she slowed, and we rolled on in silence a mile or more. Then, "Miss Weston told me your parents died at sea, caught in a storm."

I thought I might choke.

"I'm really sorry. That's awful."

I nodded, unable to speak.

"How are you doing?"

How do you think? But I didn't say it, didn't call her a thoughtless, nosy girl. At last, I responded with an island saying: "I've been better, but it costs more."

It was a little bit of home that tended to put those from away off their kilter, stop their questions. I felt Dot staring at me, speechless, for near a minute before I glanced at her.

Her eyes held sympathy. She didn't ask another question, just sat back. Finally, she spoke, watching only where we'd been. "Adelaide MacNeill, I believe we're gonna be best friends."

Chapter Three

Dot introduced me to the headmistress, Miss Weston, that night after dinner. A kindlier woman I couldn't imagine, but Dot warned me not to let her cupid-bow smile fool me. "She can be an absolute dragon when she's a mind. Walk the straight and narrow and she's true enough, but step out of bounds once and she's on you like a bobcat."

I'd never encountered a bobcat. Still, I think Miss Weston at her worst could hardly have compared to my Old Girl at her best.

On day two, I met Mildred Hammond, my very own "Old Girl." Strange how such a nightmare on two feet could have the same first name as dear Mrs. Simmons.

During the first week of school, older girls who'd attended Lakeside two years or more were assigned one-on-one to younger girls in their first term, ostensibly to welcome us, introduce us round, connect us to activities and buildings, and help our transition into boarding school, especially comforting those who'd never been away from home. The theory was sound, but in truth a few of the Old

Girls, including Mildred, were the dragons, giving cursory tours of the facilities before forcing new and younger girls to serve as something between their ladies-in-waiting and their slaves.

"Carry my books to class, Adelaide . . . Take my dirty smalls to the laundry—you'll find your way, just ask anybody . . . Make my bed before breakfast . . . Save me your slice of cake from dinner—you don't need it; you don't want to grow pudgy." The miserable list grew until the first week ended, by which time New Girls were considered connected and assimilated into the program.

"They say it's good for our souls," lamented Ruth, a second-year girl in my dorm room who sympathized when I came in drenched and heaving with fright after carrying Mildred's books from the library to her dormitory through the dark, the booming thunder, and the striking lightning.

"The only thing that's good for our souls is that we'll one day be Old Girls, too, and can pass the joy along to the next crowd," quipped Susannah, twelve years old, same as me, in a soft, slow drawl—an accent I soon learned came from one of the Carolinas.

"She shouldn't have made you go out in that storm," Dot fumed. "She had to walk that way anyway and she knew better. It was just meanness. She knew your—" Dot stopped when she caught the warning from my eyes and looked away. Color rose in the other girls' cheeks as they studied their bedclothes, their hands. I realized then that Dot had told them about my parents, or someone had.

Angry and humiliated that they'd talked behind my back and knew things about me that I hadn't wanted told, I turned away, shaking out my sopping coat and squelchy shoes. Dot was right; the storm had terrified me and reminded me of how fearful it must have been for Mother and Dad swallowed by the sea that night. At least in the rain it hadn't mattered that I'd screamed and cried. Inside the walls of the school, or outside in daylight, there was no place to mourn, not even the privacy to journal my cries. I desperately needed to grieve.

Behind the dressing screen, hands shaking, I changed into my nightdress.

"Addie?" Dot's voice came soft from the other side of the screen. "Hand me your coat and shoes. I'll lay them by the fire to dry. They'll be warm as toast come morning."

It was a conciliatory gesture, but in my hurt, I wanted to push it away, push Dot away. Who could I trust? Mildred was supposed to be my guardian this first week, but she'd waved me off as if dismissing a servant and smirked wickedly as she'd closed the door in my face, pushing me out into the storm.

"Addie, please."

Dot had given me the nickname my second day on campus. I didn't mind it then. She'd seemed friendly. She still seemed friendly, and heaven knew I needed a friend. But she'd shared my darkest, saddest secret. Still, even teachers might have shared that, or the headmistress, thinking they'd save me heartache by speaking first. Begrudgingly, I handed my sodden coat round the screen, almost daring Dot to take it.

"And your shoes and stockings."

Dot knew from my unpacking that I only had the one pair of stockings. I couldn't risk running out until more could be purchased. There was no going about barelegged at Lakeside Ladies Academy, not like on PEI. "Thank you," I whispered, handing them round.

"You're welcome." I heard the smile in her voice.

By the time I'd tied the neck of my nightdress and climbed into bed, pulling the covers to my chin, chatter in the room had resumed. Ruth did her best to draw me in to the conversation—gossip about the teachers and some of the older girls.

I liked Ruth. She hailed from just north of Halifax so knew something akin to home, though she'd never met my half brother or his family and never set foot on PEI. Ruth seemed straightforward to me. Pretty, with spare freckles, she stood tall, her posture ramrod straight even when sitting on her bed or at table. She took no guff from anybody, nor offered it.

Susannah was tallest of all and rounded in feminine ways before the rest of us. She was everything I'd imagined an American Southern belle to be with her shining gold curls and sparkling blue eyes. Her skin reminded me of a porcelain doll with a peaches and cream complexion. She was very careful to keep from the sun, even when walking to class. But I imagined, from sharp little snipes of the tongue in her Southern drawl, that she could sting with the bite of what she called "the copperheads back home" if she'd wanted. Thankfully, she never bit me.

They were nice, those girls, but of all of them Dot seemed to genuinely care about me.

Susannah lay back on her bed. "You ought to get back at old Mildred."

Dot sat up, inspired. "We should all get back at her. She treated you like dirt last year, Susannah. She's nothing but a bully—a mean one."

"I wouldn't mind a little retaliation." Susannah smiled wickedly.

"Don't make trouble for yourselves on my account," I insisted but breathed a little easier for the camaraderie. It was nice to feel I hadn't been singled out, or at least that I wasn't the only one singled out.

"Be careful," Ruth warned. "Whatever you do, you don't want to get caught or let her know who's behind it. That would make trouble ten times worse."

"Ruth's right," Dot agreed. "We need to think it through, plan carefully."

"I'll dream on it." Susannah yawned. "Inspiration always comes in my dreams."

I smiled, rolled over, and waited for the lights-out. Tomorrow I would write Mrs. Simmons and tell her that at least I'd landed among friends, or girls who might one day become friends.

～

The next morning sunshine broke brilliantly across the campus. It was the last morning of my first week, the last morning I'd have to make Mildred's bed. Susannah encouraged me to spread salt on her sheets or stuff the foot of the bed with evergreen needles. She had even gone out early to gather some.

But Ruth forbade it. "She'll know it was you and that's when she'll retaliate. Mildred Hammond's retaliation is far worse than anything she's put you through so far."

"How do you know?" Susannah challenged. "She's never done anything to you."

"It's her kind—that's how I know. There's human nature and there's nature that's barely human."

"I agree with Ruth." Dot frowned. "Too risky."

They argued as if I weren't there and I left them to it. I just wanted to get the last morning over with. I made it to Mildred's building just before the breakfast bell rang and knocked on the door of her room. Senior girls each had their own room, having aged out of the dormitories.

"You're late!" Mildred accused. "You should have come in time to wake me."

"I thought the maid woke you. The maids wake everybody." The other girls on her floor had already gone.

"Impertinent! I told the girls not to let her wake me since I knew you'd be here. I expected you to keep your promise."

"I never promised. You commanded."

"You little—" But she stopped short of slapping me. "Oh, there's no time. We'll both be late!" She held her arm out to me. "Help me with these buttons."

Obediently I buttoned the long cuffs of her shirtwaist, tempted to leave the three middle ones undone.

"Finish my braid while I dress."

I followed her around the room, braiding hair as she retrieved stockings and shoes. Ruth was right. I needed to be careful. Mildred was cross and I did not doubt her venom. Susannah and Dot were also right. Mildred needed to be taught not to lord over us younger girls.

She fairly threw her books at me, expecting me to run after her, which I did, biting my tongue and not wanting to miss breakfast either, glad beyond words that this was my last day with her.

We'd just entered the dining hall when she grabbed my arm. "Tomorrow you'll be on time, and I expect you to save me your breakfast bun. Saturdays we get sweet rolls. No teeth marks, understood?"

"This is my last day with you." I pulled away, but she jerked me back, digging her fingernails into my arm.

"You will save me your breakfast bun each and every Saturday morning until Christmas. Do you understand, little miss?"

She glowered and stood almost a foot above me so that terror ran through my veins.

"Mildred? Adelaide? Is there a problem?" Miss Weston stood at the far end of the table.

Immediately Mildred released my arm but pinched it from behind. "No, ma'am. I was just explaining to Adelaide that she absolutely must get up on time from now on. She cannot expect me to call her, especially after today."

My eyes must have grown three sizes.

"That's quite correct." Miss Weston frowned. "There are no favorites here, Adelaide, no matter what you might have been accustomed to at home. Punctuality is of the utmost importance. I wouldn't have expected your wholesome island upbringing to beget slovenly ways. If so, we must work to change that." She waited.

Giggles came from girls at the table. Some of the older girls looked down their noses at me. One whispered, "Canadian born. What can you expect?"

"Answer Miss Weston, Adelaide," Mildred ordered, smiling, while digging her fingers into the back of my arm.

"Yes, ma'am. I understand. I'll not be late again." I gritted my teeth to keep from crying out, which made Miss Weston frown further. I must have looked positively grim. She furrowed her brow, lifted her head, nodded, and turned away. More girls snickered.

"Leave my books on the side table in the dining room. After breakfast you may carry them to my class." Mildred spoke quietly, with a condescending smile, as if she were my older sister.

Tears of anger and humiliation welled behind my eyes, but I

refused to let them trickle down my cheeks. I turned away, rubbing my arm, but Mildred said, loud enough to be heard by the rest of the table, "There's no need to cry, little one. You'll do better tomorrow, surely."

Mortified, I reached my seat at the far end of the table. I didn't want to be thought of as a "little one," a child with no upbringing. It smacked not only my cheek but also the faces of my parents, my dead parents. Mother. Dad. The lump in my throat grew as girls stared at me, some in pity and some in scorn.

I'd have cried then and there if Dot hadn't kicked my shin beneath the table. I looked at her sharply across from my place setting; she made a cross-eyed monkey face, the corners of her lips turned up in a perfect monkey smile. It was all I could do not to laugh, and she winked at me.

Ruth mouthed, *"Well done, Addie."* Susannah narrowed her eyes at Mildred.

My breath caught. For all that was tragic and bereft in my life, I was not alone. Friends. Dot, Ruth, Susannah. They gathered round me like the sisters I'd never had, like the angels guarding Eden with flaming swords. Maybe I could learn to wield a flaming sword, too.

Chapter Four

Saturday morning, I did not go to Mildred's dormitory but saved her my sweet roll. I made no teeth marks in it.

Later, Dot said she'd love to have seen Mean Mildred's face when she bit into it and found it coated with salt instead of sugar.

"Try gravel next week," Susannah advised as she set down her final domino, winning a game against Dot, as casually as if remarking on the weather. "Better for her teeth."

With no Saturday afternoon classes, we four linked arms after luncheon and made our way to the picturesque gazebo by the lake on school grounds.

"This is the best spot ever," Susannah declared, stroking the intricately carved gingerbread hanging above us.

"It's beautiful! But, if it's the best spot, then why haven't Mildred and her friends taken it over?"

"Oh, they used to—" Ruth raised her eyebrows—"but on Saturday afternoons the older girls now have permission to go into town for tea and shopping."

"Once they're back, they spend the evening primping and gossiping, not wanting to muss their hair or dresses." Dot scrunched her nose.

"We're not allowed to wear makeup, but they put it on to go into town and then hide in their dormitory or the attic afterward, so Miss Weston won't see." Susannah placed a fist on her hip, thrust forward, and mimicked Mildred: "You children aren't allowed to go out on your own. You must remain on the premises or face dire punishments."

"Then this can be our place," I said in a brave moment of wonder.

"We should give it a name." Dot's brow furrowed in concentration.

"Think Tennyson," remarked Ruth, gazing skyward.

"This is Saturday afternoon!" Susannah rolled her eyes. "Tennyson is the last thing I want to think about!"

"She means," I said, inspired, "what we were just reading in class."

Ruth smiled, not looking at one of us. "Are we not—"

"The Lady of Shalott," I finished.

Ruth hopped onto the bench built along the inside perimeter of the gazebo, thrust her arm toward the lake, and intoned in her most dramatic voice:

"And by the moon the reaper weary,
Piling sheaves in uplands airy,
Listening, whispers, 'Tis the fairy
Lady of Shalott.'

She knows not what the curse may be,
And so she weaveth steadily,
And little other care hath she . . ."

"The Lady of Shalott!" we all shrieked.

27

"We are all Ladies of Shalott!" Susannah gave a dimpled smile and a deep curtsy.

"But she died once she looked out into the world," Dot observed, none too keen.

"Because she was distracted by Lancelot—handsome devil!" Susannah grinned.

"Language, ladies!" Ruth ordered.

"Well, I'm just saying that she was, so that means we must not be . . . distracted by handsome men."

"Never!" insisted Dot.

"Of course not," I agreed.

"Well, now, I don't know . . . ," Susannah mused.

"We, however—" Ruth swept her arm lakeward once more—"will one day go out and conquer the world, despite all the Mean Mildreds and dragons it presents. We are the Ladies of the Lake."

Chills of agreement ran up my arms.

Ruth hopped down. We copied her thrust of right hand to the center of our group and, hand over hand, solemnly vowed, "Ladies of the Lake!"

"All for one and one for all," Dot cried.

"That's the Musketeers," Susannah countered.

"That's the spirit of who and what we are," Ruth led again. "We, the Ladies of the Lake, will always stand for one another, no matter what, come what may—sisters to the last."

"The Ladies of the Lake—sisters to the last." Fervent, we repeated our vow, never imagining one of us would pull back her hand.

Chapter Five

Dorothy Meyer tapped her pencil over the account books. Something didn't add up, but it had nothing to do with the numbers in the columns before her.

Why would a mother refuse to attend her daughter's graduation, especially when that daughter was slated for valedictorian? Bernadette insists that her mother's scars are not that bad, that she wears a veil when going out in public, that she's not the least inhibited at home—in fact, very creative and fun-loving—and yet the woman all but hung up on me on the telephone.

Headmistress of Lakeside Ladies Academy for the last five years, Dorothy Belding Meyer was not accustomed to being told no. She'd never placed an international telephone call to personally invite someone to graduation. She couldn't imagine the expense or how she would justify such preferential treatment if the amount was noted by Mr. Shockley, treasurer of the board, or more likely his wife, the

29

spiteful Mrs. Mean Mildred Shockley—especially now with the school in financial straits.

Rosaline Murray had already received an engraved invitation. That she should decline was unthinkable after sending her daughter to Lakeside for five years. Parents returned from Europe to attend their daughters' graduations. Dignitaries and their wives vied for invitations, even when their own daughters had previously graduated. *Who does she think she is?*

The question had pestered Dorothy for two days. She was still puzzling when a knock came at her office door.

"Come." Dorothy sat up straighter, reclaiming her headmistress posture.

"Mrs. Meyer? May we come in?" Bernadette Murray and her best friend, Josephine, peeked through the partially open door.

"Come in, ladies." Dorothy was not looking forward to this conversation.

"I just wondered if you've heard from my mother." Bernadette's *just* belied the angst Dot observed as the girl twisted her fingers together.

"Perhaps we should have this conversation in private, Bernadette." Dorothy raised her eyebrows toward Josephine.

"Whatever there is to know, I'm glad for Josephine to hear. We have no secrets." Bernadette reached for her friend's hand.

"I'm here for moral support, Mrs. Meyer."

Dorothy nodded. She knew Bernadette would need it. "Very well, ladies. Please sit down."

How to frame this? How to tell her that her mother wouldn't give me the time of day?

"I'm afraid the telephone call was not successful. Perhaps we had a poor connection, but . . ."

"Then could you try again?" Bernadette raised her light-brown eyes in hope.

"What I mean to say, my dear, is that your mother declined. She won't be coming."

Josephine's disapproving frown and protective concern for her friend, who pressed her lips together, touched Dorothy. She'd had just such friends at that age, and she was grateful. She was grateful that Bernadette, now trying very hard not to cry, claimed such a loyal friend. *May they always be so.*

The thought caught Dorothy up short. She knew she had not been that loyal a friend in those long-ago days. Perhaps that was why it meant so much to her now to help Bernadette, to help all the girls in their friendships. Perhaps it could help make up for her own failure . . . if anything could. By all outward appearances, Dorothy was a highly successful and accomplished woman, but as a friend, she knew she'd been found wanting.

"I thought that if you spoke with her, surely she'd . . ." Bernadette didn't finish. "I just don't understand why she won't come. She travels other places, at least sometimes . . . not often."

Dorothy would give anything to comfort the girl and calm her pleading eyes, but what could she say? She didn't understand Rosaline Murray either. She'd never met the woman, only spoken with her on the telephone this once. "I don't know why, Bernadette, but I'm sure she has her reasons. Perhaps one day she'll explain them to you. In the meantime, you know that we're all here to celebrate you. Valedictorian! You've worked hard and should be so very proud."

But Bernadette didn't look proud. She smiled, as if trying to please, but tears clearly welled. Dorothy pressed her own lips together. She could just shake Rosaline Murray—at least someone should shake some sense into the woman. But who, and how?

Chapter Six

OCTOBER 1905

Neither I nor any of the other girls could fathom exactly why Mildred Hammond targeted me for abuse as the weeks went on, but target she did. If Mildred wanted to keep me from forming bonds and friendships among the girls at large, she was successful. No one dared befriend me and come under the vengeful eye of wealthy, well-connected Mildred Hammond . . . none but the Ladies of the Lake, who dug in their heels and raised their proverbial swords, surrounding me with a shield of protection.

I tried to keep to the straight and narrow, avoiding Mildred, but she sought me out, publicly criticizing and humiliating whenever I least expected it, especially in deportment class, in which the older girls mentored us under the eye of an assistant teacher, not much older or wiser than the girls themselves.

"It makes her feel important, superior," Susannah insisted one mid-October Saturday afternoon as we gathered at the gazebo.

"Sometimes I feel like doing that myself . . . not to y'all, of course, but it's a temptation when I don't feel so good about myself, to pick on someone else who is weaker."

"That's ridiculous—it's terrible!" Dot fisted her hands on her hips.

"Of course it's terrible," Susannah agreed, twirling a lock of golden hair. "I'm just saying it's true. It's human nature."

"For some." Dot's eyebrows rose.

"All right, for some," Susannah conceded. "We're not all equally saintly, Miss Belding, I agree." She crossed her eyes and ran a crooked halo round the top of her head with one finger.

"Well, at least this is her last year here. She'll graduate in July, thank goodness."

"I'll have to avoid her as best I can until then—the whole school year! I'm so nervous around her that I'm apt to do silly things—things she'll call me out for. You heard her call me names at table with her friends."

"So, what exactly is a Spud Islander?" Susannah wanted to know.

I shook my head. "Someone from Prince Edward Island, because we grow so many potatoes there. Who knows? Maybe she thinks everyone in Canada grows potatoes."

"But Ruth's from Halifax and Mildred doesn't call her that."

"Mildred has an entire catalog of terms for Canadians. She's just trying to show her smarts and in the process demean us. She called me a 'goon of a Haligoonian.' People living in Halifax are known as Haligonians. A clever play on words," Ruth observed.

"But not amusing," I moaned. "I'm sick of being pointed out. You heard her this noon—just because I'd helped Miss Weston carry that case of tablets to class."

"'Well, if it isn't the little bluenoser,'" Dot mimicked Mean Mildred in a singsong voice.

"And what in the world is a bluenoser?" Susannah slapped her arms against her sides. "It's like she's talking in code!"

"She's just showing off. *Bluenoser* is just what some people call Nova Scotians. It isn't bad or anything—said to come from the dark blue dye of mittens that sailors and fishermen wore in the cold. They'd wipe their noses with their mittens and end up blue . . . or maybe from the cold. It's nothing really, but everybody laughed and turned their backs on me."

"She meant to imply *brownnoser*," Dot explained. "She's just jealous. She knows Miss Weston likes you. Mildred never goes out of her way to help. She thinks it's beneath her. She thinks Miss Weston is beneath her."

"I know what she meant, but I'm sick of the humiliation and snide remarks. My stomach's tied in knots every time I walk into the dining room, not knowing what she'll say or do next. Last week she tripped me when I was carrying a full serving tray. Mrs. Potts was vexed with me for spilling dessert and breaking two goblets, but it wasn't my fault. Mildred's never fair. I'm sick of her!"

"Then, as all for one and one for all, I believe it's time we taught Miss Hammond a lesson. If it's noses she's so concerned with, why don't we see if we can put Mildred's rather out of joint." Ruth, in her quiet and studious way, smiled as if cooking up a plan.

Susannah's eyes lit. Dot grinned. And I felt a first inkling of hope— and fear.

The following Friday, Miss Weston stood after our noon meal and began to speak. I followed the example of all the other girls and placed my knife and fork across my plate.

"Ladies, as many of you know, the last Saturday of October has long been designated for our local Harvest Festival. It is the one night of the term all girls twelve and older join locals, as well as young men from Dartmore, for an evening of festivities."

A whoosh of anticipation and giggles rushed through the dining room. Miss Weston waited for the room to still. "There will, of course, be games and refreshments for younger girls here in the dining room, organized by Miss Blair." Young shoulders slumped but no one dared complain.

"This year's festival will be held once again at the Meyer family's home. There will be late-afternoon hayrides, apple bobbing, an outdoor dinner, and in the evening a bonfire with music and folk dancing. This year we will have the special privilege of a short lecture on the night sky by noted astronomer Mr. Anthony Bunitelli. He expects to bring one of his powerful telescopes so a carefully selected few of the upperclassmen and women might view the constellations through it—a great privilege.

"I know some of you have brought smaller, handheld telescopes from home to use in your astronomy classes. You must be very careful with them, but I think it will add to the delight of all if you are willing to bring your telescopes to the festival and share views of the sky with our local friends and neighbors. Some have likely never seen the moon or stars at such close range. Those willing to share their telescopes must make certain the lenses are clean and that they are carefully packed in their cases. I will take responsibility for your instruments until Mr. Bunitelli's presentation has ended.

"This, as well as the entire festival, should be quite a treat. Let me remind you that it is an honor and privilege for Lakeside Ladies Academy to be invited to the Meyer home. I expect each of you to be at all times on your most ladylike behavior for the sake of your personal safety, your reputation, and that of the academy." She waited. "You are to remain with the group at all times. There is to be no wandering off alone and certainly no visiting with young men outside of the group. Am I understood?"

"Yes, Miss Weston," the girls replied in unison.

"Very well. Those who are going will assemble in front of the library by three o'clock sharp tomorrow afternoon. Mr. Hillbrow and Mr. Potts will meet you in front of the building with wagons. Floors of the wagons will be covered in hay for our hayride, so do not wear your best stockings and please dress warmly. Make certain you thank your drivers for their kindness in transporting you, and thank Mr. and Mrs. Meyer for this invitation. I'll see you all at three. You are dismissed. Enjoy your afternoon, ladies."

"At last!" Dot whispered. "We're finally old enough to go! I've heard about the festival all my life!"

Mildred walked by at that moment and laughed with the girl beside her. "What I can't wait for is to share a telescope with Jonas Meyer! 'Oh, Jonas, do share my telescope. We'll gaze at the stars together!'"

"I'll take his brother, even if he does just come to my nose!" The other girl wiggled her eyebrows.

After they'd passed, Susannah placed a hand on her hip and mimicked the flirtatious girls. Ruth tilted her head, as if considering.

"What?" Susannah took offense at Ruth's funny look.

"Ladies of the Lake," Ruth mused, the hint of a smile on her lips, "I have a plan. Meet me at the gazebo."

Ruth was the only one among us with a telescope, the only one taking astronomy class. She carefully packed her instrument in its case but did not add it to the collection overseen by Miss Weston. She carried it in a special pocket she'd sewn into the lining of her coat.

We followed Dot's lead and huddled together in the corner nearest the wagon seat behind Mr. Potts, hoping that our intended guilt wasn't written on our faces.

"We'll be out of the wind here and can keep an eye on everyone." Dot, born and raised on the farm adjoining the Meyer land before attending Lakeside Ladies Academy, was better acquainted with the ways of wagons and horses than most of the girls. She didn't care to mention her background in the company of girls like Mildred, who came from Washington, DC, or those whose parents lived abroad in diplomatic service, served in some government capacity, or worked in big business. Having lived on the receiving end of abuse from Mean Mildred and her friends just because I was an island girl and Canadian born, I understood.

Miss Briarcliff, the music teacher, started us singing—old favorites, rounds, and finally harvest songs. Mr. Potts joined in with a fine baritone. By the time we reached the Meyer home, we sallied forth in good form and high spirits.

Three more wagons decked in hay stood at the ready. Boys from Dartmore and teens from the local village swarmed onto them, and we began a slow trek off the main road by way of a trail through the woods.

Canopies of scarlet, flaming orange, yellow, russet, and gold filtered dappled sunlight and shadow across upturned faces as we bumped along the rutted path. I closed my eyes and breathed, drawing in autumn scents of damp earth, sweet hay, and the frosty air of the afternoon's departing sun.

All the scents and friends were different, but somehow the moment took me back to PEI in autumn. To late-afternoon hayrides after we'd all worked hard to harvest a field of potatoes and the bonfires that cooked our supper—potatoes in their jackets roasted in ashes until we burst them open and smothered the white flesh in sweet butter and salt. The fragrance of apple butter simmering in outdoor vats for hours is one I'll never forget. I'd huddled with Eliza, my long-ago best friend, while the old folks told ghost stories in the shadows of the last smoldering flames.

This hayride, with its glad shouts, singsongs, and hay tosses from wagon to wagon ended all too soon. New scents, aromas made more tantalizing by the open air, drew us to the manicured back garden edging a meadow behind the Meyers' home, alive with lanterns that flamed and breathed like fireflies in the gentle breeze.

Local ladies, directed by Mrs. Meyer, loaded gingham-covered tables made of sawhorses and boards with platters of roasted pork, barbecued beef, and succulent chicken, then piled on pots of tangy brown beans, rounds of brown bread, cinnamon stewed apples, and crocks of apple butter and sweet butter until the boards groaned. Apple pies, pumpkin pies, pumpkin muffins, pumpkin *everything* along with cold apple cider, freshly pressed, rounded out the meal. We piled our plates high and dug in as if half starved. Some of the boys went back for second and third helpings. By the time we were nearly finished, dusk had fled and dark night set in.

"I'm ready to pop!" Susannah lamented, eyeing the last bite of apple pie on her plate.

"Stop eating so much!" Ruth admonished.

"But it's so good!"

Older girls and boys had begun to pair off on the hayrides, but younger ones mingled in their own small groups, shyly at first, over dessert and new cups of hot cider, meant to stave off the evening chill.

Miss Weston, pretty in her crimson woolen muffler, clapped her hands. "May I have your attention, please. Mr. Bunitelli has graciously offered to give us a lesson on the heavenly bodies of the night sky. To see well, we will need to walk away from the fire. We'll take two lanterns into the meadow to guide our way but will turn them down when Mr. Bunitelli is ready to begin. We'll pass out the telescopes we've brought with us to share and will collect them after the viewing. May I have a volunteer or two from among the young men to carry our boxes?"

Ruth elbowed me in the ribs.

I gave her a worried smile, still uncertain this was a good idea. "If she figures out who—"

"She won't." Dot linked my arm with hers and walked us steadily toward the field. The entire group pulled close together, keeping out the cold and increasing the excitement.

Lanterns were shuttered and Mr. Bunitelli gave a fascinating lecture—not long, but enough to whet our appetites for the star-filled heavens above. We saw two shooting stars streak across the sky, even as he spoke.

"Now, Miss Weston, for the telescopes, if some of the young gentlemen will be so kind as to distribute them." Anticipation sent shivers through the group. Jonas Meyer and his younger brother, Stephen, whose parents hosted, stepped up to distribute the instruments.

I inhaled the night. The deepening cold, the black sky alive with stars dancing in their heavens—it was all akin to a dream.

Ruth inched toward Mildred, who'd giggled and flirted as openly as any girl dared with Jonas Meyer.

"Here." Ruth held out her hand to Stephen. "I can distribute a couple. Let me help." Exactly how many handheld telescopes Stephen placed into Ruth's waiting hands I could not see, given how dark it was. But I knew that by the time she reached Mildred, she would pull one more from the pocket lining the inside of her coat.

It was so dark I doubted Mildred knew who handed her a telescope. She was simply giddy, focused on Jonas's return to her side.

A half hour must have passed in which we took turns with the instruments, enthralled with identifying stars and planets that looked so close and real through the best telescopes that it felt as if we might touch them. The heavens alone were such a wonder that I didn't even mind not being one of those chosen to view through Mr. Bunitelli's instrument.

Standing in that field reminded me again of home and the sky above the shore on a cloudless, windless night. Millions of points of light, more than I could ever count, had become my friends and confidants. Stars scrolled across the heavens, whose names I didn't know, shouted *Magnificent*. I wondered if Mother and Dad could see them, if heaven resided among them, if one day I'd know for myself.

"It's getting late, ladies, and we need to make our way back to the academy." Miss Weston broke the spell. "Now, carefully wrap your instruments in the velvet bags and pass them to the person to your left. They'll be collected here and returned to their proper owners tomorrow. On your way to our wagons please thank Mr. and Mrs. Meyer for this wonderful evening." Shutters on the lanterns were lifted and wicks turned up. "Thank you, Mr. Bunitelli, for this most instructive and enthralling evening."

We all clapped heartily while Ruth inched her way nearer Mildred once more, ready to accept her telescope. Mildred was too busy threading her arm through Jonas's to notice Ruth.

By the time we'd all walked back and gathered round the fire for one last song and grateful goodbyes, several of the boys from Dartmore had developed a bad case of snickers and raised eyebrows, all directed toward Mildred, who didn't seem to catch on until Jonas unthreaded her arm from his and stood back, clearly embarrassed.

By that time some of the girls from the academy giggled. Some turned away, pretending not to see. The twitters drew Miss Weston's attention and even she seemed challenged to control the upturn at the corners of her lips, a gloved hand to her mouth.

Finally, Mildred realized that the joke was on her, though the confusion in her eyes showed she had no clue what it was. "What is it? What are you staring at?"

"Quite a shiner you've got there, Miss—Miss . . . ?" one of the boys observed.

"I beg your pardon?" Mildred huffed.

That's when the laughter broke out in earnest. Some of the younger boys doubled over.

"What a stupid thing to say, you little snot. What are you talking about?" Mildred turned angry and demanding. But it was the disapproving look in Jonas's eyes at her outburst that undid her.

"Mildred." Miss Weston walked forward. "I can help you, dear. Come with me."

Mildred jerked back, not wanting to be led away by a teacher in front of Jonas or the others but looking every second more like a petulant child. "I don't need your help."

Stephen Meyer couldn't seem to stow his grin. He circled his eye with his finger to indicate the smudged but distinctive black circle around Mildred's eye. "Give a look in the mirror when you get back. You look a little like the raccoon behind our shed—well, half a coon." That was all it took. The entire group erupted in gales of laughter, which sent Mildred into a tizzy and caused Mrs. Meyer to grab Stephen's ear.

How Ruth was able to keep a straight face, I didn't know. I bit my lip and Dot looked at her shoes. Susannah needed to wipe the smug look off her face, but it was too late. The light in Stephen's eyes, despite the twist his mother gave his ear, told me he knew the culprits. His wink when his eyes met mine, which made the heat rush up my face, confirmed it. I turned away, certain Mildred would peg us.

The Dartmore boys, groomed as gentlemen, escorted the girls to our wagons and held out their hands to help us up. Even in the dark, I knew my face flamed at the idea of touching a boy's hand.

Stephen Meyer, who knew Dot from childhood and their adjoining farms, stepped up to us and offered his hand. As he helped Ruth into the wagon, he whispered, "Not sure how you girls pulled that one off, but well done. She's a bossy old thing. A little egg on her face won't hurt."

"Won't hurt a bit, I declare," Mr. Potts chuckled, gathering the reins in his hands.

I gasped, certain if it was so plain to them, we were done for, but Dot laughed, enjoying Stephen's near pun.

"Never worry." Stephen grinned and pressed my hand, looking into my eyes. "Your secret's safe with me."

"And me," confided Mr. Potts, to no one in particular.

Chapter Seven

MAY 1935

Dot, Ruth, Susannah, Stephen, Jonas, even our archenemy, Mean Mildred . . . what memories! What mischief we four girls conspired in together. We stuck with each other through thick and thin . . . at least then.

I tugged off the sleeves of my cardigan. The morning had passed; the day grew warm.

Portia knocked on the door as she entered the library. "Thought we might eat in the garden. First day warm enough to lunch out there."

"That's a wonderful plan, Portia. I'll help. What do we have in the cupboard?" I wanted to mend fences with my friend. I hated when she thought ill of me, that she believed I did wrong by Bernadette. I never wanted to hurt my daughter. She'd been hurt enough in life.

"Everything's ready. You can help carry out."

"Perfect." I stood, smiling. Portia didn't look back but turned on her heel and headed for the kitchen. I followed her down the hallway, into the kitchen, and picked up the tray she'd prepared. Still, Portia didn't look at me but busied herself pouring boiling water over the tea leaves. Her mouth remained grim—not unkind but sitting in enough judgment that I knew she nursed something in her mind.

More than anything I wanted to confide in her. Telling Portia the truth would relieve such a burden. But how could I? The outing of my secrets would hurt her now, nearly as much as they would hurt Bernadette. The lies had been needful years ago, a saving grace for Bernadette, for me. All these years later their unraveling would convince Portia that I hadn't trusted her, that she could not trust me. Devastating. I might lose Bernadette and would surely lose Portia. They'd never understand. Even losing Dot could not compare to that. Dot and Stephen . . . No. I couldn't, wouldn't think of them together. All I had, all I could possibly grasp, was this moment, this day.

Beneath the leafing maple, Portia had spread the damask cloth across the garden table, topping it with a vase of pale-pink peonies and setting it with the best china. My throat swelled. "Thank you, Portia. This is lovely."

Portia looked at me, her grimace fading. "What you do or don't do is your business. Now, I know that. And you know there's nobody left on this earth I care more about than you and Bernadette and my Silas, but I've got to say my piece. I think you're doing wrong by her. I believe you know that just as well as I do, and I don't understand why you're so stubborn when you love her more than you love your own life."

I wondered in that moment if diminished was how I'd feel standing before the judgment seat of God. Was Portia practice for that? The Almighty already knew everything about me and yet somehow, I believed He'd ask the same question. What could I tell Him? What could I tell Portia? The truth? It was all so convoluted I wasn't even sure I knew the answers anymore.

"You've got nothing to say?"

I breathed in the fragrance of peonies, hoping they'd give me answers.

"Well?"

"No."

She turned away.

"Not yet. But—"

"When? When you're done breaking that girl's heart? Because I can't wait that long, Rosaline, and neither can she. I won't be here much longer. Once Silas and I marry, you'll be on your own. If you don't make an effort for Bernadette—"

"I can't go." I pleaded with my eyes.

"You surely can. You can get on that train just like anybody else. I'd go with you if it would help, but we both know it wouldn't."

There was no more to say, not then.

"Tell me you'll think on it. For Bernadette's sake."

Portia's picture-book luncheon sat, growing cold.

"Well?"

I sighed. She'd not leave off. "Yes. All right. I'll think on it."

Portia's eyes softened. Her smile returned. "Whatever it is, whatever's got you so scared, I'll understand. The Lord already knows. You know He does, and He loves you, and I'll be here. I'll help you through, friend, just like always."

I squeezed her hand. She meant what she said, but I couldn't believe it.

⌣

There was no use working on my story edits that afternoon. My mind could no more enter a fictional world than it was able to flee the real one. When Portia climbed the stairs to take a rest, I closed the library door, picked up the nearest book at hand, and pretended to read by the open window. But all I did was remember.

~

NOVEMBER 1905

Miss Weston never asked about the telescope and we, the Ladies of the Lake, never confessed. Mildred fumed as if every girl in the school sat behind her humiliation. She couldn't leave it alone.

She whined in the dining room that it had been the most humiliating event of her life, then all but swore that whoever'd pulled such a trick was green with envy over her relationship with Jonas Meyer.

"As if there is any relationship!" Susannah rolled her eyes.

"What did you say, you little snippet?" Mildred demanded.

"Ladies!" Miss Weston admonished.

But Dot mused aloud, "It was a shame. But did you see the way he looked at you, Mildred? You don't suppose it could have been Jonas himself that did it, do you, playing you along all that time?"

Eyes around the room, including Mildred's, widened at the suggestion—at the audacity of the suggestion. Napkins flew to mouths to hide dread of Mildred and the absolute mirth of the idea. Mildred's color flew up her neck in a moment, from peach to persimmon. "How dare you! You'll pay for that—I swear it."

I kicked Dot under the table, but it was too late. The dining room was in hysterics.

"Ladies! *Ladies!*" Miss Weston rose from her chair, clapping her hands for attention. "I will hear no more of this. Girls, you must not tease. Mildred, you must simply rise above this, knowing you are better than the embarrassment. It may have been a random joke, aimed at no one in particular. Assume it was simply that and do not take it personally. There is no reason to imagine anything different."

"But Miss Weston—" Mildred, deeply offended, pleaded.

"I will hear no more. Now, ladies, finish your meal in silence."

I lifted my eyes to those of my friends. Ruth's were glued to her soup, the hint of a smile across her lips.

No matter what Miss Weston said, it wasn't the end of the story. Mildred stormed a rampage, grilling younger girls and even accusing her own friends. Finally, she settled on Dot and me—perhaps for what Dot had said and because we were both easy targets. Maybe just because she still considered me her New Girl and felt ownership.

Dot was looked down upon by some of the older girls for coming from a farm, her tuition paid in part by her grandmother in Boston, though no one was supposed to know whose tuition was paid by their immediate family and whose was sponsored. I was considered an outsider, an island girl and an orphan with the reputation of an orphan, not much better than a British Home Child, no matter that mere months ago I'd had parents who loved me, the same as any one of them. Ironically, Mildred never suspected Ruth.

Day after day we found something new—homework taken from our notebooks; my art project, left to dry overnight, splattered with ink the next day; the sheets of our beds soaked just before bedtime, made to look as if we'd wet the bed. There seemed no end to her attacks and yet we could never catch her in the act.

"Humiliation is a powerful thing," Ruth considered when we met in the gazebo, "but clearly not strong enough to stop her retaliation."

"She needs to be afraid of us." Susannah twirled a lock of her hair.

"Not a chance," Dot sighed. "What's to fear?"

"Fear itself," Ruth mused.

I'd become intrigued by Ruth's musings, but wary. So much went on behind her quiet, studious nature.

"Addie, what are you doing for your recitation next week?"

"*The Highwayman* by Alfred Noyes. I've already asked Miss Weston's permission. It's thrilling and ghostly and so very dramatic. Perfect for a cold November night."

"Excellent. Dot, Susannah, what about you?"

"We're not on for this month. We recite in December. It's just you and Addie from our form."

"Well then, I guess it's up to me." Ruth smiled and I believe the others felt the same shiver I did. "I'll ask Miss Weston if I can surprise her with my recitation and go last. It might be well to leave the group with two stark poems likely to stir the imagination come midnight."

"What are you cooking up, Ruth? Something delicious, I presume?" Susannah tilted her head.

"I'm thinking that a little tapping, a bit of rapping at Mildred's chamber door might be in order."

"Poe?" I asked.

Ruth smiled. "Edgar Allan."

"Do tell." Susannah grinned.

We huddled closer.

⌣

Dot borrowed the metal nut and fishing line from Mr. Potts's toolshed outside Young Clem's stable. Susannah, whom no one would have imagined a tree climber, faked a stomachache at dinner to be excused from the dining room and later told us how she'd scurried up the maple outside the senior girls' housing. In the meantime, the rest of us kept innocent faces over beef stew and Mrs. Potts's melt-in-your-mouth biscuits. Susannah attached the fishing line and nut to dangle outside the windowpane of Mildred's room, then threaded the long end of the line through the leafless boughs of the maple.

After dinner we gathered in the assembly room for our monthly Saturday night program—recitations or tableaus or comedy skits or debates, whatever our teachers had assigned. The first form girls created tableaus of the first Thanksgiving feast. Third form girls put on a skit inspired by Longfellow's Hiawatha. At last, it was time for second form. Two girls recited ahead of us. For the life of me I could not tell you what they said. I was that nervous.

My turn came for *The Highwayman*. I poured every ounce of dramatic flair I possessed into the poem, tossing the moon as a ghostly galleon upon cloudy seas, weaving the road in a ribbon of moonlight, brandishing my rapier to the sky, and finally grasping the bunch of lace at my throat once the highwayman was shot down like a dog— like a dog to die on the highway.

Silence followed my recitation, then an expansion of held breath. Cheers and clapping swept through the students and Miss Weston looked proud enough to cry. If ever I felt a part of something at Lakeside Ladies Academy, it was in that moment. I almost regretted what we were about to do.

Ruth recited last, *The Raven* by Edgar Allan Poe. Among the four of us, Ruth was the genius. Intellectual, studious, a scientist and engineer by nature, she also possessed the uncanny ability to quietly convince. From the moment she began, "Once upon a midnight dreary . . . ," we each sat alone in that darkened room, ghastly images from Poe's ghosts stretching their limbs against the far wall in the waning firelight, the flickering lamplight. We each heard the barely perceptible rapping, rapping at a time no mortal should walk. We observed the wretched bird perched above our chamber door with its doomed and chilling message, "Nevermore."

Tension mounted. Electric currents passed from girl to girl, rais- ing the very hairs on our arms. Each time Ruth whispered, "Quoth the Raven," we whispered, breathless, in return, "Nevermore." We leaned forward in our seats, nerves stretched taut like springs of clocks wound too tight.

By the time Ruth screamed, pleading, "Take thy beak from out my heart, and take thy form from off my door!" we were ready to swoon or race from the room. When the poem finally ended on a note so sinister and low that we had to lean forward to hear, we were spent and terri- fied to walk across the campus to our dormitory houses in the dark.

"That was quite a recitation." Miss Weston, nervous fingers at her throat, congratulated Ruth on our way out the door.

"Thank you, Miss Weston. I hope so."

We followed Ruth to the second-form house, readied ourselves for bed as quickly as possible—clothes beneath our nightgowns—and had the lights out before the dormitory monitor came through.

We waited until the downstairs clock bonged eleven thirty, then crept from our beds, tied the knotted rope, which Dot had also procured from Mr. Potts's shed, to the nearest bedstead, and raised the window ever so gently.

"Sure y'all don't want me to go?" Susannah offered. "I'm the fastest tree climber."

"No. You and Ruth have done enough. It's our necks we're risking now, and should be." I was firm about that. "Just be ready with the rope when we return."

"Right," Dot agreed, tying the rope around my waist and pulling it up beneath my armpits. "Equal shares."

The girls helped me out the window. I went down slowly. Dot followed. The rope went up a final time and the window closed.

We made our way through the shadows, hard-pressed not to let our imaginations run wild amid the wind-tossed branches in the near moonless night. By the time we reached the tree outside Mildred's window, we were freezing, our fingers so cold we could barely grasp the lower limbs to climb.

Once up in the tree, we waited for the school tower clock to bong midnight.

Dot handed me the fishing line. "You should have the first go. Remember, Ruth said gently at first, but rhythmically."

I didn't need to be reminded. I needed nerve.

"Just think of all the nasty things she's said and done. You won't regret this."

I wasn't sure about that, but I did gently tug the line until the nut tapped against the window once, twice, three times, then paused. I waited twenty seconds—we counted them beneath our breath, frosty in the night air—then tapped again. We must have done this ten times.

"She must sleep like the dead," Dot whispered, blowing on her hands. "Let me try." Dot tugged a little harder, sending a louder ping against the windowpane. Not long after, a lamp lit inside the room. The curtain was half closed, but we could see a form rise from the bed. We pulled the nut back, higher, so it couldn't be seen if she looked out the window, and waited. A minute passed.

Mildred peered through the window. We were well hidden in the limbs of the tree, higher than her point of view. She raised the window and stuck her head outside, looking toward but not seeing us in the tree limbs. It could have been a limb scraping the window, only no limb was near. She ran her hands up her arms, as if shivering, then abruptly closed the window and pulled the curtains tightly closed.

We waited, perhaps twenty seconds, then lowered the nut, swinging it against the pane one, two, three times before drawing it up.

A light went on in the next room. Another form rose from a bed. Two shadows appeared against the curtain in Mildred's room. It was all Dot and I could do to stifle our giggles. Marissa, Mildred's cohort, pushed the curtains aside and raised the window. We held our breath.

"There's no one there. You must have been dreaming. You woke me up for a dream!"

"It was no dream, I tell you. Someone's out there! Tapping—rapping!"

"And flying through the night on a broomstick, no doubt. You're letting Ruth's recitation get to you. Now go to sleep and don't wake me up again!" The window slammed shut.

If we hadn't held each other, I think Dot and I would have fallen out of the tree laughing.

We waited until all the lights went out, then waited another minute, and began again, tap, tap, tapping. Half a minute passed, and we did it again, then again. Pretty soon we were doing it nearly nonstop.

That's when we heard Mildred's piercing scream. Her light came on again, then the hallway lights and finally the downstairs light of the dormitory monitor. Pretty soon there were several shadowed forms in Mildred's room. The dormitory monitor pushed back the curtains, raised the window, and peered out. Dot and I leaned back against the tree trunk.

"There's nothing there, Mildred. You're simply hysterical."

"There is, I tell you! It won't stop rapping."

"Maybe the raven's out to get you!" one of the girls in the background chided.

"Stop it! Stop it!" Mildred was white as the sheets on our bed.

"Get some flashlights, girls," the dormitory monitor ordered. "We'll search the grounds around the house, but you must each go out with a partner and stay together."

Dot gasped. "We've got to get out of here. Pull the line in."

I tried, but it wouldn't budge. I tried again, and again. Dot pulled, but it was no use. "Susannah must have nailed the thing down."

"We've got to go! Cut it loose."

"I can't. I didn't bring a scissors or knife."

The front door of the dormitory house opened. Dot scurried down the tree, and I jumped from the lowest branch, nearly on top of her. "Run!" she whispered hoarsely.

We ran and ran, out through the back garden and through the wooded copse that separated the buildings.

"There! I see someone!" one of the girls called behind us, but we were farther ahead, separated among the trees, weaving together once we reached the hedge surrounding our dormitory.

Ruth and Susannah must have been listening at the window, for they let the rope down in a flash. I pulled it over Dot's head and beneath her armpits. She was lightest and they could pull her up quickly. "Hurry! Hurry!"

The rope came down a second time and I settled it beneath my armpits. "Pull!" I begged, and my three friends pulled with all their might. I found footholds in the stonework, finally scrambling over the windowsill as a pounding of feet and wild swings of light rounded the building. Ruth silently pulled the window closed and drew the curtains.

We scrambled into our nightclothes and stuffed our shoes and coats beneath our beds. If anyone touched our hands or faces, they'd know we'd been out in the frigid night air, but we faked the sleep of the dead for all we were worth.

Voices swelled from downstairs and up the hall staircase. Multiple sets of footsteps and shushing by our own dormitory monitor bumped along the corridor, then quiet turnings of doorknobs. Finally came the squeak of our door being opened. I kept my eyes closed and breathing even. Footsteps crossed the room. I moaned and turned over, as if disturbed in my sleep, burying my icy hands beneath the covers.

"What did I tell you? It's not my girls. That Mildred is a hysteric. Now go on with you all and let me get some sleep!" Our dormitory monitor whispered but was not pleased. At last, the door closed. Footsteps receded down the hallway and down the stairs. The front door opened and closed. We heaved a collective sigh of relief—and stuffed our covers in our mouths to keep from guffawing aloud.

∼

A week of peace without Mildred so much as seen in the dining room passed before Miss Weston called Dot, Ruth, Susannah, and me into her office and closed the door. She did not ask us to sit down but took her seat behind her desk, looking very much like a tribunal judge.

"Mildred Hammond . . ." Our headmistress's mouth turned grim.

I dared not look at the others but knew my eyes went wide.

"Mildred Hammond has been in a state of hysterics since Saturday evening when there came a mysterious rapping at her chamber window . . . reminiscent of the dramatic recitation given during our Saturday night program. In fact, as I recall, two recitations from your form that night ranked as spine-chilling, particularly yours, Ruth. Do you have anything to say?"

Ruth straightened her shoulders and stepped forward. "Perhaps Mildred's imagination is overactive?" She stepped back into line.

"Someone's imagination is certainly active." Miss Weston's fingers drummed her desk.

We held a collective breath.

Miss Weston sighed. "I am not unsympathetic to your plight, ladies. I know the older girls—Mildred in particular—can be difficult at times."

"Cruel," Dot said.

Miss Weston's brows shot up. "However, these back-and-forth pranks have gone too far. Mildred's nerves can take no more. She's convinced that someone or something has come to haunt her. She's taken to her bed for the week."

If I sighed aloud in relief, I didn't mean to, but Miss Weston shot me a glare that said I had.

"She has contacted her parents, asking to be withdrawn from the school, despite this being her final year. Do you understand what that means?"

"She won't graduate." Susannah spoke up, but there was no sympathy in her voice.

"That is correct, and that would be a crime, given the several years she's lived and studied here. The inability to graduate due to a state of nerves will do her prospects in life no good, no matter what path she chooses. I don't believe that any one of you would be so *cruel* as to want that."

Though I felt certain Mildred was faking her paranoia, I could not let my friends take the blame for what I'd done, for what had been done on my behalf. "Miss Weston, I take full responsibility for—"

"I am not asking for a personal confession, Adelaide. I do believe you will all do well to spend more time in thought and prayer. More attention to your Bible readings and to every passage encouraging love for God and holding others in honor greater than yourselves will do you good. This entire affair puts Lakeside Ladies Academy in a very poor light as well as possible financial straits."

We studied our shoes.

"Do you want us to make up her tuition?" Dot asked. "I'm not sure how—"

"No, although Mildred's withdrawal will certainly mean that her family's patronage, which is considerable, will also be withdrawn . . . patronage that Lakeside Ladies Academy can scarcely do without."

We waited, glancing at one another, uncertain what Miss Weston wanted if not a confession or money.

"Are we to be expelled?" Ruth, ever the one to get to the point, asked with only a slight quiver in her voice.

"No. But you are all under disciplinary restrictions. No walking into town with your class for birthday gatherings, no horseback riding on Saturdays, no sweets for a month. I need your guarantee that nothing like this will happen in the future. These petty wars must end."

"Yes, ma'am," we said, as one voice.

"Miss Weston?" Susannah stepped forward.

"Yes?"

"Will our guarantee convince Mildred to stay?"

"I don't know. That will be up to her parents."

"It's just that . . ."

"Fear of retribution?"

Susannah nodded.

"I will personally see that Mildred has no contact with any of you for the remainder of the school year."

"Thank you, Miss Weston."

If the headmistress could spread her mouth into a flatter, more disapproving grimace, I couldn't see how. "Now, back to class."

We filed out, knowing we'd escaped more easily than we had a right to, but thankful beyond words that our bully would either leave or be put on notice. A few years later I came to understand and appreciate the need for and importance of Miss Weston's watchful eye and proactive intervention on behalf of all her students, far more than I realized at the time.

Chapter Eight

The school luncheon bell rang, echoing through the hallways. Dorothy righted the stack of mathematics papers she'd been grading, tucked them into her portfolio, and frowned.

Bernadette's test results were not up to par. A job reasonably well done, but not her usual excellent work. Miss Webster had mentioned that morning that Bernadette's recent essay for English Literature was not her best work either, somewhat alarming for the chosen valedictorian, especially the daughter of a notable author. Bernadette's mother would not be happy to see a slip in her daughter's grades.

Dorothy sighed. Ever since she'd told Bernadette that her mother had refused her invitation to graduation, the girl had been off her stride, downhearted, as if nothing mattered. *It won't do. It simply won't do. There must be some way to encourage her. It's just not fair that her mother won't come.*

But Dorothy knew that life was not always fair. Despite her husband's assurance that it would all work out, that it was just one event in the girl's life, Dorothy wasn't sure. She knew how important the years at Lakeside were for the development of the girls' minds and bodies and emotions, how each experience moved their characters forward or backward, how these important days and relationships featured in their future connections and in their convictions of self-worth.

At least it had all mattered so much to Dorothy. Friendships, classes, and community formed at Lakeside Ladies Academy had shaped her future, mostly for good. But this sadness, what surely felt like betrayal to Bernadette, might shape her future for ill. Anger mixed with sadness had a way of doing that.

Dorothy, of all people, should know. It was what had made her do what she did—or didn't do. Anger, sadness, jealousy had changed her life, caused her to betray the friend she'd held most dear—a thing that fate had decreed could not be undone—and saddled her with guilt and remorse that could not be directly repented of or forgiven by her friend in this life.

The second and final bell rang for luncheon. She'd dallied too long. Dorothy locked her desk, smoothed her hair and skirt, and strode quickly to the dining hall. Prayers had been said and servers were already offering the first course. Throughout luncheon, Dorothy discreetly eyed Bernadette and her friends. Chatter at the table appeared normal and healthy, except for Bernadette, who shoved peas around her plate as if they were lost ships at sea.

When at last the meal ended, the girls fled the dining room for their free half hour of constitutionals and gossip before elective classes began. Bernadette was slow to leave the table and for once, even Josephine did not wait for her.

Dorothy caught up with Bernadette in the hallway, placing a hand on her shoulder. "Miss Webster mentioned concern for you, Bernadette. She believes that you've been distracted of late. Is everything all right?"

The gulp in Bernadette's throat was visible. She looked at her headmistress, set her mouth in a firm line, and looked away. "I've been better, but it costs more."

Dorothy stopped short. Her hand fell from Bernadette's shoulder as the girl walked on. Whatever Dorothy had expected Bernadette to say, it wasn't that.

The long-ago memory of the only other person who'd ever said those words to her stole through her mind, clear as the first day they were spoken—a Prince Edward Island expression that Addie had used with just the same inflection through the years more times than Dorothy could count.

Bernadette's words had the same effect of throwing Dorothy off her kilter, stopping her from asking more questions or pursuing conversation, as Addie's had all those years ago. It was like hearing a ghost speak.

The afternoon passed in a blur. Dorothy couldn't stop thinking about Bernadette. This wasn't the first time the teen had said things that reminded her of Addie. There were times when Dorothy even thought that Bernadette resembled her a little, though it was hard to tell. The burn scarring on Bernadette's face distorted her natural beauty. But it was more than looks. It was mannerisms, a tilt of the head or a play on words now and again, her love of literature, her perspective given in a paper or in an answer in group discussions.

Dorothy had always put it down to her own guilt looking for a place to resurrect, and the fact that Bernadette was born and bred in Halifax. But what she'd said in the hallway after luncheon was clearly a PEI saying, at least that's what Addie had told her the first day they'd met . . . so long ago.

Dorothy shook her head, trying to dislodge the cobwebs and anxiety growing within. She wished she could talk over her concern for Bernadette and her haunted feeling with Stephen or Jonas, but that would simply revive horrid memories and remind them that there'd been a time they couldn't trust her—a thing she tried so very hard to avoid at all costs. As much as she was ashamed to think it, she still didn't want either brother to compare her to Addie. She knew in her heart that she'd come up short.

But there was one person, possibly two, in whom she could confide, who would understand "Addie ghosts" from the past. Susannah was busy with her husband and children, helping to launch her eldest from school into the world of Southern politics. But Ruth, now stationed as a social worker in Western Canada—one of the first women social workers—would understand.

That night, after dinner, while her husband read the evening paper and fell asleep before the fire, Dorothy began her letter . . .

Dear Ruth,

You'll think I'm crazy, but I need to talk to someone. I need to talk with you. You may remember the girl I mentioned who came to us from Halifax a few years ago—the girl, Bernadette, who'd been injured as a baby in the Halifax Explosion. She's about to graduate here at Lakeside, this year's valedictorian. She's a brilliant girl and has earned that honor and more.

The thing is, she reminds me so much of Addie, the way she walks, the way she talks, little mannerisms and expressions of speech or face. I don't believe in reincarnation, but it is uncanny.

Dorothy stopped, her pen in midair, and reread what she'd written. She'd never told Ruth what she'd done to their friend. Raising these concerns about Bernadette now sounded obsessive, as if Dorothy were going over the edge, losing her mind. Without knowing the torment Dorothy had inflicted on herself all these years, it would make no sense. *Ruth will think me a mental case. It's one of the things she's trained to look for. If she knew the truth—what I did—and the guilt I bear, maybe she could help me.*

Dorothy drew a deep breath and let it out slowly. No. She couldn't do that. Not now, not ever. There were too many who would suffer if the truth came out. Deliberately, Dorothy replaced her pen in its holder. She took up the linen letterhead she'd begun to write on and ripped it in two.

Chapter Nine

Two weeks had passed since Dot's telephone call inviting me to Bernadette's graduation. Since I'd hung up on her. In all that time I couldn't stop thinking about my years at Lakeside.

Portia didn't pester but seemed to understand that I was dealing with my own torment. She didn't know how my past haunted me, or the repercussions of resurrecting that past. At least I didn't think she did. Thankfully, she was distracted by the very specific attentions of our greengrocer delivery man, her Silas. In all the years we'd lived together I'd never seen Portia so happy, glowing, often singing in the kitchen or musing through our parlor window. Love and a new life had been a long time coming, and I was glad for her, and glad she focused elsewhere.

I spent most mornings in the library with the door closed, ostensibly writing my newest novel, or in the garden pulling weeds and digging new beds. I could have hired the help and often did so for major projects, but I loved time with my flowers and vegetables, loved the exercise of digging and separating clumps, loved the scent of freshly turned earth and the rejuvenation the sun brought after a long winter indoors.

It felt good to wear myself out physically, to be so tired from a morning in the garden that I all but collapsed in a chair in the shade. Even the exertion couldn't pull the ghosts from my mind or keep the memories from tumbling over one another. Perhaps it was the red of the robin's breast splashing in the birdbath beside the holly tree that morning that reminded me of Christmas.

My first Christmas at Lakeside Ladies Academy, Lemuel and Bertha did not invite me to spend the holidays with them in Halifax. I was the outcast, "that girl" no one at home wanted, like young Ebenezer Scrooge in Dickens's *A Christmas Carol*. Though I'd written weekly to Mrs. Simmons, she did not invite me either, imagining that I'd surely be going "home" to Halifax.

Thankfully, Dot and her family invited me to spend Christmas Day with them on their farm. It was wonderful to drive over newly fallen snow in their sleigh, horse harness bells jingling, then to sit in a real home with a real family by the fire. They could not help that for me it was bittersweet. After all, they weren't my family, it wasn't my home, and Dot's mother, kind as she was, lavished all her affection on her daughter. Near the end of a long and mostly wonderful day, Mr. Belding drove me back to the dormitory, where alone in the dark, I cried myself to sleep.

Why did my parents have to die? Why couldn't Lemuel wait to sell our home? Why didn't he want me with him and his family? Each question burned in my brain, sending it in circles, and the brand *orphan, orphan, orphan* rang through the night like a blacksmith's hammer pounding its anvil.

Lemuel had written once, a brief note detailing decisions he'd made regarding my schooling and allowance finances. There was nothing sentimental or personal, nothing brotherly—or what I'd imagined brotherly after seeing Dot and her brothers laughing, cavorting in the snow on Christmas Day.

The week between the winter holidays loomed long and lonely. Since there were so few of us—two older girls whose parents were stationed in Europe for foreign service, and Miss Braithwaite, the assistant teacher who'd volunteered to stay at the school with us stragglers during the holidays—we were moved into a single dormitory the day after Christmas and ate with Mr. and Mrs. Potts in the kitchen. The kindly couple and Miss Braithwaite tried to make our meals cheerful, Mr. Potts even telling jokes and stories of Christmases gone by, but not one of us girls had much to say. The other two were probably as miserable as I.

New Year's Eve the Meyer family held a watch night service in their home and invited Dot's family and us few strays from Lakeside Ladies Academy, as well as a couple of young boys from Dartmore who'd been staying with them since Christmas Eve.

I envied the easy camaraderie between the adults and guests my age, ever grateful for Dot and her family, but still missing my parents and my PEI friends, wondering if my islanders ever thought of me, ever missed me. I'd written to Eliza for a time, but she'd stopped writing after a few weeks. Our paths had diverged. Our worlds had changed, a thing I'd never imagined could happen to best friends.

Back on the island we'd celebrated the coming of the new year at home, just Mother and Dad and me. It was always a time of quiet recollection, that closing of the old year and dawning of the new. A poignant time, a time to remember and give thanks for the harvest just gone and to pray we'd get through the harsh winter upon us and for the spring planting yet to come. Oh, how I missed my parents!

It was painful enough to think of Dad, his strength, his wit, his charm . . . but to think of my mother and to know I'd never feel her arms about me again in this life . . . never see her smile or have her kiss away my fears or sit with me after school, with a glass of milk and a slice of warm bread slathered in her home-churned butter and blackberry jam made from our own patch, ready to listen to all the commonplace events of my day as if they were of great moment to the running of the world . . . no, I could not fathom it.

"Welcome to our home, Adelaide. We're so very glad to have you, my dear." Mrs. Meyer smiled into my eyes, holding my face between her work-worn palms, greeting me in her thick German accent laced with genuine warmth, then wrapping two strong arms around me in a fierce hug.

"Thank you, ma'am, for inviting me." I nearly choked the words.

In that moment when Mrs. Meyer hugged me so tightly, I clung to her, burying my face in her shoulder. I think—I know—that is the moment I fell in love with her, with the Meyer family. Even if they would never adopt me into their hearts, I secretly adopted them.

Dot looped my arm, pulled me away, all but dragging me to the refreshment table where Stephen and Jonas and both of Dot's brothers sampled Mrs. Meyer's array of cookies, cakes, and sweet breads.

"Mrs. Meyer makes absolutely the best Christmas stollen! I've loved it since I was a toddler. You've got to try it." Dot swooned, speaking to me but smiling at Stephen, her color high.

That was the first time I suspected Dot nurtured feelings for Stephen. We were still so young, only twelve, but Dot laughed and flirted in a way I'd never have suspected of her. Of course, there were only girls at Lakeside. Still . . .

I looked between the two of them, but Stephen was intent, focusing on me in a way no boy ever had. My breath caught. I felt my own color rise, a thing that had nothing to do with the warmth of the fire in the room. He winked at me in the time it took Dot to take a bite of stollen and roll her eyes in pleasure.

If I could pinpoint a moment in which I think Dot's and my worlds began to diverge, even a little, perhaps that was it, a tiny, hairline crack in the infrastructure of our friendship. The light in her eyes told me she wanted Stephen for her beau, a boy she'd grown up with next door, a young man bound for things beyond the constraints of her own farm life, and that I'd best leave him to her. And why not? Even on PEI, girls and boys who'd known each other all our lives secretly set designs long before we were of age. We played at superstitious means to predict whether we'd marry and who our future partners might be—counting the "he loves me, he loves me not" petals of flowers, looking backward through a mirror to find the first person who passed, knocking on the chicken coop door on Christmas Eve to hear if a rooster crowed—but the truth is that we knew early on just who we were attracted to. Sometimes those attractions were returned, met with wide-open hearts that led to romantic sparks and lifetime commitments. Sometimes they fizzled out, or led later to heartbreak, frustration, and bitterness.

Dot had not mentioned Stephen to me before, but I saw it all very plainly that night, as plainly as I saw that he had eyes for me and that I had eyes for his family. If Stephen came with his family, well and good—more well and good than I dared admit.

Because I'd come with Dot and her family, I was careful not to look Stephen's way when Mr. Meyer called for the fiddler. Couples trooped to the center of the room, ready to dance.

It was surely pity and hospitality, trying to make us both feel welcome, when after a brief word from their mother, Jonas asked Dot to dance, and Stephen asked me. Stephen's warm smile and brightly lit eyes, his very closeness embarrassed me and set my heart to racing. I'd never tasted alcohol, but I was certain those racings of brain and pulse signified intoxication. Before the dance was finished, Stephen whispered, "Won't you look at me, Adelaide?"

I swallowed what was surely a lump of stollen in my throat and looked him keenly in the eye, not wavering. His breath caught; I felt and heard it. Or was it my own? The moment the dance ended I stepped back. He bowed. I curtsied, and when I looked up, something was sealed between us. Is that possible? At twelve?

Dot was furious on our ride home. "I can't believe she won't leave them alone, let them make their own choices of who to dance with."

"Maybe Mrs. Meyer was just making sure everyone had a chance to dance. At least we didn't have to sit by the wall all evening. That's something."

Dot huffed. "Well, there will come a day when those boys cut their mother's apron strings. Then we'll just see what happens."

Yes, I thought, *but it might not be what you want, Dot.*

I didn't see Dot again until the new term began in late January. We never spoke of the New Year's dance, but something had shifted between us, and I knew enough, even at that young age, to tread with care.

Chapter Ten

MAY 1935

Dorothy gave up on sleeping. Dressing quickly, she walked to the school. Dawn came early these late spring days, and it was less than a quarter mile to the academy. At least there, she could busy her hands, engage her mind. There were balance sheets to render, papers to grade, reports to write . . . something, always something to do.

Not wishing to be disturbed, she didn't turn on the hallway lights; better if no one knew she'd come in early. She closed her office door, heaving a sigh of relief. At least in this one place she could shut out the world, be alone to breathe more freely than at home with her husband. She'd never told the love of her life all there was to tell, never told a soul but God. Surely her husband knew there was a part of herself that she held back from him, but she feared that telling him could drive a wedge so deep the vein of their life together might split wide open.

Dorothy sat behind her desk, turned up the lamp, picked up her pen, and pulled the nearest stack of papers close. But it was no use.

She tried to remember when she first realized that Addie loved Stephen, or that Stephen was smitten with Addie. It wasn't a thing she cared to spend much time remembering. Truth be told, she'd spent years pushing the knowledge aside, wishing for all the world she could forget.

Perhaps it was the year Addie received the book by Mrs. Montgomery—Lucy Maud Montgomery. Her friend Mrs. Simmons sent it to her in the post shortly after it released in 1908. That book, *Anne of Green Gables*, had set Addie on a new path, a determination to become the writer she'd always dreamed of being. But it was more than that. Addie had found in the story a perfect kinship to Anne—the orphaned girl no one wanted who'd finally found a home with Marilla and Matthew Cuthbert. Anne had grown and flourished under their roof, within the cocoon of their love and the many-natured folks of Avonlea.

Addie had talked about the characters and their development nonstop, about the plot and lifelike pacing of the book. She was obsessed with the story and the author.

We were what—fourteen? Addie had dreamed of becoming a writer from the time she was little and discovered from her father that books were not created by magic, but that real people wrote them.

"By hook or by crook, I'll write that book!" Addie had declared. She'd said it often, a rhyme and determination that made all the Ladies of the Lake smile.

Dorothy smiled now, despite herself. She'd never known anyone with such determination, such drive . . . unless it was Stephen—before the war, before everything changed for all of them . . .

Addie had been thrilled to learn that another soul from PEI shared her literary dreams—not only shared them but had accomplished publication surrounding a story of an orphaned girl who loved stories and wanted to write them, things that seemed impossible to her. She'd been so proud that Mrs. Montgomery was part Macneill—"not one of my MacNeills," she'd admitted, "but a Macneill just the same, granddaughter to the old couple who ran the post office back home on PEI. If only Lemuel had asked them to take me in, too. Mrs. Montgomery and I could have been like sisters—or cousins! Still, it's a sign for me, her being published and with a book whose character is so much like me, don't you think?"

Addie had been happy, focused on her fiction writing and the mentoring letters that flew back and forth between Lucy Maud Montgomery and herself. She'd relished each letter, caressing it as if someone had sent her the crown jewels of England. So enraptured with writing and the notion that the Ladies of the Lake were all now kindred spirits, just like Anne and Diana in Mrs. Montgomery's books, that for a time Dorothy thought Addie had lost interest in boys altogether.

If only she had, I wouldn't have done it. I wouldn't—

Dorothy caught herself. *What happened that December was never Addie's fault, nor was it mine, but what I did, what I didn't do, set the rest of my life and Stephen's in motion. Still, dear God, why couldn't she leave him alone? She knew that I loved him, had loved him forever. Was it too much to ask? We were friends!*

But Dorothy could no longer ask Addie, and God did not answer the question she'd begged a thousand times, or if He had answered, it had not been in a form Dorothy could comprehend. *If there was any way to change the past, I would. You know I would, Lord. But I can't. I can't. Confession to Stephen is impossible. I can't. I won't. So how do I go on? Please, God. Please!*

Dorothy swiped the moisture from her eyes. She wasn't given to crying. She couldn't let the girls or teachers see her like this. She would not cry in front of her husband. That was one of the things he'd always said he admired about her, that she was strong, emotionally stalwart.

Dorothy had grown so used to hiding her emotions, playacting her strength. Sometimes she even believed what he thought was true. Other times she nearly suffocated from the exhaustion of hiding.

If she were truly strong, she would have told Stephen and Jonas and Father Meyer the truth long ago. She would not have taken to avoiding Bernadette now, a thing she'd done ever since Bernadette had innocently responded in words that raised Addie's ghost and all the memories of the past. *Memories. Ghosts.* She knew where some of them lay buried.

Dorothy unlocked her desk. From the back of the bottom left drawer she pulled the diary she'd started a few years before the Great War began. She'd only written in it intermittently, so the one book covered many years. She hadn't opened it in well over a decade. Perhaps now was the time. Perhaps she needed to return to the past to be rid of it once and for all. She didn't know if going back might bring her salvation or prove her undoing, but nothing else she'd done these last weeks had helped, and something must before she cracked.

She opened the book.

July 8, 1910 . . . Day Before Graduation Day

This morning Susannah, Ruth, Addie, and I wove our end of the Daisy Chain. The Daisy Chain is a longstanding tradition at Lakeside Ladies Academy.

All the girls at school were sent this week to the nearby meadow to pick daisies. We picked hundreds, maybe thousands, and for two afternoons linked them to form crowns and a long chain that we graduating girls will carry through the grounds. A real photographer will come tomorrow and take our picture. Miss Weston has already told us to practice a pose, frozen in midair, as if we were really walking down the hill all together.

Ruth, Susannah, Addie, and I have already determined our expressions, each of us helping the other to find the most flattering pose. After all, the photograph will go into the display case of archives for the school. It will be there for us and God and all of posterity to see forever!

Graduation. We've waited so long for this day, but now that it's nearly here I'm frightened at the ending of our world together. How will we navigate the years ahead without one another?

Susannah and Ruth are leaving the day after graduation. Susannah will return to North Carolina. Her mother is already planning her coming-out debutante ball. The dress she's having made costs a fortune. Susannah showed us a sketch and a swatch of the fabric. I've never touched anything so silky or seen a dress so beautiful.

Ruth—our resident genius—is off to university and then a nursing program.

At least I don't have to return to the farm. I don't think I could bear the loneliness of that. But the Ladies of the Lake . . . how can I go on without my friends? They've become family and more than family to me.

Miss Weston has agreed to take Addie and me on as assistant teachers for the next school year. If we prove ourselves, and we absolutely will, she'll recommend the board of governors hire us as full-time teachers the following year. Addie is to assist in teaching English Literature for the older girls and a class in deportment and posture to all the grade levels. I'll assist Miss Trumbull in teaching Mathematics to all the forms and Introduction to Astronomy to the older girls.

Every time I think about teaching astronomy, I laugh, remembering that night of the Harvest Festival when Ruth coal-blackened her telescope for Mean Mildred. I wonder what's become of Mildred now. I haven't heard since she withdrew from school. Overseas with her foreign service parents, I guess, maybe married to some duke or earl or something. She certainly didn't marry Jonas Meyer for all her manipulations. I'm just glad she's gone from here forever.

Jonas is almost finished with university and will be off to law school next year and is what Miss Weston calls "up-and-coming."

Stephen—dear, handsome Stephen—is already finishing his second year of university. He's doubled up on classes and is likely to graduate in another year, then he's off to law school, too. I hope he'll come for the graduation tomorrow. I know Mr. and Mrs. Meyer will. They've taken a shine to Addie. Pity for her orphan status, I guess. I'm glad for Addie but the chumminess between them is a little sickening. I know Addie misses having a mother and Mrs. Meyer missed out on having girls. Still . . .

I'm glad Addie's so taken with her writing and not thinking about men and marriage, at least not now. I don't like the way Stephen looks at her, the way his eyes light up and follow her every move when he sees her. Of course, he's just being nice to her, like I've asked him to. He's always especially glad to see me, at least I think he is, but sometimes I wonder if he actually sees me—that I've grown, that I'm not the flame-haired, pigtailed girl he played tag and red rover with ages ago after church services. Does he see me as a woman equal to those he meets at college? Equal to Addie? I don't know. I can't think of competing with my friend . . . and yet.

At least we've all planned to meet at the gazebo tomorrow night before curfew. Will it be for the last time?

Dorothy closed her diary. *How indeed did we manage to say good-bye to one another?*

December 6, 1917, ended everything. It shattered each of us in different ways. Staying in touch through Christmas cards and the occasional letter has helped. But the Ladies of the Lake have never been the same. I've not been the same.

Dorothy shoved the diary into its hiding place and slammed the drawer closed. She turned the key, locking the drawer, as if secrets long past might escape.

She pressed her fingers to her temples, circling, circling, wishing to relieve the tension. Dredging up the past hadn't helped a thing. Still, despite the angst and guilt, there was something bittersweet about remembering her friends, about remembering herself, as they all were then.

◝

JULY 1910

The entire Belding clan within a twenty-five-mile radius turned out for Dorothy's graduation. Parents, grandparents, siblings, aunts and uncles, cousins, and cousins once removed. Even longtime neighbors came, including the Meyer family.

Susannah's parents and older sister came from North Carolina. Ruth's parents and twin brother, Rodney, came from Halifax. Among the Ladies of the Lake only Addie stood alone. Neither her brother, Lemuel, nor his wife, Bertha, came, nor did they send flowers or gifts, not even congratulations. Mrs. Simmons sent her a bouquet and a book of poems, a collection by American authors. Mrs. Montgomery sent Addie her latest book, *Kilmeny of the Orchard*, signed *From One Author to One Author Soon To Be*. Addie squealed that she was starstruck and over the moon, but when we prepared to begin our graduation walk, seeing that no one came for her, her eyes told a different story.

Dorothy had urged her brothers to clap as loudly as they could when Addie's name was called. What she didn't expect was for Stephen Meyer to give her a standing ovation.

"Over the top, that's what that was," Dorothy whispered to Susannah, who stood beside her in the receiving line after the ceremony.

"You're jealous, Dot Belding, and you know it. You'd give your eyeteeth for a standing ovation from Stephen Meyer."

"I'm not jealous. Take that back! He was just being nice to her, but it came out silly."

"Well—" Susannah shrugged and smiled knowingly—"if you say so."

Dorothy ignored Susannah the rest of the afternoon. By the time parents, siblings, and cousins drove to their homes or to nearby hotels or boardinghouses, dusk had begun to fall.

At nine o'clock, just an hour before this once-a-year late-night curfew, the Ladies of the Lake assembled for the last time at the gazebo.

"I feel as if my glass slippers have crashed into a million pieces," moaned Susannah.

"Rudderless." Ruth sighed and perched on the railing. "All this time that seemed so far away and now here we are. Time to go. Time to say goodbye."

"I don't think I can." Addie's voice was small.

"Then we won't," Dorothy insisted.

"I'm sorry, y'all, but Mama and Daddy are picking me up first thing tomorrow morning. Our train leaves Hartford before noon."

"I don't mean that you won't go—you and Ruth. I mean that it can't be goodbye, can't be over."

"We must write." Susannah nodded in agreement.

"We must come back," Ruth insisted. "We're the Ladies of the Lake. We can't simply desert one another."

"Mama's hell-bent on my getting engaged within the season and married by next June. I don't see how—"

"We're modern women. We do have some say in our lives," Ruth pushed.

"Single modern women have some say in their lives. I'm not so sure Southern husbands see it that way."

"We should make a pact," Dorothy said, "not to lose touch."

"To be there whenever one of us needs help," Addie added. "All for one and one for all, remember?"

"Every two years." Ruth took charge. "We write, yes, but we also meet back here, at the gazebo, every two years to renew and repledge our sisterhood. Ladies of the Lake, always. Here, I'll write it out and we'll sign in blood. Swear it." Ruth placed her hand in the center of the group.

Dorothy knew it was easy for her. She saw her future as a teacher at Lakeside Ladies Academy; her family lived nearby and hopefully, prayerfully, she would marry and live in Farmington, or Hartford if Stephen wanted to practice law there . . . assuming, of course, that he asked her, and she would make certain he did. "Every two years, just after graduation, when the students have left for the summer." Dorothy placed her hand atop Ruth's.

"Agreed." Addie added her palm to the pledge, smiling broadly.

Susannah shrugged. "I'll just have to make this arrangement part of my marriage nuptials." She grinned, joining the pledge. "All for one and one for all."

"Ladies of the Lake!" Four voices rose as one to the heavens. And then they signed Ruth's pledge, in blood from their pricked fingers.

Chapter Eleven

"Portia, you make the best raspberry muffins I've ever tasted." It was no lie. They melted in my mouth. "I wish Bernadette were here for these. She loves them. And if I'm not mistaken, this is produce delivery day. I wonder if our Mr. Silas Clements will notice the fragrance from our kitchen and stop in?"

Portia huffed but smiled at my tease. "Breakfast here at Rosemont is the best in the world," she acknowledged, passing the butter, as if she commanded a host of chefs who created recipes the culinary world would die for rather than concocting them herself. "If that poor man's hungry, I might let him have one or two, and a cup of coffee. He does seem taken with my cooking." She couldn't keep the smile from her eyes.

"It's more than your cooking, my friend. It's good to see you so happy, Portia. I'd best write down some of your recipes, maybe try my hand in the kitchen before I'm left alone."

"You never had the patience to learn. It takes a light hand to bake. Bernadette, now, she's the one."

"Yes," I laughed, slathering the softened butter across my muffin, broken down the middle. "You've told me a dozen times."

"Two dozen, more like." Portia poured tea. "Truth bears repeating."

"How did you learn?"

Portia's smile faded. "Mama. My mama taught me everything she knew in the days before . . ."

We both knew which days she meant. My early life had been measured before and after the storm that took my parents' lives. But for every man, woman, and child in Halifax, all of life was measured either before or after December 6, 1917, the very day and hour known and observed by every Haligonian since.

But Portia didn't like to remember—at least she seldom spoke of it.

"I'm sorry, dear friend. I should have known better."

"Remembering is a dangerous thing. Sometimes it gets hold of you and won't let go." A minute of silence passed before Portia sighed deeply and blinked back tears—tears she rarely let fall in my presence. "I never thought I'd love anybody again, not after losing my husband and my baby boy, my Ahanu."

"But now you do." I was glad for her, even though it underlined my aloneness. "Ahanu. I've always thought that a beautiful name. It sounds almost musical."

Portia nodded. "We chose it the day he was born, for his smile, even that young. Ahanu—Algonquin for 'he laughs.' My husband said it was nothing but gas and a grimace, but a mother knows." She smiled at the memory.

I nodded. All the mothering I knew was in watching Bernadette grow and change. If Portia hadn't been there, I'd have been lost.

"And who taught you to write like you do? That's why you've got no time for anything but that, and a turn now and again in the garden."

"And Bernadette."

"And Bernadette. You did good by her . . . while she was here."

I ignored that little jibe. "I knew I wanted to write from the time I was a very little girl, from the moment my father told me that books were not created with magic or fairy dust, but by people, through hard work and imagination."

"That's all it took?" Portia looked doubtful.

"No. I've been blessed by mentors. Wonderful women."

Portia turned her head in a frown of disbelief and curiosity. "You don't get mail; you don't go out now that Bernadette's gone. I'd like to meet these mentor women of yours."

"From when I was young. There was a woman, a Mrs. Simmons, who kindly took me under her wing and wrote to me, often. She introduced me to a book by a woman who wrote just the kind of books I wanted to write. I studied what the author wrote, as carefully as I knew how, and sent her letters. She wrote me back many times, guiding me."

"She's dead now?" Portia's curiosity had been roused.

"Mrs. Simmons? Yes."

"No, the writer lady."

"I don't believe so." I spoke carefully.

"But you don't write to her." It was a statement. Portia saw everything that came in or went out of the house.

I shook my head.

"Sounds ungrateful to me, after all that inspiration she gave you, after the success you've achieved writing your own books."

I didn't answer.

"Does she know you're published?"

"I don't know. I don't think so."

"A woman like that, so good to you . . . she'd want to know."

I set my teacup down. My favorite muffins turned sour in my stomach. Why did all my conversations with Portia lately end in her disapproval?

"I'll be in the library. Working."

"Why do you cut me out this way, Rosaline? You never used to."

"Because you're harping on the past. Because you won't leave it alone."

"I'm sorry. I'll say that. I don't mean to hurt you. I just want what's best for you and for Bernadette."

"You can't know what that is. You don't understand."

"Then help me. Explain it to me."

I walked out, letting the breakfast room door swing closed behind me. In the library I shut the door, tempted to lock it. Instead, I pulled open the draperies and cranked open the windows, wide as they'd go, beckoning the morning sun.

Pulling a fresh sheet of paper from my desk drawer, I rolled it into my typewriter and pounded out the keys, *Chapter Sixteen*.

Sixteen. Ironic. Sixteen was supposed to be my magic number. Lucy Maud Montgomery had graciously responded to my first gushing letter, in which I begged her to tell me how she began writing for publication, when she knew she wanted to become a writer, how she would advise me to proceed. She'd written back, saying that her first real encouragement came at age sixteen when the local newspaper, the *Patriot*, published her poem—her very first publication. Letters flew back and forth between us. I don't know if other girls and would-be authors hounded her, but I certainly did. How she found time to write her own books or tend to her family is now a mystery to me. I didn't think of those things then.

I was bound and determined to prove myself to Mrs. Montgomery, to publish by sixteen, too, but I was intimidated, afraid to send my work to publishers, afraid to be shot down.

Mrs. Simmons, as always, encouraged me. I spent summers with her in Boston, living and working as her companion, though truth be told, there was little work and much joy. In failing health by the time I'd turned eighteen, she insisted I sit down and write the story of my heart and send it to a publisher before returning to Lakeside for the fall term, to get on with things and meet my future head-on. So I changed the names but wrote of the man I hoped to marry one day, who I hoped would want to marry me—the man and his wonderful, welcoming family.

I missed my publication goal by three years. Before returning to school, shortly before my nineteenth birthday, I submitted my short story, rewritten and revised a dozen times, to a local paper. When it appeared in print, spread across two issues, serialized, it ranked a miracle. I was so very proud of that first publication . . . a Christmas romance between a handsome young aristocrat—a widower with a little girl—and a teacher hired as her governess. The teacher wore glasses, a plain Jane who never imagined the man of her dreams would pay her any mind, but of course, he did, and romance ensued with a happily-ever-after ending.

Mrs. Simmons loved it and praised me to high heaven. But it was Dot who set the dream aflame.

~

DECEMBER 1913

Dot walked into the teachers' lounge, throwing the *Hartford Courant* onto the table before me, causing me to splotch ink across the paper I was grading.

"Dot! Watch out, please."

"*Watch out* is exactly what I'm thinking, Addie. What is this supposed to mean?"

"My story." I smiled from ear to ear. "They published my story. What do you think?"

"I think you've made a ninny of yourself, that's what I think!"

"What?"

"Flaunting your infatuation with Stephen for all the county to see."

"What are you talking about? It has nothing to do with Stephen. It's about a widower and a—"

"It's about a handsome, well-to-do man and a plain-Jane schoolteacher falling in love. Who wouldn't connect that with you and Stephen? Be serious!"

I felt heat creep up my neck. Of course, it was inspired by my feelings for Stephen. What girl in her right mind wouldn't fall for him—intelligent, handsome, strong, intoxicating wit and charm, a gentleman, a family of comfortable means filled with faith and love? But were my feelings obvious? Could they be read in the lines of my governess story? I didn't think so.

"You moon over him like a lovesick puppy, Addie. You think he won't see this as pitiable?"

I snatched the paper and shoved it in my stack. "I very much doubt he'll see it at all. I'm only sorry you did." I picked up my books to walk out but turned. "Dot, you of all people know how much this publication means to me—my very first after all this time trying. You're being cruel. Maybe you should ask yourself why." I didn't wait for her to respond, but walked out, letting the door slam behind me.

I knew Dot had a crush on Stephen, but as far as I knew he'd never returned her affections. We both wrote to him, just as we wrote to Jonas and Ruth and Susannah and so many others—visits on paper with friends and neighbors living away.

The Meyers had become my surrogate family of sorts—them and Mrs. Simmons. They included me in holidays, as well as Dot and her family as longtime friends and neighbors. Jonas and Stephen had always acted like brothers or perhaps cousins might, toward both Dot and me. I could lay nothing more at the feet of either brother.

It might have been my imagination, but I did think Stephen was especially glad to see me last time he was home. There were never moments when we were alone, but whenever he caught a glimpse of me, his smile seemed to broaden. Twice I looked up and realized he was watching me from across the room. His neck reddened then, and it felt as if there might be some mutual attraction, chemistry sparking a tiny flame . . . At least I hoped there might.

Dot either didn't recognize the connection or refused to. Well, I couldn't help that. I took my wounded ego, sat down, and wrote a tortured letter to Mrs. Montgomery, mailing with it a copy of my story, evidence that I was now a published writer, one step closer to becoming a world-renowned author.

Mrs. Montgomery wrote back three weeks later, severely critiquing my story, intent on helping me become a better writer . . . a critique and true gift that I took very badly. Eventually, when my bruised ego recovered, I took her instruction to heart and began my real writing journey.

Chapter Twelve

Dorothy smiled as she watched Stephen and Jonas enter the building.

"Mr. Meyer and Mr. Meyer, welcome to Lakeside!" Bernadette and Josephine, along with two younger girls, giggled, swooning over the headmistress's handsome husband and his brother as they stepped into the school's foyer.

Dorothy smiled at them from across the room, lifting her chin in recognition. It had been the same since the day she'd married. Girls flirted with her husband in a thousand different and only slightly coquettish ways, always pleased beyond reason to see him or his brother. To some of the younger girls one was a father and one an elder brother figure, but to many they were the men of their dreams.

Despite the toll the war had taken, they were still the handsomest men on two feet in Dorothy's estimation. Both tall, blue-eyed, broad-shouldered. Recently, tiny, almost indiscernible streaks of silver had begun weaving through their mostly still-blond hair. She didn't mind but teased that it made them look more distinguished. It was funny how alike they'd grown as they'd aged.

Dorothy had always despised her red hair and freckles, but over the years her hair had deepened into a rich auburn with no hint of gray—at least not yet. Her husband seemed to love it, love her fading freckles, and love her. For all of that she was grateful. She could never risk spoiling that, could never confide the anguish of her heart, and that alone kept that tiny wedge between them, a wedge he'd hinted at, wondered over, but never probed.

Leaving his brother to chat with the girls, in three great strides he crossed the room. After a quick glance to make certain the girls were not looking, he bent to give Dorothy a peck on her cheek and a wink. "How's my best girl?"

"Your only girl, thank you very much," she playfully corrected.

"Right you are, my love. Doing any better? I noticed you left early this morning."

Dorothy straightened. "Fine. Just a little tired. You know, end of term near, graduation coming . . . just everything."

"Still worried about Bernadette and her mother? Any news?" he whispered, searching her face. She knew he worried about her, grew concerned when she didn't sleep or her face looked pale.

"Nothing further since my telephone call. Imagine, calling all the way to Canada. So far, no one on the board has mentioned the expense. There's a chance it will pass Mr. Shockley unnoticed unless his dearly beloved Mean Mildred finds out. She can't seem to keep her nose out of academy business." Dorothy huffed, still annoyed that Mean Mildred had returned to Farmington and married a member of the board of governors.

"You can't change some people. I don't understand Mrs. Murray, but I can imagine Bernadette is hurting after all she's been through, all she's given to achieve what she has." Gently, he pushed a tendril that had escaped from Dorothy's chignon, catching it behind her ear. "I know you hurt when any of your girls hurt. I'm sorry, sweetheart."

Dorothy's throat caught. He knew her so well, or thought he did. He was right about the girls. They were her—their—children, the only children they were likely ever to have. Whether it was because of what had happened to him in France during the Great War or after in the flu epidemic, or if it was some inability of her own, they didn't know, hadn't sought to find out. She was simply unable to conceive, or he was unable to help her conceive. They considered it the will of God and concluded that their parenting, their hearts, were meant for the girls at Lakeside Ladies Academy and the boys at Dartmore, both schools and causes close to their hearts. They supported both, just as the Meyer family had done as good neighbors since they'd first set foot on American soil.

"We just stopped in. Thought we could pick up those skids you wanted removed. We've brought a wagon to load."

"Thank you, dearest. That will free up the staging area for Saturday's *Twelfth Night* production. I know Miss Wilson would like to use the floor for dress rehearsal."

"Will you be home for dinner? Say yes." He gave her that little-boy look she could not resist.

"On time. I promise. Mrs. MacArthur is sending home one of her shepherd's pies with mounds of fluffy potatoes, just for you."

"For us. Deliciously browned, of course." He looked so serious.

"I've instructions for thirty minutes in the oven and eight under the broiler, just so." Dorothy smiled. There was nothing so serious as a man's stomach at dinnertime.

He kissed her nose. "See you there. Oh, by the way, you might want to whisper when you refer to Mrs. Shockley as 'Mean Mildred.' Walls have ears, you know."

She watched as he rejoined his brother, two halves of a whole, one with a slight limp and the other with a sleeve empty since the Great War, neither of which stole appeal from either man. That war had stolen much from the Meyer family, far more than the damage or loss of limbs.

~

One hot July morning the Ladies of the Lake gathered at the gazebo for the second time since their 1910 graduation, two days after the Academy's 1915 graduation and one day after the mass exodus of students for the summer.

Susannah, married, came with her two small children, Harriet and Harold—twins—in tow. "So sorry to be late!" Susannah, talking a mile a minute, rushed across the grounds to join her friends. "Reginald insisted I bring the children with me. It's the only way he'd agree to let me come."

"So, where are your darlings?" Ruth, who'd made the longest trek from Western Canada, kissed her friend's cheek in welcome.

"At the hotel or the park or the waterfront looking at boats—wherever and whatever my maid and their nanny can do to keep them busy and out of mischief."

"How much mischief can they get in at three years old?" Addie's eyebrows shot up.

Susannah guffawed in a most unladylike manner. "You have no idea!"

Neither did Dorothy. She was the youngest in her family, and the girls at Lakeside Ladies Academy did not enter until at least ten years old. That age was mischief-prone enough. She knew from personal experience.

"Ladies!" Ruth led the way, placing her hand in the middle of the foursome. Each woman added her hand to the pledge. "One for all and all for one! Ladies of the Lake!"

Laughter and hugs followed, as they'd done three years before.

"It was so good of y'all to postpone till this summer so I could come, too. There was no way I could leave Reginald for the trip last summer. I really appreciate it." Susannah, suffering from a too-tight corset, still appeared breathless.

"We could never meet with three; we need all four of us!" Dorothy insisted.

"That's right. It wouldn't be the same without each one of us here," Addie agreed.

"I declare." Susannah's eyes misted. "Y'all are still the sweetest. Now, bring on the food!"

Addie, ever glad to provide hospitality, snapped an embroidered linen cloth and spread it in the center of the floor.

Dot helped unpack the picnic hamper Addie had dragged across the grounds, thanks to Mrs. Potts's generosity in the kitchen as long as the four vowed to clean up after their picnic.

"What have we?" Susannah clapped her hands.

"Scones—cherry almond, currant, blueberry lemon—the best Irish butter, Mrs. Potts's own jam, Mr. Meyer's lavender honey, and tea, of course."

Ruth's smile disappeared. "I'll pass on the honey."

"You're kidding. We asked for a jar just for you. You've always loved the Meyers' lavender honey." Dorothy held out the jar to her friend.

"No, thank you." Ruth was firm.

"Sweet tea, I hope. That's the only tea we drink in the South," Susannah insisted.

"I brought the cream and sugar bowl, just for you!" Addie smiled.

"Sugar only, if you please."

"Some things never change." Dorothy grinned.

"Thank heavens!" Susannah sighed.

For the next half hour, the only sounds were the occasional demure slurp of tea and contented moans over Mrs. Potts's melt-in-your-mouth scones.

Fully sated, the women leaned back against the benches and framework of the gazebo.

"It's so good to be back here with y'all." Susannah smoothed her skirt. "Sometimes I feel like I'll die for want of conversation beyond this fundraiser and that debutante ball and every mother's concern over new dresses for the spring cotillion, as if their offspring could manage to waltz across the floor in those ridiculous skirts! Yards and yards of silk they'll wear only once."

"Don't they know there's a war on?" Ruth snapped. "Women in Canada have gone to straight skirts."

"To conserve fabric for the military," Addie acknowledged.

"And because they're far more practical. With so many men gone, women are more in the workforce than ever."

"Not in the South. The women I know would rather die than enter a place of business or wear dresses that look like men's suits. They don't care a fig about the war," Susannah quipped, then stopped short.

"Susannah!" Dorothy gasped.

"Oh, Ruth, I'm sorry. I'm so very sorry. I didn't mean it. I wasn't thinking."

But it was too late. Ruth paled. "But you did mean it, and it's true. You all keep on as if nothing's happening across the Atlantic, as if men aren't dying by the thousands every day."

Levity disappeared. Dorothy set her scone on the plate before her. There was no way she could eat it now. She reached for Ruth's hand. "Did they ever find your—"

"Rodney. His name is Rodney. No," Ruth snapped, her voice trembling now in anger. Moments passed before it came under control, quieter, more conciliatory. "They never found his body."

"That's so hard, so very hard. How are your parents?" Addie asked.

"Grieving, what do you think? It's barely been two months."

Dorothy recognized that as the kind of sharp answer Addie had sometimes given early on when she'd come to Lakeside Ladies Academy after her parents had died at sea, when so many, meaning to be kind and sympathetic, asked questions that opened gaping wounds. Shipwreck, storms, torpedoes . . . different times and places, the same deadly effect.

"Those nasty Germans should be strung up," Susannah spat. "Torpedoing a ship of innocent civilians like that."

"There were rumors that the *Lusitania* was carrying wartime supplies for Britain, even munitions," Addie spoke softly. "We never heard if it was true."

"True or not, that had nothing to do with the people on board. Did you know that ninety-four children were drowned in that sinking? Thirty-one of them infants—babes in arms! My brother and his friends were going so they could work with the Red Cross in France—to save lives! Murdered, before he ever got there."

"But just as much a hero as if he'd died in battle," Susannah offered.

Dorothy nearly rolled her eyes. *As if that's any comfort to Ruth.*

"How are you doing?" Addie asked, reaching for Ruth's hand.

Ruth visibly shuddered, pulled her hand away. Silent for a time, when she spoke it was so quietly each of the other women leaned forward to hear. "I'm going over . . . in two weeks."

"What do you mean, 'going over'?" But Dorothy knew.

"We sail from Halifax for Liverpool in two weeks. My brother couldn't serve as he'd intended. I'm going for both of us."

"No, Ruth . . . no." Now Addie seemed the one shaken.

Ruth looked up, searching each face in turn. "Don't you understand what war means? Young men—boys—our age and some even younger are being killed, murdered. Have you heard about the trenches? Mazes of open tunnels in the earth, filled with water and rats and our men and boys while they wait for a lull in the firing from the enemy so they can crawl over the top and charge through no-man's-land—a quarter mile of rolling barbed wire—hoping to shoot before they're mown down."

Every woman held her breath.

"Rarely do they make it. Rarely do they inflict the damage they're ordered to inflict. If they live, they're mostly wounded, lying in the heat of the day until evening when a medic or another soldier can crawl through the dark to come pull them away. And then they need doctors, nurses, people to treat those wounds. I'm trained. I'm not married. I have no children. I should go. I must go."

"But you don't have to," Susannah pleaded.

"Yes, I do. For my sake, for Rodney's."

"What about your parents? What do they say?" Dorothy couldn't imagine her parents going along with such a scheme.

"You can't do this to them, Ruth. They've already lost your brother," Susannah pushed.

Ruth's mouth firmed but her eyes softened in pity. "You really don't understand, do you? You've never had to sacrifice anything, Susannah. You have every material thing a person could want in this world, but you don't understand that people somewhere have died so you can have and preserve it. Well, my countrymen, my family, and families across Britain and France and Canada are the ones paying the cost."

Susannah straightened. "We're not in the war, Ruth. It's nothing to do with the United States, so don't make it like it is. It's not my fault."

"It's not any of our faults." Addie replaced the lid on the sugar bowl and swept crumbs from the tablecloth. "But that doesn't mean it's not our responsibility. America's likely to join in the Allied effort soon. I don't see how we can help it."

"We?" Ruth's eyebrows shot up. "You're Canadian by birth. Did you forget?"

Addie's face reddened. "No, I'll never forget, but I've lived here since I was twelve."

"Don't you think you have some responsibility to Canada? We're at war, Addie. Canadian men and women are dying, fighting the Hun."

"I care. Of course I care. What can I do beyond knitting mufflers and gloves and helmet hats, and having the girls knit in the evenings? We've raised funds and sent bundles upon bundles of clothing for refugees."

"I'm not talking about knitting and packing crates from the safety of Lakeside. I'm talking about taking a stand. Taking sides."

Addie stared. "Of course I want Canada and Britain and France to rise victorious. Of course we're on the same side!"

"Then why are you still seeing Stephen Meyer? Why do you spend your Sundays with the Meyer family and accept honey from them? Why are they even still here?"

"They're my friends—our friends. They live here; they've lived here longer than I have."

"They're our longtime neighbors," Dorothy intervened, annoyed that Ruth saw Stephen as more connected to Addie than to herself.

"They're Germans."

"Stephen was a baby when they came here. They're American citizens now."

"They still have family in Germany. Don't you think they're loyal to them? It's bad enough if Dot's still mooning over him, but you, Addie, you're Canadian. How can you?"

Addie froze with two bone china cups she'd begun to tidy in midair. She looked at the others.

Susannah shrugged. "Ruth's got a point. Much as I hate to think it, it's true, we'll likely join the war before it's over. I heard Daddy and the senator talking the other day. They don't see how we can stay out altogether, no matter what President Wilson says. When that happens, it's not going to matter whether you're Canadian or American, Addie. Dating a German is not popular."

Addie gasped. "I don't want to be popular. I love Stephen. I love his family. The Meyers have been only good and kind to me, to everyone. To you, and to you, Ruth."

Dorothy swallowed the lump in her throat. Addie had never openly declared her love for Stephen. Neither of them had. Somehow, that she'd said the words aloud drove a deeper wedge into Dorothy's heart. *Does Addie have reason to think Stephen returns her love?*

"It's disloyal. Don't you understand that?" Ruth pushed.

Addie sat back. "You're not being fair."

"Fair? Is war fair? Was my brother's death fair? You've got to take a stand. You can't straddle the fence when people are dying, slaughtered."

"Not by Stephen. Not by Jonas."

"If they were in Germany, they'd have been conscripted by the enemy long before now."

"But they're not. They're here, since they were children."

"And if—*when* America joins the fight, as they should have long ago, will the Meyer brothers fight for her? Will they fight against their aunts and uncles and grandparents? Ask yourself if you can live with them refusing to fight, Addie, because I can't, neighbors or not. Not after what they did to my brother."

"Ruth." Addie spread her hands in a plea for understanding.

"Addie—" Susannah laid a hand on her knee—"the point is that such alliances are seen as unpatriotic. Besides that, we're the Ladies of the Lake. I think what Ruth is saying is that as one for all and all for one, it's disloyal to her for you to pursue a relationship with Stephen, disloyal to Rodney's memory. She can't live with that, not from friends she has a right to count on."

Dorothy blinked. *How did it come to this? But Ruth agrees with Susannah. I see it in her eyes.* In that moment Dorothy saw a path forward, albeit a Judas kiss. She barely wavered. "What Susannah says makes sense."

Addie's eyes widened, reminding Dorothy of a deer caught in lantern light. Three against one.

"You write to Stephen and Jonas as often as I do," Addie accused. She wouldn't back down, but her voice wobbled.

Dorothy shrugged. "Maybe we shouldn't, or maybe we should think more about what Susannah and Ruth are saying. We owe them that. They're our sisters of the heart."

"It's a blemish on the school," Ruth said quietly. "Just think how it looks for Lakeside Ladies Academy teachers to be writing to Germans. Think what the new headmistress would say if she knew you were taking up with one."

Addie paled at Ruth's thinly veiled threat.

Dorothy's heartbeat quickened at the very notion of being reported or dismissed from her position. But to give up on Stephen or on writing to Jonas? Stop visiting with the Meyers or acknowledging them in public? That's what Ruth was asking, demanding. Still, hoping Addie would take the cue, Dorothy nodded in agreement, as if Ruth had just supplied the nail for the coffin.

Chapter Thirteen

MAY 1935

"Rosaline, you need to stop walking these hallways at night. Those bags get any bigger under your eyes and they're going to hire you as a porter down to the station. And if you don't start eating this food I cook, you'll be nothing but skin and bones by the time Bernadette comes home, by the time Silas and I marry." Portia took me to task over breakfast, pointing at porridge covered in berries and lavender honey, my favorite. "If I didn't know better, I'd guess you were in the family way with how you pick at my good food."

"Please, Portia. I'm sorry if I woke you. I'm certainly not in the family way."

"That would be an immaculate conception." She reached for my hand. "I'm worried about you, is all."

"I have things on my mind, things I need to sort."

"Things you're still not ready to talk about?" she asked gently.

I closed my eyes, as if that might shut out the conversation.

Portia was silent for the space of a minute before pulling back. "Well, if going to that graduation has you so worried sick and off your kilter, then maybe you'd best stay home and hide."

"I'm not hiding," I snapped—a habit when I lied. That was so seldom it was no surprise to see Portia's eyebrows peak. "I'm sorry." I pushed from the table, taking my teacup and saucer with me. "I'll be in the garden."

That, too, would send Portia on alert. My mornings were nearly always spent in the library, hammering away on my latest manuscript. But I couldn't concentrate, hadn't been able to for days. Every pathway inside my brain burned. Every nerve in my body set my skin to tingling, to crawling. I needed fresh air, sunshine, open skies.

Pulling a pair of shears and a bucket from the gardening shed and donning my gardening apron, I headed for the tulip bed. Time to tie back the drooping tulip leaves and deadhead the spent roses. Perhaps I'd dig a new bed. I certainly had enough nervous tension to channel the energy required.

Despite the industry of thrusting my spade into the ground, I knew the truth. *Yes, I'm hiding . . . from Dot, from whatever is left of the Meyer family, from the Ladies of the Lake, from telling Bernadette and Portia the truth.*

Swiping my eyes with my sleeve, I threw down my spade and gloves and settled into the wooden swing hanging from the red maple at the far end of the garden. Swinging beneath that wonderful tree with its far-reaching shade had always brought me peace, ever since we three came to Rosemont. Ever since this sacred plot of ground became our home, our solace, our sanctuary—for Portia, for Bernadette, and for me.

Back and forth . . . back and forth . . . I closed my eyes and let the years fall away.

～

SUMMER 1915

After the Ladies of the Lake urged me to cut ties with Stephen, I spent the summer with Mrs. Simmons in Boston, nursing her, watching her fail week by week. Each day dawned bittersweet. Sweet, because we spent precious hours together. Sweet, because unlike with my parents' deaths, there was time to say how very much I loved her, all she meant to me, how she'd helped me, saved me in the years since we'd first met on that ship from Halifax. Sweet, because there was time to say goodbye. Bitter, because it really was goodbye, at least for this side of eternity.

In those last weeks I poured out my heart to my dear, elderly friend and mentor while she poured her wisdom into me.

"You've known your Stephen and Jonas almost since you arrived at that school as a girl. You've loved their mother and all of them as family. They cannot help where they came from any more than your friend Ruth or I can help where we are from. It's a fair wager that all Germans are not evil, no more than all Scots or Irish or Italians or Canadians are good or evil. They've never given you a reason to believe they are saboteurs or disloyal to this country, have they?"

"None. They're open and welcoming to all in the community, especially to the students and staff at Lakeside and Dartmore. It's cruel to ignore and slight them. But now, the headmistress says we mustn't lead young ones astray or come under the watchful eye of the government—that we must appear patriotic and above reproach. She says that German families and even families of German extraction are suspect for their loyalties to the kaiser, that it's likely they'll be interned before the war ends."

Mrs. Simmons shook her weary head.

"It's so unfair! Stephen and Jonas are American citizens, and America's not even in the war."

"Not yet, but I fear we soon shall be, my dear. You must face that, make your heart ready. Will there be a conscription? I don't know, but if Stephen and Jonas don't willingly join, they will surely be suspect, however unfairly . . . not simply by your friends or the school's headmistress, but by others who may prove more dangerous."

I loved Mrs. Simmons, but I didn't want to believe what she said, what I'd heard. Stephen and Jonas go to war? Stephen and Jonas be interned if they refused go to war against the land of their birth and their parents' birth? Surely the voice of reason would prevail for those who'd emigrated long ago, for those who'd been born or raised in America.

I was not prepared for the patriotic frenzy in the academy that school year, let alone what the Great War meant in our town the following year.

⌒

FALL 1916

That October was the first in all my years in Connecticut that Lakeside Ladies Academy declined the much-anticipated invitation to the Meyers' Harvest Festival. Ultimately the celebration was canceled, not because of any decision of the Meyer family but because Lakeside Ladies Academy, Dartmore School, the local church, and the surrounding community at large had declined the family's invitation. Heartbroken for Mr. and Mrs. Meyer, who'd grown as close as surrogate parents to me, and for the students, I took my concerns to the headmistress after breakfast one morning in mid-October.

Smoothing my skirt and hair, I knocked on Mrs. Evans's door.

"Come in."

"Good morning, Mrs. Evans. Do you have a moment?"

"Of course, Miss MacNeill. Is there a problem?"

"I hope not." But there was. Mrs. Evans had made her reservations regarding the Meyers perfectly clear. I, in good conscience, would make mine. "I'm concerned for our relations in the community, particularly as regards the Meyer family and their invitation to the Harvest Festival. For all the years the Meyers have been members of this community they've graciously opened their home and hosted—"

"Miss MacNeill—" Mrs. Evans held up her hand to stop me—"I believe I've made my position clear, and the board supports my decision."

"Harvest Festival is a long-standing tradition at Lakeside Ladies Academy, Mrs. Evans, almost a rite of passage for the older girls to attend."

"I am aware. My decision may seem harsh to you. I understand you've engaged in a longtime relationship with the family, with one member of the family in particular, but these are difficult times. Difficult times call for difficult measures. Associating with neighbors of German extraction presents a delicate and potentially volatile situation. It is simply not possible for the school to engage in subversive relationships."

"The Meyers are not subversive in any way. They are truly patriotic. Stephen and Jonas are both American citizens."

"Be that as it may, their parents are not citizens, and even if they were, there is every reason for caution. We cannot afford to sully the reputation of the academy for the sake of a festival, no matter—"

"But these are our dear friends and longtime supporters of the school. We've committed to teaching our girls Christian principles of compassion, kindness, generosity—"

"They are your friends, Miss MacNeill. I understand that, and I must caution you: parents entrusting their daughters to our care will not look kindly on teachers who keep company with the enemy."

"The enemy!" I gasped.

Rising to stand behind her desk, the headmistress straightened her spine even more, if that was possible. "Apparently I must also caution you against insubordination, and against allowing your emotions to rule your head. We shall hear no more of this. Am I clear?"

"Yes, ma'am." The bile in my throat formed a nasty taste. I turned to go, before I said things I could not take back.

"Miss MacNeill."

"Yes?" I stopped with my hand on the door but didn't turn.

"Do not ruin your teaching career for causes beyond your control.

Given the present circumstances, I think it best you discontinue your correspondence with Mr. Meyer. It sets a poor example for our girls to see letters arrive from Germans."

The blood drained from my head, leaving me faint. I didn't reply but quietly closed the door behind me, determined not to cry from fury or pain. I could not understand such prejudice, such unfairness, such small-mindedness.

Two months passed. It was nearly Christmas and once again I was not going anywhere. Mrs. Simmons had died in autumn of the previous year, a thing I'd not learned until her letters were returned to me unopened, marked *Deceased*. I felt her loss and the loss of my parents most keenly at Christmas.

Things between Dot and me had become more strained. Two more of my stories had been published in a local magazine, bringing modest checks and praise from Mrs. Evans. The recognition that brought me from the board of governors did not sit well with my friend, but the congratulatory box of long-stemmed roses delivered with a note from the Meyer family fell like a death blow on that open wound.

Flowers were such a rare and extravagant gift in a Connecticut winter that by day I placed the vase at the head of my classroom for students to enjoy, taking it to my room at night.

When Dot walked into my classroom and heard the girls oohing and aahing over the lavish bouquet, she grimaced but spoke to me. "Flaunting your coat of many colors, Josephina?"

That stung. Flaunting was not my intention. More, perhaps, to show how kind the Meyer family was, and yes, to celebrate my achievement. I was proud of those early publications, and who wouldn't be? Wasn't it my right to enjoy the praise? Looking back, I wonder that I didn't anticipate how those roses might hurt Dot. Surely she hoped for a future of more than flowers with that family, as did I.

Whether or not she continued to write to or see Stephen or Jonas, I didn't know and dared not ask. Dot could have letters mailed and delivered from her family's home, whereas I could not. For the first time I declined her family's invitation to Christmas dinner, saying it was my turn to stay and care for the students who would spend Christmas at the school. Dot made no attempt to persuade me otherwise.

But once the noon meal was finished and the girls were occupied with games and a round of carols provided by Mr. and Mrs. Potts, I dared ask the Pottses if they'd mind if I slipped away for a few hours.

Mr. Potts had nourished a soft spot in his heart for me ever since that first day he and Young Clem had met me at the train station—ever since the day I'd first met Dot. Often, he'd say, "You were such a slip of a thing with them brown eyes wide as saucers. Terrified of the world, you looked. I'd say to Mrs. Potts time and again that I wished we could take you in and raise you ourselves, save you the worry of them older mean girls. But we couldn't. Best I could do was to welcome you down to the barn when you needed an ear to bend or let my missus know to pocket you a cookie or two from the kitchen."

If I needed to whisk mental cobwebs and chase the wind for a few hours, he'd quietly saddle the newest Young Clem or Old Clem, whichever happened to be available, and give me free rein. "Just bring him back and if you get lost, give him his head. He knows his way home from anywhere. Smartest horse I ever knew."

That applied equally to Young Clem, Old Clem, and each of their descendants.

That afternoon I rode pell-mell for the Meyer farm, hoping against hope that I might see Stephen, trusting I could at least find the comforting arms of his mother and assure her of my love and affection. I took care to tie Old Clem to the hitching post around the back of the house so he could not be seen from the Belding farm.

I was halfway up the back kitchen steps when Mrs. Meyer opened the door, eyes wary at first, then relieved when she saw who it was.

"Merry Christmas, Mother Meyer!"

"Adelaide." She opened her arms, and I ran into them, holding her tight. It had been so long since anyone had held me.

Over coffee and warm apple cake straight from the oven, Mrs. Meyer poured out her side of the story.

"Never in my dreams would I have thought that our neighbors, our friends, would turn against us. Once, friendship and laughter, now suspicion at every turn. Women hold themselves apart in church and turn their backs at market, pretending not to see me. Friedrich has been put on notice at the bank. He's to see his regional superior after the first of the year."

"They're firing him?" I couldn't comprehend it.

"He fears so, unless he can convince them we are Russian, not German."

"But you're not Russian . . . are you?"

Mr. Meyer appeared in the doorway. I didn't know what he'd heard. "We speak no more German. If asked, we are Russian." He strode into the room, stopping before me. "You still dare to come, Adelaide? You are not forbidden?"

How I hated to admit it. "The headmistress has told me not to write to Stephen or Jonas anymore, to cut ties. That's why it's been so long since I've come. But I can't. Don't you see it would be like cutting off my arm?"

Mrs. Meyer gasped, fisting her handkerchief and pressing it to her mouth.

"Now, now, Mama. We've been through worse in life and survived. We will survive this, too." Mr. Meyer stood behind her chair, stroking her hair, her neck. She leaned into him. The tenderness between them pressed a weight of longing on my heart.

Mrs. Meyer nodded, lifting her head, and tried to smile. "You are right, Husband." She reached across the table for my hand. "You will stay for supper, Adelaide?"

"If you'll have me, I would love to."

"Always we will have you. You are part of our family, as long as you want to be."

"Forever." I smiled.

We spent the next hour in companionable silence, peeling and chopping apples for that evening's sauce and the next morning's *Apfelstrudel*, scrubbing and chopping vegetables, adding them to the already savory goose roasting in the oven. Setting out Mother Meyer's Christmas stollen reminded of the first time I'd met this dear lady, and the warm welcome she'd given me as a stranger.

I set the table, glad for the familiarity of crockery and coffee mugs, of knives and forks and spoons, glad that I knew where each thing was kept and little stories, learned over the years, of how each item came to be part and parcel of the family's store.

"I don't know if Jonas or Stephen will make it home tonight, but set their places just the same, just in case."

I didn't need to be asked twice. I knew I'd get a grilling or at least the evil eye from Mrs. Evans if she learned where I'd gone, but I was an adult now and a teacher. I needn't answer her questions if I didn't want to. The worst she could do was fire me. I'd no idea what I'd do if that happened. Now that the school year had begun, I hoped that wasn't likely. We were shorthanded enough at the academy and losing a full-time teacher would be difficult. Mrs. Evans also liked having a faculty member who'd been published, meager as my publishing credentials were.

Neither Jonas nor Stephen made it home before we sat down to dinner. Not one of us voiced the concern we felt, but I knew our worry for them was shared. Mr. Meyer reached across the table. Together, we formed a circle of hands around the meal as he prayed.

"Dear Lord and Father of us all, we praise Your holy name. We thank You for Your Son, Jesus, whose birth we celebrate this day. We thank You for His life, the death He gave, and His resurrection, for the opportunity for life everlasting through faith in Him. Help us take the lessons of His life, His love and sacrifice, to heart. Thank You for the labor and strength to do that labor given us this day. Thank You for this food, this home, for bounty in this land. Guide the leaders of this country and those around the world. Give them wisdom, discernment, and a desire to serve You and live with one another in peace. Protect our loved ones, wherever they are, and bring them safely home. Forgive us for our anger, our willful pride, our every sin, Lord. Help us to do better. Help our neighbors to see past their fear. Help us do the same. We pray all this, Father, in our Savior's name, amen."

"Amen," we echoed.

The meal was eaten in silence, at least until we heard boots stomp up the back porch steps. Hope sprang in Mother Meyer's eyes, making my heart leap. The back door swung open before we could rise from our seats.

"Merry Christmas, Mama! Merry Christmas, Papa!" Two strong male voices rang from the rafters. Laughter and hugs filled the space, crowding the balsam-scented room that had only moments before loomed cavernous.

My heart swelled, nearly exploded in my chest when Stephen drew me aside and, taking my hand, whispered, "Merry Christmas, Addie," so close to my ear.

Before I could respond, Jonas thumped him on the back. "No slinking off to corners with your lady love!"

Stephen's neck and cheeks burned crimson, and he swatted his brother's shoulder. I didn't know if he'd been angered by the sport his brother made or embarrassed when called out for his true feelings. Did Jonas know? Had Stephen spoken to him? Did Stephen even know how he felt about me?

There was no time to speak alone. The minutes sped by. When the clock on the mantel bonged eight, my throat caught. I knew I must go. The doors at the academy would soon be locked. I should have already returned to spend the evening with the girls. Mr. Potts must be frantic for Old Clem and for me. Mrs. Potts would surely know where I'd gone, even though I'd not told her.

"I'm sorry . . . I must go. It's been wonderful to be with you all. I'm so glad you're all here together. Merry Christmas." My words tumbled out, one upon the other. I'd no idea when I could slip away to see them again. There was no time, no easy way to explain to the brothers why I hadn't written. Surely Mrs. Meyer would tell her sons.

"Stephen, you must escort our Adelaide back to the school." Mr. Meyer spoke with finality.

"No, it's all right. Truly, I'll be fine."

"Not this time of night."

"No one will see me. I promise. I'll make certain." Stephen spoke quietly.

Oh, the humiliation of that moment! It must have shown in my face.

"Never worry, my dear." Mrs. Meyer gathered me in her arms. "We know your heart. Come whenever you are able. You belong to us."

I couldn't speak, could only close my eyes, savoring her hug.

She wrapped my scarf around my neck, tucking it close, while Jonas held my coat and Stephen donned his own. We walked into the cold and starry night. A dusting of snow must have fallen in the late afternoon or early evening, but wind had swept the clouds clear, the night brisk and the sky alive in stars, gleaming in their spheres.

Stephen cupped his hand for my foot, hoisting me as I mounted Old Clem, though I had no need. His hand rested on Old Clem and I thought he might speak. I knew he looked up at me, but it was so dark I couldn't read his eyes. He patted Old Clem's side and mounted his own horse, Thunder. We rode in companionable silence, my heart thudding so loudly in my chest I thought he surely must hear.

We were within sight of the school when Stephen reached for the reins of Old Clem, bringing both our horses to a stop. "Addie."

"Yes?"

"I wish we had more time. There's so much I want to say, to ask you."

"Anything. Ask me anything." My heart pounded.

"Why haven't you written? My letters, every one, have been returned."

"What?"

"*Return to Sender.* That's what they all say, but it's not in your handwriting. I wrote Mama, asking if you'd left the school, but she didn't know."

A lump began in the pit of my stomach, rising to my throat. "I never received your letters. I would never have returned them. I swear. You must know that." Even in the dark, I knew he studied my face, my form. "Mrs. Evans forbade me to write you, but I didn't imagine—I never thought she'd withhold my letters."

"Because my family is German." It wasn't a question.

"I'm so very sorry. I had no idea. I thought you'd stopped writing me."

"Never." He was quiet, so quiet I couldn't tell his thinking. "But you were at my family's home today."

"Because it's Christmas. Mrs. Evans is away, so I could come. Because I couldn't not come. Your mother—she's like a mother to me. And because—because I hoped to see you."

He swung from his horse and gently but firmly pulled me from Old Clem. We stood so close I wasn't sure if the breath before my face was his or mine.

"Addie," he whispered.

I touched his face with my gloved hand, wishing that wool did not stand between us.

"In another year and a half, I'll be finished with law school."

"It seems forever."

"But it's not. I hope by then this hateful war will be over. But I'll still be from a German family."

"That doesn't matter to me. It's never mattered." He embraced me and I clung to him. "You know that, don't you?"

He didn't answer but held me tighter. "Father wants us to say that we're Russian. He's forbidden us to speak German at home."

"Your mother told me. I heard him say, 'No more German.' He's going to try to convince the bank that he's Russian."

Stephen snorted. "But we're not. I cannot pretend."

"For safety's sake." I pulled back, just a little. "Your mother is worried that—"

"Mama worries too much."

I dared not tell him that all I did was worry—every time I heard the ravings of anti-German sentiment from locals or girls, students who knew so little of what they spoke.

A lantern lit the night outside the school's stable. I knew it was a signal—Mr. Potts looking for me, warning me to come in. He must have known we were near, but how, I didn't know.

"I must go. If I don't, Mr. Potts will come looking for me." I didn't want to. There was still so much to say, and no time.

"I'll write you through Mama, and you can write me the same way."

"You know I want to . . . but how I'll get letters to and from . . . Mrs. Evans has forbidden me to—"

"Yes, you said." He sounded frustrated, annoyed. I didn't want our time to end on that note, but the stable door opened, and Mr. Potts emerged.

"I must go," I whispered, pulling away.

But he resisted, taking my face between his hands and kissing me, long and warmly, until I could barely breathe. "I love you, Addie MacNeill."

My heart nearly burst for joy. "And I love you, Stephen Meyer. I've loved you so long."

He pressed his forehead to mine. I felt the fire of his skin, knew even in the dark that as he kissed my face again and again, he smiled, just as I did.

The sounding bell, giving fifteen minutes' warning before the doors were locked, rang out at the academy. Stephen hugged me tight once more, then helped me mount.

He took my hand and, pulling the top of my glove from beneath my coat, kissed my wrist. He squeezed my hand before dropping it. Never had my face felt so warm or my fingers so cold, not even inside my flannel-lined gloves. Before I could think what else to say Stephen had mounted, turned Thunder, and was gone.

Chapter Fourteen

MAY 1935

For the third time that morning Dorothy compared the seating arrangement for the baccalaureate banquet to the guest list, determined to keep warring political factions apart without appearing to slight anyone or to favor one party over another. She wondered if slipping in the unsuspecting guest or couple at a table might appease those who simply needed an audience. Was subjecting an innocent party to the overbearing railings of this senator or that diplomat a wise or a cowardly thing to do?

She'd spent an hour that morning trying to divert the local florist's passion for feathers. "Feathers are all the rage, Mrs. Meyer. Imagine bleached white plumage among bouquets of the academy's signature daisies. Something really must be done to dress up field flowers."

She groaned inwardly. The florist was new to the area and clearly did not understand the value of the school's time-honored tradition of daisy chains. She wouldn't mind something different for the tables—perhaps pink roses and some sort of filler to complement the daisies—but she would never agree to feathers. *White feathers, of all things.* Dorothy cringed at the memory.

⌒

JUNE 1917

It began in late spring of the year President Wilson declared war on Germany. Up until then, the girls and faculty at Lakeside Ladies Academy had limited their war efforts to collecting bundles of clothing, rolling bandage strips to donate to the Red Cross, and knitting scarves and gloves and socks for soldiers and refugees overseas until their fingers chafed raw. But once America declared war on Germany, patriotic fever took on a fervor within the town and among the girls at Lakeside that neither Dorothy nor Addie had foreseen, let alone Mrs. Evans, the school's headmistress.

Brothers, fathers, cousins, and beaus across the country enlisted in droves, including Dorothy's two older brothers, Jason and Jackson. Those who waited for the first draft registration were considered slackers, cowards.

Rumor ran that some young ladies had taken to handing out white feathers to any male not in uniform, regardless of his age or apparent abilities.

Dorothy happened to be in the school's foyer when the practice was reported to Mrs. Evans by a local police officer.

"Officer Bailey, I can assure you that none of my young ladies are involved. As you know we're doing everything we possibly can for the war effort, but my girls would never behave in such a fashion, nor would they have opportunity. They're kept quite busy here during the week, and weekends are strictly supervised."

"I hope you're right, Mrs. Evans. It seems that whoever these girls are, they've made their way through the locals and are out pestering Mrs. Salley's son. She's made a formal complaint. We don't need that kind of thing here. Most of our boys join willingly, if not yet, then when their time comes. But Cal Salley isn't like other boys and—"

"I'm sure you are correct, Officer, but I promise you, it's not—"

"I'd appreciate it if you'd make that announcement to your young ladies. Just a warning, mind, but it can't hurt."

Mrs. Evans straightened. "I don't like putting ideas in their heads, Officer. I'm sure not one of my girls has considered such a thing."

Officer Bailey pressed his lips together, looked about to speak again, but tipped his hat and turned on his heel.

"The idea!" Mrs. Evans murmured, catching Dorothy's eye and shaking her head.

But Dorothy wondered. Mrs. Evans had not heard the girls' talk over the lesson on baking victory bread in the school kitchen or the pitch of near hysterics when one of the girls claimed that her brother had run away from home to join up. Dorothy had, and she wouldn't put it past two or three of the girls at the very least to go around handing out white feathers.

Dorothy held her breath through luncheon, hoping Mrs. Evans might address the older girls and caution them, but she didn't, and Dorothy didn't think it her place to repeat what she'd overheard.

Dorothy's first free Saturday afternoon and Sunday finally came. On her walk home, she stopped by the milliner's in town to pick up a new green broad-brimmed hat her mother had ordered. Mrs. Stroop was just showing it off for Dorothy when a commotion across the street caught their eye through the store window.

Dorothy could not have been more shocked to see Emma Lockheed and Augusta Blake, two Lakeside Academy girls, neither more than thirteen—certainly not old enough to be wandering Farmington's streets alone—thrusting a handful of white feathers back and forth beneath the nose of six-feet-tall Cal Salley outside the bakery, apparently teasing him to distraction. Cal, possessing a child's mind in a grown man's body, visibly quaked, holding his hands in front of his face, doing his best to fend off his attackers.

"Please, Mrs. Stroop, box Mother's hat. I'll be right back."

Dorothy, furious and embarrassed, was determined to lecture the two across the street but stopped in her tracks when she saw Mrs. Salley, brandishing her rolling pin, step outside the bakery and confront the girls in a fury. Dorothy could not overhear everything she said, but the girls' faces reddened until they looked suitably reprimanded. Mrs. Salley forcibly turned them and pointed them back in the direction of the school, whereupon the girls took off at a dead run.

Cal had slipped off in the opposite direction. It looked as if his mother might go after him, but a customer stepped into the bakery just then and she reluctantly followed the woman inside, casting a worried glance after her son.

Dorothy breathed a sigh of relief. Apparently the girls had been taught their lesson, or at least caught and their misbehavior stopped. If their winged flight meant anything, they should be halfway back to the school.

There was little enough time to spend with her family, let alone write a letter to Stephen, so Dorothy thought it well to go on. She could deal with the girls herself on Monday. She saw no need to involve Mrs. Evans.

Mrs. Evans, ever superior in her manner, strained relations at the school. It was so near the end of term it would be a shame to have the year end on a sour note for the girls and their parents. The school's enrollment had declined since Miss Weston, dearly loved by students and alumnae alike, left to marry. Tensions ran high in every quarter, what with the war and concern for spies on every hand.

Dorothy didn't want to draw attention to herself, especially since she continued to write Stephen and Jonas through her mother, even though she'd led Addie and Mrs. Evans to believe she'd terminated her correspondence with the brothers. It would be a year or more before Stephen finished his law degree. Surely the war would be over by then. If their relationship grew as she hoped, they might need to leave Connecticut and settle somewhere more amenable to Germans or convince a new community that they were truly Russian. However it came about, Dorothy didn't much care, as long as she and Stephen could be together. She hoped Addie had moved on in her feelings for Stephen, that she'd realized she could not pursue him, but Dorothy wasn't certain. They never spoke of it. In fact, they both stayed busy and spoke very little at all.

If only that had been the end of the white feathers, if only Dorothy had confronted the girls the moment she saw them that day, perhaps none of what came later would have happened.

Chapter Fifteen

MAY 1935

It was only midmorning, but I'd given up any pretense of writing or even light editing and spent another morning in my garden, not digging, not weeding, but simply sitting, focused on the delightful sparrows alternately splashing in my birdbath and squabbling over the few crumbs Portia had scattered from our breakfast.

At once funny and frightful in their determination for food and territory, more than a few feathers flew. One landed less than a foot away. I retrieved it, marveling that something so small and plain, so needful, could be so soft. I twirled it in my fingers. Still, it was a feather, and feathers, I knew, could be dangerous things.

Portia had been right. Remembering, too, can be a dangerous thing. Once begun, it's so very hard to stop. Memories tumble down from the heavens, or up from hell, one upon another, insidious, persistent, relentless in their presentation. I didn't like remembering those long-ago days any more than Portia did. Life before 1917 was a different world, a different time, a different me . . . snatched away in a moment, forever gone, everything after changed. And what point was there in remembering? In longing for the past buried beneath the rubble of fire and destruction?

If it hadn't been for the war . . . that hateful, useless, pointless war . . . If I cast enough blame on the war, on fate, on circumstances, I could pretend I'd had no part in all that transpired.

I hadn't seen it coming . . . no more than Mrs. Salley or her son had.

Bullies. Emma Lockheed and Augusta Blake were bullies of the worst sort . . . worse in their sneaking ways than Mean Mildred had acted toward Dot and me. Their pushing, pushing, pushing cloaked in secrecy somehow gave them an inflated sense of importance, of power, and a sure belief that they were right and evidencing patriotism . . . Even now, all these years later, it turned my stomach and made my heart ache to think of it. But it was where the bullying began—at least it was the manifestation of what already fomented in the hearts of some.

There were stories in the newspapers and magazines of girls who handed out white feathers to men not in uniform. I think the girls saw it as something brave and bold, patriotic, even romantic, though they all vowed they would never dare.

Once word filtered into the academy that white feathers had been distributed to teens and men in town, whispered snippets and rumors raced through the corridors. Often I'd hear bits and pieces not meant for my or any teacher's ears as I knitted with the girls in the long evenings, though I pretended ignorance. It was the best way to keep a watchful eye. I knew from my own years growing up at the school that there were plans hatched that we'd never admit to teachers. Oh, that I'd listened more closely, kept a more watchful eye! Perhaps I could have prevented the outcome, at least warded off the offenders.

But I was too inclined to spend those mindless hours dreaming of Stephen, imagining what he was doing, wondering if he was thinking of me, worrying over things I could not change. I hadn't seen him since Christmas and had heard very little from him, though I replayed those few moments, when he'd accompanied me back to the school, over and over in my mind.

Only when I chanced upon his mother in town could I learn anything, could she slip me the letters he wrote, the ones she kept ever in her purse, and take the ones I kept in mine for him, in case we'd meet.

I took every opportunity I could invent to go into town on the chance I'd see her, in the hope I'd learn some little thing about him to keep me going. But visiting their home was forbidden, and after my late return on Christmas evening, Mrs. Evans, who'd returned early from her family's gathering and found me missing, kept a watchful eye. I couldn't afford to lose my position. It was all that kept me from poverty and in close proximity to the Meyers.

I wondered if Dorothy visited with them on her weekends home, the Meyer home being just across the field from their farm, though she never said. I had a feeling if I asked, she might deny it. All those things filled my mind as we knitted socks and helmet hats, scarves, wristlets, and even gloves with exposed trigger fingers for our troops. But there was one evening when the venom in the room broke through my musings.

"He's a coward, I tell you! Look at how muscular he is, toting those heavy bags of flour and such for his mother. He's a slacker and ought to sign up. If anyone deserves a white feather it's him—or his mother for keeping him tied to her apron strings." Augusta's menacing tones stood out from the crowd.

"But he's simpleminded, isn't he?" Margaret, a girl from New Hampshire, more timid than most, questioned. "He'd be a danger to the others in uniform, and surely to himself." Her confidence waned and she little more than whispered, "Wouldn't he?"

"He could at least dig trenches for the others with a strong back like that," Emma asserted. "He ought to sign up. He ought to be ashamed not to."

There was little I could do without revealing I'd been listening, but surely I should say something, perhaps pull the girls aside. It was nearly time to put our needles away and prepare for bed. I tucked my knitting in its sock and stood, about to make the announcement, when I heard Augusta stage-whisper to her clique. "Well, he's not the worst. Look at those Meyer brothers—both of them hale and hearty—hiding out at their university and work while our boys are dying, fighting their kind. They deserve worse than a white feather!"

"Time for bed, girls!" My voice came out shriller than I'd intended. I should have said something more, I knew it then, but I quailed—in the face of a thirteen-year-old, in the face of prejudice and the shock of their venom, despite their knowing nothing of what they spoke. I knew I should keep a watchful eye on the girls, but it never occurred to me that anything more would come of it than the stirring of their own adolescent imaginations.

It was the next Saturday afternoon when I stopped in the bakery for a box of scones, hoping to show my support for Mrs. Salley. She'd had a hard time keeping her business going since her husband's heart attack. Though I'd never confess what I'd overheard, I knew her son had grown up the butt of jokes and sometimes cruel pranks. He was a kind boy—well, a boy in a man's body—given to shy smiles and a willingness to help. Her older son was away at university. Mrs. Salley told me he'd come home to help when his father fell ill, but she'd sent him back directly, saying, "Schooling is the best way you can help our family in the long run." She wouldn't hear of him coming home to stay, though I wondered if she sometimes regretted that decision.

"Is Cal well? I haven't seen him lately." I tried to make small talk, to assure her of my concern and friendship.

She sighed, shaking her head. "Keeps to himself, ever since those girls laid into him. Afraid of his own shadow, and he never used to be."

"Girls?" I feigned ignorance but feared it was some of our girls she meant.

Mrs. Salley fisted hands into her hips. "From your school, Miss MacNeill. Two upstarts giving out white feathers hither and yon, and when they ran out of victims, they started on my Cal. Scared him half to death, telling him he was about to be drafted and sent to the trenches, that if he didn't stand up straight, the Germans would mow him down with machine-gun fire or set him alight with flame throwers."

"What?" I gasped. "Surely not. What makes you think it was our girls?"

"Who else hereabout talks so uppity, as if they're better than the rest of us? They've been here three Saturdays in a row. After the first two I made sure my Cal's sent on errands with Mr. Stroop out of town to pick up supplies."

"Only our oldest girls are allowed in town for tea on Saturday afternoons, and I can't imagine any of them doing such a thing. Mrs. Evans runs things by the book."

She raised her eyebrows.

"Can you describe the girls?" I didn't want to believe it.

"They wear long skirts, pile their hair up and rouge their faces, as if they're near grown, but for all their airs I don't figure them for more than twelve or thirteen at most. One has blonde hair, the color of cornsilk. The other, brown, with a bit of red when the sun hits. Pretty girls, but wily."

She'd described Augusta and Emma to a T. But I didn't have to guess. Out the bakery window we heard them. I'd recognize Augusta's nasal tones anywhere. I also recognized the back of the man they'd accosted, white feathers in their hands. Emma, her eyes fastened to his face in brazen coquetry and daring, tucked one in his coat breast pocket.

"There they are! I told you!" Mrs. Salley retorted.

My hand went to my throat and fury to my brain. Leaving my parcel on the counter, I flung open the shop door. "Emma! Augusta! What do you think you girls are doing, and what are you doing in town?"

They spun on their heels, eyes opening wide. Emma had the sense to look caught and frightened, but Augusta lifted her chin in defiance. "We're standing up for what's good and right in our country. This traitor's out of uniform. We're giving him the white feather of cowardice he deserves."

My heart pounded. "Mr. Meyer," I implored Stephen, all the while shaking from rage and shame for the girls and from the nearness of him, "please forgive these ignorant girls. They have behaved badly and will face consequences for their unspeakable actions."

"Our unspeakable actions?" Augusta spoke back. "He's the German! He's the one unwilling to fight for the country that took him in. That makes him a coward and a traitor."

I wanted to slap her.

"Miss MacNeill." Stephen removed his hat in my presence and smiled stiffly. "I know this is not how you teach your students to behave in public."

Emma and Augusta flicked their eyes between Stephen and me. Emma, too perceptively, said, "It's true, then, Miss MacNeill. And him, a German." She spoke the last in wonder.

"Get back to the school, girls, immediately. Take your hair down and scrub that rouge from your cheeks. Remain in your room until I return. We're going straight to Mrs. Evans."

Emma looked as if she wanted to plead, but Augusta pulled her friend away without a word, walking with her head held high to the end of the block; then the two of them tore up the road to the school.

"I'm sorry, Stephen. I'm so very sorry."

"It's not the first time. It won't be the last, and I know it's not your fault." He looked for all the world as if he wanted to take my hand in his, or my face in his hands. I wanted that touch, more than anything. "It's not safe for us to be seen together in public. You'd best go."

"When can I see you?"

His eyes looked suddenly forlorn. "When this madness is over." He replaced his derby, tipped it, and walked away.

I knew Mrs. Salley was watching out the window—Mrs. Salley and probably every storekeeper and businessman on the street. Composing my face as best I could, I turned to return to the school. Dealing with the girls was first on my list of priorities, though I dreaded it.

"Miss MacNeill!" Mrs. Salley stood on her bakery stoop, parcel extended. "Your scones."

"Thank you, Mrs. Salley." I couldn't look her in the eye.

"I expect now those girls have stepped on your young man's toes, they'll be dealt with?"

"They'll be dealt with, I assure you." Was Stephen my young man? I didn't know.

She pressed her hand on my arm. I pulled away, unaccustomed to touch, but she whispered, "Things are rarely what they seem. Don't let the locals addle you. The Meyers are good people. We're all from somewhere. Most just forget that."

Pools threatened my eyes. I grasped her hand. "Thank you. There are things none of us can change."

"That I know right well." Her smile faded as she saw Mr. Stroop's wagon rattle up with her grown son, waving to everyone like the boy he was, on the seat beside him.

An hour later I stood before Mrs. Evans, but it was not with Augusta and Emma. I was summoned to the headmistress's office the moment I returned to the school.

"Close the door, Miss MacNeill." Mrs. Evans did not invite me to sit, though she remained seated behind her desk. "It's been reported to me that you were seen amiably conversing with Mr. Meyer on the streets of Farmington."

If my mouth dropped open, I would not have been surprised. "Yes, but—"

"Have I not warned you of this very thing?"

"I was merely—"

"I do not care what you were merely doing. The Meyer family have been declared enemy aliens and the fact that—"

"Enemy—? What do you mean, enemy aliens?"

"They're German, Miss MacNeill, as you well know. Germans on American soil have been declared resident aliens. Some are being interned as we speak. To be seen consorting with the enemy is—"

"Stephen—Mr. Meyer—is not my enemy or yours. He's American."

"German American, perhaps, but he's from an alien immigrant family and not in uniform."

"That gives those girls no right to accost him on the street with white feathers!"

"I've heard the rumors and I don't know who the girls are that are doing this, and I don't want to know. A part of me cannot help but admire their courage. It's a great evil we're facing in this war. Every able man is needed."

"Their courage?" Further words failed me.

"I've decided that you must return to your family in Halifax. Summer is nearly upon us, and Miss Belding can complete your classes until then. If you believe you can maintain your distance from the Meyer family and uphold your responsibilities for the good name of Lakeside Ladies Academy, you may return to teach for the fall term. If not, well, then, I trust you will send me word before September."

"You're firing me?"

"Let us say I'm offering you an opportunity to prove your loyalty. Consider it probation if you must."

I stood speechless. Motionless.

Mrs. Evans shifted uncomfortably in her seat. "Influential parents and their relatives will soon attend graduation. I want no rumors or scandal."

Blood boiled within my veins. "Let us not forget *affluent*."

Mrs. Evans rose to her full height. "No, let us not forget that it is the affluent parents of this institution who keep it running through their tuition payments, their sponsorships and generous donations. How long do you suppose that might go on if it were known that one of our teachers brought scandalous accusations of treason down on our heads?"

It was all wrong, out of proportion.

"You may go. If you have insufficient funds for your transportation, I'm certain the school budget can supply."

"When do you want me to go? The school play is next week. I'm directing—"

"There is no need to delay. Trains run Monday morning. You have

until then to clear your desk. Miss Belding will absorb your duties with the girls beginning this evening. Mr. Potts can drive you to the station."

"Monday? But the spring play . . . the girls have all worked so hard."

"Which makes it possible for Miss Belding to take over. I'm certain everything will run smoothly." Mrs. Evans stood firm.

I felt as if the earth shifted beneath my feet.

"That is all, Miss MacNeill. You may go."

Dismissed. My heart pounded in its cage. How my feet moved toward the door, how my hand turned the knob, how I closed the door behind me to stand in the hallway, I didn't know.

Shushing behind the curtain across the way—and the feet beneath it—drew my attention. I pulled the drapery aside to find Augusta Blake and Emma Lockheed staring up at me, the hateful glimmer of triumph in Augusta's eyes.

My breath came hard and fast, and I grabbed Augusta's arm, squeezing it tighter than I realized, than I should have dared. "You think you've won, but your spite and wickedness will out for all to see. Stay away from Cal Salley. Leave him alone. He's a poor boy who through no fault of his own—"

The door behind me opened. "Miss MacNeill!"

"She's hurting me, Mrs. Evans, because she thinks I told on her!" Augusta whined, feigning tears.

I dropped Augusta's arm.

"Pack your bags, Miss MacNeill. Augusta, go to the nurse. Make certain your arm is all right."

I walked away as quickly as I could, the pounding in my ears more than I could take.

A month later, miserable and lonely in my brother's house in Halifax, I received a letter from Dot.

Dear Addie,

I'm sorry I did not see you before you left, and I'm sorry now to write the first time with bad news.

I heard the rumors of what happened in town and later with Mrs. Evans and Augusta. I know you've always carried a torch for Stephen, so I put it all down to that and figured a few months in Halifax might cure you of your crush, and that everything would blow over in time.

I know you always meant to be kind to the Meyers and to the Salleys, and I know this news will hit you hard. There's no easy way to say it.

Cal Salley was found in his mother's basement, hanging by the neck. She found him herself. She said he couldn't take the girls' teasing. They'd convinced him that he'd be drafted and sent to the front as cannon fodder, that he was too stupid to do anything but dig trenches and stand as a human shield for real men, but that it was his patriotic duty to do that. Evidently, they kept after him.

It all came out when Mrs. Salley went to the newspaper, saying how girls from Lakeside had terrorized her son. It's caused a great scandal, and upon investigation, Mrs. Evans has been dismissed for not keeping better track of the girls. Augusta and Emma cried and carried on, professing their repentance, but that cannot bring Cal back.

Augusta's parents have withdrawn her. She'll not be allowed to return for the fall term. Emma was evidently more of a follower than a leader in it all and has been put on probation, pending a talk with her parents when they return from overseas. I rather think their funding has something to do with the leniency toward her.

Anyway, I'm sorrier than I can say that it's come to this. I wish now I'd spoken up or taken the girls to task when I saw them slipping out. I truly had no idea they'd pestered Cal again and again. We all attended his funeral, though because it was a suicide, he wasn't allowed to be buried in their church's yard. Mrs. Salley is beside herself with grief. She's barely able to keep her bakery going. It hurts to look at her.

I heard that the girls gave Stephen a white feather. I saw him recently now that he's home for the summer. I think, in the end, he's going to join up, though it hurts my heart to think of him over there.

I've counseled you to forget Stephen, and I suspect you know why. It's not because he's German, though I wish he weren't. I love him, Addie. Please let go your hold. You're smart and pretty and successful in your writing. You can have any man you want. Stephen's the only man I've ever cared anything about. Now that he and I are here and you're in Halifax, perhaps you can find a Canadian, someone more like you.

I'm sorry we quarreled so long ago. I hope we can remain friends.

Your Sister of the Lake,
Dot

Chapter Sixteen

MAY 1935

Dorothy unplugged the electric lights that had been strung around the gazebo to create the school's outdoor theater garden. It wasn't her job, not really, but it had become a sort of tradition once she became headmistress of Lakeside. It felt as if she were tucking away her children's memories for another year, the only children she was likely to have.

The electric bulbs had cast a brilliant effect across young thespians during their performance of *Twelfth Night*. The late spring play had gone off without a hitch, much to Dorothy's relief. It wasn't what it had been back in the day when Addie had directed it, but it was something, and parents loved to see their daughters perform on stage, so long as they performed within the confines of the academy.

Dorothy hoped that would not always be the case, that the gymnasium/theater combination once begun—the building stalled during this horrid Depression—would be completed. She longed to see the day that Lakeside Ladies Academy's thespians would perform on a real stage, facing a packed auditorium, as they deserved. *Wouldn't Addie have loved that?*

Addie. Never was a spring play staged at Lakeside that Dorothy did not think of her friend, remembering the year Cal Salley hung himself after the girls' bullying, as well as her own attempts to bully, to pull Addie and Stephen apart.

Until Bernadette and all this sad business with the girl's mother, she'd rarely allowed herself to think long of Addie. When memories surfaced, she'd pushed them away. But not now, and never after the spring play. It had become a sort of penance for all she'd done to the two she'd loved most.

Dorothy's face still burned in shame over how she'd tried to make Addie believe that Stephen had forgotten her, that any hopes she might have had for him were doomed, that distance made the heart forget. She'd realized all too soon that distance had only made their hearts grow fonder.

—

SEPTEMBER 1917

Bittersweet was the day Addie returned to Lakeside Ladies Academy. The board of governors, realizing they needed to bolster faculty and increase admissions under a new headmistress, had written Addie, urging her to return from Halifax in time to begin the fall semester.

Dorothy and an aging Mr. Potts, driven by the newest Old Clem, met Addie's train at the station. Just as she'd done the first day they'd met as girls, Dorothy flung open the ladies' waiting room door, searching for Addie. But Addie was no longer the green forlorn-looking waif she'd been at twelve. Halifax must have agreed with and improved her. Her sister-in-law must have finally taken Addie under her wing, for the young woman before Dorothy was a raven-haired beauty with upswept hair, more Gibson girl than Lakeside girl, poised and elegant beyond anything Dorothy hoped to become.

The sight of her friend nearly took Dorothy's breath away. She'd made so little headway in her relationship with Stephen over the summer. She must do all in her power to keep the two of them apart now.

"Dot!" Addie smiled with her mouth and questioned with her eyes.

"Addie!" She made certain her hug hid her own eyes. "I'm so glad you're back. I've missed you. We've all missed you!"

That was a truth so clear it hurt. In spite of her jealousy, Dorothy had missed Addie and all their conflicted relationship. And each time she'd been with Mrs. Meyer, the woman asked Dorothy if she'd heard from "our Addie." Stephen had stopped asking her at all, which had made Dorothy wonder if he and Addie were corresponding, if they had done so the entire time Addie was away from the watchful eye of the board and the school.

"Mr. Potts! I'm ever so glad to see you!" Addie flew into the groomsman's arms, as if he were a long-lost grandfather, embarrassing Dorothy no end.

"We've missed you something fierce, my dear. Lakeside's just not been the same without you, Mrs. Potts and I agree, and don't you, Miss Dorothy?"

Dorothy had never been so warmly greeted by Mr. Potts, though she'd known him since she first came to the school. She set her mouth, smiling. "Of course."

"I brought the buggy this time. You young ladies are too grown up to be riding in the back of my old produce wagon. Here, let me help you up." He extended his hand for them both and saw them safely seated before taking his place and clicking his tongue, signaling Old Clem to walk on.

"You're looking well—splendid, Dot! I was so glad for your letters. I feel I've been gone for ages. How is everyone?" Addie couldn't seem to slow her questions.

Dorothy wasn't certain which to answer first, or whether "everyone" actually meant Stephen. So she redirected. "Much the same as when you left, except that Mean Mildred's come back to haunt us."

"What do you mean?"

Mr. Potts guffawed.

Dorothy sighed. "Mr. Shockley—the treasurer of the board of governors—has gone and married her. Can you believe it?"

"You're not serious!"

"Whatever possessed either of them I've no clue, but she gets her snaking little fingers in every pie possible regarding the school's expenditures, as if she owns the academy. I think she sees it all as retribution for her last year . . . and that mysterious rap, rap, rapping that 'ended her academic career.'"

A conspiratorial glance passed between the young women.

"One thing's for certain, we don't miss Mrs. Evans. What a battle-ax she was!"

Addie laughed. Even her laugh had grown up over the summer, sounding more like bells than the belly laughs they'd known as girls.

But she sobered quickly enough. "I can't say I'll miss her, either. She wouldn't listen, no matter what I tried to say to her about those girls, or—or anything about the war or the danger of prejudices. I'm just so sorry all that happened . . . Poor Mrs. Salley. How is she?"

Before Dorothy could speak, Mr. Potts, who'd clearly been listening, added, "We're all sorry we didn't speak up more. Can't take that blame on yourself. I saw those two slipping off in their finery a couple of Saturday afternoons."

"You never said!" Dorothy was shocked.

Mr. Potts shook his head. "I took no special notice. Girls that age have been slipping off into town of a Saturday for years, just to show they can. If I tattled on each and every one, I'd spend my Saturdays in the headmistress's office."

Dorothy and Addie exchanged another glance. They'd been "girls that age" once and had slipped into town a time or two. The thrill of not getting caught had driven them on until they decided that meeting with Susannah and Ruth at the gazebo was preferable.

"Mrs. Salley's come round a little, I think. She looked pretty bad for a time, but she's still got her husband to look after and the bakery to run. Her older son is off to France."

"Oh no. Was he drafted?"

Dorothy shook her head. "Enlisted. Said it was his duty, that he'd do it for him and Cal both."

Addie sat back, as if the wind had been knocked out of her. Finally she whispered, "How are the Meyers? I know you see them. Stephen wrote, but I can't tell if he's letting me know how badly things are going."

There it was, then. *Stephen wrote.* So, Dorothy knew at last, things had not ended between them, but how far had they gone?

"Dot?"

"Oh. I don't know, not so bad, at least not so differently than before. Mr. Meyer lost his job at the bank, but I guess you know that."

"Stephen didn't say."

So, he's not told her everything, not confided. That's something. "Well, he might not want just anyone and everyone to know. They've added chickens and a cow. Mr. Meyer put in a big garden this year—they depend on that. Mrs. Meyer doesn't come into town much. I think it's too hard."

"People can be so cruel."

"Yes, I suppose they can." Dorothy didn't want to be cruel. She didn't mean to be cruel.

"Have they hired a new headmistress?"

"Miss Fullbright's acting headmistress in the interim. They're talking about hiring a headmaster."

"For an all-girls school?" Addie's eyes widened.

Dorothy shrugged.

"I wish they'd ask Miss Weston back."

"Mrs. Earlton, now."

"Mrs. Earlton. She'd be wonderful. Do you remember how she kept us all in line but listened to teachers and students alike, how she knew when to give us freer rein or tighten those reins? She did it instinctively."

"And she seemed to know just who the mischief-makers were."

"The Ladies of the Lake?" Addie's eyebrows rose.

"Too often, I'm sorry to say."

"Have you heard from Susannah? From Ruth?"

"Ruth is in France, too near the front if I can understand her cryptic words. She's not allowed to say just where. She asked if you'd cut ties with the Meyer family. I think it's still a sore point for her."

Addie clasped her hands together and set them in her lap, sealing off whatever Dorothy had hoped she might say. Finally, she spoke. "You haven't cut ties, have you?"

"It's different for me. They've been our near neighbors forever. I've known Stephen and Jonas since we were toddlers."

Addie turned away.

"Susannah's third child is on the way."

"Another?"

"She won't be able to come to the gazebo for another year or more. But then, I don't suppose Ruth will be back anytime soon. If she makes it."

"Don't say that. It's unlucky."

"Don't you think it?"

Addie met Dorothy's eyes. "Every day. I don't know when or if we'll all meet there again. I'm sorry for how our last meeting went."

Dorothy faced forward. "Me, too. We should have been more considerate of Ruth, having just lost her brother."

"Better days will come, won't they?"

"Surely." Dorothy forced a smile she didn't feel and determined to change the subject. "Do you remember those late-night skating parties on the lake? The ones Miss Weston organized on the spur of the moment?" She smiled, genuinely.

"And the bonfires! That's the kind of headmistress we need again."

"Maybe you'd best apply." Dorothy was only half teasing. If there was one thing she wanted beyond Stephen, it was to rise to the position of headmistress of Lakeside Ladies Academy. But if Addie had any designs on the role, Dorothy knew she wouldn't stand a chance. She'd lived in Addie's shadow academically and in the hearts of the Meyer family. She'd just as surely be overshadowed by Addie as a candidate to lead the school. Still, she needed to know Addie's intentions.

Addie stopped smiling. "I'm too young. Besides, you should know that I'm only here until Thanksgiving. Bertha, Lemuel's wife, is expecting. It's been a tricky pregnancy from the start, and they need my help."

"But your teaching career."

Addie shrugged. "The board knows. I told them I'd return on the condition I could leave before the birth. I'll come back as soon as Bertha can do without me. But they're all the family I have, Dot. I can't let them down, and I owe it to Lemuel."

"I hardly see how. He never even wrote you. One letter in all those years! You were miserable there." A sense of relief washed through Dorothy that Addie's sights were not set on the role of headmistress, at least not now, not yet. Her old desire to protect Addie rose a little, and it felt good. It felt right.

"Things are better between us now. Well, at least with Bertha, and Marcus is a darling, though he'd die of shame to hear me say that. I'm glad to have this time to get to know my nephew."

"And your brother?"

Addie shrugged. "Lemuel's a different sort. He's so much older than I am that he seems more like an uncle—certainly acts like one. But we get along . . . not easily, but not poorly. I think he appreciates what I've done for Marcus and for Bertha. And there's something nice about being needed by family."

Addie reached for Dorothy's hand and squeezed it in friendship. That felt right to Dorothy, too.

❧

If things had continued in that vein, how sweet it would have been. But Stephen came to Lakeside the next day. Dorothy happened to answer the door, and all he asked of her, all he wanted was for her to give Addie a note.

Of course, she'd smiled and agreed. When she closed the door, she slipped open the envelope. It wasn't tightly sealed.

Meet me at the gazebo at 10 tonight.

All my love,
S

Twelve short words. That's all it took to break Dorothy's heart.

⌣

MAY 1935

They met here, at the gazebo . . . the gazebo where we four had pledged our sisterhood, the place that was ours. They made it theirs. Dorothy pulled the last string of electric lights from their clasps with a greater jerk than the task warranted. *Perhaps if I'd not delivered that note, he would have waited and waited, and when she didn't come, perhaps he would have believed that she didn't love him after all. It could have ended then, couldn't it? Things could have been so different. But now, even if I tell the truth of all that happened later, it can never make things right.*

"Still here, Dorothy?"

Startled, Dorothy jumped, dropping the last electric bulb, sending it shattering across the floor of the gazebo.

"Darling! Are you all right?" Her husband, gallant as ever, was beside her in a moment, lifting her palm. "Did that cut your hand?"

"No, no, it didn't. You startled me." She wanted to pull her hand away but kept it there, within his, until he released it.

"You did seem far away. Everyone has gone and I only saw one lantern burning. I wanted to make sure you're all right. This play always seems something of a melancholy time for you."

Dorothy nodded, her heart too weighted by conflicting emotions to speak.

"Be careful where you step. It's too dark to see now, but I'm sure there are shards of glass everywhere. Let me help you down the steps. I'll get someone to clean this up in the morning."

"Wait."

"What is it?"

"Do you love me? Do you really, truly love me?" The ache in Dorothy's throat made the words come out raspy.

He hesitated only a moment, then took her in his arms, pushed the wisp of hair from her forehead and kissed it, her ear, her cheek, her lips. "Does that answer your question? Dorothy, you are my life; you know that."

She nestled in his arms, determined to push the ghosts of the past away, determined to make this moment the new memory forged in their gazebo.

Chapter Seventeen

I settled into my favorite high-back library chair and unfolded the new letter, thicker than usual, from Bernadette. I would share the letter with Portia but wanted to savor it alone first.

> *Dear Mother,*
>
> *Last night was our spring play performance, Twelfth Night, by William Shakespeare. You'll see my role, listed in the enclosed program.*
>
> *I think it not bragging to say you would have been proud of me. I remembered all my lines and delivered them soundly.*

I laughed aloud, the first time in days. "Yes, my darling girl." I took up the program and spoke to the empty room. "There you are! I am so very proud of you! I'm always proud of you."

Returning to the letter, my laughter faded.

Mrs. Meyer said I performed wonderfully, and that when the electric lights illuminated my face beneath the vines overhanging the gazebo, I reminded her of another girl from Nova Scotia who attended the school long ago, when she was a student. I asked her who, and she said the girl's name was Adelaide MacNeill—Addie—that she'd been her best friend and the best performer of their class. She'd even become a teacher and directed the play each spring she taught here, in the gazebo, as we had done. I asked if her friend ever came back for the spring play or for graduation, but she said no, that her friend had died long ago.

That was so sad, Mother. Mrs. Meyer looked as if she might cry. I don't think she has a best friend now, besides her husband.

It made me think of Father, with not so much as a grave to visit. You must miss him terribly, even after all these years. For me, it's almost as if he never lived. I wish I'd known him. We were so fortunate, you and I, to survive the explosion, and the war. Despite my burns, I'm glad I lived. I'm glad we lived. It's a gift to be alive, don't you think?

I must ask you once more, Mother, won't you please come to my graduation? It would mean so much to share that day with you, and I want to show you everything that has been my life here these last years. I want to take tea with you in town like the other girls will do with their mothers. I want to show you the gazebo where we perform our plays by the lake—the lake itself where I've learned to ice-skate in winter. Oh, I do love to skate! The freedom of it all! And there is someone very special I want you to meet, someone you can only meet here.

I'll show you the school. Did I ever tell you that the work horses here are all named Old Clem or Young Clem—no matter how old or young they are? It's some sort of tradition started by a groomsman who used to work here. There's so much I want to show you before I leave these halls forever. Then we could travel home together for the summer. It would be a grand adventure!

Mother, you must know that I never see your burns. I never did. You are simply my beautiful mother and everyone I know will see you as I do. I miss you. I love you, with all my heart. Please come.

Give my love and hugs to Portia. I can't wait to see you both.

Your Bernadette

The letter lay in my lap, its weight more than I could bear to hold. I rested my head on the back of my chair and closed my eyes, willing the ache in my chest to stop.

Bernadette, my darling girl, if only I could undo the past, I'd be there in a moment. But if I unknotted that past, our life would not be what it has been. It might not ever be again.

Does the gazebo look the same? Our gazebo? How have the Ladies of the Lake changed?

Stephen. The last time we met was in the gazebo . . .

~

SEPTEMBER 1917

Dorothy gave me the note Stephen had dared to bring to the academy when I returned after Mrs. Evans's dismissal. I saw in Dot's eyes what it cost her to do that, and I was sorry. But I knew that Stephen didn't love her, not in the way she hoped, not in the way she dreamed. He loved me. And was I to give up the love of my life because she wanted him, too? Would she not be able to finally move on once that door was closed?

They were questions I had no answers to. I only knew that through Stephen's and my years of letters and sympathies, our love had grown, had blossomed, and that I loved him with every fiber of my being.

I waited until 9:45. All the doors had been locked and lights were out in all the dormitories. I slipped out the back kitchen door, careful to leave the latch unhinged so I wouldn't make noise returning. By the light of the half-moon, I made my way down the hill toward the lake. I couldn't see his face, but there, in the shadow of the overhang, I saw a form.

"Addie?" His whisper of my name came through the dark, an invitation so pure and sweet I ran into his arms.

He nearly smothered me in kisses, his arms wound round me so tightly I could barely breathe. He kissed my hair, my wrists, my face, my neck, and I kissed him back with a fervor I didn't know I possessed. If I could have died in that moment, I would have passed from this life transported.

How long before either of us spoke, I've no idea. Up the hill, the clock in the school tower bonged 10:00 and then 10:15.

"I didn't know if you'd come." He was breathless.

"You doubted me?"

"No, but . . . I wasn't sure Dorothy would give you my note."

He knows. "She did."

We held each other then, simply snuggled, resting in each other's arms. I felt alive, content, joyous, hopeful, and secure.

"I passed my bar exam, Addie. I'm done."

"Stephen!" It was the thing he'd worked toward, studied for, for years. "Congratulations! I'm so very proud of you! Will you practice here, in Farmington?" I wondered and doubted and hoped. That had always been his plan, but now . . .

"No." He pulled away. "Not with how things are here, and not with the war on. I'll have to do my service first."

"What?" I knew he might be conscripted; I'd heard what Dorothy had said, but I did not expect him to enlist. "Can't you wait to see if you're called? Not everyone is."

"You know I can't."

"Why not? Please, don't do this."

"You know why. If I don't volunteer, I'll forever wear the badge of shame, the proverbial placard that reads *German Coward Go Home*. Who would solicit services from a lawyer with that hanging on his shingle?"

I sat down hard on the bench. "We've only just—and you're going away."

"You'll be going away, too. You wrote that you'll be returning to Halifax."

"For the birth of the baby, and a couple of months to help. But I'm coming back."

His voice held a smile through the dark. "Then I'll know where to find you." He sat beside me. "This war can't last forever. With American help, the tide will surely turn."

"But the trenches . . ." The news reports I'd read were horrendous . . . mud, rats, dysentery, and that's if the Germans didn't mow our soldiers down with machine-gun fire or burn them alive with flame throwers or poison and blind them with mustard gas.

"We can't know where I'll be sent. I speak German, fluently, so that can be useful. It may not be the curse it is living here."

"When will you go?" I could barely speak past the knot in my throat.

"I've promised my old professor that I'll address his class in November; then I hope to make it home in time for Thanksgiving."

"I'm leaving before Thanksgiving. Will I see you again?" Slipping out in the dark of night was one thing—a thing that could not be accomplished often—but if he returned to school, and I returned to Halifax, then he was shipped overseas . . .

"There's something else I want to do before the Army takes me, somewhere else I need to go." His voice was low. "I'd like to see Halifax. What do you think? Would Halifax have me? Will you?" He reached for my hand.

"What?" I tried to clear the fuzz in my brain but it was all too murky with worry.

"I'd like to visit you in Halifax, Addie, to meet your brother, to have a conversation with him."

"With Lemuel?"

I heard the smile in Stephen's voice. "That's his name, isn't it?"

"Why do you want—?"

"I have a very important question I'd like to ask him, one I would have preferred to ask your father, if that were possible."

I sat up straighter.

"Once I've asked Lemuel's permission, I'd like to ask you that question . . . if you're willing." He removed my glove and cradled my hand in his own, caressing my palm.

"Yes. Yes, I'm willing." My mind raced, nearly as fast as my heart. "When? When will you come?"

"Soon after Thanksgiving. I owe it to my parents to spend a few days with them here. Let's plan on early December, before I enlist. I want to go away knowing you'll be waiting for me, that when I come home, God willing, we can—"

"Yes!"

He pulled my head to his shoulder. "We'll meet, then, in Halifax. Let's say Sunday, December 2—the beginning of the week for the beginning of our lives."

"You know the date?"

"I've thought of little else, Addie. I thought this time would never come. It hasn't come fast enough for me."

"I don't want to meet you at my brother's." I couldn't explain, but I wanted that moment, the moment Stephen asked for my hand in marriage, to be ours alone, not shared with a family I only felt slightly a part of. "The gazebo . . . in the Halifax Public Gardens, beside Victoria Park. It's my favorite place in Halifax, and it reminds me of this gazebo."

"Our gazebo." His voice smiled again. "I'll aim to get to Halifax by Saturday night. I can speak with your brother on Sunday. It shouldn't take long."

"He'll be home then, after church. After luncheon."

Stephen laughed. "Yes, I don't think I'd want to ask him before he's eaten. The answer might not be the same as it would on a full stomach."

I smiled, too. "He should be free by one thirty, then. I'll wait in the gazebo for you. It's only a ten-minute walk from the house."

"I'll meet you at two, or two thirty, depending on how much of a grilling your brother gives me."

"I'll be there. Two o'clock . . . in the gazebo . . . in the gardens." What could be more perfect?

~

MAY 1935

The afternoon had worn away while I'd savored those memories. I folded Bernadette's letter with her program and returned them to the envelope. I wasn't certain I wanted to share this one with Portia. I'd add them to the packet of Bernadette's letters that I'd saved, tied in pink ribbon. I'd saved each and every note and card. She was, after all, the love of my life, the child of my heart.

The time was coming, I knew, when I might be forced to tell Bernadette the truth. Not yet, but soon. She was old enough now that her questions might outweigh, outrun, outlast my ability to divert her attention when she pressed too close. Bernadette had been content with my evasions before, but she was seventeen now and that was a far cry from ten or twelve.

I didn't believe there was anyone else who would tell her—who could tell her. But Dorothy's reminiscences and comparisons of Bernadette to her long-ago friend might precipitate more questions than I dared answer, might even bring things to a head. I couldn't risk that. Still, I wasn't ready, and I wasn't about to attend that graduation and watch as Stephen escorted his wife through the procession. What would I say to them? What could I possibly say?

Chapter Eighteen

MAY 1935

Dorothy had been glad to leave their automobile at the school and stroll home in the moonlight after the play. It had been both a pleasure and a relief to walk to the school the next morning with her own thoughts. Even now, days later, she loved remembering the strength of her husband's arm about her that night, the nearness of him. She realized she'd been foolish to give in to her worries, to give her doubts a voice. He'd shown his love in so many ways. At the time she thought she could put the ghosts of Addie to rest. Only her own foolishness had kept them alive, she was certain, and high time she ended her remorse. Still, she'd taken great comfort in those moments' response in the gazebo. She'd needed the words, needed to hear her husband say them aloud.

Twice on the walk home, he had brushed her hair with his lips. She smiled now, remembering his face as she'd smiled up at him, content, happy in the moment.

By the time they retired, they were both too tired from all the preparations and festivities to do more than kiss goodnight and lie back-to-back. She'd nearly succumbed to the sandman when he sleepily said, "Did Bernadette remind you of anyone tonight?"

Dorothy's eyes opened but she replied, in as sleepy a voice as she could muster, "Not particularly . . . Why?"

"It's nothing, I'm sure. Just that in that last scene she reminded us of Addie—Addie MacNeill."

Dorothy swallowed, her mouth like cotton. "Us?"

He half chuckled. "The 'other' Meyer brother."

"Mmm," she responded. "Addie was Canadian, like Bernadette. Maybe it's the accent." Though Dorothy knew that was not true. Addie had always maintained her PEI accent, somewhat different from Bernadette's Halifax inflections.

He sighed. "I don't know. Something more. The look on Bernadette's face, her profile—something—just put us in mind of her. Funny, we both thought it. I haven't thought of Addie in a long while." He rolled over then, and, spooning his wife, nuzzled Dorothy's ear.

"Were you thinking of her long? Of Addie?"

"No." He smiled—she heard it in his voice, still sleepy. "Only because she always loved directing the spring play . . . . and seeing Bernadette tonight reminded me of her. Go to sleep, my Dorothy. I love you."

"I love you, too." But there was no chance Dorothy could have slept. She'd soon given up the attempt and given in to remembering. Though days had passed, she still played that night and all of the past over and over again in her mind.

~

SEPTEMBER 1917

Dorothy left her door ajar the night Addie was to meet Stephen at the gazebo. Even then she didn't know if she took some perverse pleasure in torturing herself or if she half hoped that for whatever reason Addie would return to her room across the hallway in frustration, anger, or tears, that she and Stephen would argue, call off their relationship.

But when she heard Addie creep in around midnight and softly shut her door, there were no tears from her room. Only Dorothy's.

The next morning Addie glowed, despite her lack of sleep. Dorothy didn't want to know but needed to know where things stood.

After breakfast, on their way to chapel, Dorothy fell into step beside Addie. "So, is Stephen all right?"

Addie smiled but kept her face forward. "Very all right. He's passed his bar exam. Once the war is over, he'll be ready to set up practice or join an established legal practice."

"That's wonderful. That's what he's always wanted."

"Yes." But Addie's glow was beyond her pleasure for Stephen's accomplishment.

"He needed to meet you in the dark to tell you that?" Dorothy probed, knowing she'd regret it.

Addie slowed to a stop, glancing from side to side. When the girls had passed, she pulled Dorothy aside. "This is a secret, for now, so you can't tell anyone."

Dorothy did her best to swallow the lump forming in her throat.

"He wants to ask Lemuel for my hand, Dot. He's going to ask me to marry him." Addie fairly trembled with excitement—excitement Dorothy couldn't share.

"Did he actually say that?"

"After Thanksgiving—early December, when I'm in Halifax, he'll come speak to Lemuel. We're to meet in the Public Gardens afterward, where he wants to ask me . . . a question. *The* question." Addie's breath came fast and in short gasps. "Please be happy for me, my friend!"

The concern in Addie's eyes drove a knife through Dorothy's heart. "Of course I am. I wish you both the best." Dorothy pulled away then, walking quickly toward the room where chapel was surely already underway.

"Dot—Dorothy!" Addie called in a stage whisper, but Dorothy couldn't turn, couldn't think, and Addie ought not expect her to.

To Addie's credit, she didn't rub it in, didn't talk nonstop about

Stephen or her hopes and dreams—their hopes and dreams—as Dorothy herself might have done had the tables been turned. In fact, they spoke very little, though Addie made attempts.

Dorothy maintained civility and a reserve that neither young woman knew she possessed, an internal temperature to match the marching autumn's chill, right up until the time Addie left for Halifax.

The night before Addie's scheduled train, a knock came on Dorothy's door.

"Please, Dot, may I come in?"

Reluctantly, resentfully, Dot opened the door. "What is it?" She wanted to say, *What more do you want from me?*

Addie stepped inside, gently closing the door behind her. "I'll be gone for a few months, Dot. I want to go knowing we're okay, that things are going to be okay between us—you and me."

"What? Ladies of the Lake, and all that? Is that what you want?"

"Yes. Yes, it is. Forever friends, like we've always been."

"I think you left that behind when you set your sights on Stephen, knowing I loved him. You horned in and stole him from me, Addie."

"I didn't. We just—just loved each other. It was never to spite you; you know that."

"Do I? Is that what you want—for me to say, 'Oh, it's all okay. I don't care that you ripped my heart out of my chest.' Well, I don't think I can do that, so don't ask."

Addie stood there, staring at Dorothy as if she'd been horse-whipped. Dorothy looked beyond her.

"I'm sorry," Addie whispered. "I'm so sorry, Dot. I never—we never—meant to hurt you. I love you. You're the best friend I've ever had, and—"

But Dorothy turned her back, folding her arms tight across her chest, gripping her waist, desperate to keep from crying. "Please, Addie, go. Just go."

A full minute passed before Dorothy heard Addie close the door, as gently as she'd done the first time, only now, Dorothy heard it click, closure in all its finality.

Chapter Nineteen

MAY 1935

I was used to Portia housekeeping around me as I worked at my desk. She all but ran her feather duster over my typewriter keys as I struck them. There was no use asking her to wait. Portia was as much in charge of our house as I was. Our work simply revolved in different spheres. Neither of us could do without the other, though I knew I would soon have to. Her wedding was scheduled for August. If I was smart, I'd hire someone for Portia to train in housekeeping by July, but I didn't want anyone other than my dear friend, didn't want things to change, at least not until I was forced.

My only complaint was that Portia talked aloud to herself while she worked—a distraction when I was deep in the middle of hatching a plot or a character's musings or attempting to draw a conclusion. I was never quite certain if she was talking to me or herself. If I asked, she grew annoyed, saying to never mind, that she only carried on her conversations with the most intelligent person in the room—herself. If I failed to answer, she called me uppity and stuck-up. There was not a way to win, so I often ignored her until she poked me in the side or slapped my head with her feather duster. That happened far too often.

Slap against my head, feathers tickling the back of my neck.

"Why don't you answer me?"

"I didn't know you were talking to me."

"Well, pay heed. I asked—" she reiterated with exaggerated patience—"if you think Bernadette will be here in October this year. I'm thinking of Thanksgiving. If they'll let her come for the holiday once she's not a student anymore."

"Of course she'll be here. Where else would she be?"

"Well, she's been at that school every fall for the last six years. I doubt they'll let her go if she's working for them. Those Americans don't even celebrate Thanksgiving the same time we do, so it's no holiday to them."

"What?"

"If she becomes assistant teacher there, like she's talking about."

"Who said anything about Bernadette teaching at Lakeside?" My heart flew to my throat.

"Bernadette did. In her last letter. I figured she must have talked it over with you already if she wrote it to me."

"No . . . no, she didn't." I thought I might be sick.

"Here now, you've gone pale. Don't take on. She didn't say she was going to, only that that woman had offered her a place. She's just considering it."

"That woman—you mean—"

"Mrs. Meyer, I believe that's what she wrote. That woman who called here about the graduation, I imagine."

"Yes, that woman."

"I'd just been thinking how nice it will be to have Bernadette home in the fall, home for the Thanksgiving holiday. How maybe Silas and I'd come over for the day, roast a nice, fat turkey and stuff it and make that apple pie she likes so, maybe some cranberry chutney—I mean if you haven't hired somebody on by then. I suppose now we'll just have to wait and see."

"Thanksgiving. Bernadette. Yes, I hope she'll stay home. And, yes, of course I'd want you and Silas to come. We're family."

"Well, I hope she'll come but that won't be likely for long, no matter what she does. She's nearly grown. We'll have to face that, the both of us. You realize it'll more than likely be up to you to go to her if you want to see her." Portia patted my back and left the room.

Why had I not considered that Dot might offer Bernadette a position? Valedictorian. Of course she would, just as Miss Weston had offered places to Dot and me when we graduated. If Bernadette stayed on at Lakeside, I might never see her—only in summer, unless she married someone from the States, and then . . . oh, I couldn't think of it. *What if she never finds time to come home? My only choice would be to go there . . . but I can't. She must come home for Thanksgiving.*

I pulled the sheet of paper from the roller, too full of mistyped letters to keep or mend. I crushed it into a ball and threw it in the trash.

～

NOVEMBER 1917

I left Lakeside just before the American Thanksgiving holiday, full of anticipation for December and Stephen's and my moment-of-promise date in the Public Gardens. I hoped there'd be snow. I'd always loved early snowfall—so romantic. Perhaps, I mused, we could rent a horse and sleigh—more romantic still. But there was nothing romantic in the way Lemuel took our news.

I'd written Lemuel and Bertha about Stephen's plans. It was easier to put everything in a letter, where I could rewrite and edit and rewrite again, than to speak to my austere half brother in person. Lemuel did not reply, so I had to wait until I reached Halifax to receive his reaction. It came in the form of a confrontation in his study.

"He's German, Adelaide." Lemuel sat at his desk, much like a judge over a tribunal. Bertha sat across from him. He kept his voice even and his eyes cold. "We're at war with Germany, or have you not understood that?"

He'd not invited me to sit, but I did so, beside Bertha, and leaned forward, desperate to make them understand. "Stephen and his brother are American citizens. He's going to serve in the American armed forces, he and his brother. He's passed the bar, Lemuel! After the war he's going to practice law in America. Stephen's a good man, a hard worker."

"In need of an income, no doubt, to set up his practice."

"Well, you certainly don't have to worry that he's after my money. I haven't got any. He loves me!"

"But he will profit from the marriage, Adelaide," Bertha interjected. "Has Lemuel not told you?"

"Bertha! You speak out of turn."

"What do you mean?"

Lemuel looked as if he'd like to stuff a sock in his wife's mouth, nearly bursting with baby though she was, but she was not deterred.

"Your brother's been quite savvy with your inheritance, and his. We've stayed in this district, saving and scraping every penny till stones bleed, but the truth is we're doing so well, Lemuel's just bought land and we're building a new home—a mansion—in Halifax's South End, come spring. You really ought to tell her, dearest. She's of age, and her portion of the trust is legally at her disposal anyway. It might have some bearing on her plans."

"My plans are to marry Stephen, as soon as he returns from the war."

"If he returns from the war." Lemuel spoke evenly.

"That's cruel. *When* he returns." It was rare for me to stand my ground or speak against my older half brother. I loved my nephew and had grown closer to Bertha but didn't like Lemuel, though there was a family attachment. That counted for something, I supposed, and he'd kept me in school after Mother and Dad died. I thought he'd financially supported me. I'd no idea of any trust.

"You're right; that was uncalled for." He sighed. "My apologies." Lemuel stood and walked across the study to the fireplace, where he studied the flames. "Bertha spoke truly, of course. There is a trust for you, an inheritance from Father that I've managed since he drowned."

I'd always hated the way he'd spoken of our father drowning—so matter-of-fact—and dismissed my mother, never mentioning her, as if she'd not existed, as if she and the most monumental loss of our lives were no more a thing than the change in weather. "What does a trust mean, in practical terms?"

"It means that as of your birthday last year you came into a great deal of money. I've done well in managing our finances, if I do say so myself. Your allowance heretofore may have seemed meager, but not ungenerous, I hope."

"It's been adequate for my needs. I presumed you were supplying—"

"Father had his will set up so that half of everything would come to me and half of everything go to your mother, should she survive him. If she did not, then her half was to come to you or any other children they bore in trust until each child turned twenty-three."

"You and your Stephen will want for nothing, Adelaide." Bertha smiled. She was fully on my side, I realized, much to my surprise.

"Horatio Emberly, my attorney, has handled our affairs and possesses the necessary paperwork to transfer the administration of your funds. I've arranged a meeting for you after Christmas. He'll explain everything and wishes for you to sign papers now that you've come of age for the trust."

I nodded, still trying to absorb this new possibility for Stephen's and my future. "Thank you. But you've waited a full year—and more—to let me know this?"

Lemuel ignored my question. "I encourage you to delay embarking on this engagement until your intended returns from the war, Adelaide, then decide if you wish to continue such a course." Lemuel spoke coldly, but in that moment his eyes changed, softened somewhat. "I say this for your own good. You can't know what sort of man the war will make of him, beyond his nationality."

"The loss of a limb will not change my mind."

"The loss of his mind might. Canadian veterans, even now, are being treated for what they're calling shell shock, the aftermath of war no one wants to talk about. You've no idea—"

I stood. "I will marry Stephen with or without your blessing, Lemuel. We would both prefer to have it, and I am glad to know there are means for me to bring to the marriage. Stephen will be here in a few days. Please be ready to receive him." I straightened my shoulders and walked out of the room, not looking back. I'd lost my parents long ago and my best friend more recently. Losing my relationship with Lemuel, Bertha, and Marcus would hurt, but it would not upend my world. The thing that would do that would be to lose Stephen.

Bertha had a tray sent to my room shortly before dinner. I didn't know if that was because she was ousting me from the family or protecting me. But after dinner, once I heard Lemuel's footsteps retreat to his study, she slipped into my room . . . or waddled, to be precise.

"Did you like the mutton, Adelaide? It's Mrs. Abernathy's best recipe, I think."

"Everything was delicious. Thank you. I'm quite happy to take meals in my room, so if you—"

She looked horrified. "No, my dear sister! I only sent the tray because I didn't think you could stomach sitting across from your brother after that exchange. And I do believe it did him some good to see that he can't lord over you. Well done, Adelaide. If you truly love this Stephen of yours, you must stand your ground. That's one thing you'll learn about my husband . . . he'll declare and forbid and grouse, but once an opponent stands their ground, he better respects them."

"Is that what I am? His opponent?"

She sighed, lowering herself into the chair by the fire. "We're all Lemuel's opponents at times. Then again, we're all his cheering section. The trick is in learning when to wield the sword and when to offer honey."

My sister-in-law was a wise woman, wiser than I knew how to be. But then, she'd survived well over a decade of marriage to my brother. Perhaps I could learn a great deal from her.

"I'm thankful you've come back to us, Adelaide. I'm nervous about this baby."

"You said that when I was here before. But you look so well. You've done so well."

"Perhaps, but I'm not young, not as young as when I birthed Marcus."

"But you're strong and healthy. The doctor said he expects all to go well. Remember?"

She smiled, but the worry lines did not leave her forehead. "Lemuel and I are both worried. His mother died in childbirth, you know. He's never been able to get beyond that. I want you to promise me something."

"Anything I can do; you know I will."

"Which is why I can speak of this, why I know I can ask." She reached for my hand, her grip strong.

"Bertha, what is it?" I knelt beside her chair.

"I want you to promise me that if anything happens to me, if I should not live—"

"Don't say that! You'll be fine. You and the baby both. You must know that, believe it."

But she ignored my outburst. "If anything should happen to me, I want you to promise that you'll care for my child, for my children."

"What? Oh, Bertha, nothing will happen. All will be well, but you know that Lemuel will love this baby as he loves Marcus—both his children."

"We don't know if Lemuel will even yet be called up, sent to the war, and if he is, whether he'll return. So far, his work here is considered essential for the war effort, but even he does not expect that to last. What I do know is that your brother is a man who, for all his genius and bluster and love to command, cannot live alone, won't live alone for long.

"I'm not so worried for Marcus. At twelve, he's nearly grown. Lemuel is so very proud of him that I know if he's here, he'll see him settled well—into boarding school and later in business. We've talked about it, planned."

"But I've seen what happens to young children when their widowed father remarries. They're too often ignored or abused or neglected. Sometimes they're sent early to boarding schools or worse yet, to orphanages. Even if kept at home, they're not loved as a mother loves her own children."

"You can't think Lemuel would—"

"I don't know what he would do. I saw what he did with you when your parents perished—his own sister."

There was nothing I could say to that. I had no idea what went round in Lemuel's head. My brother was not outwardly affectionate, not even with Bertha or Marcus, certainly never with me.

"If all is well, if this baby lives and he or she and Marcus are loved by whomever he marries, well and good. But please, Adelaide—" she clasped my hand so hard it hurt—"promise me that you'll watch over my darlings. Be the aunt to them they will surely need no matter what, and if they need a mother, if your Stephen is willing for you to take them and some other woman Lemuel marries doesn't want them, then . . ." She couldn't speak more for the sobs that racked her body.

I cradled her in my arms, rubbing her back. "Oh, Bertha, dear Bertha. I'll be there for them always, as long as you want me to, forever if you or they need me. But you must push these morbid thoughts away. They're not healthy, not good for you or the baby. Think on how well you are, how strong you are, how beautiful or handsome this baby will be, and how you will love it as you love Marcus. Think how you'll grow as a family—a beautiful, healthy, strong family. And Christmas is coming—less than a month away. You'll birth this baby and be on your feet by then. Just think, Christmas morning before the tree, snuggling your new baby in the bosom of your family."

Gradually, Bertha's sobs subsided. As she pulled away, I handed her my handkerchief. She mopped her eyes, her nose and mouth. "You're right, of course . . . but I need to know, I need—"

"I understand, and I promise, but we won't speak of this again, all right?"

She nodded, pressing her lips together, seeking some form of composure. A few moments passed before she spoke again. "In any case, Lemuel and I were going to ask if you'll be the baby's godmother. You will, won't you? Say yes, Adelaide. We've never designated a godmother for Marcus, but you'll do it—won't you? Please say yes."

"Yes, of course. Of course, I'm honored. But Lemuel agreed?"

"We both saw how you were with Marcus this past summer. He's smitten with his aunt Adelaide, and you've taught him so much. You've been tender and helpful with me. There's no one we could better trust our child's care to. The godfather we chose for Marcus—Lemuel's childhood friend—has gone to war. We don't know what's happened to him. He's not on casualty lists—Lemuel checks them every day—but he's not responded to our letters for nearly five months."

"Mail gets lost—the war—"

"Yes, mail gets lost . . . but we can't be sure. It's something you'll have to remember when your Stephen goes. It's hard not to fear, not to imagine the worst."

I knew she was right. It was the thing I didn't want to think about, Stephen going to war, what it would be like for him, and for me, waiting at home for his letters or for a dreaded telegram from strangers.

Chapter Twenty

DECEMBER 1917

Bertha's projected due date came and went, considered by the doctor unusual for a second baby or one carried by an older woman. I was careful to stay nearby and to keep an eye on Marcus as best I could.

There was a sweep of whooping cough going through the area and at all costs it must not be brought into the house, so Marcus was ordered to go to school and come home, nothing more, not even drilling with the Richmond School Junior Cadet Corps or attending practice at the indoor winter rifle range, which was the highlight of his young life, this being the first year he was old enough to join. He'd just been fitted for his uniform at Clayton's, a huge and important store in the center of the city. He strutted the grounds with his chest puffed out like a peacock's. "Not being able to drill with the fellows is the worst thing that's ever happened to me!" he declared.

He stalked the hallways like a caged lion, fretting about the Cadet Corps, then nearly beside himself because there'd been no snow yet and he and his friends were itching to get their toboggans flying down the hill toward the harbor. He begged to no avail to prowl the wharfs to investigate the newly "dazzle-painted" ships intended to thwart German submariners and declared that staying home was a "horrendous and unpatriotic ordeal." I couldn't keep up with his changing moods and moans, but they reminded me of the cabin fever Dot and I had felt as girls each spring, desperate to escape the confines of classrooms and dormitories for the open air.

The doctor, who could not be swayed even by a twelve-year-old's pitiful pleas, and the midwife both declared that Baby could come any day, any moment, and that we must all be available and ready. We walked on tenterhooks.

But neither the doctor's nor Bertha's anxiety, the war news, or Marcus's fractious behavior could keep my excitement from mounting the morning of December 2, the day Stephen intended to ask Lemuel's blessing for my hand, the day he would meet me in the Public Gardens at that magnificent gazebo and bandstand.

Though the cost was prohibitive across borders, I'd half expected he might send a telegram or even telephone to confirm our meeting— at the very least a letter—but I'd heard nothing since the first letter I'd received from him, the one waiting for me upon my arrival in Halifax. I knew he was traveling to give his lecture, then traveling home again for the holiday. Surely he was winding up his affairs before he enlisted, and most especially before he came to meet me.

To while away the morning, I signed a Christmas card and penned a long overdue letter to Mrs. Montgomery, thanking her for her new book, *Anne's House of Dreams*, that she'd signed and sent to me. It was the perfect gift for 1917—the story of Anne and Gilbert's wedding and their settling into life together. It seemed a premonition of my life to come. In my letter I confided my hope and expectation for a proposal that very afternoon—further proof that Mrs. Montgomery, Anne, and I were all kindred spirits.

When the time came to leave for the gardens, I could barely button my coat for all my excitement.

The shops I passed that afternoon boasted windows bright with displays of elegant china, fine jewelry, toys, and goodies of every imagination. Being Sunday, their doors remained closed, but holiday music from a local children's choir practice poured into the streets.

It was just three weeks before Christmas and I'd not done one bit of shopping, but those shop windows, as colorful and enticing as they were, did not give me pause. I walked toward the gardens quickly, partly because of the cold, mostly because of excitement, doing my best to avoid the winks and stares of the many soldiers and sailors in town awaiting deployment.

Even in winter, the Public Gardens were beautiful. Not filled with curtains of wisteria or mounds of cascading roses and bubbling fountains as they were in summer, but magnificent in their stark beauty—in the frosty, frozen lake and the black naked limbs of trees set against a brooding sky.

One thirty was too early to arrive, but I hadn't been able to wait at home a moment longer. By two o'clock I stood shivering, even in my heavy coat, wearing fur-lined gloves and a muffler wound twice around my head, most elegant gifts from Bertha. I danced, stomping my feet to make certain the blood flowed through my toes and legs, to know I could feel them through my boots and woolen stockings in the below-freezing temperature.

Twice, gentlemen dressed in dark coats and derbies strode through the gardens on their way to somewhere. Once, a gentleman headed toward my gazebo. I was certain it was Stephen, his head down against the wind. But shortly before reaching the gazebo the man looked up, raised his hand in greeting to someone beyond me, and fairly flew to the side of a woman dressed in furs. They embraced, laughing, and walked off together toward the far side of the gardens. I bit my lip in frustration.

For all I knew, Lemuel was keeping Stephen deliberately, going over his expectations and demands. Well, I wouldn't give in. Stephen had said he'd be here, had even imagined it might be closer to two thirty, so I would pace and wait.

By the time the town clock bonged three, the light had begun to gently fade. *Something must have happened to delay him. Maybe he's waiting at the house. Could he have missed his ship from Boston? Is he well?* I thought of every contingency, every possibility . . . None of them presented a scenario or outcome I wanted.

By three thirty I could no longer stand the cold. I'd go back to Lemuel and Bertha's. Surely Stephen must be there, or they must have received a telephone call. If not . . . I couldn't, wouldn't consider that. On stiff and sore legs, I trudged back to the house, taking the steep hill, already slippery, down toward the harbor. When the house came into view, I recognized Lemuel's automobile in the drive rather than the carriage house—an unusual and concerning sign. I hurried along, as best my frozen feet allowed.

Chaos reigned inside. Both the maid and the cook rushed up the stairs toting pitchers and basins of hot water, their faces pinched with worry. Lemuel snapped at a clearly frightened Marcus in the downstairs hallway. The moment he saw me, Lemuel bellowed, "Where have you been? Bertha's in labor! She's been calling for you the last hour. The midwife needs your help—go—go!"

"I don't know anything about birthing babies," I protested. "Where is Stephen?"

"Who?"

"Stephen." I wanted to shout, but I could barely breathe.

"Well, he's not here, is he?" Lemuel did shout.

"He's not come? Did he telephone?"

"No! For mercy's sake, go to Bertha!"

I took the stairs, confused, worried—frightened, too, for both Stephen and Bertha, as her alternating groans and piercing screams echoed throughout the house. I'd much rather have comforted Marcus than enter the birthing room, but Lemuel brooked no refusal, and I knew Bertha needed me. I stepped inside, gently closing the door behind me.

Bertha lay on the bed, groaning through the middle of a spasm, a contraction so hard it stole her breath and reddened her face and neck and chest. I'd never attended a birth, not more than the birthing of Old Clem in the stable at Lakeside. At the sight of my sister-in-law in such pain, my heart seized in my chest. My feet felt rooted to the floor.

Once the contraction subsided, Bertha looked up and gasped in relief, breathlessly reaching for my hand. "Adelaide!"

That was all it took. I fell to my knees beside the bed and clasped her hand. "I'm here, Bertha. I won't leave you. I promise."

She nodded, nearly too weak to speak.

"Miss—" the midwife spoke calmly from her place at the end of the bed—"mop her forehead and face and neck with the wet flannel, if you will. It won't be long now. Baby's coming quickly."

A mercy. A short and intense labor. It didn't look as if Bertha could take much more. Even so, it seemed to go on for hours. Wringing the flannel in the basin of cool water, mopping Bertha's forehead, I wondered if I'd ever be strong enough to do this, this birthing of a child. But if it was Stephen's child—Stephen's and mine—I knew. *Love is a powerful force. It overcomes everything.* That's what I thought as the miracle of Baby finally slipped out of Bertha and into the hands of the midwife in a gush of blood and fluids.

"A baby girl! You've a fine baby girl, Mrs. MacNeill!"

A hint of a smile crossed Bertha's lips. Her arms reached for her child.

"Let me just wash her a bit and give her a swaddle. She'll be in your arms in two shakes of a lamb's tail."

"Well done, Bertha. So well done," I whispered, pushing sweat-plastered tendrils of hair from her forehead as she clasped my fingers.

"Did you see her? Is she . . . all right?" Bertha's breath came shallow.

"Yes, she's beautiful. She's perfect." I smiled.

"All ten fingers, all ten toes," the midwife affirmed from her post on the far side of the room, where she washed the screaming newborn.

But those newborn screams, piercing as they were, came as music to our ears, and I laughed out loud for the relief and joy of it all.

"A son and a daughter! You've a rich woman's family," I enthused.

Bertha's hand clamped mine. "I'm still having contractions."

"It's the placenta coming, my dear. Remember? Same as when your Marcus was born." The midwife thrust the infant into my arms and attended Bertha, massaging her lower abdomen.

"What are you doing?" It looked strange to me.

"Getting the placenta to move, to come along."

"Oh. That looks like it hurts her. It won't come on its own?" The baby had come. I didn't understand the hurry now.

"Hurts a bit, but all will go easier once it's out. She had a time with the placenta after her first. I want to get it moving."

"Wait—wait a moment . . ." Bertha tried to speak, but the midwife kept on.

The placenta did come in a rush. The midwife deftly swept it into towels and stuffed everything into a bin for the maids to clear. "There, now. We'll just get you washed up and comfortable."

But Bertha had gone deathly pale. In the time it took for me to turn away and lay the baby on the bed and finish swaddling her as best I knew how, a broad gush of red blood spread across the bed linens, far more than when the baby had emerged.

"Something's wrong!" I didn't know what.

The midwife swore.

"Surely that's too much blood for her to lose," I whispered.

But the midwife, in another moment, had pulled the sheet aside and worked one hand inside Bertha with the other massaging her belly.

Bertha groaned, but her strength was clearly waning.

"Should I—should I have Lemuel call for a doctor?" I could barely speak.

"Yes. Yes!" The midwife's urgency frightened me further. Bertha was too far gone to know.

"Lemuel! *Lemuel!*" I called from the top of the stairs. "Send for a doctor—quickly!"

"What's wrong?" Lemuel stood at the bottom of the stairs with Marcus by his side.

"She's losing too much blood. The midwife can't stop it. Call him now!"

I heard the telephone receiver lift and Lemuel speak urgently into the phone while I returned with the baby to the bedroom. Bertha's eyes looked as if they were trying to focus on the bundle in my arms.

"What can I do?"

"Keep talking to her. Keep her awake."

"Your daughter's here, Bertha. She has your eyes. She's just as lovely as you. Stay awake, Bertha. Stay with me, with—with your daughter." My heart raced so I hardly knew what I was saying. I lifted her hand to her daughter's face, but Bertha's eyes rolled to the back of her head, then forward again. Her breath came in shallow spurts.

"You promised, Adelaide. You promised me." Bertha's voice was a rasped whisper.

Another moment and Lemuel was in the room at her side. I stopped babbling as he leaned in, but the sight of blood nearly undid him, and he faltered.

"Do something! For pity's sake, do something!" he begged the midwife or God or me, I didn't know who. I couldn't look but simply held the baby as she squalled in my arms, closing my eyes for a moment against the nightmare.

"Hush, hush, now," the midwife ordered. "It's letting up. Talk to her. Keep her with us."

But Lemuel looked stricken and didn't speak. I pushed between them, holding the baby near Bertha's face. "Your daughter's here, Bertha. She wants you to hold her. Open your eyes."

Her eyes fluttered. She did her best to focus.

"That's it. That's it, dearest! Your baby's beautiful. She's absolutely lovely and pink! And look, she has a wee birthmark on her chest, like a locket—an angel's kiss."

Somewhere in the midst of my babbling the doctor rushed in, dropped his bag, and washed his hands while consulting with the midwife. What they did there, from the foot of the bed, I didn't know. I wouldn't take my eyes from Bertha's, willing her to stay awake, to stay alive.

"Close those blackout curtains and raise the lamp. I need more light." The doctor ordered us right and left, which I remember as a sure relief, as if doing something, keeping busy, might change the outcome. We waited on pins and needles.

In the time it took for night to fall in earnest, the gushing of blood stopped, at least what the doctor considered an abnormal amount of bleeding. Bertha and Baby were washed. Clean linens were provided all round. The midwife put Baby to Bertha's breast until she suckled a little. That woke Bertha but exhausted her. She and Baby slept. I felt as if I were waking from a long nightmare.

The doctor stayed an hour longer, then left with instructions to telephone him if the hemorrhaging started again, though he did not expect it to. Lemuel, pale and spent, kissed his wife on her forehead and left the room without a word. I nestled in the chair nearest Bertha, holding the baby close for her whenever she woke. Periodically the midwife took her from me to help Bertha nurse.

"Give me the baby. Let me show you how to get her started. Mrs. MacNeill's mother's milk is yet to come in, but she's got what Baby needs for now." The midwife pulled Bertha's gown aside and nestled the infant against her breast, tickling the baby's lower lip until she opened her mouth to suckle. Bertha did not seem to notice.

"It won't be much, but this will give her a start. In the meantime, you must speak to Mr. MacNeill and have him procure a wet nurse right away. I know Mrs. MacNeill had planned to nurse Baby herself, but she's too weak, and will be for some time. We nearly lost her." She whispered this last.

I nodded mechanically, having no idea about such arrangements.

"I think, on second thought—" her eyes beseeched mine—"that you may be the one needed to make these arrangements, miss, and see to the care of the baby for now. I'm not sure Mr. MacNeill is . . .

is ready to do what's needed. Mrs. MacNeill told me, before you came today, to rely on you should anything go amiss."

"I don't know any nurses, anyone able to nurse a baby." My heart beat faster; I was completely out of my depth.

"There's a woman in Africville, part Mi'kmaw, just north from here, that delivered a baby boy not a month ago. She's got milk come in to spare. I recommend her, if the MacNeills are all right with that. I don't know who else might take her on just now." She stared at me as if asking a question.

I returned her stare. How could I know what Bertha and Lemuel were all right with? I knew the Mi'kmaq were indigenous peoples, that most in Africville were black, and that some in Lemuel and Bertha's circles might scorn either, or the mix. But milk was milk and Africville was close; wasn't that a good answer?

"You'd best make certain . . . or when you interview the woman, don't say whose the baby is. The MacNeills may not want word to get out that a—well, they may not want word to get out. Just until Mrs. MacNeill is strong enough."

When I went to ask Lemuel, I learned he'd gone to his office, even though it was Sunday, leaving no instructions about anything.

The weight of it all fell on me then: Bertha's request that I care for her children, her certainty that Lemuel could not manage alone if something happened to her—apparently even temporarily—and now the need for a nurse. I must help a worried Marcus understand that his mother could not see him, not until she regained some of her strength . . . all while this tiny pink newborn flailed her arms and screamed, doing her best to latch on to life.

Chapter Twenty-One

MAY 1935

There was something potentially healing for Dorothy in rising while it was still dark and leaving her husband snoring softly, in making the trek to the academy in the cool of a late-May morning as the sun broke over the trees, in pulling the journal from her desk, in reading words she'd written as a young woman—a girl-woman who'd poured her heartaches and triumphs in equal measure onto pages where it had felt safe.

But even then, she'd never written down what she'd done, not fully. There were hints in the diary, surely, but the terrible worry that someone might one day find it kept her from ever penning the tale. It had even stopped her from journaling altogether, though she'd never thrown the book away.

What if I wrote it all out now, confessed everything on paper? Could it help? Could it heal?

But Dorothy knew she would not. She knew, firsthand, that

sometimes things happened—unexpected, tragic things—that could not be undone. She could not bear the idea that one day, some catastrophe, some unexpected disability or death might overtake her before she could destroy the diary. If that happened, someone dear might read it and condemn her long-ago actions, might cease to love her, even after she'd departed this earth. No, she could not write it down, but neither could she forget.

It was as if she stood outside herself and saw that young woman in early December of 1917, the young woman who'd spent the last hour in the chapel wrestling with her heart, the one who answered the knock at the front door to the academy two full hours after it had been locked for the night.

DECEMBER 1917

"Stephen—you look half frozen. What are you doing here?" He stood on the doorstep, distraught, his hair disheveled, but still the most handsome man she'd ever laid eyes on. She pulled him in from the cold, knowing he shouldn't be admitted to a girls' school so late at night. Still, the lateness of the hour and the cold and the needing look of him thrilled her.

"I'm sorry to come so late, but I'm desperate, Dot. Help me. Please."

"Anything, you know that."

"I was supposed to meet Addie in Halifax—supposed to meet with her brother to ask for her hand. She must have told you."

Dorothy felt every muscle tense. But he was here, with her; he hadn't gone. That must mean something. "Yes."

"You haven't heard? Bricks were thrown through our windows two nights ago. Our stable was torched."

"What?" She'd heard nothing of the kind, but then, she'd been in classes every day, and the girls were not allowed off school property during the week or on weekends for now. No newspapers or local gossip had come her way.

"Mama was hit by one of the bricks—a brain bleed, the doctor says. She's not opened her eyes since. I think . . . she will not live."

"No. No!" Dorothy could not comprehend it. "Who would do such a thing?"

He shook his head miserably. "We don't know who—but we know why. Authorities are patrolling our property, insisting we stay home to forestall further violence, but it feels more to keep us in than to keep anyone out."

It was too cruel. *Surely the tormenter meant to frighten, not to kill. Surely.*

"Papers came for Jonas and for me today—for military service—translation work. We're to report this week."

"So soon?"

Stephen shook his head. "Somehow they were delayed getting to me—or the date sped up. I don't know, but I need to let Addie know. There's no way I can get to Halifax before I must leave. I tried to convince them to let me stay until Mama . . . but they say no, that they'll escort me themselves if I don't go voluntarily. I don't know that they won't do that anyway, or that Mama will last another day."

The layers of bad news stole Dorothy's breath.

"Our phone lines were cut. I've no way to phone Addie. I had to slip out, and I have to get back before they know I'm gone. They'll arrest me if they think I've run. They searched our house and found letters to family in Germany—accused Mother and Father of being spies. There's talk of interning Father under suspicion because of the letters and since he's not an American citizen. I need to use your phone—please. I'll pay for the call to Canada." He pulled a wad of cash from his pocket.

Dorothy's heart nearly stopped. She'd do anything for Stephen—but this?

"The school only has one phone. It's in the headmistress's office—locked. She won't be back until morning."

"Can't you get in? Does no one have a key?" Stephen looked ready to break the door down.

"No." Dorothy felt horrible about Stephen's mother and his enforced draft, but she wouldn't lose her job to shorten Addie's worry by one day. "You can come back tomorrow, but I can't guarantee she'll let you use the phone. Go to my parents. They'll let you telephone. I know they will."

Stephen shook his head. "I've already tried your farm, but the lines there have been cut, too. You've all remained friends with us, and we're grateful, but it puts your family at risk. Please, can't you try to get the door open?"

Dorothy drew a deep breath. How could she say no? "Come with me, but be very quiet."

Together they crept to the office of the headmistress, conscious of every creaking floorboard. Dorothy tried the door handle just in case Miss Fullbright had forgotten to lock the door. *Locked.* But in his desperation, Stephen wrenched the doorknob from side to side, shaking the frame.

"Please," Dorothy begged. "Don't break it. I'll lose my job."

Stephen pushed long fingers through his hair. "What can I do?"

"Write her. It will only take a couple of days—no more than a week to reach her."

He slumped against the doorjamb. "They'll never let me out to get to the post office. I have no stamps for Canada."

"Then give it to me. I'll mail it." Dorothy didn't want to, but she'd do it for Stephen.

The first glimmer of something akin to hope crossed Stephen's eyes. "Will you? Thank you. Thank you, Dorothy." His smile cut Dorothy's heart. "Do you have paper?"

"Wait in the foyer."

He crept back the way they'd come as she slipped up the stairs to her room, walking past Addie's closed door. She could hardly believe she was doing this, saving Addie's feelings. *I must do this for Stephen. For Stephen, not Addie.*

She creased a fresh sheet in her journal next to the binding and carefully tore it from its home. She rummaged through her desk for a pen, then tiptoed down the staircase. Stephen sat, slumped forward on the mahogany visitors' bench in the foyer, his head in his hands. How Dorothy wanted to sit close to comfort him, to hold him! But she offered him the pen and paper, while digging a knife in her heart.

He grabbed her offering like a lifeline and, going to the window, scribbled in the light cast by the moon. When finished he pressed the paper to his heart and breathed deeply.

Each motion, each breath drove Dorothy's knife deeper.

When he placed the note in her hand, he stood so close Dorothy could feel his breath, uncertain whether the hammering in her chest came from his heart or her own.

"You'll mail it, first thing tomorrow? Promise me?"

"Yes, of course." She swallowed the burning coal in her throat. "I promise. I'd do anything for you."

He touched his forehead to hers. "I knew I could count on you, Dot. Thank you."

She savored the warmth of his forehead against hers in the dark but did not trust her voice.

⌣

MAY 1935

Dorothy closed her journal. From the flap at the back of the book's cloth cover she pulled the folded sheet of paper, slightly yellowed with age. Opening it, smoothing the crease with two hands, she read the words she'd long memorized and ran her fingers over Stephen's handwriting. She should have burned the note long ago—would have, if only Addie had lived. *Mail goes astray all the time.* It surely did during the war. That's what she'd always told herself, had been prepared to say to Stephen, even to Addie, if necessary. But of course, it hadn't been necessary, and she never did, not even when she learned of Addie's phone call to the school, a call she was certain was made in search of Stephen.

Chapter Twenty-Two

Sunday was our day for church and rest, but Portia spent part of every Sunday midday walking out with Silas, then late afternoons in Bernadette's room, tidying a room that needed no tidying, watering and deadheading the African violets that bloomed in profusion on the windowsill, running her hands over the girlhood treasures of rocks and pine cones that our Bernadette had collected over the years.

I stopped in the hall, watching Portia through the doorway, and smiled, albeit a little sadly. "You miss her, too."

Portia startled.

"I'm sorry. I thought you knew I was here."

"I was the one not here. I was back, oh, seventeen years ago now, I guess." Portia's shoulders rose and fell in a deep sigh. "Just remembering that day." She replaced Bernadette's hairbrush on the dressing table. "I came to your house with Bernadette, after the midwife told me to bring her home."

I remembered, too. "I was so grateful to you for taking her on."

"When you couldn't make the milk come." Portia looked at me keenly.

I blinked.

"I always thought that strange . . . a young strong woman like yourself unable to produce milk for her baby."

"We're not all as gifted as you were, Portia." I tried to make light and turned away.

But Portia stood, stopping me with her words. "A fine, slim figure for a woman who'd just given birth not three days before."

"You'll appreciate those are days painful to remember."

"Oh, I do. I appreciate that. I lost every member of my family, my husband, lost my own sweet baby, my home, and every stitch of clothing I owned, you know."

I'd reached the stairs but stopped, closing my eyes. "I do know, Portia, and I'm sorry, so very sorry. That was terrible of me."

"After I lost my Ahanu, Bernadette took my milk. I tried to think of her as next to my own child after that, nursing her as I did, caring for her every day of her life, even while you recovered in the hospital. I couldn't always do that. My arms, my breasts ached for my own sweet baby boy."

"I know. I'm sorry. I'm so sorry."

"Time and again I wished I'd been home with my son and husband, wished I'd been taken with them in that blast."

"Please don't say that."

"Why not? It's God's own truth." She tilted her head, but her mouth formed a straight line. "But I always wondered why your milk never came in."

"What? Oh, the blast, I think. It changed everything . . . changed us all." I kept going down the stairs but heard Portia's words trailing me.

"It certainly did, coming as it did days after her birth."

I closed the library door behind me. That was the closest Portia had ever come to asking me directly. I knew it would not be the last time. I wanted so much to forget those days, wanted her to forget them, every last one of them. Yet what is determination to forget but an invitation to remember?

~

DECEMBER 1917

The midwife swaddled the new baby and wrapped her in a fur lap rug—the tiny girl baby who'd not yet been named—and as it seemed the best arrangement, carried her to the woman in Africville, a woman whose name I didn't know then, a woman who nursed a recently born boy child of her own.

Even then I wondered which child would be fed first. If it were me, I'd feed my own first, care for my own first. I worried for Bertha's baby. Mostly, I worried for Bertha.

She did not rally. The maid and I fed her beef broth, a spoonful at a time, around the clock, hoping she'd strengthen, but her eyes remained glazed, her pulse weak.

Two days passed before the midwife returned to check on her, just after noon. "I don't like it. I don't know why she's not improving."

"She's fading, if anything," I whispered out of Bertha's hearing.

"Baby's thriving. I stopped in to see her this morning. Still, I believe we'd best bring her back to her mother. I'll give her another day, just so Baby gets a good start. Maybe seeing her newborn will help. I don't know what else to do. Has the doctor been back?"

"Once. He said to keep up the broth, let her rest, give her time."

The midwife shook her head. "When Marcus returns from school, have him come in, sit a while, and give a hug and a croon to his mother. He's been the light of her life, so she said. See if that helps. I'll have Mrs. Cadeau bring the baby here day after tomorrow."

"Mrs. Cadeau?"

"The mother from Africville, wet-nursing Mrs. MacNeill's baby. We'll see if having the baby brings her round. I'm sure Mrs. Cadeau will agree to come nurse here if needed, provided you can discreetly arrange a room for her and her child."

"Yes. Anything you suggest. Just anything." I was ready to surrender responsibility. I was bone weary and worried sick for Bertha, but I was also worried about Stephen. Why hadn't he come or called or written? I checked the post in the hallway twice each day.

"You need rest, my dear. You look dead on your feet. It will do Mrs. MacNeill no good if you break down from exhaustion. Once Marcus gets home, you go on and lie down. She'll be all right without you for an hour or three. I'll stop back in the morning."

I nodded, too weary to argue. As long as the midwife thought Bertha would be all right.

Marcus argued with me from the moment he came in the door. He and his friends had planned to go down to the docks and catch a closer look at the big Norwegian ship, the *Imo*, anchored there.

"It will sail tomorrow; I don't want to miss it. Maybe one of the sailors will sell me a button for my collection."

"No, Marcus. Your mother needs you, and I want you to spend time with her. She needs to know we're all with her, that we want her to get well. You do, don't you?"

"Of course I do." Marcus looked conflicted, as any twelve-year-old boy might. But goodness won out. "I'll go right away, Aunt Adelaide. I'll sit with Mother as long as she likes."

"Thank you, Marcus. I need to lie down a bit. If you need me, come knock on my door." I gave him a hug, a thing many boys his age might have resented or pushed away, but Marcus hugged me in return.

"Thank you, Aunt Adelaide, for being here."

That warmed my heart. I touched my palm to Marcus's cheek and gave him a smile that I hoped let him know I cared.

No sooner did I lie down but my worries turned again to Stephen. Finally, unable to rest, I rummaged through the desk in my room for my address book and made my way downstairs to the telephone in the hallway. Few families in the Maritimes vicinity boasted telephones at home. That Lemuel had one spoke of how well he was doing. That the Meyer family possessed one spoke well of them, but for how long they'd keep it without Mr. Meyer's job at the bank, I couldn't imagine.

Lemuel had gone to his office on business. There would never be a quieter, more private time for me to telephone.

I spoke to the operator, gave her the number, and waited while she put the call through to the United States. The cost for such a call would be ridiculous, but Lemuel had said I was now a wealthy woman. I could afford it.

After a time, the operator came on the line again. "I'm sorry, madam, but that number has been disconnected."

"Disconnected? Are you certain? Could you please try again? Shall I repeat the number?"

The operator sighed, repeating the number back to me. "Once more, madam. Please hold."

The wait felt interminable. Surely there was some mistake. Finally, I heard the line click and the operator came back on.

"There is no mistake, madam. This line has been disconnected."

"Thank you." I hung up the phone, frustrated. Had the Meyers' phone been repossessed? I searched my address book again and lifted the receiver, ringing the operator once more. "Please, Operator, could you place a long-distance call to the United States, to Lakeside Ladies Academy in Farmington, Connecticut?"

"Number, please."

I gave the number and waited. Finally, a familiar voice came on the line, but not one I was overly pleased to hear. A senior student, best friend of Augusta's older sister, was, I supposed, no worse than talking with Miss Fullbright.

"Lakeside Ladies Academy, Emily Jones speaking."

"Emily? This is Miss MacNeill. Is Miss Belding there? I know she's likely to be in class now, but I must speak with her. It's urgent."

"Oh, she's not in class; she's run off. That's why I'm on telephone duty. Miss Fullbright is fit to be tied but she's filling in for her class till she gets back."

"I don't understand. Run off? Is Miss Belding ill?" I could think of no other reason Dot would miss teaching her classes.

Emily all but snorted. "Ill in the head, if you ask me."

"Emily, I don't have time for this. Please explain." Between my fatigue and her nonsense, my head pounded.

A moment passed before Emily's venom took on a condescending note. "So you don't know? I suppose the other woman's always the last to know. She's over to the Meyer house, is my best guess, to cozy up with her Germans. Those Meyer brothers are finally being sent to war. Everybody knew they were on their way out. I wouldn't want to be her when Mrs. Shockley finds out!"

"Sent to war? Now?"

"Everybody knows it—apparently everyone but you. You needn't worry they'll be lonely, Miss MacNeill." Emily laughed. "They'll find a girl in every port, as long, that is, as Miss Belding comes back single. Look, I've got to go. Time to ring the change of class bell. Bye now!"

The phone slammed in my ear, but I stood frozen, the receiver still in my hand, Emily's words ringing between my ears. *Off to war? If Miss Belding comes back single? Stephen? But you were supposed to be here, to meet me, to propose to me. Weren't you?*

In a daze I climbed the stairs to my room, found a chair. Throughout the afternoon and evening, I sat, too numb to brave the questions I needed to ask.

The maid had promised to sit with Bertha through the night, but I finally sent her away. There was no point in both of us going without sleep. In the dark of Bertha's room, the questions I'd been too afraid to address finally took form.

Why had Stephen not telephoned? Or written? Had he really planned to go off to war without seeing me first? Was his plan to come to Halifax, to ask Lemuel for my hand, a joke? *No, it can't be. He wouldn't . . . But has he changed his mind about asking me and been too embarrassed, too ashamed to contact me? What does Dot have to do with it?*

It didn't sound like Stephen. I didn't want to believe Emily, but what could I believe? Her words ran round and round my brain—*"I suppose the other woman's always the last to know."*

To know what? That everybody else knew they were going? How is it Dot knew to see them off? Why would Stephen have told her and not me?

All these thoughts tormented me through the night—a dark night of the soul. By morning, when Alice, the chambermaid, came with tea,

I'd written a hurting and angry letter to Stephen, hoping he'd receive it before being shipped out, or that it would somehow catch up with him if he'd gone. I wrote a remorseful one to Dorothy, asking what she knew, asking her to forgive me in the name of our longtime friendship. I could not believe that Dot would go after Stephen now, no matter what Emily implied. Surely she wouldn't do that, knowing that I expected his proposal any day. But at least she would know the truth. She would have answers.

"Will you post these for me, Alice?"

"Yes, miss. I'm on my way to market for Mrs. Abernathy. I'll hand them in directly."

"Thank you."

How I made it through that day, that fifth day of December, I never knew. I stayed by Bertha, never bothering to so much as change my clothes, wash my face, or brush my hair. What did it matter? What did any of it matter?

But late in the afternoon, during another visit from Marcus, who came in breathless from his quick trip to the docks to see the *Imo* up close, Bertha began to rally just a little, and that took my focus off my own heartache.

"You should see it, Mother! She's a ship bound for Belgian relief and was to have sailed today. I was afraid I'd missed it. But she's still in harbor and the gates are about to close. Tom, from down at the wharf, says there's a boat due to unload coal into her first thing in the morning. That must be why she's not sailed. The captain won't like the delay! Missed a whole day on the sea. Maybe she'll sail before school tomorrow, and I can still see!"

Bertha smiled. "My young sailor, bound for his sea of dreams. I hope you do get to see the sailing, but you mustn't be late for school."

"No, Mother. I won't. I promise."

Marcus was the picture of boundless energy, portrait of the future of the family. It struck me then that Marcus was just a little younger than Lemuel had been when I was born. I wondered what he'd think of his baby sister, the sister he had yet to lay eyes upon.

When Marcus left, Bertha closed her eyes to rest. "Where is Lemuel? Has he been in to see me?"

I could not tell Bertha that her husband—my brother—had not been in since the birth of the baby. The one time I'd seen him he'd not looked well—pale, as if he hadn't slept, as if he'd not kept up his appearance, even though I knew he'd gone to his office, or somewhere.

But Bertha smiled. "You needn't pretend for him. I know my husband, Adelaide. He's a frightened little boy, terrified that I will not live, that childbirth will take me from him." She pushed up onto her elbows, lifting her head onto the raised pillow behind her. "You may tell my kitten husband that I have no intention of dying, that I'm a little blue and weak, but coming round."

"It was a strenuous birthing. You've lost a great deal of blood."

"Which I'm gradually recovering from. Now, where is my baby?"

Her question was a great relief. "She's being well looked after, nursed by a mother who's recently given birth, too. The midwife is having her brought back first thing tomorrow, so rest up today. She'll be here in the morning."

Bertha closed her eyes, as if the thought alone was tiring, but the faint hint of a smile formed on her lips. "I'll be ready for my darling."

I could not help the niggling ache in my chest. Bertha possessed a beautiful new baby; a fine, stalwart son; a home of her own; and a husband who, though terrified of losing her as he'd lost his mother in childbirth, loved her with all he was capable of. I'd had what now felt like the audacity to entertain those hopes of love, of husband and home and family for myself, and now . . . nothing. Worse, I felt foolish and betrayed. All I could do was wait for Dorothy's response to my letter, but I doubted it would bring news I craved.

～

The next morning Bertha really had improved—at least a bit of color stained her cheeks. At my urging, Lemuel stopped in early to see her, greatly relieved to find his wife smiling, acknowledging his presence, and aware of his kiss to her forehead, much like the kiss a child might give the forehead of a porcelain doll. It struck me as amusing and endearing, this fear of his that she might yet break, this slim hope that each of them tentatively nurtured.

When it came time for Bertha's morning ablutions, Lemuel knelt by her bed, prayed a quiet prayer of thanksgiving, then disappeared.

Alice and I aided Bertha in her washing and change into a clean gown, then helped her sit in a chair while I changed the bed linens and Alice built up the fire once more. By then, Bertha was weary and glad to return to bed. Alice went to fetch the breakfast tray. She was back in minutes.

"Miss, there's a dark woman waiting in the kitchen."

"A dark woman?"

"Yes, miss, with Baby. Mrs. Cadeau, she says." Alice looked as if she disapproved.

"Mrs. Cadeau . . . I'd nearly forgotten. Is Mr. MacNeill here? Could he see to her?"

"Mrs. Abernathy says he's gone into Richmond, miss. He's off to see Reverend Crowdis to arrange for Baby's christening at Grove Church. Have they decided on a name, then, miss?"

"I don't know. I hope so, but I can't imagine Mrs. MacNeill will be well enough to attend soon. When Mr. MacNeill returns, please let me know. I'll be down to see Mrs. . . . Mrs. . . . ?"

"Yes, miss. Mrs. Cadeau—that's what she says." Again, that near grimace.

"Please tell her I'll be down directly." My head was nearly splitting from lack of sleep. I needed to wash, to dress, and comb out my own hair.

I did the bare minimum to make myself presentable and had just reached the bottom stair when I saw the front door standing wide open and Marcus on the front porch without a coat.

"Marcus! You'll catch your death. Do come in!"

"Aunt Adelaide! Aunt Adelaide, come and see! Take my binoculars. Look! Those ships in the harbor—the *Imo* and something else—look as if they're headed straight for one another. They're blasting their whistles, but neither is budging from the lane. They're going to crash—I know it!"

I didn't need binoculars to see that the two ships in the harbor below were set on a collision course, but surely the captains and harbormaster knew what they were doing and would right their courses. More worrisome to me at the moment was the notion that Marcus stood in his shirtsleeves in the freezing weather and might catch pneumonia. That would be the worst outcome for him and certainly dangerous for Bertha and the baby.

"Come inside. You can watch through the bay window, but you must get out of the cold, and we cannot leave the front door standing wide. It must be past eight thirty. You don't want to be late for school."

"But Aunt Adelaide—"

I wasn't in the mood to argue with my nephew. At the same time the insistent cries of an infant called me from the back of the house. "Marcus, come inside, now. I've got to see to your sister."

Marcus came in, but the moment he took his watch at the bay window, he yelled, "Fire! They've hit and there's fire!"

I forgot the wailing baby and the woman waiting and ran to the window, my hand on Marcus's shoulder as we knelt on the horsehair sofa and watched. Orange flames rose amid rising plumes of black smoke from the deck of the smaller ship.

"That's no coal fire. Must be an ammunition boat! Look at the way she's going up!"

"The *Imo*? You said she was a Belgian relief boat! There's no red flag to indicate munitions." I immediately thought of Ruth's brother, Rodney, who'd drowned when the *Lusitania* was sunk by German torpedoes under the claim that she'd been carrying munitions, though the British denied it.

"No, the smaller one—*Mont-Blanc*, it says on her side. There's barrels loose on her deck, and likely lots of explosive stuff below—bullets and dynamite and such."

"Will she explode?"

"Hope not. Look! They're lowering the lifeboats—and sliding down the tackles!"

Even I could see the man waving his arms through the air, shouting something and pointing toward Halifax for all he was worth as columns of flame shot into the air, but of course neither of us could hear what was said so far away, and certainly not with Baby crying.

The hallway clock bonged eight forty-five as something smashed in the back part of the house—crockery or crystal, I didn't know what, followed by a long string of words I knew Bertha would cringe over. Instant, more-insistent baby wails rose from the kitchen, and I could just imagine Mrs. Abernathy turning purple. "I'll be back as quickly as I can, but you really must go to school. You're running late already. Wrap up warm." And I left Marcus there, staring through his binoculars at the blazing fires as men abandoned ship.

In the kitchen stood a bronze-skinned woman, nearly my height, with sharp cheekbones and thick black hair bound in a braid down her back, jiggling Bertha's screaming baby as Mrs. Abernathy, loudly complaining, swept a pile of crockery.

"Mrs. Abernathy, please. That's quite enough."

Mrs. Abernathy straightened and huffed. "I'm sorry, Miss MacNeill, but I'm not accustomed to screaming babies and . . . and dark women in my kitchen."

I ignored her. None of us were accustomed to anything that had happened in the last few days, let alone that morning.

"Mrs. Cadeau? I'm Miss MacNeill. Perhaps we can step outside where we can speak more freely."

The woman nodded, sending a look I could only call *daggers* in Mrs. Abernathy's direction. "That would be a pleasure, ma'am."

I pulled a shawl from the hook by the back door over my head and shoulders. "Baby's wrapped warmly, I see. She'll be all right?"

"Better than in here."

I couldn't keep the smile from my lips. I think that was the first connecting link between Portia Cadeau and myself.

As we stepped through the back door and into the side garden,

Marcus slipped through just behind us, one arm in his coat, his leather book bag swinging from his shoulder and binoculars in hand, tearing for the road.

"Marcus! School!" But I just knew he'd head toward the docks. I could see the street from the side garden and two other boys, boys he often walked to and from school with, were also headed down the hill, none of them toward the school. His father would have to deal with him later.

"There's a terrific fire in the harbor—one of the ships caught fire." I felt the need to explain my nephew's rude behavior.

Mrs. Cadeau turned away from the house. Cradling Baby against the wind and the rising stink of a billowing black smoke, she settled onto a bench behind the stone wall. "I expect that's where he's headed, then. Half of Halifax and all of Richmond will surely go."

"We saw it from the window." I rounded the wall, intending to sit beside her. "I just hope those boys won't get too close or make a nuisance of themselves."

And then abruptly, a deep, unnatural silence fell. Even Baby stopped wailing. I looked up.

Nuisance of themselves . . . The words echoed through my brain as a fireball of blinding light erupted and ripped open the belly of the house, shooting shattered window glass and splintered clapboards toward us before I could cover my eyes, sending me up into the air and away, away from the woman with the baby clutched in her arms, wonder and horror written across her face. A deafening roar filled the air, ringing in my ears as I flew backward, twisting through a world of black debris, flying steel, fierce wind, and putrid smoke. A perfect tornado, a thousand hurricanes, and earth's destruction all at once forced me higher, higher, until I was upside down, spinning, then falling, not breathing, unable to see my hands or arms for the wood and glass and metal debris of houses and walls flying past me, shooting high, raining down, while the earth rushed closer, closer. I felt an unbearable rush of pain, and then nothing.

Chapter Twenty-Three

JUNE 1935

Rarely was Dorothy called to meet with the Lakeside Ladies Academy Board of Governors. Usually their decisions were rendered typed, with flowing signatures, bound in a leather portfolio, and placed on her desk where she would find them the next day. Dorothy had always considered that means of dispensing their commands a not-so-gentle reminder that they owned the keys to her office, that her position was by their grace, her life's work by their command. Thankfully, the desk was her own, a ten-year anniversary gift from her husband, and only she possessed the key.

She'd known the school was in financial trouble. Who wasn't, throughout this horrid Depression? Cutbacks in staffing, reduction in salaries and spending, delays in completing the new gymnasium—the Adelaide MacNeill Memorial Gymnasium, if she and Ruth and Susannah had their way, where they would hold not only classes and sporting events but theater productions that had been dear to Addie's heart—were all to be expected. But she'd never anticipated anything worse, not until that morning's summons to the afternoon board meeting.

"Please sit down, Mrs. Meyer." Mr. Blankenship, the head of the board of governors, indicated a seat at the far end of the table.

Dorothy sat. The long table and the reserved and frowning businessmen surrounding it gave her the feeling of being on trial. For what, she couldn't guess.

"Let me begin by saying, Mrs. Meyer, that we have appreciated your years of dedicated service to Lakeside Ladies Academy. Your work here has been exemplary, and we hold you in no way responsible for these financial straits."

"Thank you, sir. I appreciate that." Dorothy, uneasy with wherever the conversation was headed, didn't know what else to say.

"However, enrollments are down, and operational costs continue to rise. Taxes and the upkeep on the school's properties, in addition to staffing and the day-to-day costs of running the school, exceed tuitions—have, indeed, exceeded tuitions in these troubling times."

Dorothy braced herself. Did they want her to take a cut in salary?

"As much as it pains the members of the board, we have reached a point of no return."

Panic raced from Dorothy's chest to her throat. "I'm sorry, Mr. Blankenship. I don't understand." She forced herself to swallow. "Surely, gentlemen, you can't mean to close the school."

Mr. Blankenship heaved a sigh and spread his hands, as if the weight of his words had done him in.

"But the school's an institution—for over seventy-five years. Daughters of diplomats and senators, generations of the very elite of our country depend on its doors remaining open, depend on the education and the lifelong connections their daughters foster here."

Mr. Blankenship looked truly sorry, as if this cut him deeply. Mr. Shockley, the school's treasurer and financial adviser, pulled back, stiffening his spine. His hands folded on top of the account books, as if closing himself off, preparing for battle. "You must understand, Mrs. Meyer, the gravity of the situation. Enrollments are at an all-time low."

"Because of the Depression, I know—which surely can't last much longer." But Dorothy knew that was a weak argument. There simply seemed no end to hard times in sight. "Perhaps we could lower the cost of tuition—more students at a reduced price should generate more income overall, surely."

Mr. Shockley shook his head. "That wouldn't prove sufficient."

"The school and its lands are paid for, are they not? There is no lien, is there? What about endowments, legacies?"

"Do you actually think, Mrs. Meyer, that we have not considered every possibility, each and every alternative? We are simply informing you as a courtesy before making an announcement to parents and guardians." Mr. Shockley's condescension knocked the wind from Dorothy and sent a flame up her neck.

Members of the board looked away in embarrassment, but Mr. Blankenship spoke up. "I believe Mrs. Meyer has a right to know these things, Mr. Shockley." He turned to Dorothy. "When we agreed to build the new gymnasium, it was because we took out a bank loan, a loan we believed could easily be repaid over the next several years, and all things being equal, it certainly would have been. As you know, we began construction right away. Unfortunately, construction costs were much higher than we'd calculated and world events being what they are, we were forced to delay the completion of that project. Those monies have proven essential in covering operational costs as enrollments have declined throughout this Depression. Now, the bank is calling the school's note due."

Dorothy inhaled. She'd had no idea.

"For several months we've worked quietly, though unsuccessfully, to sell a portion of the acreage, hoping to appease the bank and forestall closing. The bank has agreed to wait until this class graduates to take possession of the property, but no longer. We will inform alumnae by letter ahead of time, and an announcement will be made at graduation: 1935 is Lakeside Ladies Academy's final graduating class."

Dorothy felt as if someone had grabbed her by the throat and punched her in the kidneys. Every teacher at Lakeside would feel the same. Surely there was a better solution. She closed her eyes to shut out the men, to calm her brain. *Lord, what is the answer?* But she didn't wait to hear.

"What if instead of closure you asked those attending the baccalaureate, or even the graduation, for significant donations? Wouldn't the parents of graduating students, most of whom are alumnae, prefer to empty their pockets than to see their alma mater closed?" Dorothy knew she would if she possessed that kind of money.

Eyes shifted uncomfortably among the board members, giving Dorothy the distinct impression that they'd discussed this very option and disagreed upon its execution.

"Mrs. Meyer, it is one thing to encourage legacies from willing parties; it is quite another to beg for money from parents who have already paid for their daughters' educations. Nearly half of our students now come from local homes—homes likely unable to donate that amount of funds. Besides, Lakeside has never reduced itself to begging." Mr. Shockley huffed, as if it pained him to explain what Dorothy should already have understood.

"Lakeside has never needed to," Dorothy countered, much to the displeasure of the gentlemen around the table. Men, Dorothy knew, who thought a woman shouldn't be guiding their discussion of finances. "Perhaps in these short remaining weeks the girls and staff can work on fundraisers. I believe that most of our staff would willingly take a reduction in pay if it meant keeping the school open another year. I would."

"You would have our young ladies participate in cookie and baked goods sales? Really, Mrs. Meyer!" Mr. Shockley shook his head, disgusted.

Dorothy's head pounded. She didn't know, didn't have a clue how to raise funds, especially substantial funds, but there must be a way. *The school simply can't close. It can't!*

"You may inform your staff of our decision, in the interest of their pursuits for future employment, and of our willingness to write each a letter of recommendation, but do not allow students to hear of this," Mr. Blankenship counseled. "Under no circumstances do we wish to cause alarm, and there is to be no scandalous newspaper reporting so near the end of term."

As if I can do anything about that. As if this won't break the hearts of parents and students and staff alike.

"Please, Mr. Blankenship, Mr. Shockley, members of the board— please do not make this decision final yet. Surely there must be means we haven't considered."

"I assure you, Mrs. Meyer, there are not." Mr. Shockley spoke with authority, but it was not his job on the line.

"Two weeks, please. Give me two weeks. If I cannot conceive a plan guaranteed to succeed in that time, well, then . . ."

"Then you will go quietly?" Mr. Shockley's sarcasm reeked. "Accomplishing a miracle in that time is impossible."

"Improbable," Mr. Blankenship echoed, but sympathetically.

"Please," Dorothy begged.

Mr. Blankenship hesitated, weighing Dorothy's sincerity, her ability, she was certain. He looked to the other members of the board. Almost imperceptibly, two shrugged, and one nodded. One looked at Mr. Shockley's disapproving glare, considered, and looked away.

"I don't know what you might accomplish in two weeks' time that we have not, Mrs. Meyer, but you may have your two weeks. It will not hurt to delay the announcement that long. I wish you Godspeed in your endeavors, and may I say, I am truly sorry. Closing the school is the end of an institution of great value to this community, to our country." Mr. Blankenship's eyes spoke regret, and for that Dorothy was grateful. "This meeting is adjourned."

How she would accomplish the miraculous in two weeks' time, she had no idea. *Impossible. Improbable. Perhaps.* But she would give it all she had.

Chapter Twenty-Four

Once Portia stimulated memories of that day, I could not set them aside.

For years, each time calendars turned past November, Haligonians had asked one another, *Where were you that December morning?* To a man, woman, or child they remembered the moment, the place, what they'd said or done or thought before the Halifax Explosion, and their first conscious thought after.

One moment I was looking at a babe in Mrs. Cadeau's arms and the next, after the earthquaking blast, the whirlwind tornado, the hurricane of fire and soot, I woke, buried beneath a pile of rubble, cold and wet and shivering, as a great wave—a tsunami—receded, leaving me covered in slick black oil and soot. Heartrending wounded-animal cries—or were they the human dead and dying?—pierced the air. A fiery inferno, still roaring and crackling, had swept the landscape clean.

I could not move my leg, twisted at an odd angle, from the beam that pinned it to the ground. Bone jutting from my wrist, my left hand dangled from its socket, my skin the color of rich garden dirt. I remember thinking that was odd, and then nothing.

Next I knew I was bumping along the road in some sort of garden cart—perhaps a wheelbarrow—driven by a man I didn't know. My shoes and stockings were gone and half my skirt and shirtwaist ripped away, exposing my naked legs and shoulders for all to see. I thought of my mother's red heeled shoe—the only one I found after the drowning. I wondered if our shoes might be joined together now, might become friends. I became aware of something jagged sticking out of one eye, but my hands would not move to shift it. And then all went dark again.

I opened one eye to bodies lined like cadavers in a morgue. Only some moaned and groaned, a few twisting in pain. Red blood pooled from open wounds and seeped through bandages, but we were all covered in black oil so that only the whites of eyes showed like raccoons'.

I thought of Mean Mildred and the shiner Ruth had temporarily given her the night of the Harvest Festival. I wondered where Mean Mildred was now, where Ruth and Dot and Susannah might be. And then I thought of Bertha, and Marcus and Lemuel and Baby. Were they alive?

Halfway between asleep and awake, I saw that a woman stood over me in her faded dress, her hands stained gray from all the soot and oil she washed from my twisted, broken limbs.

"Ah, open your lovely brown eyes wide so I can see. Did anyone ever tell you that you have beautiful eyes, my dear?"

No one had, but it made me open the remaining one wider with the wonder of such a thought—which is what I think she intended. I could see nothing out of the other and later learned that a bandage covered my empty socket.

"Time and a half you woke up; you're sleeping the day away—three, as a matter of fact."

A woman on a pallet next to mine moaned aloud, then screamed,

"Germans! They've attacked! Invasion!" More screams, more cries penetrated the line of pallets.

"Germans?" Panic electrified my sluggish mind. Fear of German invasion raced rampant through Halifax. "Germans, here?" Fear for Bertha, for Baby, for all of us coursed through my aching limbs.

The woman nursing me motioned for another to go calm the screaming woman. "Germans? No, no. A rumor, fear like a fire through her dreams, but it isn't true."

"Then what?" I turned my head to better hear with my right ear, for my left ear received no sound, as if stuffed with cotton or bandaged, like my face. Somehow the groaning of others stole through my senses, pounding a rhythm in my brain.

"Two ships collided in the harbor, a French one loaded to the hilt with munitions of all kinds and another bound for Belgium relief. Such an explosion! Felt like the end of the world had come."

"A ball of fire, and a roar."

"That and more." She straightened and sighed. "There, now. That's as much washing as I think your skin can take for a bit. We'll try again tomorrow."

My head throbbed and half my face and my eye were bandaged, but looking around, I appeared one of the lucky ones. "It's so cold. Where am I?"

"It's a makeshift hospital for now, best we've got under the circumstances. Quite a blizzard blew in the night after—everything's covered in snow. Doesn't look real out there." She penciled something to a tag, then stood, poised to write more. "And what is your name, my dear?"

I opened my mouth, but no words came out. *My name? What is my name? Bertha? Who, now, is Bertha? I just thought of her a moment ago.* "I know the answer. I do."

"It's the shock, dear. It will wear off soon and things will come plain. Do you know where you live? Names of your family members?"

I knew. Of course I knew. Why couldn't I tell her? Why couldn't I remember?

"It's all right. Don't fret yourself. It will come back. Give it a bit of time. When it does, tell us soon as you can, and we'll write down everything needful. Lists of names are posted in the newspapers, helping folks find loved ones. Are you up to a cup of tea?"

Cup of tea. Tea? I nodded, at least I must have, for she lifted my head and poured something warm and sweet down my throat. I choked. Everything swam and muddled. The room tilted, swaying, the floorboards and earth rising as they had before. Nausea and blood fought their way up and out my throat.

"Doctor! Doctor!" the woman called. "Help!"

The cup fell away just before darkness came.

Chapter Twenty-Five

Dorothy's legs barely carried her back to the school. If anyone spoke to her before she reached her office, she couldn't remember. She wanted only to close the door, lock it, and reach the stability of her desk.

She closed her eyes, willing the board meeting to have been a dream, a nightmare from which she would awaken any moment. But when she opened her eyes, the room looked just as it had before. She lifted the pages she'd taken from the meeting. Facts and figures, numbers she could crunch without blinking an eye stood out before her in stark black and white. So much money, gone, and the gymnasium the loan was taken out for never completed. *Close. Lakeside Ladies Academy will close. No!* She wanted to scream, to curse, to pound the desk and weep, but she sat, frozen.

At last the clock in the foyer bonged four. Classes dismissed.

Footsteps, scurrying, hurrying, joyful in their freedom, stampeded the hallway. Any other day Dorothy would have opened her door and admonished, "Walk, ladies. Decorum, please." And the girls would laugh, smile, chant, "Yes, Mrs. Meyer," and gladly comply. But soon those hallways would empty—empty, and never fill again.

No! Please, God! Please! Dorothy rarely prayed, or more truthfully rarely listened for the answers she begged, but now there was no one to turn to, no human who could help, barring a miracle. *Miracles are Your department, aren't they, Lord?* Dorothy wondered if that was sacrilege, to beg God when she needed Him and ignore Him when things were fine. *But things aren't fine, Lord! They've never been fine, not for a long time.*

A knock came at the door. "Mrs. Meyer?" It was Miss Milton, the academy's secretary.

Dorothy could not speak with her now, could not look in her eyes and not tell, not cry in the telling. If she said nothing, Miss Milton would think she hadn't returned; she could wait to speak with her tomorrow. At last footsteps receded in the hallway. Dorothy heaved a sigh of relief.

She sat, staring out the window, listening as teachers and staff left the building, watching the light fade. How long she sat she didn't know. It didn't matter. Her husband would naturally think she was working late, so near the end of the school year.

Dorothy closed her eyes, willing herself to remember the first day she'd come to Lakeside, gratis of her grandmother in Boston. She thought she'd died and gone to heaven, leaving the farm, exchanging her work clothes and apron, and donning a skirt and shirtwaist, new stockings, and button shoes. And then, her friends, the Ladies of the Lake . . .

Close Lakeside? Shut out all the memories she'd made, the place that began lifelong friendships? Impossible. Impossible for her and impossible for all the girls who'd ever walked these hallways, who'd graduated and entered the world as women richer for their time here—generations past and present.

How would she tell Ruth? And Susannah? No more Ladies of the Lake? No more meetings at the gazebo? In the years after Addie's death, their meetings had stretched from every two to every four or five, but they'd kept their vow to meet and bless their friendship as best they could. Each time they met they remembered Addie, toasting her memory with tea and tears. Dorothy had toasted their friend with unconfessed guilt.

Each time they'd met, they'd vowed to keep the gymnasium project—started as the Lakeside Ladies Academy Gymnasium—before the board of governors, even though the foundation of the building sat incomplete. Delays in building in such times were to be expected, but Dorothy, Ruth, and Susannah had resolved the moment building resumed, Susannah would flood alumnae with requests to petition the board to name it in Addie's honor. Susannah was a genius at convincing, a well-connected woman of means, if somewhat reduced means in recent years. Still, she and her family's name were respected and could be seen as independent of Dorothy or any staff member of the academy. Now there would be no gymnasium to name in Addie's honor, no secret means to assuage the guilt in Dorothy's heart, no need to write to alumnae or ask them to petition the board . . . or was there?

Dorothy's pulse quickened. Many of the mothers of girls enrolled now had known Addie, had gone to school with her, or their younger sisters had sat under her tutelage during the short years she taught at Lakeside. Many knew she was likely to be named headmistress, if only she hadn't—if only the explosion never happened.

What if Susannah wrote those women now? What if Susannah boldly asked those women and their husbands to support the school in these uncertain times and to help raise funds for the delayed building of the gymnasium, asked them to request it be named in Addie's memory, reminding them of all the good she'd done the school, of the kindness and light she'd brought? Reminding them that Adelaide MacNeill was forever, at least in memory, one of them?

~

DECEMBER 1917

The first news of the Halifax Explosion came to the academy from Hartford with the post. Miss Fullbright believed Boston newspapers had spread the word across New England, maybe the world.

But Dorothy wasn't there when word reached the school. She couldn't let Stephen and Jonas face the death of their mother alone. It wasn't right, not after their longtime friendship, not with how she felt about Stephen. What kind of neighbor, what kind of friend would she be if she didn't show support? She'd taken a week's leave, with or without Miss Fullbright's blessing.

At home with her mother, Dorothy had cooked and baked, taking food to their neighbors that the authorities would only allow them to leave on the porch. But at least the Meyer men would know they'd come, know that they could claim and depend on their Belding friends nearby, even if others had turned their backs.

Dorothy would not have known of Mrs. Meyer's death except that she'd come to deliver a meal the day she saw Stephen and Jonas and Mr. Meyer standing by a long mound of dirt in the fir grove behind the house, heads bowed. Mr. Meyer held his Bible, open to the middle, surely the Psalms. Mrs. Meyer had loved the Psalms. Dorothy knew that.

Where was the pastor? Why was no one there? Why was she buried in a grove of trees and not in the churchyard?

But Dorothy knew, and her heart broke for the Meyer men, for Mrs. Meyer, whose life had ended so cruelly.

Police no longer guarded the door, but men in black coats waited by two dark cars on the side of the road. No one stopped Dorothy as she approached the gravesite.

The brothers stood together, caps in hand, heads and shoulders bowed. Dorothy set her food basket on the ground and stepped between them, linking her arms with theirs, hoping to infuse strength, support, love.

Jonas clasped her hand as if it were a lifeline. Stephen shuddered at her touch.

She couldn't look in their faces, knowing she, too, would break down if she did. But she looked up at Mr. Meyer as he read aloud from the Bible, words in German that she could not understand. It was only when he finished praying that he seemed to see her and nodded, his eyes glazed, his mouth grim.

The men in dark coats coughed loudly, a reminder of their presence and apparent impatience.

"They're taking Father to an internment camp." Jonas spoke, still clasping her hand, unable to look in her eyes.

"What? No!" It didn't seem possible.

Mr. Meyer stepped closer, pulling something small from his pocket. "I do not know when or if I will see any of you again."

"Father!" Stephen shook his head, unable to say more.

"You must be strong, and safe. You must look after one another—always. Promise me."

"We promise. We promise, Papa." The brothers spoke as one.

"You must survive this war and live your lives. Do not let them break you. If I am able, we will be together again once this war is past. It cannot last forever."

The men by the road coughed again.

"Dorothy Belding, you and your parents have been our faithful friends. I ask one thing more of you."

"Anything, Mr. Meyer. Anything at all." Dorothy meant it.

He pressed his German Bible and a thin gold band into her hand. "My Greta's wedding ring. I know they will take it from me. Keep these safe, I beg you, until I return, or until my sons return."

Dorothy gasped. The weight of things so dear and so small, emblems of a lifetime of love and faith, nearly undid her. "I will. I'll keep them safe."

Stephen looked at the ring in Dorothy's hand then. "We'll come back to claim it, I swear, Father."

"Give Mama's ring to your wife, whichever of you marries first."

Stephen stood straighter, as if taking the commission, but Jonas slipped the ring on Dorothy's finger—her right hand. "Don't lose it."

It was a futile attempt at levity. Both brothers gave crooked smiles. Dorothy nodded, her heart too full to speak.

Two of the men from the road began walking toward them.

"It is time, my sons." Mr. Meyer's voice broke. Jonas grasped his father in a bear hug, only letting go so his younger brother could embrace their father before the men reached them.

"I will write; I will tell you where they've taken me, if allowed."

Despite their attempts to look strong, wretched sobs escaped the sons.

Dorothy's fury at the cruelty of it all stoked a burning flame. She stepped between the men and Mr. Meyer, ready to spew her anger, her indignity, but Mr. Meyer pulled her back. "Let me go, Daughter," he whispered.

The love in that last word stopped Dorothy, flooding her soul with warmth and light that she knew she didn't deserve. It should be Addie standing here, accepting the family's precious ring and Bible, hearing the word *Daughter*. Dorothy knew she was a surrogate, a proxy-in-waiting, second in all their affections. Still, to be enfolded in the trust and love of these three men at any level meant everything to her.

It was Mrs. Meyer, she told herself in that moment, who had chosen Addie to dance with Stephen so long ago, who had enfolded Addie into the family, and now Mrs. Meyer was gone. Perhaps Dorothy could be the daughter Mr. Meyer had never known, the wife Stephen would need upon his return. She was, after all, the one sharing this life-altering moment that could cement them as family. All these things sped through her mind as she watched Mr. Meyer being led away, thoughts thrilling and heartbreaking and shameful.

The car door had not even closed on Mr. Meyer when the men came for Stephen and Jonas.

"Where are they taking you?"

"Train depot for now. Uncertain after that. They want to make sure we won't desert before we're in uniform." Jonas pressed her hand. "Take care, Dorothy. Write us—write us both, and Father if we learn where he is."

"I promise." Dorothy watched the two men she'd known all her life walk away, toward the waiting car. Their bags were tossed into the car's trunk. The door opened. Overcome by the knowledge that she might never see either of them again, Dorothy cried out, "Wait! Wait!" She ran, as fast as her unbelieving legs could carry her.

Stephen turned and, seeing her, opened his arms. She ran straight into them, and he gripped her as tightly as she held him. He kissed her forehead and held her close. "Goodbye, Dorothy."

He was cut off by the taller man in a dark coat, who pulled him away. "Let's go, soldier."

Dorothy's legs might have given way if Jonas hadn't caught and held her, turning her toward him. He held her face in his hands and kissed her fully, on the mouth. Not passionately, but as a question. "I'll be back. I swear it. Don't forget me."

She nodded, her head going up and down, then sideways, vowing she would never forget either of them, wondering what exactly had just happened.

How she retrieved her basket, how she walked back across the field toward home, she could never remember. But when she walked in the door, she saw the pallor on her mother's face as she handed Dorothy the newspaper with sprawling headlines:

HALIFAX IN RUINS; STREETS LITTERED WITH DEAD; FRENCH MUNITION BOAT COLLIDES IN THE HARBOR WITH A BELGIAN RELIEF SHIP AND BLOWS UP; TWO SQUARE MILES A BURNING RUIN

"Addie," she whispered.

Chapter Twenty-Six

With raised eyebrows, Portia read the letter from my publisher.

Dear Mrs. Murray,

Your request for a further extension on the due date of your manuscript has been forwarded to me by your editor, Mr. Whitley.

While I appreciate that there may be circumstances beyond your control, please understand that a further extension must adversely affect our publishing schedule and disappoint your readers anticipating this novel—a delay in neither your best interests nor ours.

To be included in our spring catalog, your manuscript must be in-house no later than July first.

Please advise immediately if you are unable to comply.

Sincerely,
Melvin Richards
Publisher

"You've hardly touched that book since you got caught up with worry over Bernadette's graduation. What will you do about this? And why are you telling me?"

"I'm telling you because I need my friend, my prayer warrior." I folded the letter and returned it to its envelope, as if sealing it away might make it disappear.

"And just what is it you want me to pray? That you finish this book? Is it the money you need?" Portia's tone came as part challenge, more concern.

I faltered. "The money is not as important as my readers. I need . . . I don't know what I need." I needed help—desperately—but how could I ask Portia to pray to cover my secrets?

"Help in time of need."

"Yes, I need help."

"The Lord said, 'My grace is sufficient for thee: for my strength is made perfect in weakness.'"

"Weakness, yes." *He never promised to make us strong in our lies.*

As if Portia had heard my thoughts, she took my hands, led me to the settee, and peered into my face. "Jesus came to free us from our sins, our every shame. We only need confess and ask His forgiveness. He'll help us make it right, right as we can in this life. He'll do that for you; you know that—whatever's worrying you so."

My breath hitched and a sob escaped.

"You've been falling into the past, Rosaline, remembering, and remembering is hard. You lost everything and everyone but Bernadette in that explosion, but something tells me you've never faced it, never mourned what you need to. Why not?"

I looked away, but Portia didn't let go of my hands. She shook them, which shook me and forced me to face her again.

"I said, why not? What is it you're afraid of? What is it you've never said out loud in words meant to free you?"

I swallowed. I wanted to tell her, to tell someone, but how could I? After all these years? And would she tell Bernadette? What would that mean?

"You're not Bernadette's mother, are you?" Portia spoke so softly I might have pretended I hadn't heard. Her eyes held only sympathy and love. Both undid me, opening my floodgates.

She pulled me to her, resting my head on her shoulder, stroking my hair. I clung and cried, cried as I'd not since the day I learned that Stephen was lost to me forever.

"There, there, now. Did you really think I didn't know? I'm not telling you to hush, I'm saying cry it out. Cry it all out."

I did. Light faded from the room before I stopped, before I pulled away and saw that I'd soaked the shoulder of Portia's dress. She handed me her handkerchief. I mopped my eyes and cheeks and nose until it, too, was soaked.

She pulled my own handkerchief from my shirtwaist cuff and handed it to me.

"How? How did you know?"

"The day I met you, the day the world as we knew it exploded and was gone, you introduced yourself as Miss something or other. I could never remember what, but it wasn't Mrs. I remember that. And I don't think it was Murray."

"You knew—from that?"

"And the fact that you looked too hale and hearty, too slim and trim to have just birthed a baby. The idea that milk wouldn't come in for one so young and strong made no sense. That, and the midwife told me the baby's mother was poorly, not likely to live, at least not rally anytime soon—that I'd be needed to nurse longer, but to come to the house with the baby that day."

"She never told me she didn't think . . . didn't think her mother would live."

"Maybe just trying to convince me to take on the baby to nurse. I don't know. She didn't need to stretch the truth; we needed the money, Henry and me."

"Henry."

"My husband."

"I never knew his name."

"You never asked."

"I'm sorry, Portia. I'm so sorry I never asked. I didn't want asking in return."

Portia nodded. "I figured there were things not meant for me to know and I didn't need to. The two of you needed help I could give, and I needed a home. That's all I had to know."

"I'm sorry. I'm sorry for everything."

"It's not me you should be saying sorry to. Bernadette doesn't know, does she?"

"You know she doesn't."

"And you're the one that has to tell her."

"I can't. At least I can't now. I've always known there would come a day when I must, but it has to be later, after she's come home."

"How does that keep you from going to that graduation, from celebrating the most important day of her life with her?"

I wasn't ready to say.

"It's got to do with that woman on the phone, doesn't it? You've been off your kilter in every way since she called. That woman you put your handkerchief up to disguise your voice to. None of that's like you, Rosaline. Not like you at all."

I pushed my head to the high back of the settee and closed my eyes. Already I'd said too much.

"There's no turning back. You may as well out with it now."

A minute passed. I hoped if I kept my eyelids closed, Portia would take the hint and go away.

She didn't. "I'm going to start remembering out loud, and when I hit the nail on the head, you tell me."

"No, Portia—"

"Don't you 'no, Portia' me." She huffed and settled back. I knew she was in for a long speech. I wanted to close my ears but couldn't.

"I came to the house with that baby—that beautiful, hungry baby girl with no name. I thought that the saddest thing in the world, to bring a child into the world and not name her, not show God and everybody how grateful the parents were to have her . . . unless she wasn't wanted. Unless she had no daddy, and the mama couldn't care for her."

"No!" I opened my eyes and sat up. "No, that wasn't it at all."

"Then you best tell me the truth, because if you die of shame and remorse and I have to tell Bernadette the truth, that's the only truth I can imagine."

My mind raced. My heart beat a rhythm likely to make it jump out of my chest. Portia was right. Bernadette had a right to know. The truth was horrible, but not as potentially ruinous to Bernadette's reputation as Portia's conjecture. "They died. They both died in the explosion. My brother and his wife—and their son. None of their bodies were ever found."

"They lived in that house—that house up on . . . What was the street name?"

"I don't remember. It was all so long ago. North, up the hill from the harbor, somewhere near Gottingen Street, but that wasn't it. Funny, I've never been able to remember."

"Go on."

"Bernadette's father was my half brother—we had the same father but different mothers. By the time I was old enough to really know him, Lemuel had left home. Mother and Father and I lived on Prince Edward Island. I was nearly twelve when they both perished in a storm at sea."

"So young to lose your mama and daddy. Then you came to Halifax to live with your half brother. I hope he was good to you."

"He arranged for my education. Boarding school." I said the words carefully, knowing I would regret giving away too much.

"Like Bernadette, but here in Canada," Portia concluded, nodding.

I didn't answer. "He was already married, with a son. It wasn't until several years later that his wife birthed another live baby. The pregnancy was risky. I'd come to stay with them for a time, to help with the birth and with my nephew."

"Bernadette's mother was the one who was poorly, with no milk to speak of."

"Yes. Yes, you saved our girl, Portia, nursing her as you did."

"Because I could. Because I nursed my own sweet baby. But that day . . . the day of the explosion . . . Bernadette lived in my arms, but my Ahanu and my Henry died."

"I'm sorry—sorrier than I can say. But if you'd been there, with them, you would have been killed, too."

"Most nights I wished I had been, that I could be with them now."

I reached for Portia's hand. She'd said that before and I knew she meant it. I could not imagine her pain. "And yet you loved our Bernadette."

"I love her still. She's next to my own, but that didn't stop me from being angry with the Lord, from railing against Him for the loss of my own sweet child. Do you understand that? The unfairness of it? Do you have any idea?"

"Yes, a little." I swallowed all I might have said. A minute passed, both of us lost in that past. "You saved me, Portia, in every way."

"Didn't know so much as your own name after the explosion."

"But you recognized me."

"Only by God's grace was I working in that hospital, scrubbing floors. They let me work and sleep there so I could nurse the baby I came in with. So many babies left without their mothers, and I had milk, but no child.

"Plenty of people were ready to adopt a newborn, but I kept claiming that her mother was alive, that I'd been with her at the time of the explosion, seen her alive with my own eyes. I figured even then you weren't the mother, but you'd know who she was. They just had to find you.

"I knocked on the door of that morgue set up at the Chebucto Road School time and again until they finally let me in. Searched every day till they held those public funerals. Then I figured there was no use. You'd have been brought in by then. You were out of your head in that hospital for more'n ten days."

I hadn't known anything. "I was blown away—clear up Needham Hill, I was told."

"And the house gone to splinters, everybody inside incinerated."

"But you'd already suspected I wasn't Bernadette's mother?"

"Don't you see? That didn't matter. I needed that baby, and I needed that job. My husband, my child, my home were all gone in an instant. I had nothing. My breasts were full of mother milk, my heart broken in two, my arms left empty. I hung on day after day nursing that baby, crying out for my child every moment she suckled my breasts. Still, I insisted—hoped and prayed and begged the Lord that you'd show up, that you'd need me. Finally, you did."

"How you recognized me, God only knows."

"God does know, Rosaline. You are His child and He called you by name. It was the voice He gave you that told me who you were."

~

DECEMBER 1917

I'd been gently scrubbed clean over a period of days, but my skin, like that of every other person in Halifax caught in the aftermath of the explosion—in the hailstorm of oil and soot, wood and metal and glass debris that poured from the sky—was still gray. At least the parts that weren't badly burned and flaming red. Besides, I wore a bandage over my face on one side. I couldn't have looked like the woman Portia had first met.

When I opened my eyes, I was aware of sounds in the long ward of beds and pallets: nurses speaking in soft tones, the muffled clatter of crockery and utensils, the gentle swishing of a mop. Everything came to me in a fog, until I pushed matted hair from my good ear.

There was a bronze-skinned woman with sharp, high cheekbones, mop in hand, scrubbing the aisle between my bed and the next one. She looked familiar, but I couldn't place her, couldn't think where I'd seen her before. She glanced at me, looked twice, nodded, and moved on.

For days I'd not seen a soul I knew, not that I'd known many people in Halifax. But as I'd lain there day after day, I'd gradually remembered Lemuel, Bertha, Marcus, and the baby girl with no name. I remembered the cook in the kitchen, and Alice, the maid who'd worked so hard. I couldn't remember the name of the midwife who'd come to help birth the baby, or the name of the doctor, or the woman who'd come, nursing Baby. I couldn't even remember the house.

Two days and nights had passed since I'd remembered my own name, and then Stephen's and Dorothy's, and all my life before. But no one asked me about my name or address again, and the longer I lay there, the more I wondered if I wanted anyone to know I'd survived. I could not see my face, but from what I could feel, I knew the burns were bad and could imagine the horror of my disfigurement.

My broken leg and wrist were temporary troubles. But the burns shot pain through my body and into my brain—down the left side of my body and up my neck and face—and wouldn't mend. The hair on that side of my head had been shorn in the blast and my left eye socket sat empty. Whether the fog would clear from my ear, I didn't know. I had one good eye and one good ear, and for that I was thankful—at least I tried to be.

I lay there thinking, trying to decide all the while if I wanted to live or die, and then the woman with high cheekbones who'd been scrubbing the floor came back.

"Excuse me, ma'am."

"Mrs. Cadeau," I blurted, astonished that some part of me recognized someone—anyone—and more that my brain had recalled the name of a woman I'd known for less than five minutes before the blast.

She straightened, resting her mop in the pail of dirty water. "Something told me to scrub this floor first thing this morning. Praise God I listened." She stepped closer. "I told them you were alive. I told them."

I didn't know what she meant, but memories and fragments of memories flew through my brain. "You were holding Baby—"

"When you flew high in the sky. Like the Lord took Elijah, just like that."

I groaned at the memory. "Is she—?"

"She's burned, but your baby's fine. She'll be fine." The woman looked away.

"The house exploded."

"Yes, ma'am. Every person inside gone—had to be."

Bertha . . . the staff . . . "But the boy that ran down the hill, the one—"

"Those boys—no, ma'am. Gone."

The weight of knowledge, of things I'd inwardly known as I'd listened to the talk around the ward, of all that had been lost that fateful day, sat like an anchor on my chest. "The church—the Presbyterian church in Richmond."

Mrs. Cadeau's eyes went darker yet. "I'm sorry, ma'am. Grove Church was destroyed. Anybody inside—gone." Each pronouncement weighed on her, too, deepening the circles beneath her eyes, and I realized that Mrs. Cadeau had likely not slept for days. Had she lost loved ones of her own?

"Your baby—is he—?"

She looked away. "My boy's gone. My husband's gone."

I could not fathom it. *Please, God, let me go to sleep and wake up again where none of this is true.* "I'm sorry . . . I'm so sorry."

"Your baby, she's alive. Burned bad, but she'll mostly mend."

"She's not—" I stopped. I'd promised Bertha . . . *what*? That I would care for her children. That I would be a mother to her baby if she could not, if she did not live. *Well . . .*

Mrs. Cadeau leaned closer. "You want me to keep nursing her? The hospital's had me do it so far. They wanted to let her out for adoption. People are calling from all across Canada and even the United States ready to adopt children orphaned from this mess. They said they can't wait much longer, figure you must have died, too. If nobody claims her, then—"

"Orphaned?"

"So many families dead, so many little ones left to wander. Next of kin can come claim them, but if they don't, they've got to find homes for them, and quick. I told that man I saw you alive. I told him not to give away your baby, that she has a mama, just not found yet."

Orphaned, like me. Sent away, to . . . where? But what else is there? She needs a family—a mother and father. I'm a teacher, I'm—no. Wait.

"Now I ask you again, do you want me to keep nursing your baby? You'll have to tell them if you do, because otherwise, they—"

"What do you think you're doing, woman?" A nurse in starched uniform jerked Mrs. Cadeau away from my bedside. "You know you're not to disturb patients. Get back to scrubbing before I have you sent from the floor. I'm sorry she bothered you, miss. I've no idea what she—"

"Please. She knows where my baby is—she's seen my baby."

The nurse's eyes went wide. "Your baby? You have a baby? You remember your name?"

"I remember my baby. Please, Mrs. Cadeau was nursing her for me before the explosion."

"You know this woman?" The nurse looked as if she didn't believe me.

"I wouldn't have my baby nursed by someone I didn't know." My brazenness surprised me.

Mrs. Cadeau kept her eyes on the floor, as if looking up might jinx all we said. The nurse looked from one of us to the other, weighing whatever she needed to determine. "I'll have the clerk stop by to see you."

"My baby's alive. I need to see her."

The nurse pursed her lips, uncertain. "I'll send for the registrar right away. Mrs. Cadeau, is it? I suggest you remain here."

"Yes, ma'am." A hint of a smile passed Mrs. Cadeau's lips as soon as the dragon nurse stepped away.

Chapter Twenty-Seven

JUNE 1935

Dorothy wrote Susannah the next morning, swearing her to secrecy about the potential closing of the school but pouring forth the urgency to raise funds within the next two weeks to repay the bank note and fund the building of the gymnasium—the gymnasium that would never be built in Addie's honor without a miracle. *If there is anything you can do to persuade our Ancients to help, I will be forever in your debt,* she wrote. To aid the process, Dorothy enclosed a full list of the names and addresses of the parents of graduating girls, alumnae, and potential donors, with the deliberate exception of Mean Mildred and members of the Lakeside Ladies Academy Board of Governors.

Susannah did not disappoint, guaranteeing her support by return telegram.

Persuasive as she was, Susannah flooded the mailboxes of alumnae, affectionately known as Ancients, and parents of alumnae, reminding them of the years of stellar education and finishing that Lakeside Ladies Academy had provided them and their daughters, even their mothers in some cases, and of all that the academy had done to prepare them to take their places as capable and leading women of society. She encouraged them to donate immediately so that the announcement that work would continue on the much-needed Adelaide MacNeill Memorial Gymnasium could be made at the baccalaureate dinner the evening before graduation in a few short weeks. Not only would every graduate and her family attend the dinner, but it would be a formal occasion to see and be seen by everyone from the governor to statesmen. Susannah ended with an impassioned, emotive call to join forces as women eager to make their voices heard. If Dorothy possessed the funds, she would have written a check on the spot.

But a week passed, and no checks arrived. Dorothy paced her office at the academy. She paced her living room at home.

"Dot, you're going to wear out the carpet. You're wearing yourself to a frazzle." Her husband set the newspaper down, pulling the reading glasses from his nose.

"I simply cannot believe no one has responded! Not one check. If I'd received Susannah's letter, I'd have taken out a loan to donate!"

He smiled. "Rather defeating the point?"

"It's not funny." Dorothy rarely snapped, especially at this man she loved so dearly, but her rope had frayed. She rubbed worry from her forehead, or tried. "I don't know what else to do."

He was behind her in a moment, pulling her into his embrace, nuzzling her neck in the way that only he could, the way that had calmed her nerves for well over a decade. "It's only been a week, hardly enough time for responses to reach you."

She turned to him, burying her face in his chest, willing his arms to tighten around her. This man was everything to her, had been, and would be forever, as long as he never knew all that she'd hidden in her heart.

"I know you love the girls, and I know you love your work, sweetheart. You've done wonders there these years. I know you love the school, that it's part of you, of who you are. But if you're at all worried about the income, don't be. We'll be fine."

Dorothy wanted to scream. It wasn't only her job, the school, the income. From the moment discussion was raised about building the gymnasium, she'd dreamed of its dedication and so had Susannah and Ruth, the remaining Ladies of the Lake.

If only she could see that it was named in Addie's memory, wouldn't that make up, at least in part, for the past? It couldn't send the letter she'd never sent. It couldn't change the fact that Addie never knew Stephen had truly loved her, had desperately wanted and fully intended to go to her.

Two days after the explosion, Dorothy had received Addie's anguished letter written when Stephen never came, believing he'd deserted her, regretting the fracture in their sisterhood, and begging Dorothy to tell her what she knew.

In the months that followed, when Dorothy became part of the Meyer family—the one thing Addie had longed for, besides her writing—Dorothy pushed her guilt and regret aside, determined to forget. But nothing could change the fact that Addie was dead or that Dorothy was living so much of her friend's dream, had as good as stolen her friend's dream.

The board of governors had sent Addie telegrams after the explosion. When there was no response, they'd sent letters of inquiry to officials in Halifax and finally sent an envoy to search for Addie.

But the searches were futile. Addie's body was never found. Her brother's house had been blown to smithereens, and with it, every soul under its roof. Eventually those who'd lived and worked within the household were listed among the dead, even though there were no bodies to recover, nothing to so much as bury.

Only then had Dorothy written the bleakest letters of her life to Stephen and Jonas in service, and to Mr. Meyer, who her parents discovered had been interned in North Carolina.

Dorothy had learned, through the board of governors, that Addie had been slated for the position of headmistress in two years. It was only because she was truly and forever gone that the position was in time offered to Dorothy.

Dorothy knew she'd been second choice—second choice as head-mistress, second choice as a Meyer—and that she'd failed as a friend. Even now, twisting the gold band on her left finger, the wedding ring that should have been Addie's, Dorothy felt the sting of those memories.

Somehow, the gymnasium had to be built.

Chapter Twenty-Eight

Mail to Canada from New England took less than a week. When Susannah's letter, addressed to Mrs. Rosaline Murray of Halifax, Nova Scotia, parent of graduating student Bernadette Murray, arrived pleading for funds to build the Adelaide MacNeill Memorial Gymnasium, it was as if the paper burst into flame, as if ghosts raised from the long-ago dead screamed in my hands.

I recognized the voice of the letter and the handwriting of the signature immediately, though I'd not seen either in seventeen years. Susannah's strong and fluid script was unchanged, along with her powerful persuasion, her ability to convince you not only that you wanted to do what she asked but that if you didn't, you'd be found morally wanting, and who in the world would want that? But it was the cause that made me catch the side of my desk for fear I would faint. *The Adelaide MacNeill Memorial Gymnasium. The Ladies of the*

Lake. Friends and confidants to the last. All for one and one for all. How I have betrayed you . . . betrayed you all.

But what could I possibly do now? If the letter had come to me, an unknown party in Nova Scotia, it must have gone out to all the parents of graduating girls, at least. Knowing Susannah, it would have gone out to all the Ancients, and perhaps many other persons of influence and financial stability in these uncertain times.

My fleeting imagination of telling Bernadette the truth, of entertaining Portia's urging to attend the graduation, disappeared.

And yet, how can I allow them to name a building in my memory when I'm alive? But Adelaide MacNeill is not alive. She died in the Halifax Explosion. She was declared dead. Her name is listed among the dead. I have not been that woman for seventeen years.

Dear God, how has it come to this? Why?

I tore the paper in bits and threw it in the fireplace before I realized there was no fire. I'd dig it out later. I couldn't stay inside; I couldn't breathe.

I left the house, slamming the front door, regret, fear, anger, frustration, humiliation coursing through my veins. Every moment, every memory leading to my decision to disappear ran rampant through my brain.

～

DECEMBER 1917

The clerk did not come right away, nor did the nurse return that morning. Mrs. Cadeau did as she'd been told and waited by my bedside. I feigned sleep, not wanting to say more than I'd already committed and needing time to think through my story.

What would I tell them? My name? If I did then I could be traced. Traced by the Lakeside Ladies Academy Board of Governors, traced by Dot and the Ladies of the Lake, traced, perhaps, even by Stephen.

But Stephen hadn't come. He'd enlisted without so much as contacting me. *What clearer message of his change of heart could there be? If there was ever any hope of winning his love, it's gone now. These burns, and my eye. He'd be unable to look at me the same, and who knows how my leg will mend? Will I be crippled? Blind? Half deaf? A crippled, half-blind, burned wife? A crippled, burn-scarred teacher with no hair on one side?*

There was no way I could return to Lakeside, not like this, not now, not ever. And how could I go back on my promise to Bertha—a promise made in the heat of a moment that seemed too impossible to imagine? *But when the registrar comes, I must tell him my name, my relationship to the baby. If I say that I am her unmarried aunt, will I be allowed to keep her? How will I support her? How will I support myself?*

To change a life in the twinkling of an eye—how can one plan for that? How can I make this decision in a moment? Yet if I don't, she'll be put up for adoption. What will that mean for her, a child burned and scarred? Better she stays in Halifax where there are so many injured like her, where she won't be so noticed for being different, where she'll be seen as one of the lucky ones because, like me, she's alive. Is that true? True for her and true for me? Am I claiming her for her sake or for my own? Dear God, I don't know. I don't know.

"Madam?"

I opened my one good eye to a man standing at the foot of my bed and Mrs. Cadeau, standing beside me at the head.

"I am Mr. Matthews. I've been commissioned with finding homes for orphans of the explosion. I've been told by Nurse Hillshire that you believe we've found your child. Is that correct?"

I moistened my lips, willing them to speak with a confidence I didn't feel. "I hope so. Mrs. Cadeau, who was nursing my daughter, said that my baby is here, somewhere, that she's seen her, that she's continued to nurse her."

"Mrs. Cadeau," Mr. Matthews acknowledged, but turned again to me. "Can you tell me your name? Your baby's name and age?"

What name? Adelaide MacNeill? Or someone entirely new with a clean and uncomplicated slate? Murray—Mother's maiden name. She said it meant "settlement by the sea"—and that's what we are, where we are.

"Madam?"

"Murray." *I've always wished my name was Rosaline—a perfect rose name.* "My name is Rosaline Murray."

"And your child?"

She should be named after Bertha, but not Bertha. That might raise suspicion. What were the names we found in the baby name book? "Bernadette." *Bernadette means 'brave as a bear.' She'll need to be fearless.* "Bernadette Murray."

He wrote down the name on his tablet. "And the age of your daughter, please."

"She was born—" I had to stop and think, to close my eyes to concentrate. "Just a few days before the explosion."

"December 2, I believe," Mrs. Cadeau offered.

"Yes. Yes, that's it." I put my good hand to my head as the pain returned. Thinking was still a challenge.

"And your address?"

"My address?"

"Yes, here in Halifax."

"I'm not from Halifax."

"Oh?"

I felt heat creep up my neck. "I was visiting a friend—of my cousin and her family."

"And they are?"

"Lemuel and Bertha MacNeill."

"Address?"

"I'm sorry. I don't remember. Halifax—the north end of Richmond."

He hesitated, tapping his pad with his pen. "And how is it you know Mrs. Cadeau?"

"The midwife took my baby to her to nurse. I'm afraid the birth rather did me in. Mrs. Cadeau was holding Bernadette when the blast came. We were in the courtyard. The house was destroyed. I saw it go up—and everyone . . . I'm told . . . no one could have—I don't think there's anything left. There couldn't be." I didn't have to feign my trembles at the memory, or the choking back of tears.

"I'm sorry, Mrs. Murray. I'm afraid there was a great deal of that, and the fires that followed."

"Fires everywhere—for days," Mrs. Cadeau supplied. "What the blast didn't start, turned-over coal stoves did." She shook her head. "Fire's what took my house and my family, right down to the ground."

"I'm very sorry," Mr. Matthews said, returning to me, intent on his task. "Do you have friends or relatives in the area, Mrs. Murray? Anywhere you might stay?"

The realization that I was homeless, without so much as shoes or clothes, set in. "No."

"You'll need temporary housing, until you and your baby are able to travel. You'll need to return home, of course. You understand that we are overrun here. And where is home?"

Where, indeed?

"Mrs. Murray?"

"I—we were going to relocate here, with the MacNeill family. So, I—I don't know what to say."

"Your husband? Does he know of the explosion? Was he in the house?"

"My husband died in the war, Mr. Matthews."

He looked away, becoming all business once again. "I see." He'd surely heard many such stories from unwed mothers in these times, women who'd succumbed to the wiles of soldiers or sailors looking for a night to remember before sailing to war. I saw in his expression that I was suddenly one more. "Well . . ."

"Maybe the best thing is for Mrs. Murray to work on getting herself well and on her feet so she can care for her baby." Mrs. Cadeau rested her hand on my back. "Maybe she needs to see her baby now."

"Yes, please. Please," I implored.

Mr. Matthews softened then. "I'll see what can be arranged." He turned to go.

"I want Mrs. Cadeau to continue nursing her."

"Under the circumstances that would probably be best." He left without another word.

"He means he thinks you don't deserve better than a mixed-blood woman to nurse your baby."

I reached for her hand. "He's no idea how lucky my baby is to have you. Thank you, Mrs. Cadeau, for all you've done, for all you're still doing for—for—"

"Bernadette. And you're welcome. You call me Portia; that's my given name. I hope you won't forget. I hope you'll still need my help by the time you get out of here . . . that is, if you've got someplace to go."

I couldn't answer that. *Where will I go, and when?*

❧

"Mrs. Murray?" A hand touched my shoulder, pulling me from the depths of sleep next morning, just as daylight stretched across the ward. "Mrs. Murray?"

Who do they want? Who is Mrs. Murray? Something jogged my memory, and the word came without my bidding. "Yes?" I did my best to open my good eye, to focus on the face in front of me: the nurse from yesterday.

"There's a gentleman here to see you."

Stephen?

My eye opened wider. "There must be some mistake."

"There's no mistake, ma'am. Something to do with the MacNeill household—where the baby was found in the yard with that colored woman."

"Mrs. Cadeau."

"I think it best if I help you to a chair and you speak with him in the consulting room. He says it's private."

"Have they found more of my family—my friends?" My words stumbled over themselves.

She looked at me skeptically. "You'll have to ask him about that. Come, let's get you up. I've a dressing gown of sorts we can cover you with. There, now, gently."

The idea of placing another layer on my burned shoulder made me want to scream. The idea that someone wanted to speak with me—Mrs. Murray, who didn't exist—made me want to hide. "Must I see him today?"

Her eyebrows rose. "The man says it's imperative, something to do with the baby."

"My baby?" I said the words in wonder.

She looked at me sympathetically then. "I believe he's likely to wait."

What more could I lose? Bernadette? My heart raced and head ached, nearly as much as my shoulder.

Nurse wheeled me into a small room and the gentleman turned around. He had the courtesy to wait until the nurse closed the door behind her before speaking.

"Mrs. Murray, I'm told."

My mouth tasted of cardboard.

He offered his business card. "Horatio Emberly, attorney-at-law."

Lemuel's lawyer. I couldn't speak.

"May I?" He gestured toward a chair beside the table.

I nodded, doing my best to summon manners and some form of confidence. "Please."

"I see by your expression that you recognize my name."

"Yes." There was no point in denying that.

"Mrs. Murray, I'll come straight to the point. I've been given to understand that you intend to claim the baby found at the MacNeill property as your own, the child born December 2."

I didn't know what he knew, how much he knew. "Mrs. Cadeau—Portia Cadeau, her nurse, was holding her when the blast came. Until yesterday I thought everyone had died."

He stared at me longer than was comfortable. "I should tell you that as his attorney, I represent the interests of Mr. MacNeill."

"Lemuel is alive?" If I could have jumped from the chair, I would have.

He hesitated. "Forgive me, the late Mr. MacNeill. I'm sorry. You knew him?"

Tears came, unbidden. Mr. Emberly waited. His demeanor seemed to soften, if only a trifle.

"I know that a girl child was born to Bertha and Lemuel MacNeill on December 2. Mr. MacNeill contacted me to include the child in his will and establish trust arrangements for his children." He waited, leveling me with his stare, taking my measure. "How did you know the MacNeills, Mrs. Murray?"

I'd known they were dead. I'd believed it, but some part of me had not accepted the horror, the finality, the eternity of life without them, without another living being who knew Dad and Mother, who knew me. Tears flowed down my cheeks, the salt of them painful in my burns.

"Can I get you something, Mrs. Murray? Water? Tea? Should I find a doctor?"

No. I shook my head.

"Is Murray your name?"

I gasped. If I told this man the truth, would I lose Bernadette? If I didn't, would the weight of my lie consume me? I heaved a sigh. It was all too heavy a burden. What I was about to do would cast the die. I shook my head.

"What is your name?" He leaned forward, taking my hand in his.

"Adelaide. Adelaide MacNeill. Lemuel was my brother, my half brother."

He nodded. "I thought as much. Your brother told me about you. I'm so very sorry for the loss of your family, Miss MacNeill."

He leaned forward, handing me his handkerchief.

"It should have been me that—not them. Bertha struggled so hard. She was a good mother, and just on the mend. The birth was so hard on her."

He waited several moments, but I could not continue.

"Can you positively identify their baby?"

"What?"

"The MacNeills' baby. Can you positively identify her? Have you?"

"I haven't actually seen her since the explosion."

"Then what makes you think—?"

"Mrs. Cadeau was with her. She saved her."

"Mrs. Cadeau?"

"The midwife recommended her. Portia Cadeau had taken the baby to nurse, along with her own. Bertha didn't have the strength. That morning, Mrs. Cadeau brought Baby back. The midwife believed seeing her daughter again might help Bertha rally. We were just outside, in the courtyard, when the blast came. Portia was holding the baby." It was a relief to tell the truth.

"And you've seen this Mrs. Cadeau? She survived, she and the baby?"

"Yes, I've seen Mrs. Cadeau. She told me the hospital is caring for Baby, that she was badly burned, but I've yet to see her."

"Then you cannot know if the child is genuinely . . ."

What was he suggesting? That Portia had lied? That the child was not Bertha's? "I will recognize her."

"How? A newborn infant you saw for what, a few minutes? A few hours? And now she's burned? There are many infants orphaned as a result of the explosion, Miss MacNeill. I need to ascertain that this child is indeed the child of Lemuel and Bertha MacNeill."

How can I do that? How can I know for sure? My head ached so that I closed my eyes—my eye. I tried to remember Baby—after the birth, as I held her. "Something . . ." I tried so hard to think.

"Miss MacNeill?"

"A locket. I thought—as if she wore a locket."

"I beg your pardon?"

"A tiny pink splotch—where a tiny locket might rest on her chest, just between her collarbones. I remember thinking it was a sign—like an angel's kiss—that she would live, that Bertha would rally and live." I bit my lip at that memory and drew a deep breath to compose my face, but I couldn't control the shudder through my body.

He nodded, not indicating more than a belief in what I said, though even I knew it must have seemed a feeble thing to lay the baby's identity on. A pink mark like that could have been the result of birthing. "It might not still be there. I saw it shortly after her birth, but I don't know if—"

"I'll see the baby for myself, and then we'll speak again, Miss MacNeill."

"Please," I all but begged, "please do not use my given name here. I've given them another."

"Why? MacNeill is a well-reputed name in Halifax."

"Look at me, Mr. Emberly. Don't you see? I can never go back to my life that was. That woman no longer exists. Adelaide MacNeill is dead. Everyone believes that and I want to leave it at that."

"But, Miss MacNeill—"

"Please. You have no right to thwart me in this." I didn't know if that was true, but I stood my ground—all the standing I was likely to do for a very long time.

He sat down again. "Mr. MacNeill told me that you are a teacher at a highly regarded and well-known ladies academy in the States, that you have longtime friends there and are well thought of by their board of governors. He believed in time that you might even be asked to—"

"None of that is true any longer. Look at me, Mr. Emberly. I cannot hear out of one ear. I am missing an eye. My hair is shorn from my head and lurid burns have ravaged one side of my face, my neck, my body—I can feel them. My leg and wrist are broken, and though they will likely mend in time, the rest of me won't. I'm horrified to look in the mirror. The board of governors of Lakeside Ladies Academy will not hire me to teach the daughters of diplomats and statesmen. They will not ask me to lead or represent their academy in any way."

"But your friends. Surely you mean to let them know—"

"I do not want their pity, and that is all they could offer me now. I am unmarried and will not become a burden to them. I will not. Let them draw their own conclusions. Everyone in the MacNeill house died that day. There is no reason to assume otherwise, or that I am an exception."

"Miss MacNeill, I can't see—"

"The point is you can. Your sight is what it was before the blast, Mr. Emberly. You were nowhere near its epicenter. Your life is intact. Allow me the opportunity to go forward, not as Adelaide MacNeill but as Rosaline Murray." The speech exhausted me to the point I trembled, barely able to breathe.

He hesitated, frowning, debating. "And what of the child?"

I drew the deepest breath I could. "You must tell me what is possible. I want to raise her as my own."

"Legally, you would need to adopt her—Adelaide MacNeill adopting her niece, Baby MacNeill. Does she have a name?"

"As far as I know Lemuel and Bertha had not yet named her. If they did, they did not tell me. I choose to name her Bernadette, in honor of her mother. But I don't want her to know about her past. I don't want her to be raised with the stigma of being orphaned. I've lived that label since I was twelve years old, and it is a lonely one."

"She'll no longer be an orphan once you adopt her."

"You've never suffered the cruelty of children or borne the label of orphan in our society. I want her to grow up believing—and the world believing—that she is my daughter."

"And her father?"

"I'll say he died in the war. That's true enough. Lemuel died in the explosion, one that never would have occurred but that we're at war."

Slowly, thoughtfully, he nodded. "Will you tell her one day? The truth?"

"No . . . Perhaps. When she's grown, when she can bear it. For the sake of my brother and your years of service to my family, will you help me?"

"If that is what you wish. If you're certain."

"I am."

"You may sign your name as Murray on the certificates here. No one is likely to question or follow through with those; they are that eager to reunite families. I will draw up papers with your names as MacNeill for legality—in private. Once the adoption is complete, and once the inheritance and trusts are transferred, I can legally change your names if you still wish it."

"Inheritance?"

"Mr. and Mrs. MacNeill's estate should be held in trust for their daughter, do you agree?"

"Yes, absolutely. I didn't think, with the explosion, that there would be anything left. I thought—I didn't know how—financially—I would raise her."

"Already the Canadian government is talking of establishing a relief commission for those disabled from the explosion, but you'll be pleased to know that Mr. MacNeill's investments were not affected by the blast, nor were your own, which, held in trust, will of course now be transferred to you. You needn't worry about money for a very long time, Miss—Mrs. Murray. I hope that will be of some comfort to you, and a help in raising Bernadette."

An ally, at last, and help and relief I'd not anticipated. "When? When will you see her?"

"I'll go now. If the identifying mark is there, we'll—"

"Take me. Please take me to see her."

"I'm not sure you're well enough to—"

"Mr. Emberly, I need to see her. She—she's my only living relative. From this moment on she's my child—my daughter." The thrill of that stole through me—the thrill and the fear. What did I know about raising a child?

"Are you prepared to accept her, no matter what you find? Consider carefully. The state of her burns might—"

Heat flared up my spine. How dare he! "Of course I am. She's my flesh and blood." *She'll need me.* The realization of that flooded my soul and filled it with such love—love and longing—I could scarcely breathe.

Mr. Emberly nodded and stood. "We'll go, then. May I push your chair?"

"Please . . . thank you."

"It is my pleasure, Miss—Mrs. Murray. I will be at your disposal."

"Thank you. Thank you, Mr. Emberly."

We left the room and he pushed me down hallway after hallway. With each corridor my heart beat faster and my longing for Bernadette grew, along with fear that I'd not be up to the task ahead. A short sprint was one thing—the long haul, a lifetime, was another. Had I made a mistake in my assertions to Mr. Emberly?

Finally, we came to a room that may at one time have been a dining room or a large waiting room now converted into an emergency nursery. Several young children napped. A few stared wide-eyed at the man pushing a strange-looking woman in a wheeled chair.

Immediately, seeing small children and babes with severe burns, bandaged eyes, or missing limbs, some looking in near-critical condition, set my heart aflame.

A little boy glanced hopefully, hungrily my way, struggled to smile, and raised his bandaged arm in a half wave as if hoping I'd recognize him. His hand was missing.

I inclined my head toward him, giving him the most smile my face could muster, but it wasn't one of recognition and his face fell as he turned away.

"Bernadette." I whispered her name, impossibly begging her, infant of days, to call out to me . . . afraid for her, afraid *of* her, afraid for myself.

Mr. Emberly softly, reverentially read aloud the names written on cards at the foot of each bed or bassinet until he came to one labeled *Baby Unnamed.*

"Stop."

"Do you think—"

"Please push me closer . . . to the other side."

"Of course." I heard the blush in his voice. His embarrassment embarrassed me. I'd have to get used to that, to the discomfort others felt in my eyeless presence, my inability to see on one side.

He pushed my chair as close to the bassinet as possible. I leaned forward as best I could but still could not see the baby's face.

"Can I help you?" A voice came from outside my line of vision. I'd not heard her approach.

"We're hoping to identify this baby," Mr. Emberly said. "Perhaps you can help us, Nurse."

"My little girl, my Bernadette." I could not control the tremor in my voice.

"Well, this can't be her, my dear."

My heart fell. "Are you certain? How do you know? The sign—it says the baby is unnamed."

"This is a little boy, madam." The woman sounded patient, kind even.

"Oh." I felt so stupid, but how was I to know? I could barely see out of my one good eye, and the child was wrapped and swaddled.

"Let me show you the girl babies. How old is your child?" She leaned close, careful not to touch my burns.

"Less than two weeks. Mrs. Cadeau, of Africville, has been nursing her for me."

"I don't know Mrs. Cadeau. We've hoped to find families for the infants unclaimed. It's good you came . . . but you must be prepared—"

"Please take me to my baby." My voice strengthened with resolve—resolve borne of desperation.

"Right away. This way, if you will, sir."

Mr. Emberly returned my chair to the aisle, and we followed the nurse into an adjoining room. There was a row of cribs and bassinets, an odd assortment certainly donated for the tragedy, lined against the far wall. The smell of burned flesh and hair mixed with antiseptic still permeated the air. Somehow, I'd imagined that would not exist in a nursery, not like it did in the adult wards.

The nurse stopped beside a bassinet about halfway down the row. "I'm afraid some of these little ones are rather badly burned. You won't be able to pick her up—not yet. It would be too painful for Baby."

"Which child, Nurse?" Mr. Emberly spoke, for I could not.

"There are three girl babies we've yet to identify. Our registrar knows the circumstances in which they were found but nothing more. I'm not sure which baby your Mrs. Cadeau has been nursing. I'm not always on duty in this ward. Will you—will you be able to recognize her, do you think?"

I couldn't tell if she spoke to me or to Mr. Emberly.

"I need to check for her birthmark. I'm not sure if it is still there or if it was a mark from delivery. Please, I need to get closer. I can't see very well."

"Of course." The nurse pulled my chair closer to the first bassinet. "Where is the birthmark? I can pull her little gown aside if we need to."

Close to the bassinet I first saw tiny hands—burned raw and red—and I gasped.

"It's hard to see, I know," The nurse spoke low. "But, if she's your baby—"

"Can we check for the birthmark?" Mr. Emberly spoke to the point. "On the chest, didn't you say, Mrs. Murray?"

"At the base of her throat, between her collarbones—a little oval shape, like a locket." I struggled to keep my voice steady. "An angel's kiss," I whispered, more to myself than to them.

A moment passed while the nurse searched. "No, nothing like that here."

I didn't know whether to cry or to sigh in relief. Bernadette might be even more badly burned. And why should I cringe? How could I, knowing my own body—?

"Here, let's take a look, my little love." The nurse was already searching the next baby, pulling back her gown, as the tyke sent up unholy howls of pain. I thought I might vomit. "I can't tell. There's not enough unscarred tissue to—"

"Check the next child, please, Nurse." Mr. Emberly's urgency matched my own.

"I must get this child something for the pain. I hate to wake them like this, but you really must say if one of these is your daughter."

How can I say such a thing when I can't tell? Is it a mercy to take a child—any child—who needs a home? What if I take the wrong child, someone else's child, and leave Bernadette because I can't identify her? Please, God, please help me! Help Bernadette!

"Here." The nurse searched the baby in the third bassinet. "What's this? What have we here?"

"Is it there? Do you see it?" I begged.

"Well, I don't know. It's not much of anything. She's badly burned but I can lift her for you to see. Her back's all right."

It seemed to take forever but the nurse lifted Baby from the bassinet. Much of her face and neck was burned. Her eyes were bandaged, so I didn't know if she could see at all, if she was even awake, until her tiny hands flailed and she whimpered.

Carefully, the nurse pulled back the gown near her throat. I tilted my head to better see, pain shooting up my neck. I squinted my eye to focus, uncertain of what I saw. I wished I could reach for her, hold her. But all I could do was blink and squint again. There, between tiny collarbones, sat a small oval, more pink than red.

"Your angel's kiss." I heard the smile and relief in Mr. Emberly's voice, the absolute benediction.

"Bernadette," I whispered, salty tears stinging my cheeks. "My Bernadette. My darling Bernadette."

Chapter Twenty-Nine

Dorothy closed her office door, hoping to encapsulate the tirade of Mr. Shockley. Students and staff did not need his venom.

"Do you realize what you've done, Mrs. Meyer? Not only have you deliberately flouted Mr. Blankenship's instructions regarding the utmost discretion of the school's affairs, but through Mrs. Whitmore's letter you've gone begging alumnae—families once affluent but who, in these times, cannot afford to fund outrageous building projects on a property that will be repossessed by the bank. You have breached our confidence, our trust, Mrs. Meyer! If the board is not yet aware of these indiscretions, I assure you they soon will be."

"Mr. Blankenship gave me two weeks to see if I could turn our financial situation around, to find a solution. He said nothing that would forbid fundraising for the auditorium, and there is absolutely no mention of the school's financial straits, nothing at all to indicate the academy might need to close its doors—a declaration which you have already proposed be written to them soon anyway. I don't see how—"

"No, clearly you do not see. You have no idea the cost of a gymnasium of this size!"

"No, I don't. Please tell me, then explain to me how far in arears we are in repaying the loan, what the costs of the school are that have put us so far behind."

That raised Mr. Shockley's color from his collar to his hairline. "The board's decisions regarding school expenditures and operating costs are not your concern, Mrs. Meyer. You will confine yourself to your duties and leave matters beyond your jurisdiction to the board of governors."

"I'm simply asking—theoretically. What would it cost? Fifteen thousand dollars? Twenty? Forty? I'm trying to understand. You will appreciate what the closing of the school means to countless women and girls, and to their families. If you don't know the answer to my questions, or if you prefer, I shall ask Mr. Blankenship." Dorothy held her breath.

The man looked as if he might rupture a vein. "The building alone would cost a minimum of thirty-five thousand. That does not include the operational expenses of the school beyond this year's graduation. Raising that kind of money is formidable in these times. Within the call of the loan, it is impossible. I'm warning you, Mrs. Meyer, mind your own business."

He slammed Dorothy's office door behind him. Dorothy flung it open and followed, desperate to plead, but he cut her off in a final biting threat. She watched the furious march of Mr. Shockley from the building.

Her knees gone weak, she leaned her head against the door's window glass, hot from the afternoon sun.

Normally careful to observe eavesdroppers or neutralize upsetting events among staff or students, distracted as she was, Dorothy simply returned to her office sanctuary and quietly closed the door.

What she would do now that the cat was out of the bag, Dorothy couldn't imagine. Mr. Shockley's final words rang in her ears. *"You've taken far too much on yourself, presumed beyond all imagination. We shall see what the board has to say about this, Mrs. Meyer, but I assure you, they will not be pleased. You would do well to begin searching for a new position at your earliest convenience—before graduation, if I make my meaning clear. Do not expect a letter of recommendation from the board."*

There seemed no alternative but to begin packing up her desk. According to Mr. Shockley, once the board was apprised of what she'd done by writing to Susannah, she could not hope to keep her position, even if the school by some miracle remained open.

The headache building behind her eyes was monumental. The last thing she needed was a knock at her door. But whoever it was must have seen and probably heard Mr. Shockley leave. She couldn't pretend she wasn't in her office. "Yes?"

The door opened to a meek and worried-looking Miss Milton, academy secretary. "The mail's come, Mrs. Meyer. I thought you might like to see it."

Dorothy closed her eyes. "Only if there's anything you urgently need me to handle today, Miss Milton, because it's really not a good—"

"You'll want to see this, ma'am." With a half-smile and more confidence, Miss Milton set a stack of opened letters before Dorothy.

There sat, atop the first letter, a check for one thousand dollars. Dorothy's breath left her body in a whoosh. She picked up the check with trembling fingers.

"We just need another twenty-nine or thirty of those," Miss Milton whispered.

"You heard?"

"I think anyone within a hundred feet heard. Don't give up hope, Mrs. Meyer. Mrs. Whitmore wrote a brilliant letter in good taste. I believe the Ancients will rally. Give them time."

Dorothy inhaled. "I hope you're right, Miss Milton. I'm afraid there's not much time. That's not to be shared."

"I understand. I'm praying."

"Thank you, that's what we need—prayer, and an answer to prayer. A miracle."

Miss Milton hesitated, her hand on the doorknob. "It's hard to imagine that the operating costs of the school these last two years have exceeded the loan—if it really was for so much as Mr. Shockley projected the cost of the building."

"What do you mean?"

"I'm surprised, is all. I intend no disrespect or to cast aspersions, but from what I understand there is no longer a mortgage on the grounds, and from what I see in the salary envelopes I prepare each month and the accounts for operations that I deliver to Mr. Shockley, I cannot imagine what additional costs could add up to such a figure."

Once Miss Milton closed the door behind her, Dorothy paused, considered, and scribbled some calculations of her own. At length she sat back, dropping her pencil, and stared into space. She could not imagine what those costs were, either.

Chapter Thirty

JUNE 1935

I'm sure every woman bears a thorn in her side of some sort. I simply didn't expect both of mine to come from those closest to me.

Portia made tea and brought the tray with scones to the library, where we settled in to share Bernadette's letter, delivered that morning. Most often we saved our girl's epistles to either of us to read aloud over afternoon tea—a reward for the day's work—where we could relax and smile and reminisce. I was blessed with a friend, the one person on earth who loved Bernadette as I did, who'd known her from infancy.

> *Dear Mother,*
> *I'm writing today with the utmost urgency.*

Portia and I looked at one another and smiled. Bernadette often wrote with "the utmost urgency." What now?

I've learned—don't ask me how, you wouldn't approve—that Lakeside Ladies Academy is in jeopardy of closing its doors forever. I don't know all the reasons, but they appear to be financial—and something to do with a gymnasium and a loan the school took out that's being called in. Whatever it is doesn't matter. What matters is that the school is in trouble and will have to close if a lot of money isn't raised at once.

"Close?" My heart leapt to my throat. *Close Lakeside? How is that possible?* I returned to Bernadette's letter.

I cannot imagine this world without Lakeside Ladies Academy. I know I didn't want to leave home when you sent me here, but I tell you, truly, Mother, Lakeside Ladies Academy has been the making of me, the saving of me. I never imagined I could be accepted and achieve like other girls, girls without burns or scars or a missing eye, girls who are truly beautiful and whole. But I have made friends, friends like sisters that I know will be mine forever. We're already planning reunions once we've graduated.

I stopped reading, willing myself not to cry.

"What is it, Rosaline?"

"I'm just so grateful it's been good for her. Sending her away was hard. Do you remember?"

Portia picked up the letter. "I do. Thought my heart might break all over again when she went away on that ship. Do you ever regret not keeping her over to the Halifax School for the Blind?"

"Never. She was there just long enough. Their long-term program required that I board her as a young child, and I didn't want that for her. She needed to be home with us—her family—and we needed her in those early years. I think we taught her well, don't you?"

"Best little reader I ever knew, and she could scramble an egg better than you." Portia smiled at the memory.

"When she did go to the School for the Blind, she learned more, things she needed to navigate the outside world."

"Sending her on to that academy in Connecticut was such a big step—for all of us. Surely seems like that was the right thing to do."

I nodded. "She's come so far. It's what I wanted for her, the step forward she needed to realize she could do the things other girls, girls with both eyes, could."

"I can still hear her, the day she asked you about her name. I marked that as the turning point for both of you."

I nodded again, remembering aloud. "'Mother,' she said, 'did you name me Bernadette because of my burns?'" Even now I ached at the memory.

"Poor child, to think she'd been wondering that all her life."

"It had never entered my mind that she would think such a thing. I named her after . . . after someone very dear and special, and because her name means 'brave as a bear.' I knew she'd need that courage to face life as she was. But later, I knew that she needed to go away when she could, that she couldn't remain forever in this house, in this city, and thrive. She had to see herself as separate, as individual from me, from us, from the explosion."

"I believe she does. She's never known anything different than who she is and what she looks like. She's not let her scars hold her back, near as I can tell, though I know she often feels not so pretty as other girls." A moment passed before Portia spoke again, hesitantly, softly. "I've always felt you hide behind your burns. You've come to let them define you."

I swallowed. Portia knew me too well. "I never intended—never wanted that for her."

"Bernadette's grown beyond all that. You can see that in her letter. You did right, sending her away. You're a good mother, Rosaline." Portia picked up Bernadette's letter and continued reading.

I want Lakeside to live on, to be here when and if I ever marry—something I never imagined possible, before—for when

227

I have a daughter. I want her to come here, to learn here, not only academics, but about herself. I want her to develop the kinds of friendships I have—forever friendships I'll take into all of life. You know, Mother—that "all for one and one for all" kind of friendship, the thing you said you wanted for me when I left home. I'm so glad you made me come.

The point is that none of that will happen without funds to keep the school going.

Once you told me that before Father died, he prepared a trust for me that would become available when I'm twenty-three. Is there any way I can access those funds now, or that you can do it for me? I want to give all I can to keep the school open. Please, Mother, answer quickly. Act quickly. Time is of the essence.

I must ask you one last time, please come to my graduation. Earlier this semester Mrs. Meyer asked if I'd like to consider a position here as an assistant teacher next year. Now, with worries about the school remaining open, that invitation will surely be withdrawn. It's possible that graduation will be the only opportunity you have of ever seeing Lakeside Ladies Academy. It's so important to me. I want to share this monumental event with you. Please come.

All my love,
Bernadette

By the time Portia finished reading, our tea had gone cold.

"Not much smiling there," Portia observed.

I closed my eyes.

"Money. That's the same problem that Susannah woman wrote you about."

I opened my eyes. "How do you know about that?"

"I empty the trash and scrape the ashes around here, or did you forget? You've got the money, even in these desperate times. Why won't you help? Why are you letting our girl dig into her future to do the rescue when you've got the means?"

"I'll not allow Bernadette to 'dig into her future.'"

"So you're just going to ignore their need?"

"No." My head pounded. "I didn't say that. Of course, if it's a question of the school remaining open, I'll send a check for that—one that does not include Bernadette's money."

"But not for that Adelaide MacNeill Memorial Gymnasium."

I felt the blood drain from my face. "No."

"That's because that Adelaide woman's not dead, is she?"

"Portia, please. This is none of your business."

"Family is my business. You and Bernadette are my family now."

I didn't answer.

"I racked my brain for years, trying to remember the name you gave that day outside the house, just before the explosion. I knew it wasn't Murray. It wasn't until I saw it in writing the other day that I remembered. MacNeill. 'Miss MacNeill' is what you said."

I won't answer her.

"You're the woman who went to that school. You're the woman who was a teacher there, who they meant to make headmistress, who they want to name that new gymnasium after. Adelaide MacNeill. That's some honor, but hard to do in memorial if you're not dead."

I kept my eyes closed, willing Portia to stop.

"Why did you let your friends believe you died all those years ago? Do you think they couldn't bear to see your scars? Is your pride too much for an ounce of humility?"

I set my teacup down with a clatter. "Stop. Just stop."

"Why? What kind of friend would I be if I just let you hide away, keep hiding behind those scars, knowing the truth? It's one thing that you don't tell Bernadette she was orphaned in that blast because you know the pain of growing up orphaned. It's another thing to let people who care about you, maybe even love you, believe you died. Do you know what it is to grieve the death of someone you love?"

With one hand I swept the teapot, the sugar bowl, the cream

pitcher, and the plate of scones to the floor where they crashed, spilling tea and cream and sugar across the rug. Then I stood, ready to flee in my fury.

Portia's eyes widened, but she rose and stood her ground, grabbing my arm. "Yes, you know. Then why did you do that to that woman— that friend who loved you enough to beg people for money to build a building in your memory, in your honor? I'm trying to understand, Rosaline. Don't shut me out. Don't pretend you don't hear me with your bad ear because I know you do, and I see good and well you're not dead, standing here before me. Why? Tell me why?"

That broke my dam, my refuge of pent-up anger and fear and aloneness. "Because she betrayed me! He betrayed me!"

"What are you talking about?"

I sat and buried my face in my hands. It was too much. I couldn't hold it in. "There was nothing and no one to go back to. How could I return, scarred and half blind and nearly deaf? I couldn't teach. He'd left, and even if—they'd look at me with pity or worse, revulsion, and I couldn't bear that. There was nothing I could do for any of them, and I had a child to raise, a child I'd promised Bertha I would raise if anything happened to her. Better they all believed me dead. Better they forget me." The words poured out, racked in sobs—all those years of pain withheld, shadowed, sharpened. I wept, desperately and long. Portia let me, until it was safe for her to take me in her arms.

"At last. At last. You let that go now. You get that out. I always wondered if there was some man you'd run from."

I wanted to pound those words away, erase that truth. Up and down my back Portia's hands went, pulling the pain from between my shoulder blades.

"You've been carrying that ugliness in your soul all these years. What's on the outside is nowhere near as ugly as you fear, Rosaline. You're a beautiful woman, inside and out. You've got nothing and no one to fear, nothing to be ashamed of."

In time I pulled away. "But I am ashamed. Now that they're on about this building. Why are they doing this? If my death was a relief, if it enabled them all to move on, to form lives together, why do they want to remember me now? I don't understand."

"I don't know what you mean by a relief, but clearly they didn't want to forget. Appears you meant more to them than you realized at the time. You won't know unless you ask them."

"I can't do that."

"You mean *won't*."

I ignored that. The telling had all gone too far. "I'm sorry about the tea, about the pot, everything."

"*Hmmf.* It's your pot." Portia knelt to pick up the pieces. I joined her, pulling bits of food from the carpet. "Suppose we'll be looking for something better to eat by and by than these soggy scones."

I half laughed, a tearful, plaintive, pitiful laugh. Portia smiled.

We cleaned the rest of the mess in silence. When it was done, we stood. I was spent, ready to go to my room.

"What are you going to do, my friend? You can't pretend that letter didn't come."

"I won't touch Bernadette's money. I'll send a donation for the school. Once I finish this book—if I finish this book—and am paid, I'll send more. I'll tell Bernadette that."

"That's not the *her* I meant. What will you tell that Susannah woman wanting to name that building after you?"

"Susannah. She was one. There were four of us who bonded as friends—Susannah, Ruth, Dorothy, me."

"Dorothy Meyer—the Mrs. Meyer who telephoned."

I couldn't answer. Portia was too quick, too perceptive. All these years later and the pain of her married name, of such a betrayal, still burned raw. "We fell out."

"A young folks' falling-out made you abandon ship?"

"It wasn't like that. She—"

"She what?"

"Please, Portia. No more." The weight of my shoulders felt too much. The weight of memory too great.

"All right, then. All right." Portia placed her hand over mine, touched the scarred side of my face so gently. "That's enough for now. You rest. Go on up to your bed and sleep the sleep of those confessed. James tells us, confess your faults one to another, and pray for one another, that ye may be healed. It's not the shame that needs telling, it's the burden needs letting go, and you've done that. Be glad."

"It isn't done."

"No matter. Tomorrow's a new day, a new beginning. Rest with the good done today. Lay yourself down in the peace of the Lord."

A new beginning. That's what I intended when I signed adoption papers for Bernadette, when I signed away my name and identity as Adelaide MacNeill. It was all I could see to do at the time, and I wanted to do it. Dorothy had called me Josephina and my writing a braggart's coat of many colors. If there was any truth in that analogy, I was then Josephina thrown into a cistern. My friends went on with their lives, believing me gone or dead, but I was on a journey to the unknowns of Egypt, and there was no peace in that.

—

WINTER 1918

Skin grafts, battled infections, glass eyes, temporary housing, makeshift lives—experiences Bernadette and Portia and I all shared or helped one another endure. We were fortunate, blessed to receive the medical care that we did, but it couldn't take away Portia's limp or give Bernadette or me back the sight in one of our eyes. It couldn't take away the shiny-smooth grafting of skin or the burned places that would not grow hair. It couldn't take away all the scarring or disfigurement. We were what we were.

We were not alone. Often I reminded myself that nearly 2,000 people had been killed in the explosion, and more than 2,500 injured, some far worse than ourselves. All of Richmond and many surrounding areas were blown to bits, leveled to the ground. Families, churches, schools, the orphanage, houses, and businesses of every kind were crushed or burned in the resulting toppling of coal stoves that set fire to large sections of the city . . . so many burned alive. Fire, wind, water, and the hailstorm of metal, brick, and wood were no respecter of persons.

Less than twenty-four hours after the explosion, a wild December snowstorm had covered the ash and soot and oil that had colored our skin. Clean and white, but deceptive in its destruction. Hundreds froze to death before they could be dug out of the debris. When I felt sorry for myself, for Bernadette or Portia, I reminded myself how lucky, how blessed we were.

We grieved, especially Portia for her lost baby and husband. Sometimes I heard her screaming in the night, until the nightmare passed. Mornings I'd find her in the kitchen, streaming silent tears that had nothing to do with the eggs she cracked or the vegetables she peeled. Hers was the greater burden, even worse than my loss of Stephen, and I wondered how she bore it. Part of me was afraid to ask, to open that grievous wound afresh.

We knew we did not grieve alone. All of Halifax cried in a state of perpetual mourning.

Yet in no time, amid the chaos of destruction, whirlwinds of activity arose. Nurses and doctors in the hospitals could not have worked harder or moved faster if their shoes had become roller skates. Medical personnel and aid came from Toronto, from across Canada, from Boston and countless places in the United States, even from faraway England.

Despite the outpouring of help and goodwill, many of us had lain in beds unattended for hours at a time. There were simply too many to see to, too many with horrendous burns and open wounds, missing or lacerated eyes, broken or severed limbs—all needing immediate attention. Because the explosion occurred before school started, and because of the fascination with the dance of ships in the harbor, countless Haligonians had stood at their windows to watch. Shattered window glass left too many people blind.

We were a city of walking wounded—once we could walk. People learned not to look twice at disfigurements or limping or glass eyes;

there were so many of us. I couldn't imagine living anywhere else, someplace where the populace ran and danced with clear skin and unclouded vision, with perfect hearing. I was thankful, then, in a perverse sort of way, that Stephen had deserted me, would not be searching for me, would never see me like this. In his memory, if he ever thought of me, I would still look like Adelaide MacNeill.

There was a part of me that longed to reach out to the Ladies of the Lake, to Ruth and Susannah and Dot, the family of close friends I'd known for so many years. But a rift had grown between Ruth and me over my continued correspondence with Stephen. More than a rift separated me from Dorothy. Susannah had sided with Ruth regarding patriotism and Germans and was caught up in the busy raising of her family. Despite all this, I wanted, needed the love and support of my sisters. But I did not want their pity. Better, I decided, to walk alone. At least I had Portia. She needed me, grieving as she was, and I needed her. We both needed Bernadette.

Days turned to weeks and weeks to months, months to years. We mourned together and grew together, moving from temporary housing to temporary housing, enduring surgeries, scarlet fever, and influenza, but escaping the smallpox epidemic. Finally, we moved into a large and finished house with garden space to tend and our dear red maple tree out back—a home Bernadette could grow up in.

Sometimes I wondered if Joseph of the Old Testament had claimed such friends during the years he was imprisoned. For even though we had food and housing and the financial security Lemuel's investments procured, with so much of the life we'd expected snatched away, I felt imprisoned in my body, with no hope of release. Thank God most truly for Bernadette and Portia.

In Joseph's story there was a joyful reuniting with his family and insights of good the Lord intended through his exile and suffering. I could not expect a reunion with my sisters of the lake, nor could I see that ultimate good for them could come through my life.

Chapter Thirty-One

JUNE 1935

"Mrs. Meyer?" Bernadette Murray stood on the threshold of Dorothy's office door, breathless, her hands nervously twisting what appeared to be an envelope. "May I see you?"

"Bernadette, please come in." Dorothy smiled, genuinely glad to see her although wondering what might prompt a visit. She'd been concerned about Bernadette's growing reclusiveness for weeks, but something seemed to animate the girl now.

Bernadette crossed the room in three great strides and triumphantly placed a folded sheet of paper on Dorothy's desk.

"What is this?"

"Open it and you'll see." Bernadette laughed, nearly giddy.

Dorothy picked up the paper and opened what appeared to be a short letter. A smaller paper fluttered to her desk. She picked that up, turned it over, and read the designation: *Lakeside Ladies Academy*. "Ten thousand dollars?" Dorothy could barely say the words.

"From Mother!" Bernadette laughed again, clapping her hands.

"She says it's not to be used for the gymnasium but for the operation of the school. I believe she'll send more if it's needed. Isn't it wonderful? Lakeside Ladies Academy can remain open."

Dorothy could not think, could not speak. She'd never seen a check for that amount of money.

"Is it enough? With tuitions and everything, is it enough to keep the school going?"

Bernadette's joyful enthusiasm cut Dorothy to the quick. There was something in her laughter in that moment, in the beauty of her smile, dimpled on one side, that so reminded Dorothy of Addie, enough to steal her breath. She shook her head, trying to clear the fog from her brain.

"It's not?" Bernadette's face fell, the scarring on her cheek suddenly red, more visible.

"I—I don't know what to say. That will be up to the board."

"Read the letter, Mrs. Meyer. Mother is firm that it's to be used to keep the school open, nothing else."

"How did she know we—?" But Dorothy stopped. Best not to look a gift horse in the mouth.

"I'm sorry, Mrs. Meyer—well, no, I'm not really. I was in the hallway the day Mr. Shockley was here. Boy, was he angry!"

Dorothy felt her face flame. To be dressed down in such a fashion by a member of the board was bad enough, but to think that one—or more—of her students had heard it . . .

"I wrote Mother, telling her how much I wanted to help the school remain open. She won't let me or can't—something about a trust I'm not old enough to access—but she was willing to help, and I think glad to do it. Read for yourself."

Fingers trembling, Dorothy lifted the page again.

My dearest Bernadette, my lovely, precious daughter,
Your heart shines through the pages of your letter. I'm so thankful that your years at Lakeside Ladies Academy have brought you joy and friendship. I see such growth in you and admire that you reach out to help others.

*I'm glad, too, for the friendships you've found there. That is
what I wanted for you, trusted you would discover. Friendship
is a most precious and delicate thing—a rare gift that must be
handled with integrity and care, nurtured throughout a lifetime
if it is to flourish. Believe me when I say that I know the value
and the loss of such a gift.*

*Yes, I will do everything I can financially to help Lakeside
Ladies Academy remain open. Enclosed you will find a check,
which you must personally hand to the school secretary. Do not
bother the headmistress. My only stipulation, which I have
noted on the front of the check, is that it be used for the property
and operational costs of the academy. This means, my dear, that
it is not to be used for the building of the gymnasium.*

*If more is needed to help the school remain afloat, I will see
what I can do.*

With all my love,
Mother

The letter was typed. Only the signature, *Mother*, was hand-written. *Is it the handwriting? The wording? The speaking of the value of friendship and its loss? The need for integrity?* Dorothy felt as if someone had shamed her or walked over her grave, or resurrected the dead, or some strange combination of it all. *Addie.*

She looked up at Bernadette. *Am I losing my mind?*

It took moments for Dorothy to regain her composure. "Bernadette, please remind me, what is your mother's given name?"

"Rosaline. She said it was because her mother loved roses. I never knew Grandmother; she and Grandfather passed in some kind of accident at sea before I was born. Mother won't talk about it. I think growing up an orphan was awfully difficult for her."

Dorothy's heart tripped. *Orphan. Accident at sea. Rose was Addie's middle name.* "Where is she from, your mother?"

Bernadette looked puzzled. "Halifax, I think. She's never mentioned living anyplace else."

"And has your family always lived in the same home there? Is it a family home?"

"As long as I can remember. Mother said our family home was destroyed in the Halifax Explosion, shortly after I was born." She shifted uncomfortably. Dorothy knew the girl did not like to be reminded of the cause of her burns. "Is there something wrong? I thought you'd be glad about Mother's gift."

"I am—oh, I am, Bernadette." Dorothy reached for her hand. "It's just that . . . I'm astonished. It's a monumental gift that I—that the board, I am sure—never imagined."

"Mother doesn't flaunt, but she's a well-known writer and lives rather simply. I think she can afford it." The pride in Bernadette's voice was unmistakable. "I know she said not to bother you with this, but I thought it might be a help to know the school won't have to close, to see it for yourself."

"Thank you." Dorothy could barely breathe.

"I asked Mother again, begged her really, to come to the graduation. She didn't answer this time. I don't think she's coming." Worry lines crossed Bernadette's forehead.

"No, perhaps not." Dorothy's heart beat faster. "She was quite firm with me."

Bernadette's lips formed a straight line. "I should give it to Miss Milton. Mother is likely to ask if I handed it to her directly, as instructed. She's a stickler for obedience." She reached for the check, but Dorothy held on to it. "It's okay, isn't it, that I give it to Miss Milton?"

"What? Oh, yes, yes, of course." Dorothy released the check.

Bernadette forced a smile, her good eye focused, the other staring into the space over Dorothy's shoulder. Never had Bernadette's glass eye bothered Dorothy before, but now it felt as if the girl could see something, someone beyond that Dorothy couldn't. As Bernadette turned to go, Dorothy shuddered at the notion.

Chapter Thirty-Two

I typed scenes with a fury I'd not known in years. To finish the book by my new deadline and to receive the balance of my advance, which I hoped to send to Lakeside Ladies Academy, I needed to increase my daily word count, estimated roughly by my number of typewritten pages.

Since mailing Bernadette the check, my stack of pages had grown, as if by sending aid to Lakeside, the school through which Bernadette and I had both grown and found purpose, a part of my brain that had been sealed off, hindering creative thought, was somehow freed.

Since my broken-teapot confession, as Portia called it, she'd obligingly left me alone for hours each day to work, until the day she strode purposefully into the library without knocking. "Been to market and happened by the bookshop, that one you're so fond of near the harbor. Guess what was standing there, big as life, in the front window?"

"No idea. What?" I was still thinking of my final chapters, wondering if I'd given my characters enough trouble to make their resolution matter.

Triumphantly, Portia drew a book from her bag.

I all but squealed. *"Mistress Pat!"*

Portia grinned from ear to ear. "That sequel you been waiting for. Thought that might bring a smile to your face."

"Thank you, Portia!" I had been waiting, for eons it felt, ever since I'd read Lucy Maud Montgomery's *Pat of Silver Bush*.

"I'll not be bothering you about tea. I know you'll bury your head in that book. About time you took a break from your typing anyway." Portia chuckled as she closed the door.

I didn't even finish the sentence I was typing but sank into my favorite chair by the window—my reading chair.

Reading *Mistress Pat* was like visiting a dear old friend, one who knew me and loved me and whom I knew and loved.

Closing my eyes, I could imagine, if only for the moment, that letters still flew back and forth between us . . . Well, they'd flown from me, but I'd had to wait, sometimes for weeks, for Lucy Maud Montgomery's letters. It was a wonder to me that she bothered to write at all, but she had, and those letters encouraged me, kept me writing, learning, striving toward each new goal in those early years. Surely in the fervor of my young imagination I'd made much more of the relationship than was due. I no longer possessed those letters. They, along with every other earthly possession, had been destroyed in the explosion, but I'd read them so often that most of her words still burned in my memory, still mentored and guided my writing.

Halfway through I set the book down. Portia was right. How was it that I'd allowed Mrs. Montgomery to believe I'd died—the author I'd followed since the first publication of her Anne books? The woman, fellow islander, who'd been so gracious and patient with a young orphan from PEI? She must have assumed my death in the explosion when her letters were returned, perhaps marked *Deceased* or *No Forwarding Address*. Being Canadian and living in Toronto, she would surely have heard the gruesome details of the explosion.

Did she grieve or say, "Oh, that's too bad," or was some part of her relieved to no longer be pestered? She must receive hundreds of letters each month. She couldn't possibly answer them all and still write books that nurtured the soul, reminding readers of the childhood and young adulthood we all wished we'd lived.

The last book I'd received from her before the explosion, the one she'd personally signed to me, was *Anne's House of Dreams*. Oh, how I'd loved that book, the story of Anne and Gilbert's marriage, of their new life together. It had seemed almost a premonition at the time of my life about to be joined with Stephen's. And yet that book had been blown to smithereens, just like my own house of dreams.

Through the years I'd wondered if Mrs. Montgomery had read any of my books, if perhaps she'd recognized my writing from stories I'd sent her early on. Once I dreamed that she'd noticed a similarity in styles and written to me, demanding to know why I'd plagiarized her dead friend's words. I'd woken in a sweat and cried, wishing more than anything that she had confronted me, that I'd been forced to tell the truth and give an account of myself, forced to say, *"Yes, I am Adelaide Rose MacNeill from PEI, truly an author now—the one you fostered and mentored, and not Rosaline Murray of Rosemont."* To know and be known was a freedom that could never be mine.

And yet what I'd confessed to Portia hadn't alienated her. She'd understood, perhaps even pitied me, forgiven me, still seemed to love me, was still my friend. Did I dare hope that would be true of Bernadette when the time came that I must tell her the truth of who I was, the truth of who she was and what we were to one another—aunt and niece, not mother and daughter?

And what of the Ladies of the Lake? Would they understand? Could Dot, being married to Stephen? Does Stephen even remember those long-ago days as I do? If he met me now, would he feel shame for not having come? Remorse? Nothing? Would my appearance cause a hardship in their relationship?

Those questions haunted me. Still, I recognized a change in the wind of my thinking. I'd not responded to Bernadette's final plea to attend her graduation. In my last letter to her I had not mentioned it at all, but for the first time I'd not said no.

Chapter Thirty-Three

Dorothy knew her handwriting appeared atrocious, but she trusted
Ruth to understand, if anyone could, why her hands trembled so in
the writing of her letter.

> *Dearest Ruth,*
>> *I hope you are well.*
>> *You're going to think me absolutely mad, but because you
>> are my sister of the heart, I am going to risk it, believing you'll
>> love me even so.*
>> *There is a student here, Bernadette Murray, from Halifax—
>> a brilliant young woman who was born days before the Halifax
>> Explosion in 1917. I've mentioned her in letters before. She's to
>> graduate valedictorian next month.*

*This afternoon she showed me a letter from her mother,
Mrs. Rosaline Murray, a noted Canadian author whose
name you may recognize, and a check, an extremely generous
donation slated for the operational costs of the school—one that
was stipulated should NOT go toward building the Adelaide
MacNeill Memorial Gymnasium.*

*None of this may seem unusual, until you learn that
Rosaline Murray was an orphan—both of her parents died in
a tragic accident at sea. Bernadette does not know the details
because her mother refuses to speak of it and said that her
mother suffered a difficult time growing up as an orphan.*

*Now, do you remember that Addie's parents were swept
overboard in a storm and drowned? Do you remember how
Addie grieved for them? How she hated being an orphan?*

*Bernadette said her mother was named Rosaline because her
grandmother loved roses. Addie's middle name was Rose. Even
the address, the name of the home Bernadette comes from, is
Rosemont. Bernadette never knew her father. Her mother told
her he was killed during the war.*

*I know this sounds outlandish, as if I'm seeing ghosts where
there could be none, but I tell you, Ruth, sometimes, when
Bernadette turns her head just so, she reminds me of Addie.
After the annual Twelfth Night performance even Jonas and
Stephen remarked on the similarity. You can imagine how that
affected me.*

*If there were only one of these "coincidences," I could put it
down to a figment of my imagination. But now, to receive this
sizable check, a check I will confide to you the academy is in
desperate need of, with the stipulation that it not be used for
the building of the gymnasium in Addie's memory . . . I simply
don't know.*

*Addie's body was never found after that horrific explosion.
The house where her brother and his family lived, where she*

was staying, was leveled to the ground. Not a soul survived or could have. But what if she wasn't in the house?

And who is Bernadette, really? I was with Addie, here at Lakeside, shortly before Thanksgiving that year. I know she was not in the family way . . . at least I don't believe she was. And yet Bernadette is so like Addie in a number of little expressions—verbal and physical—things I've put down to being Canadian, but that can't be all.

Addie had great hopes and expectation of Stephen's proposal. I never told you that. I believed you wouldn't approve, but Addie loved Stephen, Ruth, with all her heart. Much as it pains me to write it, for so many reasons I cannot explain, I know he loved her.

If only we could turn back the clock and make better, more honest choices, but we can't.

So, I'm going to ask, since you are there in Canada, though I know you're far west, will you go to Halifax? Will you ring the bell at the Murray household and see for yourself? There is no one else I dare ask. I've telephoned Mrs. Murray, and she all but hung up on me. This is not a request from the headmistress of Lakeside Ladies Academy, but a plea from your sister of the heart. All for one and one for all. Will you go in search of our lost Lady of the Lake?

My love always,
Dot

Hastily, before she could change her mind, Dorothy addressed the envelope, pressed the stamp into place, walked to the corner, and dropped her letter into the mailbox, sending it on its way.

Chapter Thirty-Four

JUNE 1935

I'd not walked through the Public Gardens in years, not since Bernadette had gone to school in Connecticut. When she was a child, I took her there on Sunday afternoons to run among the flowers in summer, to watch skaters on the frozen pond in the shimmering winter sunshine. Always, no matter the season, I was careful to avoid the gazebo, the place I'd waited in vain for Stephen.

Now, with the past opened to Portia and so much begging to be revealed to Bernadette, I knew I must confront my ghosts and chase my demons.

Saturday afternoon, the day I typed *The End* on my manuscript, I walked the many blocks to the gardens.

White clouds chased one another through an azure sky. Maples in their varied shades of green provided canopy to the walkways. The warm breath of a late-spring day tickled my neck and sent pleasant shivers up my arms. June roses unfurled petals in a first bloom—yellows and creams, scarlets and pinks, corals, purest white, and those whose petals were stained with tints of blush. Blue lobelia; geraniums in pinks, corals, and reds; and flowers in vibrant hues of blue and purple surrounded the gazebo in a lavish parade of color and scent.

This was where I'd dreamed of meeting Stephen, of hearing his proposal, albeit in the cold of December. I'd imagined that we'd return here, year by year, to renew our profession of love and life to one another, that we'd bear our own children together, grow old together. *A young girl's house of dreams. Fantasy.*

Those were images I'd imagined writing about but never did. Of all the tender scenes I'd written, I'd carefully avoided writing of trysting places set in gazebos or declarations of love in Victorian gardens.

If I dared return to Lakeside, to attend Bernadette's graduation, could I bring myself to look at the gazebo by the lake? The one that now meant so much to my daughter—*my niece*? Could I face the Ladies of the Lake—Ruth, Susannah, and most of all, Dot? Could I see Dot and Stephen side by side and still stand, still hold my head high? Could I wear my veil, so I could see them but they not see me? Could I possibly maintain my secret or would all my broken dreams inevitably be revealed?

Dear God, I prayed, *these are hard questions, and I don't know the answers. So much of what I did I chose out of fear—fear of losing Bernadette because I was a single woman determined to adopt her; fear of facing those who'd professed to love me and yet didn't stand by me, didn't prove true; fear of being pitied for my scars, and worse, fear of them looking away because they couldn't bear to see.*

I granted them no opportunity to prove me wrong, to be better than they'd appeared. And yet, now I'm the one ashamed. Ashamed of having hurt them, if indeed I did. From Susannah's letter about the building of the gymnasium in my memory, it appears that perhaps I misjudged them, underestimating their concern. Perhaps they grieved for me after all, missed me, wished I'd lived. Perhaps if my actions had been different, there could have been reconciliation, at least between the Ladies of the Lake. We'd vowed to be there for one another forever, all for one and one for all. And I'm the one who abandoned them. I'm the betrayer of—

"Madam?"

I jumped, startled from my prayer by a man I'd not seen approach as I wrung my hands on the metal bench, eyes closed.

"Are you all right? Can I do anything for you?" Middle-aged, he was handsome in his way, his eyes kind and his face posed in concern.

My first reaction was to rebuff him—to tell him no, that I was perfectly fine and needed no assistance. But then I realized that tears had streamed down my cheeks and I must look a sight. Still, I shook my head. "No, thank you. I'm all right." I pulled my handkerchief from my purse and held it to my cheek, automatically shielding the scarred side of my face. "Indulging in memories, so silly of me." I was taken off guard and hoped he'd go away.

He tipped his hat but stood there, gazing in the direction of the gazebo, as I had done. "I do that myself from time to time, especially here." He didn't move on. "Do you mind if I share your bench?"

"No, of course not." But I did.

"I come here often. It's one of the few places I know that doesn't remind me of the past but speaks to me of the beauty of the present, especially in springtime."

"You sound rather like a poet," I mused, working to compose myself.

"Simply a man grateful for life."

That struck a chord in my heart.

He sat in silence for a time. "I lost my family in the explosion. I was away on business when it happened. I come here for memory's sake. My children loved to play in these gardens in summer."

Are we all walking wounded? "I'm sorry, very sorry."

"Thank you. Halifax is the only place I know I can say that and someone, a complete stranger, will know what I'm talking about—the only place I don't have to apologize for bringing up the past, at least that past."

"Yes," I agreed. "We understand the loss. I understand the loss."

"Do you?" He turned toward me, curious, sympathetic. "I'm sorry if you do."

His sympathy nearly undid me. But he had suffered more than I, the loss of his wife and children. Yet who's to say how much suffering is more than another's?

After a time, he rose, never offering his name, and walked on, shoulders rounded, subdued. *A kindred spirit.*

Dot said Bernadette had overcome so much in her years at Lakeside. It certainly was a healing place for me as a girl. Could it be that again? What of my friends? Dot, Ruth, Susannah, Jonas, even Stephen? What about their suffering?

Can I possibly—no. What was I thinking? Declaring myself alive can only result in my everlasting shame—the one demon I cannot chase away.

Chapter Thirty-Five

Dorothy straightened her hat and smoothed her jacket and skirt before opening the door to the office of Meyer Brothers, Attorneys-at-Law. She'd never confided the full extent of the school's financial woes to either her husband or his brother, but she needed their legal advice now.

They knew of her push for the Adelaide MacNeill Memorial Gymnasium, a goal they knew she championed but neither spoke of, at least not to her. She wondered if they both still mourned Addie, if perhaps both brothers were still a bit in love with the memory of her. She believed they had been at one time. It was something she'd never directly asked for fear of hearing their answer.

Regarding the rest, she'd been sworn to secrecy by the board. She'd been certain she could turn the tide, find a way to keep the school afloat, at least until her meeting with Mr. Shockley.

"Dorothy! What a pleasant surprise." Stephen rose from his desk, kissed her on the cheek, and offered her a chair.

"We've just brewed some coffee, m'lady. Have some?" Jonas winked.

"I'd love some." Dorothy forced a smile, doing her best to keep nerves at bay.

"What brings you here, my darling?"

Dorothy looked from her husband to her brother-in-law. The brothers had grown so alike as the years had passed, except to see them as the public did. Jonas bore a limp from the shrapnel he'd taken in his leg during the war. Stephen was missing an arm, and disfigurements from mustard gas spread across his neck, above his collar. They both carried carefully guarded internal scars that few but Dorothy ever knew.

The brothers shared a large one-room office, never having hired a secretary, so visiting one at work meant visiting both. She didn't mind. They were as close to one another as the Ladies of the Lake were to each other. She trusted them implicitly.

"Everything I've got to say must be kept in strictest confidence." She was firm about that.

"Of course." Levity left the room as Jonas handed her a cup of coffee, sweetened and with cream, just as he knew she liked it.

"What's happened?" Stephen led her to the consulting table in the middle of the room.

Dorothy sat, glad to take a sip of the sweet, warm coffee. "I haven't told you before this, and no one outside the board of governors is supposed to know, but the academy is in extreme financial straits. We may have to close the school after graduation."

"What? Why?"

"I thought your enrollment was three-quarters full. Even with the Depression, that should carry the school throughout an academic year."

"That's just it: I thought so, too. But there was a loan for thirty thousand dollars taken out to build the new gymnasium—taken out ten years ago, long before things looked so grim. And now the bank is calling the note due. They've given us until after graduation before they take over the school."

"The gymnasium's not been finished—not nearly—and you said there's a major fundraising effort in progress. What's happened to those funds—the loan money?"

"They're gone—gone, Mr. Shockley says, for the operating expenses of the school and its grounds. Susannah Whitmore and I are behind the fundraising. Mr. Blankenship gave me two weeks to see what I can do, and fundraising is what we did, but Mr. Shockley is furious that I've gone to the alumnae. He says it won't be nearly enough, no matter how much is raised, as if the school's operating expenses exceed the cost of repayment of the loan."

"That makes no sense."

"He seems determined that the school fail, and he's thwarting my efforts, threatening to have the board side against me. He refuses to disclose the exact amount the school needs to raise."

"I don't understand that," Stephen said. "Clearly you, as headmistress of the academy, should be told."

"Yes. I'm responsible for the well-being of all those young women, the teachers, the staff. I have every right to know."

"Have you seen any of the financial records?"

"Only what is made available to alumnae and what little the board shared with me, nothing more."

Jonas sat back in his chair. "Why the secrecy? Why the subterfuge?"

"Sounds like he's hiding something." Stephen and his brother locked eyes.

"We need to tread carefully. I don't know if it's only Mr. Shockley, my imagination, or if there's something monumental the board is not telling me. I don't want to cause a scandal for the school, but—"

"You want us to look into it."

Dorothy nodded.

"Mr. Shockley is responsible for all the accounting, all the school's accounts?"

"Yes, as far as I know. He's the treasurer. Miss Milton, my secretary, is also puzzled. She said—confidentially, of course—that based on what she sees of the pay envelopes for staff and the operational costs she turns over to Mr. Shockley, she can't imagine what other huge costs there could be."

"Sounds like an independent audit is in order."

Stephen agreed. "One that investors in the school will be interested to see, though I don't know if the board would allow that kind of transparency."

"I'm not sure I can convince Mr. Blankenship or the board of an independent audit. I don't think I can get his ear without Mr. Shockley shutting me down. I don't want to destroy anyone's reputation or cast aspersions, but I believe . . . I mean, I can't help but wonder if—"

"If there's some sort of inappropriate diversion of funds? Embezzlement?"

"Possibly."

The brothers exchanged worried glances.

"If that's so, you've got to be careful. With that much money at stake . . . You're in a delicate position, my dear. But I believe we know someone who isn't, someone whose influence with the board will go far."

"I'm reading your mind, Brother. Dorothy, leave it to us. Be discreet. Be careful."

Chapter Thirty-Six

JUNE 1935

The sun rose hot for a June morning. I pushed my wide-brimmed garden hat to the back of my head, letting the ribbons trail down my back.

With my manuscript completed and posted, I now spent mornings in the garden, weeding beds, deadheading flowers, inhaling the fragrance of everything I loved. I'd received a telegram from my publisher by the third week in June that the manuscript was in hand, by the fourth week that they loved it, that it needed only minor editing, and that my check would be forthcoming.

But dig as I dared, weed and deadhead as I might, I could not still the voices in my head, particularly Bernadette's plea for me to attend her graduation next month. It nagged at me night and day. The idea of being loved and wanted and yet of so cruelly disappointing my daughter frustrated my heart. Even so, I could not bring myself to go, to risk revealing my wounds of body and soul. If only Dot wasn't there, if Stephen wasn't there—but they were, and they weren't likely to disappear in the days left before graduation.

I pulled off my gloves and threw them to the bench beside me. Water, I needed water. Just as I opened the back kitchen door, I heard the front doorbell ring. I couldn't answer with my face sweating and hands filthy, my hair sticking out all over my head, so I ignored it, trusting Portia would answer, and filled a tumbler with cold tap water.

I stepped to the kitchen door, just to listen.

"Yes, ma'am," Portia said, "this is Rosemont."

I couldn't hear what the other person said.

"If you'd like to step inside and wait in the parlor, I'll see if Mrs. Murray's here, if she's available."

I groaned within. I didn't care who it was; I was in no condition to greet callers. Surely Portia knew that.

"Come right in, Miss Hennessey. You've traveled such a long way. Can I get you a cup of tea while you wait?"

Miss Hennessey. Ruth? I nearly dropped my tumbler, barely managing to set it on the counter beside me.

"Thank you, that would be lovely," Ruth replied, her kind but confident, no-nonsense voice as clear and memorable as it had been twenty years ago, as the front door closed behind her.

My heart had not raced so fast in years. Was it from the possibility of a friendship renewed? Fear of discovery? Ruth's straightforwardness that I'd never been able to dodge? I didn't wait to analyze. Portia's steps clipped down the hallway as I ran for the open back door.

I heard the swoosh of the hall door opening into the kitchen as I fled onto the back porch and down the steps, around the corner of the house. I stepped behind the rose arbor. Portia couldn't see me unless she rounded the house in a deliberate search.

"Rosaline? Rosaline, are you out here?" I heard Portia call softly through the back garden. "There's someone here to see you. You here?" And then she hissed, "I know you're out here, somewhere. It's a Miss Hennessey, come a long way from out west. Came to see you specially."

Why? Why would Ruth come here? She can't possibly know . . .

"Rosaline?" Portia called again.

I held my breath, closed my eyes, and pushed into the shadows against the wall, needing to make myself invisible.

At length I heard the back door close. I breathed, my eyes still closed.

The windows of the front rooms stood wide open. I could hear Portia talking.

"I'm sorry, Miss Hennessey, Mrs. Murray must have stepped out. You're welcome to wait, but I've no idea how long she'll be or where she's gone. I'll get your tea directly. There, I hear the kettle whistling now."

"Please don't bother. I did not have an appointment. I just stopped on the off chance I might catch her—see her."

I could not hear everything she said but held my breath until I heard the front door open. I remained hidden in the shadows, tight against the house, but crept toward the front porch, behind the tree at its corner. I wanted to see Ruth, to see if she was the Ruth of our youth or someone new, someone older and different. Of course, she would be.

She'd just stepped down the porch step when she turned again toward the front door. My breath caught. It was Ruth, my Ruth, not so very different than in our school days. Older, a little gray around her temples, but her back was still straight and her angular face was very much the same—lined, perhaps. Her voice resonated a little deeper.

"Let me ask you something, Mrs. Cadeau, if I may."

"Yes, ma'am?"

"Has Mrs. Murray ever mentioned a woman named Adelaide MacNeill? Or Addie?"

Portia was silent for a moment too long.

"Mrs. Cadeau?"

"I—I can't answer that, Miss Hennessey. That's a question you'll need to ask her."

"I see." I feared Ruth did see. "Perhaps I'll stop in again if I may."

"Best that you call first—ma'am."

"I'll tell you what. Please give Mrs. Murray my card and ask her to telephone me." Seconds passed, perhaps a minute. "There, I've written my hotel name and number on the back. Please. I'd like very much to speak with her. I think we may have gone to school together. If I am right, we were in a group of the very best of friends—Rosaline, and Dorothy, Susannah, and me."

Be still, my heart. It felt as if it might jump out of its cage. I wanted to fly into Ruth's arms and yet I pushed myself tight, back behind the hydrangeas, where I could barely see her.

"I'll give her your card, ma'am." Portia sounded uncertain.

Thank You, God. Portia did not commit me.

"If I don't hear from her, I'll stop by again when I can. I'll be working in the city for another week."

"Like I said, best you call first."

"Yes, I understand. I'll see what I can do. My schedule is uncertain. Thank you, Mrs. Cadeau." Without looking back, Ruth walked away, her very sensible shoes making good time.

A full minute passed before I heard Portia's voice above me, speaking through the open window. "You can come out now. She's gone."

Chapter Thirty-Seven

The telephone on Dorothy's desk rang at her elbow.

"Lakeside Ladies Academy. Mrs. Meyer speaking."

"Dot, it's me, Ruth. I've only a moment and this is costing a bundle, so listen carefully. I went to the address you gave me, Rosemont, the home of Rosaline Murray, but she wasn't at home. At least her maid said she must have stepped out. I couldn't wait as I had a meeting with the hospital's staff. I'll try to stop in again before leaving Halifax."

Dorothy nearly interrupted, but Ruth rushed on.

"I must say that I felt there was something odd in the manner of Mrs. Murray's maid, Mrs. Cadeau, as though she held something back, but at the same time as though she genuinely wanted me to meet her employer. I hope you're right about Addie being alive, Dot, but I'm afraid this is a goose chase, and your hopes will be dashed."

"Ruth, I have to know. I—"

"Do you ever wonder, my friend, regardless of the truth, if it's best to let sleeping dogs lie? Just a question to ponder. Look, I've got to run. If I learn anything else, I'll let you know. Hold fast! Bye now!"

The line went dead.

Dorothy sighed, replacing the receiver in its cradle. *The trouble is, those dogs won't sleep for me and they won't lie. They're prowling around in my dreams, night and day. I need resolution, badly. I need forgiveness.*

The telephone on her desk rang again, making Dorothy jump. She lifted the receiver.

"Lakeside Ladies Academy. Mrs. Meyer speaking."

"Hello, Dorothy."

"Jonas?"

"We've got some news, albeit not necessarily good news. Can you stop in the office on your way home? We've something you'll want to see."

"I'll be there in twenty minutes."

"See you then." The phone clicked.

Jonas was never so matter-of-fact and all-about-business. She could hardly imagine what he and Stephen had discovered, and in less than two weeks.

Chapter Thirty-Eight

Once Ruth had gone, I went back to my garden beds along the far fence, though my hands were shaking, my pulse racing, and my mouth dry as cardboard. I worked until the sweat poured down my face, but still my heart pounded.

Some time later Portia carried a tray with two tumblers and a pitcher of cold water to the garden table.

"Water! How did you guess?" I tried to make light.

"Little bit of bread from the oven and butter, too, in case you're hungry." She frowned.

"Wonderful!" I knew that was too bright.

"Bread and water." Her frown went deeper still. "Likely better than you deserve, treating an old-time friend like that."

Portia had become my champion, my protector, my friend over the many years we'd lived and worked to build a home together. She was, as much as the Ladies of the Lake had ever been, my sister of the heart, and I loved her for that. However, I did not appreciate it when she took on the role of a disapproving schoolmarm. I wanted to deny knowing what she was talking about, who she meant, but it was no use. Lies were what had landed me in this position.

"She seemed like a nice woman, Rosaline, a friend reaching out to you. There's no reason for you to be ashamed, to hide from her."

"It isn't about Ruth." I poured water for myself and drank haltingly, letting the cold liquid wind its way down my constricted throat.

"Then what?" Portia stood with hands on hips.

I didn't have to answer her, so I turned away. "You wouldn't understand."

"Stop that. Stop that nonsense. Tell me what I wouldn't understand. I understood everything you've told me so far, and I still love you, still care about you like my own blood even when I think differently than you. Can't you grant me that?"

I stopped. A sigh so deep, from my toes right up through my torso and heart to my mouth, came out in a near groan.

"Time you let it out, Rosaline, or Addie or whatever your name is. Whatever this is, you've got to let it go because it's eating you alive, destroying the good between you and Bernadette. You turn your girl away on what's so important to her and you will rue this day."

Portia spoke the truth. The truth is hard to hear, to face. If I spoke the words, I could never take them back. Would saying them out loud kill me? Somehow, I'd thought they would. *Shame. Remorse. Self-pity. Anger. Hatred. Jealousy. Love unrequited. Does any of that matter if I lose Bernadette's love, her respect?*

"Whatever those people did to you, or didn't do, won't matter in years to come. You've lived without them since the day that munitions ship exploded in the harbor. But the love you've given and the love you've received is bound up in your daughter—and she is your daughter, no matter that another woman birthed her. You're the only mother she's ever known. What can possibly be more important than that?"

I turned to face Portia and felt as if I were standing before a jury. "Sometimes I think you can read my mind."

She smiled, and I saw the love and worry in her eyes. "Sometimes I can. Come and sit here. Tell me. Confess what you need to. You know it won't change anything in this world with me."

I did know that. Portia was rock solid in her love, in her faith, in her character. All these years I'd thought of the Ladies of the Lake as my sisters of the heart and believed that in one way or another they'd betrayed and left me, even before I betrayed them. I hadn't granted to any of them the assurance and acceptance of faults and failures that existed between Portia and me. Why not?

I sat in the chair at the garden table, let Portia refill my glass and place a slice of bread, spread with her own homemade butter, creamy as silk, before me on a rosebud china plate. *Grace. Portia offered me grace at every turn, even when I didn't deserve it.*

I sat, fingering the scallop along the plate's edge. Portia didn't rush me, and for that I was grateful. At last, I began in the language I knew best. "Once upon a time, not so many years ago, there was a girl, a girl a lot like Anne."

Portia smiled. We'd both loved reading *Anne of Green Gables* and the books that followed. I'd read them aloud to Portia and Bernadette through long evenings until Bernadette was old enough and began reading them to us.

"The girl was an orphan, from PEI, just like Anne. She wanted to become a writer, just like Anne. But this girl was sent away to school, to Bernadette's school. Just like Anne and Diana, this girl made friends, dear friends—kindred spirits." My tongue thickened. My throat tightened. "There were four of them together. They called themselves the Ladies of the Lake, after the lake by which they met to share their deepest secrets, the very fabric of their lives. Like the Lady of Shalott, they looked out upon the world, but the worries of the world could not touch them because they had one another. Until two of the girls—this girl, and her closest friend— loved the same boy."

"One day, the boy, who'd become a man, a very handsome man, asked the girl the most important question—or said he would. He said he would come to her brother's home in Halifax to ask permission, then meet her at the gazebo in the Public Gardens and ask her the same question. Their courtship caused a great rift in the friendship of the girls, so much so that the girl believed in order to have the love of the boy, she must lose her friends, especially her best friend.

"The day of the proposal came, and the girl waited in the shivering cold. She waited and waited, until the daylight waned, until she could wait no more. He'd promised, but he never came. He never called or wrote or explained."

I didn't know if I could go on. Portia reached for my hand. "All she knew was that the boy went to war, without telling her. But she learned he'd told her best friend, that she'd gone to see him off. She wondered if she'd lost both of them forever. She wrote to her friend, begging forgiveness. And then the explosion came."

"And you never heard." Portia squeezed my fingers, but I continued, determined, having gone this far, to get the rest out.

"After the explosion, a long while after, the girl telephoned the school and learned that her best friend had married the boy, and that she was the new headmistress."

"Everything the girl wanted." Portia did not let go of my hand, but I heard the heartbreak in her voice.

"Everything she'd ever dreamed . . . except her writing. She had that."

"And Bernadette."

"And Bernadette. And you." I looked up and found the love and forgiveness I'd so longed to find in Dot's eyes all those years ago.

Portia took me in her arms and rocked me back and forth, like a little child. "You dear girl. You poor, dear girl."

I sobbed then, sobbed until I'd soaked Portia's shoulder once again. Finally, pulling away, I shook my head. "This has got to stop. You're going to be a sopping mess."

262

Portia smiled. "No better cause. You got that out. Is it the last? Is it why you changed your name and disappeared forever from those that knew you?"

"At first it was just the hurt that Stephen had never come. The boy . . . his name was—is—Stephen. He'd left for the war without ever even telling me, with no explanation of why he'd not come, not even to tell me he'd changed his mind. I couldn't bear the idea that he would ever see me like this—burned and scarred and . . . and broken. When I learned he and Dorothy had married, well, I couldn't face them, couldn't bear to. And then I had Bernadette to raise."

"You poured all your love into that child."

I nodded.

"But what about those other two Ladies of the Lake? What about this Ruth? She seems to be a good woman, the kind who could be your friend now—again."

"If I let her, is that what you mean?"

Portia waited.

"Ruth's brother was killed when Germans sank the *Lusitania*—her only brother. She hated Germans. She never wanted me to marry Stephen and thought I should break things off with him because his family was German. The war, you see."

"Hmm." Portia took that in. "Seems to me that doesn't matter to her as much as friendship now. She mentioned you and your friends, and you say that Dorothy woman married your German Stephen. It seems she's friends with them."

I looked at her, wondering if that could be true.

"And that other one that sent the fundraising letter . . ."

"Susannah."

"Looks like they're all still friends—friends wanting to honor you but thinking you're dead and gone. All these years later, and they still remember you, still love you."

I let out a shaky breath. "But Stephen and Dot—I couldn't face them, not together. And look at me. No."

"A lot of years have passed. The war's come and gone. Who knows

what's happened to them. Would you think any less of either of them
if age and life haven't treated them kindly?"

"No, but—"

"It's that they're together, and you still love him. Is that right?"
She spoke kindly, still holding my hand.

I nodded. Truth, at last.

"Well, if you love him, and he came back from that war believing
you were dead, would you want him to live alone all his life, even if
he loved you? To wither away in aloneness and grief? Is that love?"

"No—no, of course not, but they married so soon after that I can't
believe either of them truly loved me, grieved me."

"How do you know they weren't comforting one another in their
grief over losing you? How do you know anything about them since
you cut them out of your life?"

"I can't, and neither can you."

"No, but then again, what if they failed you in the worst way?
What if they betrayed you, just as you think, as you accuse?"

"They cut my heart out!"

"Yes, they did—maybe something like you cutting the heart out
of your only child by refusing to share the thing that matters most
to her. Now, tell me, what if Jesus did that? Cut us out because we
fail Him ninety-nine times out of a hundred? Where would we be?"

I had no answer.

"Think on that, Rosaline. Think on the grace you've received
in this life, not just what was taken away." She squeezed my hand
between both of hers, then stood and walked back into the house.

I sat long, remembering the past and reliving the sound of Ruth's
voice at my front door, thinking of how she'd come searching for
me. The only way she could have learned my address was through
Susannah or Dot and their access to addresses at the school. If one
of them suspected who I was, they all must . . . and she came to find
me. *All for one and one for all. Am I ready for this?*

*And now, Bernadette's graduation is at hand. If I do nothing, Ruth's
suspicions will not go away, yet the die will be cast in my relationship*

with Bernadette as surely as it was with my friends when I changed my name. I've lived without those friends for seventeen years, just as Portia said. Can I risk hurting Bernadette in this way? If I fail her in this, I can never bleach the stain on our relationship.

There was but one place I could think to go to find the answers.

Chapter Thirty-Nine

Dorothy sat in what her husband termed "the seat of honor" as the brothers triumphantly spread paperwork before her—columns of figures in balance sheets, years' worth of them, bound in black leather ledgers, each book with its binding labeled *Lakeside Ladies Academy*.

"I don't understand. How did you get these? You didn't break in and—"

Wide grins spread across both men's faces.

"Stephen said you'd say that!" Jonas slapped his thigh.

"You owe me for that bet!" Stephen returned.

"All right, you two." Dorothy could not help but smile while pretending frustration. "Explain. Please."

Stephen sobered. "Everything you told us sounded off base."

"Thank you very much." Dorothy kept her mouth grim.

"I mean it didn't add up. The academy, even in these times, should

266

be covering their operating expenses through tuition payments. At the very worst, they should be skating just below the line."

"But they should never be in the red for a thirty-thousand-dollar loan made in 1925 for the building of the gymnasium. Even if poor management led them to dip into the coffers for a couple thousand for a short-term loan, they should have been making regular payments to the bank all this time, especially given that only the foundation was laid for the gymnasium."

"All right, I agree, but I don't understand how you—"

"Before the Depression, Judge Cromwell sent three of his daughters through Lakeside Ladies Academy. Let's say he has a vested interest in the reputation of the school."

"You bribed a judge?" Dorothy knew her mouth dropped open.

"No, of course not. We invited him to lunch, told him of the school's predicament as well as some of our concerns, and that Mr. Shockley has not been forthcoming in the details of missing funds. We simply asked if he might have the influence to look into the matter."

"You didn't! The board will have my head on a platter when they learn that I told—"

"We've approached the board with our findings. They'll decide what comes next. I don't think it's your head going on that platter, my love."

"No?" Dorothy wasn't so sure. "What happened to the money?"

"Euclid Brick and Mortar, does that name ring familiar?"

"No."

"I suppose not. You'd have no reason to have seen those invoices," Jonas agreed.

"Euclid Brick and Mortar is the name of the company through which Mr. Shockley purchased building materials for the building of the gymnasium."

"Okay."

"The thing is, Euclid Brick and Mortar bought those materials from . . . local companies for one quarter of the price at which they sold them to Lakeside Ladies Academy. Euclid Brick and Mortar made a fortune while Lakeside's loan ran out before the building could be so much as framed."

"That's highway robbery!"

"Yes."

"Then, can this—this Euclid Brick and Mortar be held accountable? What they did is unconscionable . . . It's illegal—isn't it?"

The brothers raised their eyebrows.

"Well?"

"There's more. Euclid Brick and Mortar is a company that exists only on letterhead."

"What?"

"They're not a company at all, simply a name with a post office box in Hartford, where Mr. Shockley sent payments—payments he pocketed."

"Mr. Shockley? Embezzlement?"

"Theft. He made a fortune."

"Then the money can be returned, surely. The school can go forward . . . can't it?"

"Unfortunately—" Stephen rounded his desk to sit beside Dorothy—"our greedy Mr. Shockley invested heavily in the stock market before it crashed in '29. He lost everything. He and his wife have been pilfering from tuitions ever since, just to stay in their house."

Dorothy felt as if the world had shifted beneath her feet, as if she'd lost a day or a year and was about to lose a lifetime. "Then it's all gone. The school is really and truly destitute."

"And in a pile of debt. That's why the bank plans to take the school. I'm sorry, darling."

Chapter Forty

The Halifax Public Gardens' roses bloomed in vibrant profusion. Their heady fragrance spoke to my fragile heart, my broken heart. Having confessed all to Portia left me bereft but cleansed in a way I'd not felt in years, in a way I could not remember feeling.

Every step I took, bringing me nearer the gazebo, became a prayer. In front, across the grass, there was a bench that gave me the full view of the place Stephen was to meet me. That bench had heard many of my prayers over the years. I bowed my head and clasped my hands for one more.

Dear God, I can no longer do this alone, not even by sheer force of will. Portia's right. I don't hate Stephen, or Dot. I love them both, have loved them so long. If they've found love in each other's arms, well . . . that hurts . . . but I wouldn't want either of them to have lived all these years sad or alone. They're the two people I loved most in this world so long ago.

Help me love them together; help me love them being together. Forgive me for my anger, my self-pity. Lord, please, show me a way forward. Give me the courage to go to Lakeside, for Bernadette's sake, for—

"Addie? Is it you?"

My head jerked up. "Ruth?"

A smile, like the east to west of the sun across the sky, broke out across my old friend's lined face. She opened her arms, and before I could gather my wits or stand, she swept down upon me in a great bear hug. "I can't believe it! I told Dot it couldn't be true, was too good to be true."

I searched her face, her eyes, but there was no recrimination there, no judgment or anger, simply astonished gladness and perhaps love.

"Ruth." It was all I could say.

"Yes, it's me. We've missed you, Addie. You've been here, in Halifax, all along?"

I swallowed, trying to find words. "How—how did you find me?"

"Dot thought she was losing her mind with how much one of her students reminded her of you. I don't know all the reasons, but she became convinced that you must be her mother, that you were alive. She asked me to come and see."

"How did you know I'd be here, in the gardens?"

Ruth's color rose. "I received a telephone message, at my hotel. The message didn't say who it was from, just, *The woman you seek may be at the Public Gardens. Go quickly.*"

"Portia."

"Is that Mrs. Cadeau?"

"Yes."

"Then I believe so. No one else here knew I was looking for you." Ruth scooted close on the bench and took my hand. "You've no idea how much we've missed you, how much I've missed you all these years. The Ladies of the Lake are nothing without all four of us."

I looked away. Ruth had approached me and was sitting even then on my good side. From her vantage point she could not see my scars. As glad as I was to see her, to have her beside me, I wanted to hide. I wanted to hide and yet I wanted to be seen and known. So jumbled were my thoughts and emotions that I couldn't form a coherent thought, couldn't speak. I just said her name again—a blessing in my mouth. "Ruth."

Ruth's eyes softened. "Why, Addie? Why did you let us believe you were gone? Why did you change your name?"

I pulled my hand away. There was nowhere to hide. *Dear God, please help me. Help me do this and help me live with whatever change I see in her eyes.* I pulled from my hair the thin scarf that partially covered my face and neck, turning to Ruth head-on so she could see. I dared to look her full in the face, to let her see my eye that would not, could not follow her movements.

Ruth's eyes widened just a bit but softened more. Her brow wrinkled slightly in concern as she raised her hand to my face, to the scarred side, and gently held it with her palm.

I closed my eyes against the tear that insisted on falling at the kindness of my friend, the friend I'd believed estranged for nearly two decades.

"You left us because of this? Oh, Addie, dear Addie." Ruth pulled me into her embrace. "I'm so sorry for the explosion, so sorry for all you must have lost. But don't you know that you're still beautiful? You're still our Addie."

Tears know no quota; mine couldn't seem to stop. "I couldn't face you, Ruth, not after—" *Not after you were angry with me for loving Stephen, not after my scars made me hideous to the world, not after changing my name and identity in a moment, not after lying about being Bernadette's mother.* But I couldn't say all that. It was too much, too soon. I'd become so good at hiding my thoughts and emotions, so good at hiding the truth that to pour it out without time to think through the ramifications was too dangerous, too much a thing that once done could never be taken back.

"It must have been awful for you. We heard that the house—your brother's house—was destroyed, so we assumed that you and everyone there were killed."

I pulled away, reaching for my handkerchief. She wanted facts. Facts I could give. "Everyone was, everyone inside at the time."

"Your brother?"

I shook my head. "He wasn't there. He'd gone to the church to—it doesn't matter. He was killed, just the same. And Marcus, my nephew. Bertha, my sister-in-law. The cook, the maid—everyone else."

"I'm so very sorry, Addie."

"It was a long time before I could walk or see or hear well. One good eye, one good ear, one cheek unscarred. I'm one of the lucky ones . . . so they say." I tried to smile. This was the time to be brave. I'd lived with my deformities so long I should be used to them. In the everyday in Halifax where so many bore scars from the explosion, they didn't matter so much, but seeing Ruth, strong, clear-skinned, unscathed from all I could tell . . . It was hard.

"You're still beautiful, still so much the same. You know that, don't you?"

A laugh, derisive, escaped me. "You don't have to lie."

She took my hands in hers and swiveled round to face me until my good eye could not look away. "I'm not lying. If no one's told you that for a long time, they should have. You must see it when you look in the mirror."

Looking in the mirror is something I do as little as possible.

"I'm so sorry about your husband. Dot told me he was killed in the war."

"How did Dot know? Oh. Bernadette." *This is getting in too deep, too soon. My story could unravel before I tell Bernadette the truth. That can't happen. She deserves to know first. But must I lie to Ruth now, after she's sought me out?*

"Yes, she said that Bernadette told her. He must have died when Bernadette was a baby or before she was even born." Ruth waited, obviously curious, her eyes penetrating.

"In the war." It was all I would say.

She nodded, watching me closely, still holding my hand. A minute, perhaps more, may have passed as the ghosts of years gone by marched past. "You've never remarried." She waited but I didn't answer. Let her draw her own conclusions. *Dear Father in heaven, who would marry me now?*

At length she sat back against the bench, keeping hold of my hand. "I understand that better than you know . . . how you'd never want to marry after the war, the explosion, everything."

Not for the first time I wondered if Ruth ever married, and worried how it had been for her, on the trenched and bloody battlefields of France during the Great War. "Serving so near the front must have been horrific."

"It was." She sighed. "I'm not making light of your scars, Addie, truly, just saying we're all scarred in one way or another."

"How did you manage—day after day? How do you cope with the memories?"

"Not always well. I broke down a couple of years after the war, ended up in hospital myself. I've learned—had to learn—that when things get too dark, I must step back, get away, seek peace and beauty. Music helps. It's always helped me, but it isn't enough."

"No, it isn't. I garden and write and listen to music on the Victrola, but those things are never enough."

"Nothing is, at least nothing in this world. You'll hardly believe it, but I've started going to church again. For years after the war, I wouldn't go. I figured if God could let such a war go on, a war that wreaked such destruction in people's lives, then I didn't want to have anything to do with Him."

"He's not the one that makes us hate one another. He doesn't make our wars. We're very good at that . . . all by ourselves."

"I know that now, but I didn't then. I wanted someone to blame, and blaming the Germans for all the evils in the world wasn't working. There was evil before them, beyond them."

"So you no longer ostracize the Meyers? You're still in touch with Dorothy, and you must know she married—" I couldn't finish.

Ruth pulled her hand away and clasped her own, as if seeking composure or strength. "I've long been sorry for how hurtful I was to you over Stephen. I'm sorry, Addie. I was angry and grieving the death of Rodney. I took it out on everyone, even those least responsible. You're the last person I should have ever hurt—you and Dot. I've asked Dot's forgiveness and I thought the opportunity long gone to ask yours. But I'm asking now. Will you forgive me?"

Forgive you? Forgive you for ripping our friendship in two? For making me feel I must choose between loving Stephen and my sisterhood of friends? I drew a deep breath. There was much I could say about that, but in that moment, with Ruth sitting beside me, caring about me and all I'd gone through, sharing her hurts and journey toward healing, I didn't want to. I loved her still, my sister of the heart. *And how can I hope to be forgiven if I don't forgive? Each day I pray the Lord's Prayer—"Forgive us our debts, as we forgive our debtors." Dear God, forgiveness depends on both of us; I know this. We're in this hole together and together we can climb out. That's where freedom is born, isn't it?*

I reached for Ruth's hand. "I forgive you, my friend." It felt so good to say that, the words foreign and delicate in my mouth. "I forgive you." Then, bravely, I asked, "Will you forgive me?"

Ruth looked at me, squeezing my hand. "How can I not? I love you, Addie. Of course, I forgive you. Just so long as you don't go hiding from us again."

Of course, there must now be conditions to move forward. Now that Ruth knows, Dot and Susannah will soon know. And Stephen.

"Dot told me that your daughter is begging you to come to her graduation."

"Yes, but I—"

"Now that there are no more secrets, you'll go, won't you? Dot says it will mean the world to your Bernadette."

"How can I—?"

"You were always the bravest among us, the one who'd faced the most and worked hard to overcome, to excel, to go after your dreams. I work with people who bear much more visible scars than you and they live full and public lives." She stopped. "I know it's not always about the scars we see, but . . ."

"Susannah and Dot have a fundraising campaign going, asking alumnae to support the building of the Adelaide MacNeill Memorial Gymnasium. How would I look—how would they look—if I show up living and breathing? The Ladies of the Lake would all look like fools—or worse yet, charlatans, frauds, and swindlers! I don't see how—"

"Is that what you're worried about? That's nothing compared to finding you alive, Addie!"

"I'm not Addie anymore and haven't been for a very long time. I'm Rosaline Murray. My daughter is Bernadette Murray, and she knows nothing of my past, not even that I ever attended or taught at Lakeside Ladies Academy. This can't all come out as a surprise to her."

"Then tell her the truth, tell her whatever you must." Ruth locked eyes with me as if it were all so clear, so simple. "Someday, some way, she'll find out everything. Don't you want to be the one to tell her? Don't you want the hiding to end?"

Chapter Forty-One

JUNE 1935

The Saturday before graduation Dorothy received a telegram from Ruth.

> LOST IS FOUND STOP HAVE B MEET US AT
> HARTFORD TRAIN ALONE THURSDAY 13:15
> STOP ALLOW B TIME WITH HER MOTHER STOP
> CONTACT SUSANNAH STOP LADIES OF THE
> LAKE REUNION SATURDAY STOP DISCRETION
> REQUIRED STOP R

Dorothy's heart hammered in her chest. *Addie. Alive! Addie. Alive . . . Bernadette will have her mother at graduation. The Ladies of the Lake will reunite.*

It was what she'd wanted, what she'd prayed for. The search she'd set in motion had at last produced the results she'd suspected. Dorothy told herself over and over that she should be overjoyed, thankful, relieved.

But the question she'd buried since she'd first suspected that Bernadette might be Addie's daughter forced itself to the foreground of her mind. *Is Bernadette also Stephen's daughter? Is that the real reason Addie went away, not for the birth of her brother's child but because she knew she was pregnant? Could she have hidden that? She didn't look pregnant, but all along she'd planned to be away at that time, saying her sister-in-law was pregnant. Whose daughter is Bernadette? By not sending Stephen's letter, did I lead Addie to believe he'd abandoned her? Did I set in motion an entire cycle of events that's led Bernadette to live without her father, and Addie without her husband? If Addie was pregnant, did Stephen know? Did he lose Addie and his child because of me?* The questions wound poisonous vines around Dorothy's heart, pulling so tight she thought it might stop beating.

She couldn't know for certain the reasons behind Addie's choices all those years ago. Only Addie could say. Only Addie should say, might say now. Dorothy shuddered to think what that might mean.

I mustn't tell Bernadette. That's up to Addie.

What did Ruth mean by discretion? I never told her that Stephen intended to propose to Addie. Dare I tell Stephen and Jonas that Addie is alive, forewarn them? I can't betray her again, but can I possibly live with such a secret between us? Don't they need to be prepared—to know she's alive before she comes?

Everything will come out now. Dear God, what will Stephen think of me? What will Jonas think? She could barely breathe, barely imagine and remain sane.

The one thing she could do was to give Bernadette the desire of her heart.

A timid knock came at Dorothy's door.

"Come in."

"Mrs. Meyer, you sent for me?" Bernadette had lost weight in the last few weeks. Was it heartache over her mother's refusal to attend graduation? Was it the strain of final examinations or the fear of going out into the world without the sisterhood she'd found here? Graduation was a blessing, a longed-for goal and rite of passage, but for some it was also the ending of the happiest of years spent in the company of friends, the closest family any of them had.

Dorothy had seen all of that in other students. She hoped the news she was about to deliver would lighten the girl's heart, giving her a gift to look forward to.

"Close the door, Bernadette, please, and be seated."

Bernadette did so but eyed Dorothy warily, as if waiting for a shoe to drop.

"Don't look so grim, my dear; nothing is wrong. In fact, things are looking much brighter for you."

Bernadette looked up quizzically.

"I've received a telegram. Your mother is coming on the train next week in time for graduation. She wants you to meet her at the station."

"Mother's coming? Here? Do you mean it? I mean, are you sure?" Bernadette looked flabbergasted but broke into the broadest smile Dorothy had ever seen from the girl. "I can't believe it! What changed her mind? Oh, I don't care. I'm just so glad she's coming."

Despite her worries, Dorothy smiled, glad to see Bernadette happy at last. "She'll arrive Thursday afternoon, on the one fifteen train. She wants you to meet her at the station so you'll have a good long visit. You have permission to stay overnight in town with her. I'll arrange to have Mr. MacLaren drive you. Be ready by the front door at twelve forty-five. That should be time enough."

"Thank you! Thank you so much, Mrs. Meyer. This is the best news ever!"

"I'm glad for you, Bernadette. You deserve every happiness." Dorothy meant it.

Bernadette fairly danced through the door and into the hallway. She'd have good news to share with her friends. Dorothy closed her eyes for a moment, then closed the door to her office and returned to her desk. She opened her locked drawer and withdrew her journal, pulling the yellowed paper from its back and running her fingers over the words scribbled in Stephen's handwriting. Minutes later she returned letter and journal to their hiding place. Whether she wanted to or not, next Saturday she'd have a long-overdue letter to deliver.

Chapter Forty-Two

JULY 1935

Ruth insisted we go shopping for a new hat and dress for the graduation. I didn't want to. It wasn't that I couldn't afford it. I hated looking at myself in mirrors. Trying on clothes required exactly that. No matter what I said, Ruth would not budge.

"Shopping is good practice for going out in public." Ruth opened the door of the boutique and ushered me through.

"I go out in public. I'm not a recluse."

"Really?" Ruth raised her eyebrows. "Well, a new and fashionable suit or two will do you wonders." She steered me toward the women's suits. "Look at this blue." She pulled a neatly tailored and belted suit from the rack and held it up to me. "It's a perfect shade for you. It highlights your eyes, sets off the color in your cheeks."

"My burns?"

She nearly dropped the hanger in frustration. "Addie, we all have 'imperfections,' if you want to call them that. You really don't see what a treasure you are, do you?"

"Please stop calling me that," I hissed.

"What? Treasure?"

I glared at her. She knew perfectly well what I meant.

"Do you want me to call you Bob?" Ruth was as forward as when she was a girl.

"My name is Rosaline."

"Is it?"

"Yes, legally. It's what I've answered to since 1917."

"Is it how you want to be known? Really?"

I considered that. "Yes. Yes, it is. I've built my life as Rosaline Murray."

"I thought you'd chosen that as a pen name. Rosaline. Rosemont. You were always crazy about roses."

"It is my name," I answered stubbornly, if weakly. "Rosemont is where I live."

"Then own it."

"I do."

"I mean, speak with confidence. You're Rosaline Murray, well-known Canadian author, mother to the valedictorian of 1935 for Lakeside Ladies Academy, for pity's sake. Stand tall. Don't round your shoulders as if you're a child caught with your hand in the cookie jar."

While growing up together at Lakeside I'd not received the sharpness of Ruth's tongue. She'd become quicker to give out what she thought. Well, I had changed, too, and didn't have to take it, certainly not as a child with her hand in the cookie jar.

I grabbed the suit, marched into the dressing room, and was a little surprised to see how well it fit, how it flattered me. Only my long hair looked out of place, a little forlorn, with so stylish an ensemble.

"There, didn't I tell you?" Ruth gloated.

I lifted my chin. "I need a hat, and gloves, and a purse and shoes to match, or at least to complement."

Ruth grinned. "That's the Add—the Rosaline I know. Here are a few more dresses I think you'll need. Try them on. And then we're off to the beauty parlor. It's high time you cut those long tresses and entered the modern world. A little makeup won't hurt, either."

That was the Ruth I knew.

~

After dinner, after Ruth had gone back to her hotel, Portia helped me combine clothes and accessories and pack my case for the trip to Connecticut. It had been so long since I'd made public appearances beyond going to church, I hardly knew what to take, what to wear besides the new outfits Ruth had helped me choose.

"These are awfully smart outfits. You'll cut a fine figure in these." Portia held up the suits and dresses and smiled. "And by the way, I like what you've done with your hair and that bit of makeup. Just right."

"Ruth helped me. Oh, Portia, am I doing the right thing? Going? Telling Bernadette? It will change everything."

"Some things need changing."

We packed in silence for a time and finally locked the case. On her way to her room, Portia paused and turned, her hand on the doorframe. "Just make sure you're doing what you want, not what these other women think is best for you or for them. You and Bernadette are the ones who have to live with whatever you decide."

I nodded. "That's all I can think of. The truth is, I don't want to resurrect Adelaide MacNeill. She was a sad and lonely girl—one full of hopes and dreams unfulfilled. I'm not her anymore. In so many ways she died in the explosion."

"And God brought Rosaline Murray to life. She rose from ashes, kind of like that phoenix."

I half smiled. "Kind of like. She rose, not at once, but in time."

"Then why not let Rosaline live? Who's to know or care besides these Ladies of the Lake and Bernadette?"

"MacNeill is Bernadette's birth name, her parents' legacy."

"You think she'll be wanting to change the name she's lived with all her life?"

I couldn't answer that.

"Hard to imagine when she's so proud to be Rosaline Murray's daughter. Who else on this earth will it matter to?"

Not Stephen. Not anymore. "But the gymnasium they're building, or wanting to build—the memorial to—"

"To Adelaide MacNeill, who died in the Halifax Explosion, December 6, 1917. Let her rest in peace, Rosaline, if that's what you truly want. God's made you a new woman, a new creature in Him. Don't you want to celebrate what He's done for you?"

"Isn't it wrong to let it go forward like that?"

"Is it? Now, I wonder." Portia's head tipped to one side, considering. "You sent that second check to the school, didn't you?"

"Yes, and later I can send more if it's needed, but that's for the operation of the school, what I hope will enable it to stay open. And what does that have to—"

"Makes me think of Joseph, in the Bible, is all. Way down in Egypt, working hard, serving, and working away under a different name, different clothes, different life than he'd grown up with, no thanks to his brothers. He'd lost everything and yet the good Lord blessed him in time as he was faithful and did his best in whatever he put his hand to. Pharoah was so impressed he gave him a new name, named him Zaphnath-Paaneah, even made him governor of Egypt. After all those years the Lord used Joseph to bless his own family— some that loved him like no other and some that had abused him, betrayed him, were even still afraid he might not be good to them now that they were on the needful end.

"I don't suppose Pharoah started calling his appointed governor Joseph once his relatives showed up, do you?"

I sat down on the side of the bed, broadsided by such a thought, such an outlandish analogy. Or was it?

"I'd guess Joseph just went on doing what he'd been doing all those years working for Pharoah . . . the best he could. While he did that, he helped and blessed his own family, his own people, so they could keep going. Sound like anybody you know?"

I tried to take that in.

"You remember what Joseph said? He told his brothers that what they meant for evil, the Lord used for good. Seems to me that a lot of those dreams of Adelaide MacNeill's have come to pass in Rosaline Murray, and now she's able to help those that helped raise her . . . as well as those who betrayed her. No shame in that. And a lot to be thankful for."

If there were tears in my eyes they came from a flicker of hope in my heart.

"Sleep well, Rosaline Murray." Portia smiled and closed the door.

⁓

Ruth and I took a ship from Halifax to Boston Harbor, and a train to Hartford, Connecticut.

Every mile, as Ruth spoke or slept or we ate, I thought of Portia's words. *Let her rest in peace.* Could I do that? Was it the right thing to do? My name change had begun as a means of hiding from the world and creating a new existence for Bernadette and me. But hadn't I also grown into that identity? Rosaline Murray was more than a pen name for me; it was who I'd become, who I'd grown to be by God's grace. Resurrecting Addie MacNeill felt like returning to myself as a child, as a young woman in love with a man no longer free to love me, if indeed he had loved me.

The truth that it was young Addie who'd loved Stephen the young man seeped into my brain as the train rumbled over miles of track. I shook my head and smiled at the sad irony of accepting something I'd wasted years of longing and hurt over.

Stephen is no longer that young man any more than I am that young woman. Who is he now? Who am I without the shield of memory I've built to protect myself? Lord, you've built an identity in me while I've stood unaware, grieving a broken monument. The wonder overwhelmed me.

"Are you all right?" Ruth covered my hand with her own.

"I will be." I smiled. "Seeing everyone, meeting them again after all these years is going to be hard. Perhaps the dread of these meetings and explanations is worse than the reality, at least I hope that's so. In twenty-four or forty-eight hours they will be done, and life, whatever shape it takes, will go on."

"Bernadette will still love you, you know. You're her mother, whatever your name might be. And Dot and Susannah will be thrilled to see you, just as I am." She squeezed my hand and let go.

The conductor came through at that moment. I pulled my scarf more closely about my neck and face.

"If you didn't work so hard to hide those scars, I don't believe people would take a second look."

I shifted in my seat. "Hiding has become a habit. I'm not sure how else to—I don't know—to live."

"Maybe this 'coming out' will change those habits. We all have things we'd rather not show the world, and I assure you, you will find our friends have aged and changed as well. None of us have stayed the same."

I smiled. "Well, you're not so different, just more so."

Ruth laughed. A minute later she confided, "Dorothy has become more anxious over the years. I don't know what it is. I think her marriage is happy but it's like she carries the weight of the world on her shoulders. I've wondered if it's because she hasn't been able to have children or if it's all the worry about keeping the academy afloat.

"Susannah has become the matriarchal socialite she was destined to be, so don't mind it when she says things she thinks the world ought to know."

"That sounds like Susannah, only more so." I smiled again.

"I haven't wanted to say this, but you'll find Stephen and Jonas changed."

"What do you mean?"

Ruth sighed. "The Great War. Jonas came back with a bad limp. He caught shrapnel at some point and lay for a couple of days on the battlefield until medics could retrieve him from no-man's-land. It's not so pronounced now, but his leg hampers some of what he'd like to do, all he once did. Stephen lost an arm."

"An arm?" I had never imagined Stephen as a middle-aged man without an arm, unable to have children. My heart went out to him and Dot, and for the first time my love and pity, my empathy, felt pure and honest.

"Surgeries have been done on his face after mustard gas burns and he's still quite handsome, but there's a long scar down his cheek.

"The war changed us all, really. Some scars we carry on the outside, but some we carry deep within. Both can be devastating. We're just better at hiding the inside scars from the world." She huffed. "In the end, I think hiding them makes the pain go deeper, longer."

I surely understood that. "What scars have you hidden?"

Ruth's eyes misted and her mouth straightened. "There was someone . . . in France. A doctor. Working in a field hospital you bond quickly with those you're working with every day, shoulder to shoulder, nearly every moment in life-threatening circumstances, never knowing if the breath you take will be your last."

"What happened?" I whispered.

"The war. The bloody, stupid war." Ruth leaned her head against the seat. "Our hospital was bombed. Jack was in the middle of a surgery . . . working to save a life while the enemy worked fiendishly to take ours. I would have been working with him that day, but I'd gone to the next post for supplies."

"I'm so sorry, Ruth, so very sorry." This time I reached for her hand, and we rode in silence for a time. *We're not so very different after all, you and I.*

"It made me realize the utter futility of it all. After the war I couldn't return to nursing in a surgical ward. It's why I went into social work. Not that that's easy, mind you, but I just couldn't go back. Every time we scrubbed up after—I not only saw the hundreds of broken men whose eyes I closed in death; I saw him—saw Jack."

Sometimes there are no words. We sat those last few miles, holding hands, each struggling with our demons, gathering courage to survive our memories and walk into the present.

As the train pulled into the station, memories of Dot as a young girl and later as a young woman meeting me at the station forced themselves to the front of my mind. Mr. Potts and Old Clem—or was it Young Clem coming to meet me?—and of how green and sad and uncertain I'd felt.

But even those memories faded into the background by the time the train lurched to its stop, for there, on the platform, waving for all she was worth, was my beloved daughter, my Bernadette! I'd seen during the Christmas holidays that Bernadette had grown more womanly, more confident and lovely, but in that moment, seeing her from the train's window, the years swept away and a woolen-stockinged ten-year-old bedecked in giant hair ribbons jumped up and down with the excitement of seeing her mother once again.

"Mama! Mama!" I saw her mouth form the words, though I knew her training in deportment would not allow her to call across a train platform.

Whatever I'd feared flew away in that moment, fears I couldn't even fathom in the light of my daughter's smile. And she was my daughter, raised from infancy, nurtured in love and all the imagination I possessed.

"She's beautiful!" Ruth whispered as we gathered our things and made our way up the aisle.

"Yes, she is." I laughed for joy—joy of seeing her, joy of seeing my daughter's freedom from fear. A glass eye had not kept Bernadette back. Burns and skin grafts and a decided limp had not. *How much I've missed through my fears, letting them rule my life. Forgive me, Lord. I won't miss another minute, come what may. I promise.*

Right there on the train platform for all to see Bernadette wrapped me in a hug so warm, so fierce and welcoming, I could barely breathe. I was the one to pull away first, determined to control my emotions.

"Mummy," she whispered. "Your hair—I love it! Oh, I'm so glad you've come."

She hadn't called me Mummy in years. "So am I, my darling."

Ruth, standing off to one side, coughed discreetly.

"Forgive me, Ruth." I swallowed and stepped back, determined, but still holding Bernadette's hand. "Ruth, this is my daughter, my precious daughter, Bernadette. Bernadette, this is my friend Ruth Hennessey—my dear and longtime friend."

"And valedictorian of our very own alma mater, I understand. Congratulations, Bernadette! I'm so glad to meet you!" Ruth beamed, clasping Bernadette's hand warmly.

Bernadette's smile checked for only a moment. Puzzlement flicked through her eyes as she searched mine.

"Oh." Ruth inhaled. "I spoke out of turn. Forgive me." It was the first time I'd seen Ruth blush in embarrassment.

"There's so much to share." I looped my arm through Bernadette's, hoping to brush aside Ruth's untimely comment and hold onto this moment, to her.

"I'll find a porter and see to our luggage." Ruth fidgeted with her purse and the luggage receipts, more than ready to make her exit. "Where shall I meet you?"

"In front of the station. Mrs. Meyer sent a car." Bernadette, distracted, spoke to the air.

"Excellent." Ruth nodded and was gone. I attempted to gently pull Bernadette forward, but she wouldn't budge.

"What did she mean, 'our very own alma mater'? Was Miss Hennessey a graduate of Lakeside?"

"Yes. Oh, a long time ago." I pulled Bernadette with me down the platform, toward the end where the ladies' waiting room used to be. *Confession time.* I drew a deep breath. "As a matter of fact, my darling, we both were."

Bernadette stopped, pulling her arm from mine. "What? You went to school here? You graduated from—"

"It's a long story and . . . complicated."

"One you've never told me." Bernadette's color rose and a flicker of hurt, of betrayal crossed her eyes.

"I should have. One I will tell you now. But not here."

Bernadette allowed me to pull her along then, down the platform that had been rebuilt since my last time here—since 1917 when I'd taken the train to begin my journey to Halifax. So much had changed, and yet the landscape was still the same—like walking past ghosts that only I could see.

Of course, there was no longer a separate waiting room for ladies, no longer hitching posts for horses and buggies or wagons. It was all automobiles and buses and a parking lot now. How I wished for the smiling face of Mr. Potts.

"Where is the car you mentioned?"

Bernadette was looking at me, slightly worried, as if she didn't know me, but pointed vaguely toward the middle of the lot.

"Perhaps we should wait here for Ruth, so she'll know where to join us."

"Mother, I don't understand. How could you not tell me something that important?"

"Because . . . one thing leads to another. There's so much to explain."

"When? When were you here?"

"Long ago. Before you were born."

"Before you and Father married?"

I bit my lip. *Lies upon lies. I can't tell her another one.* "Please, let's wait until we're alone, where we can talk. I'll tell you everything. I promise."

"Everything?" she challenged. "Because you never have."

"Yes." I looked her squarely in the eye. It was time. "Anything you want to know."

Chapter Forty-Three

JULY 1935

Dorothy had unlocked the front door of the academy before the sun rose, stopping in the school's kitchen long enough to pour a cup of coffee and search out a biscuit before retreating to her office. It was not unusual for her to spend long hours at the school in the few days before graduation; there was so much to do.

That's what she'd told herself, what she'd told her husband that morning when he asked why she needed to leave home so early and why she wanted to talk with him tomorrow instead of today, why she needed to meet with him and his brother at their office the next day.

If she spent much time at home, she'd blurt out the entire story, from sorry beginning to end. She'd put off her confession as long as possible, some small part of her almost hoping that Addie would decide at the last minute not to attend graduation, not to reveal herself. Dorothy knew that hope was fearful and selfish on her part.

The day passed in slow agony.

When the school clock finally bonged three, Dorothy swallowed. Addie and Ruth were surely in town. She must tell Stephen and Jonas that Addie was alive before she appeared on campus. She must confess to both men her failure to send Stephen's letter all those years ago, and she could only do it once.

The brothers had turned to one another as much as to her in their grief over losing their mother, then Addie, and later their father. They might need her, but they would surely need and confide in each other, especially since she was the one who'd failed them all. Who knew how they would react? How could they possibly understand her jealousy at the time? Would they forgive her? Would her husband ever look at her in the same way? Would he trust her—could he? Dorothy didn't know. She knew only that she owed them this and so much more.

Dorothy unlocked her desk drawer and withdrew the faded letter from her journal, tucking it into her pocket. She bowed her head to pray, needing God's strength and mercy to prepare for the meeting with her Meyer men.

The four o'clock bell rang. Even though her office door was closed, Dorothy heard the tramp of eager feet bounding through the front door and thundering down the hallway toward the dining room. *There must be no hallway monitor on duty.*

Dorothy remembered just how unruly she and her friends had become near the end of the school term. She couldn't begrudge another generation the same restless exuberance.

A knock came at her office door. Nerves already on edge, Dorothy jumped, spilling her afternoon tea across the papers before her. *Blast.* She mopped the spreading brown stain as best she could with her handkerchief. "Come in." The words came more clipped than she'd intended.

The door opened a handbreadth. "Mrs. Meyer?" Bernadette's timid voice came. "May I come in?"

"Bernadette. Come in." She stood. "I expected you to spend the evening with your mother."

"I met her—and her friend—at the station. We had graduation rehearsal this afternoon I couldn't miss, and I wanted to help with weaving the final garlands of the daisy chain. Mr. MacLaren said he'd drive me back to Mother's hotel in a few minutes. Before I go, I need to tell you something, to ask you a question."

"Yes?" Bernadette's reticence and pale complexion gave Dorothy pause. *She knows something, but what does she know? I must be careful what I say.*

"I feel the fool, Mrs. Meyer."

"You've never been a fool, Bernadette." Dorothy could say that without reservation.

"At the station, my mother told me that she was once a student here, that she graduated from Lakeside Ladies Academy."

"I see." Dorothy waited, unflinching but without further comment, while Bernadette searched her face.

"You've always told us that you spent the most wonderful years of your life here. My mother is in her early forties, Mrs. Meyer, the same as you."

Dorothy stiffened.

"I know how old you are because of the candles on your last birthday cake. Mr. Meyer thought it would be great fun for us to put that many candles on your giant cake, do you remember?"

"I remember fearing we might burn down the school!" Dorothy tried to make light, but Bernadette didn't smile.

"That means my mother must have gone to school with you here, and yet you've never said you knew her." Bernadette stood her ground, determined but clearly afraid to push boundaries.

What can I say? Dorothy drew a deep breath. "I didn't know—I didn't know your mother's married name, Bernadette."

"But you spoke with her on the phone, at least you said you did."

"I didn't recognize her voice."

Bernadette didn't look convinced.

"Do you doubt my word?" Dorothy asked as gently as she dared. *How can I tell her that her mother pretended not to know me?*

Bernadette blushed. "No, ma'am. I'm just trying to understand why my mother never told me, why you never told me. She introduced me to a woman she went to school with here—Miss Hennessey. She said they were friends from school. You must have known her, too. You must have all gone to school here together."

"Yes. Miss Hennessey was—is—a great friend of mine, but as for anything more, you really must talk with your mother. I cannot answer your questions."

"Because you can't, or won't?"

"I'm not able. I can only say that I very much look forward to meeting with your mother tomorrow night, Bernadette, to seeing her again. She's—she's a woman who clearly loves you with all her heart and has accomplished a great deal in life despite its setbacks. She's certainly been very generous to the school—far beyond anything I ever hoped or imagined."

"Does that mean the school can stay open?"

Dorothy nearly bit her lip. No official word had come yet. "I don't know. You mustn't say anything about the school's finances to the other girls or their parents, Bernadette. The academy's future is in the hands of the board of governors. They must decide how they will handle that information should the time come. Please remember that you wouldn't know so much if you hadn't eavesdropped. I'm trusting you."

That took the starch from Bernadette's stance and the set of her mouth, but it also robbed the girl of her confidence. "Yes, Mrs. Meyer." She turned to go.

"Bernadette?"

She stopped by the door but didn't turn around.

"When you see your mother this evening, please tell her that I'm very much looking forward to seeing her tomorrow night. Tell her—tell her that I've missed her terribly. Will you do that for me?"

Bernadette nodded once, at least Dorothy thought she did, before slipping through the door and closing it behind her.

Dorothy hadn't yet caught her breath before the telephone on her desk rang, causing her to knock the remainder of her tea clear across the desk. Her sodden handkerchief would do no good now. Dorothy covered the liquid with her blotter and plucked the receiver from its cradle, knowing the school secretary would have left for the day. "Good afternoon. Lakeside Ladies Academy. Mrs. Meyer speaking."

"Dot!" Susannah squealed through the line. "I've just talked with Ruth and Addie. It really and truly is our Addie! She's alive! She calls herself something else now—Rosaline—can you imagine? But you were right; it's her!"

Dorothy sat down in her chair, hard. Of course, she'd known Ruth told only the truth, but somehow Susannah's confirmation made it all the more real, made Dorothy's path forward all the more imminent and perilous.

"Are you there?"

"Yes, yes, I'm here."

"Aren't you thrilled? You don't sound thrilled."

"Of course I am. It's just . . . oh . . . graduation—and everything. There's so much to do." Dorothy knew she'd become altogether too good at lying, at covering herself.

"Well, you have one more thing to add to your calendar. Tomorrow, at two o'clock, meet us at the gazebo. The Ladies of the Lake will return for our first proper reunion since before the war!"

"Not tomorrow!" Dorothy nearly croaked. *It's too soon.* "We'll see her at the baccalaureate dinner. I can't possibly tomorrow afternoon—not with—"

"Dot! This is Addie we're talking about—the one we thought was lost and dead and now is found. Our very own prodigal has returned and we're going to run to welcome her with open arms. Do you understand me? Ruth says she's fragile and we must let her know we want her back, to the devil with the past. Two o'clock! Be there!" The phone slammed on the other end of the line while Dorothy held her breath and held the receiver in midair, coming to terms with Susannah's ultimatum.

~

Dorothy had come in early so many days that she no longer had the million and one things to do she normally would have before graduation. She'd intended to meet with Stephen and Jonas tomorrow morning, but that might be too late. With Addie and Ruth and Susannah in town, who knew who Stephen and Jonas might see, what they might say? Who knew if Addie herself might not call at the house? With them all coming to the gazebo tomorrow, everything could come out before then. She picked up the phone and dialed the operator.

"Stephen? I know my meeting is set for tomorrow, but it's imperative I come and speak with you both before you leave the office. Now. I'm sorry. I know it's late in the day. I'll be there in fifteen minutes." She didn't wait for him to respond or demand an explanation. She replaced the receiver in its cradle, checked her pocket for Stephen's letter, and walked out the door.

Chapter Forty-Four

I spent the hour before Bernadette returned to the hotel in prayer, asking, begging God to give me words my precious daughter could understand, words that would bind us closer and not rip us apart, words that would not destroy her graduation memories but let these days remain among the proudest, most joyous of her life.

When the knock came at my door, I opened it, drawing a deep breath.

"Mother." Bernadette smiled, but in that smile I saw reservation, longing to understand, and a veil of self-protection.

I closed the door and pulled her to my heart, still praying.

"There's so much I want to know," she whispered. "You promised. You promised you'd tell me everything."

"Everything, yes. Everything you want to know. This will take some time, so let's get comfortable. Would you like tea?"

"I don't want tea. I want the truth." Bernadette sat cross-legged on the bed, a pillow across her stomach, as if she might need protection. Protection from me, from what I might say. "So, when were you here? How old were you when you first came to Lakeside?"

I pulled off my shoes and sat beside her, on the opposite side of the bed, leaning back against the headboard. I wasn't sure I could look at Bernadette and tell her my story. Watching her reactions might make me amend it, alter it, shape it, and I mustn't do that. The truth, from beginning to end, was what she deserved. "I wanted to wait until after your graduation to tell you, to not steal one moment of this crowning glory for you, and to give you time and space to absorb everything I'll say, all that's happened in my life . . . and yours."

"I want to know now."

"Yes." I smiled. "I see that. You want to know about Lakeside."

"Yes, Mother. I can't believe you didn't tell me you went to school here. I don't understand."

"I know, my darling. How could you? Lakeside, yes, but there's so much more. Let me tell you . . . from the beginning." A deep breath filled my lungs. I turned back the pages of my life, back to PEI and the night of the storm, the night that stole my parents forever. I told her every detail I could remember, down to Mama's red shoe.

I told her about Lemuel, about leaving my best friend and every rock and shell and feather collected on my windowsill and being sent to Lakeside Ladies Academy at twelve. I told her it was the death of one life and the beginning of another, the one that would make me, shape me into the woman I once was, the woman I still was, in many ways.

I told her of Mrs. Simmons, my mentor, and of Mrs. Lucy Maud Montgomery and how she and all that happened in my years at Lakeside sparked and inspired my dream to write, how I'd finally decided, after all this confession, that I must write her and tell her, too, my life's story and apologize for simply disappearing. It would read like something from one of her books, after all. Through this telling I heard little gasps, or notes of sympathy, but I dared not look at Bernadette's face.

I told my daughter of my friends, Dot, Ruth and Susannah, how we were four musketeers and the Ladies of the Lake all at once. Friends for life, friends forever.

And then I told her about a young man—without giving his name. How I'd loved him and his family, how his mother was a second mother to me, how we'd hoped to marry, and about the Great War and the terrible prejudice they endured. I told her that I taught at Lakeside and loved teaching but went to Halifax to help my brother's wife through her last days of confinement, how I'd waited for my beloved's proposal in the Public Gardens to no avail and gone home, brokenhearted, to share in Bertha's delivery of her baby, the most beautiful baby girl I'd ever seen.

"But Bertha wasn't well, and we had to temporarily give the baby to a young mother from Africville, to nurse. When she returned to the house with Baby, Lemuel had just gone to the church to arrange for Baby's baptism and to register her name. I never knew the name they'd chosen, for in that moment, the moment the woman from Africville came to the door with Baby and I stepped outside to talk with her, the explosion came." I stopped, not sure I could go on.

Somewhere in the telling, Bernadette had slipped her hand into mine, as though she knew where the story was going, as though she could guess the end and needed help to face it.

"The house blew into a million shards of glass and wood and stone before me. I was thrown far up the hill—all the way to Needham Hill. When I woke, I was taken to a makeshift hospital for a month. For days I thought I was the only one of my family left alive, until Portia found me. Our Portia, the woman from Africville who'd nursed Baby from the beginning." I turned, positioning myself so I could see Bernadette clearly with my good eye. "And then Portia told me she'd found Baby. My niece, my precious, beautiful niece lived—a miracle, even in infancy." I stopped, letting the words settle, waiting to hear the inhale and exhale of Bernadette's breathing.

A minute passed, and then another. Bernadette withdrew her

hand from mine. I feared my heart might stop beating. *What are you thinking, my dearest? Can you bear this?*

"They were all dead?" she whispered.

"Yes," I whispered back. "I'm so sorry, so very sorry. What I've always said about your father dying in the war—he died in the Halifax Explosion during the war. At least that part was true, in its way."

She didn't speak. The light in the room had faded. I knew the time for dinner had come and gone, but we were standing on sacred ground, and I dared not move.

"I named you Bernadette to honor your mother, Bertha. She was a wonderful woman, a beautiful and kind woman."

"And not because of my burns, after all."

"No, never. I'm so sorry you ever thought that. I named you Bernadette, my darling, because you are beautiful, because she loved you so and I loved her, and because I knew that Bernadette means 'brave as a bear.' You are brave. You've always been brave. You had an older brother, Marcus. I loved him, too."

"I have—had a brother . . . Are there graves?"

"No. I'm sorry."

"In Fairview Cemetery, where *Titanic's* dead are buried, there's a memorial for the remains of those unknown, recovered from the Halifax Explosion. Is that where?"

"I want to think so."

"I need to go there. That's where all our Murrays are."

"We'll go together, if that's all right." I closed my eyes, summoning strength. There were so many layers to unfold. "They weren't Murrays. They were MacNeills. I took the name Murray for myself and for you, to start over, to begin anew. It was my mother's maiden name."

She stared at me blankly, frowned, and nodded slowly. "My name is Bernadette MacNeill."

I reached for her hand, wanting her to know I was there, would always be there for her, as long as I drew breath.

How many minutes passed, I couldn't guess. The silence seemed to go on forever. At last Bernadette withdrew her hand from mine once again. "You should have told me."

"I'd planned to tell you . . . after your graduation."

"You weren't going to come. What changed your mind?"

"Dot—Dorothy—Mrs. Meyer guessed who I was and sent Ruth to see."

"So you came for them."

"No. I came for you. I wanted to come for you all along, to be with you, but I couldn't before telling you everything . . . and I couldn't face the shame."

"Look at me. I bear the same scars."

"It's not my scars—not entirely. Facing my friends, having let them believe I died so long ago . . . I just couldn't, and I couldn't reveal myself to them without revealing myself to you first. Can you understand that?"

"I'm trying. I'm trying to understand why you never told me about my . . . my parents, my brother, even that you went to school here—you taught here! Do you have any idea how any of that—all of that—makes me feel?" She stood from the bed and brushed her skirt, as if brushing away something distasteful.

"Bernadette," I pleaded, standing and facing her across the bed.

"No more. Not now. Please. I need some time to think this through."

"Will you stay the night?"

She hesitated. I couldn't read her face. Longing? Anger? Hurt? Frustration? I couldn't tell. "I don't think so. I can't. I need to walk. It's not far to the school. I need to be alone."

"Is there anything I can say?"

"Is there more? Anything you haven't told me?"

I shook my head. I'd bared my soul. "Only that I love you, have always loved you, and will love you as my daughter until I die."

Bernadette's lip quivered. Her chin trembled. She picked up her purse and walked to the door. Her hand on the knob, her back turned to me, she paused. "The man you loved. Do you still love him? Did you ever learn what happened to him?"

He married my best friend. "No," I lied. That was one secret, one lie, the only one I'd take to my grave. "I've never seen him since." That much, at least for now, was true.

Chapter Forty-Five

Dorothy marched through the door of the Meyer Brothers, Attorneys-at-Law office with solemnity and fear, wondering if she was experiencing the racing heart one felt when going to face a firing squad.

She couldn't look in her husband's face. What she was about to say would reveal as much about the past as it did the present—a past sure to hurt him deeply, a present for which he would feel betrayed. For both, she was so very sorry.

She couldn't look in her brother-in-law's face. What she was about to say would not only cut him to the quick but convince him she was a conniving, manipulative woman, something she'd worked desperately over the years to persuade him was not true.

"What's this all about, Dorothy?" Her husband was a loving and long-suffering man, but for the past few weeks she'd pushed his patience to the limit.

"Please, both of you, sit down. I've something to say and I can only say this once. I should have told you both years ago, but once a lie is told it becomes so hard to cover . . . and then for so long it didn't seem to matter, as if resurrecting the past was worse than burying it." She knew her voice quaked, but she couldn't seem to control it.

"You, tell a lie?" Her brother-in-law looked as if he didn't believe it. "What lie could you possibly have told both of us?"

"Please. Don't say anything . . . either of you. Let me get it out. Let me get everything out." Dorothy stood at the far end of their consulting table, the picture of one condemned facing a tribunal, which she knew she deserved. Still, she couldn't do it standing. She pulled out the chair, sat, locked her hands atop the table, and looked each of them fully in the face. How she loved these men—her husband, who was everything to her, and his brother, who had all these years been a true brother to her, more than those of her own flesh and blood.

"Dorothy? What is it?"

"You both know Bernadette Murray."

"Valedictorian—brilliant girl, magnificent voice. Has something happened to her?"

"Do you remember at the spring play, how you both thought she reminded you of Addie?"

"Yes. Yes, she did. Odd, that, but Addie loved the play, so—"

"She's long reminded me of her, too. The play, yes, but other things—little things Bernadette would say, a turn of phrase or a look in her eye, a mannerism—so many little things."

"She's Canadian—you've always said." Stephen spoke warily.

"It's more than that. It became so much, so strong a resemblance that I wrote to Ruth Hennessey and asked if she'd go to Mrs. Murray's home—Bernadette's mother—and see if perhaps Mrs. Murray was truly Addie MacNeill."

"What?" Stephen's eyes filled with compassion, as if he pitied her. "Dorothy, Addie's dead. We've all known a long time."

"Dorothy?" Jonas looked concerned for her sanity.

"I know it sounds outlandish. I'm not crazy, though there were times I thought I might be. The thing is . . . it's true. Rosaline Murray is Addie—our Addie."

"Dorothy, you can't mean—"

"Ruth saw her, met her, talked with her."

"Impossible. That can't be."

"Ruth said that Addie's alive?" Jonas, ever the attorney, pinned her down.

Bewilderment, confusion, fear to hope flashed through Stephen's eyes.

"She was injured—evidently very badly—in the Halifax Explosion back in '17. Her family, everyone in the house, was killed—their bodies never recovered. The board even sent someone to search, but she was never found . . . so we all believed she'd died."

"Addie wouldn't have done that. She wouldn't have let us believe—let me believe . . . so violent a death . . .'"

"Ruth is absolutely certain?"

Dorothy nodded. "She is. And Susannah is. She's spoken with her by phone."

"This is impossible. Why? Why would she—why did she never—?"

"I don't know. At least I don't know everything. I understand from Ruth that she was badly burned . . . She lost an eye and some of her hearing."

"That would never matter—not to me, not to any of us."

Dorothy could no longer bear to look at either man. "No. But she didn't know that. There's more, possibly the main reason she never came back, never contacted any of us—not even the Ladies of the Lake."

"What could possibly—?" Stephen tried to control himself. Even that brought pain to Dorothy's heart.

She drew a shaky breath and mustered the courage to look in his eyes, so blue they made the sky pale. "I failed you, Stephen."

"What?"

"You came to me at the school that night—the night before Mother Meyer died. You wanted to telephone Addie and we couldn't get into the headmistress's office. You wrote a note and asked me to send it, made me promise to send it the next day."

"Explaining why I couldn't come, why I couldn't meet her. Of course, I remember."

"I never sent it."

"What? Dorothy?" Now Jonas was on his feet. "You swore you'd—"

Stephen looked so deathly pale Dorothy feared for his heart. "Why? Why would you do such a thing?"

This confession came harder than the first. "Because I was angry with her, angry with you for loving her . . . and not me. I was young and jealous and stupid. I'd planned to send it later—just to make her wait a few days for your explanation. And then—then the explosion happened . . . and it was too late. I know those are not excuses. I'm sorry, so very sorry. I've been sorry all my life . . . ever since that day."

"Sorry because you—"

"That means Addie never knew I wanted to come, tried to go to her—"

"She'd have believed you'd abandoned her." Jonas looked far away, as if a wall had come between Dorothy and the brothers.

"I would have died for her."

That confession sent another arrow to Dorothy's heart.

"What else could she think?"

Dorothy didn't know which was worse, the stricken pain and disbelief in Stephen's eyes or the disappointment in the shake of Jonas's head, the rigid disapproval in his turned back, long fingers raked through his hair in frustration.

"Addie's coming to Bernadette's graduation."

"She's coming here? When? Where has she been all this time?"

"She lives in Halifax—with Bernadette, her daughter, and a woman who helped to raise her." She'd said it. If Stephen put two and two together, would he come up with parental rights? She didn't know, but waited, holding her breath. Dared she ask? "Is Bernadette—do you think—"

It seemed to sink in. "She married someone else."

"Ruth said Addie's husband died in the war. That's what Bernadette's always told me—about her father. When Addie comes, I'll confess what I did—what I didn't do."

Jonas laughed bitterly. "And you think she'll forgive you just like that for ruining her life, for letting her believe Stephen didn't love her?"

Dorothy felt the breath leave her body. "No. I've no right to expect that. I've no right to expect either of you to forgive me . . . or to understand. But you have a right to know, and needed to know . . . before Addie comes, before you see her."

Stephen covered his eyes with his hand, ran it down his face. "Addie? Alive? I can't think. I can't take it in. Or that she married someone else." He pushed away from the table, looking to Jonas's back as if for strength.

"Can't think what might have been?" Jonas glanced pityingly at his brother, then accusingly at Dorothy. She looked away.

"When will she arrive?" Stephen turned away, doing his best, Dorothy knew, to keep his voice steady.

"She arrived today. She's coming to meet the Ladies of the Lake tomorrow. I'll tell her then, once we're alone. I imagine she'll come to the baccalaureate tomorrow night and graduation the next day."

"I need to see her. I want to see her the minute she arrives." Stephen picked up his hat and suit jacket.

"Come to the gazebo at four tomorrow. After the Ladies of the Lake meet. You have to wait until I've explained everything to her. You have to give me that."

"Give you—I don't believe I need to give you anything. Knowing you—"

"None of us would have known she was alive if I hadn't sent Ruth looking for her. What I did all those years ago was wrong—horribly, unforgivably wrong, and I'm forever sorry. But she was my friend, too, and I failed her. I have to tell her. She may never believe you meant to go to her if I don't tell her that you tried." There. It might mean the end of her marriage and the end of her closeness with her brother-in-law, but it was out. All of it.

Stephen didn't speak, didn't acknowledge Dorothy or Jonas, but, picking up his briefcase, walked out the front door, leaving it to swing wide.

"What will he do?"

Jonas turned to face her, hurt, disappointment, and anger she'd rarely seen in his eyes. "What would you do?"

"Jonas, please understand—"

But Jonas held up his hand. "Stephen needs time." He turned to his desk, as if to do something, to take up some work, but shook his head, picked up his briefcase, and swearing under his breath, brushed past her.

"Jonas!"

"You've got to give us both time. You know how to lock up." He walked out the door.

Chapter Forty-Six

Ruth stood behind my hotel dressing table, hands on hips, staring me down through the mirror. "You can't wear that veil, Rosaline. It's hideous. Makes you look a hundred years old and as if you're in Victorian mourning. It calls more attention to you than if you walked out half dressed."

"Please don't say that. It's vulgar." I straightened my veil. "You must understand. I'm terrified of going. The veil helps—"

"It helps you hide, but you're done hiding, remember?" She snatched off my hat and ripped the veil from it, destroying it in the process.

"Ruth!"

"Rosaline! You said you were sick of hiding. You said you were willing to make a clean breast of things. Well, it's time. The explosion was when your hiding began. This is where it ends."

308

CATHY GOHLKE

"You don't know—you can't understand how hard today will be."
My palm covered my cheek. No matter how far I'd come in surren-
dering Stephen and Dot to the Lord, I still did not want Stephen to
see my scars. It was too humiliating, too great a reminder of all that
had never been, of him, of my love for him that had simply never
gone away. Fantasy or real, even though I knew I should not covet
another woman's husband, I couldn't make those vulnerable feelings
disappear.

*For him to see me like this—for her, his wife—I can't. No more hid-
ing? Ruth's wrong. Today I'll have to do the best acting, the most convincing hiding of my feelings that I've ever done.*

I'd vowed to the Lord yesterday that I wouldn't waste one more
moment of my life in fears and regret, but carrying that out was
harder than I'd imagined. I tugged the collar of my blouse higher, but
there was no way it could cover my scars.

"I understand what it is to want to disappear. We've both done far
too much of that in the past, but we're done with that now. We have
everything in the world to live for, to enter into life for.

"Look at you, Rosaline. You've no idea how regal a woman you
are. You have a brilliant daughter who loves you with all her heart,
friends who would lay down and die for you, a writing career anyone
with half a dream would envy—everything and more than the career
that Addie MacNeill dreamed of as a girl. You should be shouting
hurrah from the housetops."

"Shouting hurrah from the housetops?" I bit my quivering lip
and attempted to smile, hoping above all that what she'd said about
Bernadette's love for me was still true.

"Well," Ruth conceded, "maybe that was excessive. But you
understand, I know you do." She took my face between her palms.
"It's time, my friend. You know it's time."

Chapter Forty-Seven

JULY 1935

Despite her lament to Susannah of not a moment to spare, despite yesterday's grueling meeting with Stephen and Jonas, and despite the fact that she'd slept little while her husband spent a silent night on the living room sofa, Dorothy had plenty of time to meet the women at the gazebo. She just didn't want to go and dreaded the walk down that hill alone.

Her fingers knotting and unknotting, Dorothy waited by the academy's front door until Susannah's long black limousine pulled into the circular drive at a quarter to two and a slightly overweight but still beautiful belle of the ball Susannah stepped out of the door her driver held open.

Dorothy smoothed her dress and hair, moistened her lips, squared her shoulders, and stood as straight as she and the Ladies of the Lake had been taught in their first deportment class. She patted Stephen's letter burning a hole in her pocket, determined not to wrinkle it with her fidgeting.

This is not a firing squad. You're doing what you must, Dorothy Meyer. You've already received more grace than you deserve. Face what comes. Dorothy repeated those words again and again in her mind as she stepped through the door, crossed the drive, and forcing herself to smile, stepped into the widespread arms of the effervescent Susannah.

—

"It's only right that we're here first, to greet her. Ruth says she's fragile—in a way—and steeled in others. I don't know what that means but you know Ruth, she's all about psychology these days with her social work and everything. What I absolutely don't understand is why Addie's going by a different name and why she didn't tell us she was alive. The idea—making us all think she'd been violently killed all these years. Ruth says she's ashamed of her burn scars. Did she think we'd care about that more than about her? Do you know what happened to Bernadette's father?"

Dorothy shook her head. She couldn't keep up with Susannah's runaway monologue and didn't know anything.

"I was counting the years and months since Bernadette's birth and they just don't add up, not unless—well, I wonder if that's part of the reason she 'disappeared.' But I shouldn't have said that. Who knows and who cares? I'm just so amazed and glad Addie's alive." Susannah gripped Dorothy's arm. "Look! Here they come now."

Dorothy sucked in her breath. Even from a distance and after all these years, she could recognize her friend—still elegant and stylish—and the years fell away. Based on all Bernadette had said in the past, she'd fully expected her mother to appear in outdated clothing and a dark veil from hairline to shoulders, her hair pulled forward to cover scars. But the woman keeping pace with Ruth wore a trim sky-blue and white suit, belted at the waist and cut on the bias—something she'd expect from a Claudette Colbert film—and an angled Garbo slouch hat, her hair cut in a cascade of close brown curls that framed her face.

It was only when the two came close, Ruth smiling broadly and Addie's eye alive with uncertainty, that Dorothy saw that one side of Addie's face was softly scarred and that the eye on that side gazed straight forward, unblinking, no matter where her other eye roved. Makeup had done an admirable job of taming the red that peeked above her collar.

But nothing could steal Dorothy's love for her friend or the sadness for Addie's fears and her own selfishness that had kept them apart. Tears threatening, she opened her arms and walked toward Addie, folding her friend to her heart.

Addie shuddered and Dorothy held her tighter. *Perhaps if I don't let go, the bad will all go away and only love will survive.* "I'm sorry. I'm so very sorry." Dorothy said the words over and over and meant them from the depths of her heart.

Chapter Forty-Eight

JULY 1935

It was as if the years had fallen away and we were girls again—girls in the dormitory—and I'd walked in after Dot had told the others that I was orphaned. Her arms about me made me tremble in my hurt, broken anger and longing to be held, to be loved.

I wanted to pull away from this woman who'd married Stephen the minute she'd thought I was dead, but I didn't want to be angry anymore and I didn't want to hurt Dot or Stephen. I was also responsible. I'd allowed them to believe my lie.

Stephen hadn't come to me, hadn't loved me as I'd hoped. But I wanted to be loved now. I wanted my friends. I wanted my sisters of the heart, Dorothy—Dot, my first real friend apart from PEI—most of all. I wanted to frame those thoughts into words, but she didn't let me speak. She just kept apologizing, and with every apology more of my hurt over her marriage to Stephen softened.

"If I could take back the years, all I did, I would."

Finally, shaking my head, I pulled away, gently as I could, swiping at the tears that surely must have made a wreck of the makeup Ruth had helped me apply. "Neither of us can take back those years. I'm the one that's sorry for letting you think—"

"That was cruel, you old thing, but I'll forgive you if you let me hug you!" Susannah bubbled, pulling me from Dot's arms. Susannah, still the tallest among us, hugged fiercely, until I couldn't breathe, until we pulled apart in tears and laughter that spread through the four of us.

Ruth looped her arm through mine and marched us all around the lake and to the gazebo. I bit my lip to push past the memory of the night Stephen had declared his love to me beneath its roof. I wondered if he'd met Dot there, and how often, if they courted there even now, after long years of marriage.

Dot must have read my mind, for she looked at me and again whispered, so that the others could not hear, "I'm sorry, Addie."

I nodded, my throat too tight to speak.

"Ladies of the Lake!" Ruth *ahem*ed to get our attention. She thrust her hand, open and palm down, to the middle of our circle. "All for one!"

We joined ours on top, one after another, mine last of all, until together we chorused, "And one for all! We are the Ladies of the Lake!"

We fell quiet then, staring at our hands bound in friendship, in trust. I'd been the one to pull back long ago, and I did so again. One by one our hands came away, until only Ruth's was left.

Ruth drew a deep breath and began. "It would be so easy to let the past remain in the past, to go forward in some stilted way, not a word spoken of all that wedged its way into our sisterhood. But if we do that, we're bound to drift away from one another, to persuade ourselves that little slights and hurts don't matter, to pretend we needn't address them because we've 'overcome' the most tumultuous rift in our lives, in our relationships. That would be a shame greater than the shame we've allowed these seventeen years because now we know better. We know where our bullying one another leads."

"Oh, Ruth, you're always so dramatic. I wouldn't say we bullied one another. We were just girls."

"We were bullies, Susannah. I was a bully. I bullied you all into siding with me against Stephen and Jonas and the Meyer family because I was devastated by my brother's death." She looked at me. "I should never have tried to talk you out of your friendship with Stephen and Jonas, your mother-daughter relationship with Mrs. Meyer. I'm sorry, Addie—Rosaline—and I'm deeply ashamed that I did that."

"You've already apologized, Ruth. You needn't—"

"Yes, I need to confess it here, before our sisters. And Dot, I'm sorry because I know I put you in a terrible situation. Siding with me meant driving a wedge between you and Rosaline and forcing you to hide your relationship with the Meyer family. I didn't even congratulate you on your wedding when you wrote me, not even after we lost Addie. I'm sorry. It was wrong of me."

Dot took Ruth's hands in her own and held them long, doing her best to gather her emotions. "I understand, better than you know."

"Well, I'm sorry, too," Susannah admitted. "Since you put it like that, I guess I bullied you both about the Meyer family, figuring it was only patriotic and right to stand by Ruth. I guess we all could have done better . . . should have done better.

"And I'm sorry I've been so taken up with my family that I've neglected you, Dot, and you, Ruth, all these years. Addie—or Rosaline, or whatever you want us to call you—I'm sorry for all that's happened to you. You didn't deserve that explosion or any of it. Let us make up these years to you; let's all make them up to one another as best we can.

"I don't want to lose another minute of our friendship, girls. The truth is, children grow up and move on with their lives. Husbands become busy with their work and who knows what. But women need friends, real, true friends, and we're the best we've got."

It was the longest speech I'd ever heard Susannah make and we all looked at her, slightly aghast.

"We're the only ones we've known so long, the only ones who knew us when we were that young." Dorothy still looked sad.

"Young and foolish," Susannah amended.

At that moment Susannah gave a wave over our heads. We all turned to see a man in chauffer's uniform standing at the top of the hill. He picked up what looked to be a large picnic hamper and carried it down the hill and around the lake toward us.

"Rosaline, you're off the hook for baking this time since you traveled from Canada. You always made the best cherry scones—or did you get Mrs. Potts to make them? My cook has never been able to come close—so I do want those next time, but just this once I'm providing the tea."

"Susannah, you're the hostess extraordinaire!" Ruth enthused.

"Where shall I spread the tea, madam?" The chauffer spoke so formally but with such a strong Southern accent that we very nearly giggled.

That made Susannah lift her chin. "I think on this ledge here, Roland." She turned to us. "I'm afraid we're going to have to use the benches for seating, ladies. I'm no longer up to sitting on the floor."

"As if any of us are!" Ruth agreed.

Dot and I looked at each other and smiled. I figured we'd both be up to exactly that. There was something lovely in knowing what the other thought, even after all these years. Perhaps we could rekindle our friendship. If it was just the two of us, perhaps. But with Stephen beside her, I wasn't sure.

Roland, evidently experienced in the practice, spread the tea quickly and with grand presentation, then disappeared up the hill. Susannah smiled, quite pleased with herself.

"There are some advantages to old money. We'd not too much invested in the stock market when it crashed. Daddy never trusted it and Reginald's head is in politics. Well, ladies, may I serve you?"

Our bone china cups and plates filled, Ruth offered a sincere prayer of thanksgiving for restoration, for friendship, and for peace between us.

"Amen," Susannah said, "with a P.S. that we appreciate the good food, too."

Dot smiled.

How I loved these women, these sisters of my heart. How I'd missed them. Each one different, each one special, each one her own unique creation of the Lord.

While we all sipped the sweet peach tea and tasted the dainty chicken salad and cucumber sandwiches Susannah had provided, we fell silent for the first time.

It had been so many years since I'd been there that the calls of the birds from the trees, the gentle breeze blowing off the lake, the smell of the emerald freshly cut grass, and the sugar sweetness of the tea filled my senses like music of the soul. My heart overflowed in gratitude for receiving all I'd believed lost. Handel's "Hallelujah" chorus came to mind.

Then I thought of all that could never be, and my heart perversely ached. How could two such things thrive in the same breast? I gritted my teeth, determined not to lose the gift before me for want of the hope unattained. *Lord, help me.*

The clock in the school tower struck three thirty.

"Where has the time gone?" Susannah sighed. "I hate to say it, but duty calls. I must get back to the hotel. Reginald's expecting me to meet him. We're to entertain some senator or other and his wife this afternoon." She rolled her eyes. "I'm supposed to be impressed and feel privileged, but I'd much rather while away the afternoon with y'all."

Ruth smiled. "Ah. But we're no longer girls and our time is not always our own. A telegram came in from my office just before we left, something I must attend to."

"Not bad news?" She'd not mentioned a thing on our ride to the school.

"No, but I really must reply during business hours."

"I'll go with you."

"No, Addie—sorry, Rosaline—please. Please stay." Dot reached for my arm. "I want—I need to talk with you privately, and Stephen and Jonas want to stop to see you. I made them promise not to come until four so we'd have plenty of time."

Stephen and Jonas. "I—I can't. I really must go with Ruth."

"I'll make certain you get to the hotel. The school has a car. Bernadette asked permission to go back with you. I promise we'll send the car whenever you want to go," Dorothy all but pleaded.

Ruth gave me no chance to respond. "That's a splendid idea. In the meantime, the two of you can catch up a little more."

I tried to give Ruth my panicked eye as she stood, dusting off her skirt, and turned to go, but she refused to look my way. "Really, I don't want to be any trouble. I'll go back with Ruth and see them—see you all at the graduation tomorrow."

Now Ruth did look me fully in the eye. "You need to meet with each of your old friends for the first time in private. We need that from you, Rosaline. You can do the meet and greet with all the unknowns at tonight's dinner or tomorrow, but your friends need this time. We've all believed you were taken from us in a horrific moment, and we've grieved—each of us, terribly, for a very long time. We've missed you more than you'll ever know. You owe Stephen and Jonas that, as much as I owed you all my apology." With that, she walked away.

Susannah blushed over Ruth's blunt directive but busied herself with packing the hamper, while motioning to Roland to come and retrieve it. "There, that's done. I'm off. I'll see you sweeties tomorrow! Save us seats together as usual, won't you, Dot?" She waved over her shoulder without looking back and was gone in Ruth's footsteps in moments.

I stood, frozen in time and space, unable to look Dot in the face. Meeting all together was one thing, but being alone with Mrs. Meyer was another, the idea of meeting with Stephen and Jonas all but impossible. I stared after Susannah as if she were the departing rescue ship *Carpathia*, leaving me stranded in the sea after the sinking of *Titanic*.

"Addie," Dot whispered.

I couldn't turn to face her, not just then.

She set her hand on my back and the very humanity of her touch nearly undid me.

"I know you want us—want me—to call you Rosaline. And I will. But for this moment, before Stephen and Jonas come, I need to call you by your old name. There's something I need to say, to confess to Addie MacNeill, and then I promise to use your new name—your name—forever."

Still, I couldn't turn to face her but stepped away, leaving the conflict of her touch behind. "You've already apologized, Dot. You've nothing to confess. You thought I was dead, and I let you. There was no reason you shouldn't marry him, shouldn't be happy." It was what I'd told myself, rehearsed a hundred times.

"But I took the life that was yours, the family I knew you wanted more than anything."

Stop. Please stop. Please, God, make her stop. "I can't do this, Dot. I want to be happy for you." I turned to face her. "I'm trying. To love and be loved is the greatest gift on earth, and I'm glad you have that."

"But you could have had it, too, and if I'd done as Stephen asked me, everything would have been different. He's never stopped loving you, you know. He's never stopped grieving for you. When we believed you'd died, it nearly destroyed him."

"But you were there to pick up the pieces."

"Of course I tried, but no one could do that. No one could take your place."

"He didn't love me, Dot, not as I believed. He never came to Halifax as he'd promised, never asked my brother for my hand, never even telephoned to say he'd changed his mind—which, obviously, he had."

"No, he didn't. He couldn't phone, not because he didn't love you. He loved you with all his heart. That's what I'm trying to tell you."

"Please, don't lie to me, Dot." *He couldn't have loved me one minute and married you the next.*

"But it's true, and you would have known if word had reached you before the Halifax Explosion—if I'd mailed his letter. But I was angry and hurt and so blind with jealousy . . . that I didn't. I'm sorry, Addie. I've been sorry every day of my life since."

My head ached. "What are you talking about?" I wanted to push her away and I wanted to understand. The conflict spun a wheel in my brain.

"It was the war. Remember all the anti-German sentiment against the Meyer family? How Mr. Meyer lost his job, how even Ruth and the headmistress of Lakeside treated them?"

I could not forget.

"A brick was thrown through their window—a brick with an ugly, hateful message shattered their kitchen window and flew straight into Mother Meyer's head as she stood at her sink washing dishes."

I'd known from Ruth that Mr. and Mrs. Meyer were both dead and gone, but she'd not told me this.

"It happened shortly after you left for Halifax. She died, Addie. She died without ever regaining consciousness."

My hand flew to my mouth. It was years ago, but I'd loved Mrs. Meyer with all that was in me. I remembered her more clearly than I remembered my own mother.

"The authorities kept Mr. Meyer and Jonas and Stephen under what amounted to house arrest until they left for military duty, saying it was for their own protection. Their phone lines had been cut. Guards were placed by their drive. There was no way for Stephen to leave or phone you or even write."

I needed to sit down. The horror was too much. "Mrs. Meyer? Who would do such a thing?" I closed my eyes. "Poor Mr. Meyer. What did you mean? You said there was a—"

"A letter." Dorothy sighed as if shedding the weight of the world from her shoulders. "Stephen snuck out, came in the dead of night to the school and begged me to help him. He wanted so much to telephone you, to explain why he couldn't come. The headmistress's office was locked and, in those days, hers was the only telephone, you know. So he wrote you a letter explaining, a letter I promised to mail for him right away—the next day. I vowed, but I didn't do it. I'm sorry, Addie. I'm so very sorry."

The idea that Stephen hadn't deserted me, hadn't abandoned me, flooded and overwhelmed my thinking.

"I was infatuated with Stephen. I wanted him to love me instead of you. When I saw that he loved you, planned to marry you, I was so angry, crazy with hurt. Surely you remember."

I did. And now I began to see that it wasn't Stephen who'd deserted or betrayed me, but Dot. "Infatuated? You said you loved him."

"I thought I did. I would have, if he'd given me a chance, but the truth is we were all wrong for each other. He could never love anyone but you. It was selfish and mean of me, and I've no excuse—not then and not now." Dot pulled a faded letter from her pocket. "This is long overdue, but it's meant for you. It was always meant for you."

She held the letter out to me, but how could I take it—a letter written before he was her husband?

"I meant to mail it, eventually, but then we heard about the explosion. When your letter came—your last letter—I wrote to your address right away, but it was returned, marked *Deceased*. The board of governors sent a man to investigate in the hope that you made it out of the house somehow, but he came back saying everyone was killed."

"And Stephen—"

"Didn't even know about the explosion for weeks because he was forcibly detained in the States and then sent to Europe to help with German translation work in the field. Jonas was here for two weeks more but then sent, too. They were heroes for the war effort, both of them, but each came back with his own injuries."

"You married soon after the explosion."

"Yes, we did, before he was sent overseas. Jonas and Stephen were both grieving beyond measure. They were prohibited from corresponding for the security of their work, and probably because they were suspect for their nationality. There were long stretches of time when I didn't know where either of them was, if they were even alive, and all that time I believed I'd lost you. I can't tell you how hard that was—how lonely.

"It wasn't right for me to marry. I didn't love him—not right away, not like that, but I felt so guilty about everything, and I thought, by helping one through his grief, it might somehow help them both, might even be something you would want me to do."

I shook my head, devoid of understanding. Yet somewhere in her convoluted explanation, I'd taken the letter, unfolding just enough to recognize Stephen's handwriting—*My Darling Addie*. I nearly choked before folding it again. I couldn't read it, not then, not in front of Dot, though she'd surely read it a thousand times.

"Yesterday I confessed to Stephen and Jonas what I'd done. I've carried that shame all these years, Addie."

You want me to feel sorry for you?

"Stephen was hurt and angry when I told him—horrified to realize that you never knew why he hadn't met you, that you might have believed he didn't want to. I hope—in time—he'll forgive me. I'm not sure Jonas will, and I'll have to live with that. Please, Addie." She reached for my hand. "I know I've no right to ask, but please, will you forgive me for not mailing that letter when I should have, when there might have been time for it to make a difference?"

In Halifax the north face of the city hall clock was broken, having stopped at 9:04 the morning of—the moment of—the Halifax Explosion. It had never started and would never be replaced. I felt like that clock face, broken, unable to move forward, and that I must exist in this broken state forever, a memorial for all to see.

Dot was right. Her failure to send the letter was immature, self-ish, but a part of me understood. I'd known she loved Stephen since we were little more than children. I knew she'd felt hurt and betrayed by us both. But how she could see that as the ultimate betrayal and yet consider marrying him an act of rescue, I didn't understand. And yet, here we were. Here we all would be soon. I could have the friendship of both, perhaps, but not of one, alone, not if it meant straining their marriage. If I refused Dot, I would lose them both forever.

Father, help me, please. Help me release them to You. Help me see and forgive and love them as You love them, as You have loved and forgiven me.

"If I could in any way undo the past, you know I would. You have to believe that."

I did believe her. I of all people knew the truth of that. "Not one of us can change the past. If I had only known Stephen wanted to come to me . . . that would have made all the difference. Still, the truth is, I didn't want him to see me after the explosion. I wanted to disappear, to die, perhaps would have . . . except for Bernadette."

Dot seemed to have stopped breathing. A minute must have passed before she sat down beside me. "Bernadette is wonderful. She's you in so many ways. She's why I first wondered . . . But I have to ask you, Addie . . . is Bernadette Stephen's daughter?"

If she'd asked me if the moon was woven of cornsilk and sand I could not have been more shocked. "How can you ask me that? Imagine that? You can't possibly be jealous of—" I stopped. "Is this because you've not borne children? You want to take mine?"

"No!" Dorothy's color rose in a peak of shame. "I'm counting the number of lives I've ruined. Has Bernadette lived without her father all these years because I didn't send the letter?"

And that was when I saw Dot's heart—the Dot I knew as a girl, the Dot who'd climbed the maple tree with me and tap-tap-tapped on Mean Mildred's window, the Dot who'd risen to my defense the night Mean Mildred sent me out into the storm alone, the Dot who'd overcome the stigma of befriending an orphan girl from PEI and invited her to her home for Christmas. She was worried for Bernadette, as well as for me, sorry for what she'd done or might have done to both of us.

"You don't have that much power, Dot. God is Father to the fatherless. He's been my husband and Bernadette's father since we lost everything and everyone in that explosion." I watched the color in my friend's complexion gradually return, saw years of anxiety and dread lift from the corners of her eyes. "There's more to Bernadette's story, but Stephen had no part in it. I'm sure he loves you, that he has loved you through all these years. You've no reason to fear any claim to him on my account or Bernadette's."

"Claim on Stephen? No, Addie—"

"You've confessed and apologized. I forgive you. Now, please accept me as I am and call me Rosaline. You promised. Going forward is our only option."

"But you're mistaken. Stephen doesn't love me—" Dot stopped midsentence and looked up the hill behind me, her eyes growing wide, her brow furrowed. "It's them—Jonas and Stephen."

"No, please. I'm not ready." I must have whispered for Dot never acknowledged my plea.

She stood and pulled me to my feet beside her. "Turn around, Rosaline. Turn around and face them."

I might have run the other way but for Dot's strong arm behind me. Ruth had warned me of Jonas's limp, of Stephen's missing arm, of the gas burns on his neck and face. But the men walking toward us looked perfect to me—tall, distinguished, broad across the chest and shoulders. The nearer they came the faster Stephen walked, half running as if he could not wait to reach us. Jonas, with his stilted gait, came on more slowly, but I couldn't see him, for my gaze took in only Stephen walking in front, a broad smile crossing his face and filling his eyes.

"Addie! Addie!" He spoke as a man in a dream, and climbing the gazebo stairs two at a time, he crushed me to his chest, and lifting me off the ground, swung me around. I closed my eyes and breathed in the scent of him, the scent I'd imagined night after night for seventeen years. His scars were nothing, meant nothing to me.

But my racing heart was wrong. My love for him was wrong. He was Dot's husband, my friend's husband. I pushed him away. "Stephen, no." The name came out in a half breath.

He set me down, surely sensing my resistance. "Addie. Forgive me. It's a miracle. Seeing you here, alive."

Jonas had reached the gazebo by then. "Addie." He hugged me gently, as an old friend might. "It's good to see you, good to have you home."

"Home." I hadn't thought that word about Lakeside in years.

And then Jonas astonished me by taking Dot in his arms and kissing her hair, holding her close beside him, both of them smiling at Stephen and me as if the world had righted itself after a very long time off-kilter. I couldn't understand it. They were brother- and sister-in-law, but they didn't look it, didn't act it.

It dawned on me in the same moment that I believe my thoughts were known to Dot. Her eyes grew round, and her hand went to her heart. "You thought I'd married Stephen all those years ago, didn't you?"

"You did. Didn't you?" My heart's pace before was a slow turtle crawl compared to its ripping speed in that moment. Or perhaps it stopped, dead. I couldn't tell, knew only that I could not breathe. I looked up at Stephen, who hadn't taken his eyes off me, who hadn't stopped pouring love into his smile, hadn't stopped nearly laughing for joy.

But it was Jonas who spoke first. "Never. I swept Dorothy off her feet before they sent me overseas. I wasn't about to wait and lose the love of my life."

"The love of your life?" She looked up at him, hopefully. "Do you forgive me?"

"Always." He kissed her hair again and then her hand, still proudly holding her by his side. "I'd be stupid not to. Stephen convinced me of that." He smiled at his brother and me, giving his blessing.

I dared to look up into Stephen's face then, dared him to clearly see my scars, my glass eye. "Then, you—"

"Have been waiting a lifetime, and at last you've come home." He smoothed the hair back from my face, his palm against my scarred cheek. We stood there, looking into each other's eyes. I tried so hard to decipher the years and what they meant.

"I believe," said Jonas diplomatically, "that we need to give these two time alone. They've waited long enough. We'll see you at the dinner tonight, Addie—or Rosaline, if you prefer. I think my brother would like your full attention."

Dot smiled, her face still awash in the wonder of our misunderstanding—of my misconception, of all that meant and all it might come to mean.

Neither Stephen nor I spoke. There were no words to fill the space. We didn't wait to watch them leave but turned away. He drew me to the nearest bench. We sat, my hand in his, our knees and shoulders touching. He felt my arm, my shoulder. I touched his face, cupping my hand over his burns, and felt the love and fear and uncertainty pour out of me.

Can this gift be real? Can this man be real and not a dream? If not, I didn't want to wake, not ever. *Dear God,* I prayed, *I'm content to die here of happiness.*

"Dorothy told me you never received my letter, could never have known why I didn't come."

"I thought you'd abandoned me. I wrote you the most hateful letter. I'm sorry."

"I never got it. We were escorted away to service—as soon as we buried Mama."

"I can't even comprehend the pain of losing her like that. Your mother was the dearest—"

"She loved you with all her heart—the daughter she never had."

I nearly sobbed, but there was so much more to say. "When I learned that Dot was Mrs. Meyer, I thought that you'd married. I knew nothing about your mother or father or the authorities taking you away until Dot told me now—none of it."

He shook his head, still holding my hand, bringing it to his lips. "When you didn't come back, when we heard nothing all these years, we believed we'd lost you in the explosion. But Dorothy said you married someone else . . . that he died in the war."

I couldn't let Stephen believe I'd given my heart, my life to another or borne another man's child. "Bernadette was my brother's child—Lemuel and Bertha's. She was born just a few days before the explosion. That morning, I was with Portia Cadeau, a woman who nursed the baby. We were outside the house, more protected by a stone wall, when all the world blew up—the house and Bertha and everyone in it. Lemuel and Marcus were killed as well. Portia's entire family—her husband and child, her home, everything disappeared in a moment."

"Addie!"

"For days I lay unconscious. When I woke, I believed I was the only one of my family left, until Portia found me. She'd saved Bernadette, and together we've raised her."

"But . . . your name is Murray."

"Murray is a fiction—my mother's maiden name. I changed my name and made that up about her father because I didn't want to be found, and because I didn't want Bernadette to bear the stigma of being orphaned—that's just too hard. I'd lost my parents when I was young. I wanted Bernadette to believe that at least she still had a mother.

"When you didn't come, I thought you no longer wanted me. Between my injuries and need to care for Bernadette, I knew I couldn't teach. I thought there was nothing for me to come back to." I held my breath, needing to confess the truth, no matter how he reacted. "There has never been anyone else for me."

"Addie. My Addie. Scars would have made no difference to me— make no difference. Look at me. Would you—will you turn away from me because my arm is buried somewhere in France? Because my face and neck and chest are covered in mustard gas burns?"

I shook my head vehemently. "Never."

"I never loved Dot. Only you, always you. Please tell me we have a chance at last—a future together."

They were words I'd never dared imagine I'd hear. I closed my eyes and leaned my head against his chest. He wrapped his arm around me, pulling me close, and time stood still.

Chapter Forty-Nine

JULY 1935

The Lakeside tower clock struck five. It seemed only minutes since I'd seen Stephen for the first time in all the years of Bernadette's life. But this night was to honor Bernadette and her graduating friends at their baccalaureate dinner. We couldn't allow our reunion to interfere.

There was time to meet Bernadette as Dot had said, drive back to the hotel for tea and a change of clothing, then return for the formal dinner and service at eight. Since Bernadette had asked to spend time with me, I dared hope that the prying open of my Pandora's box of secrets hadn't proven beyond redemption in our relationship.

Stephen took my arm and walked me round the lake and up the hill. Bernadette stood on the front steps of the school, already dressed for the evening's dinner and service. Her eyebrows rose to see my arm in Stephen's.

328

With Ruth long gone to the hotel, Stephen insisted on driving Bernadette and me the short distance into town, though how we could possibly behave like disinterested parties before her I could not imagine. To my surprise, he didn't try.

He held open the door for each of us as we stepped into the shared backseat. Once settled behind the wheel, Stephen fumbled with the ignition, gave a half laugh, and smiled into the rearview mirror. "I've never chauffeured two such lovely ladies at once. I'm afraid it's gone to my head."

Bernadette's eyes widened. She leaned over and whispered in my ear, "I can't believe you know him, too. You've got to tell me everything."

"I will," I promised, "as soon as we're alone."

"And anything she won't tell you, just ask me." Stephen winked at Bernadette.

It wasn't until we reached the hotel minutes later and he helped us out of the car that Bernadette whispered to Stephen coyly and conspiratorially, "You were eavesdropping!"

"Only when it counts." He grinned, and couldn't stop grinning as he looked at me, which of course led me to a ridiculous amount of grinning, too.

Bernadette's good eye shot back and forth between us. "Something tells me there's quite a story here."

"That's enough now." I did my best to stand straight, to act prim and proper and slightly miffed, but Stephen laughed simply for the joy of the moment, and it was no use. "Come along, Bernadette. Mr. Meyer, we thank you very much for the ride into town. I imagine we'll see you later this evening."

"I'm counting on it, Mrs. Murray." He tipped his hat as he held the hotel door for us.

"Mother, he winked at us!" Bernadette exclaimed the moment the door closed behind us.

"Surely you're mistaken." I held my head high as we ascended the stairs, but my heart flip-flopped like a fish out of water. By the time we reached our floor I was breathless, not from the exertion but from the hope that beat like a wild and feathered thing in my heart.

"Okay, Mother," Bernadette ordered, once in my room, "I thought all the surprises were out. Tell me. What's going on?"

I pulled the pin from my hat and set it on the dressing table. I watched Bernadette's reflection in the mirror, praying all the while for words that would help her understand, help her know how very much I loved her, how my world had revolved and still revolved around her. This new discovery would not change that, could never change it. "It's another long story and not nearly as important to me as you are." I reached for her hand. "Have you had time to think about . . . everything?"

She looked away and shrugged, a little helplessly. "It was a shock. I never imagined you were not my . . . my mother. But you are. You're the only mother I've ever known—you and Portia. You're my family."

"I wish with all my heart you could have known your birth mother and father, and Marcus. They loved you so. I'm sorry for all you've missed, my darling."

Bernadette shook her head. "I wish that, too. But how can I miss people I haven't known? What in life have I missed—except maybe meeting Lucy Maud Montgomery in person?" She smiled. "What I know is that I've always had you, the best mother, and Portia, the best aunt in the world. You taught me at home, sent me to the school for the blind for that bit of time where I learned everything I needed to come here. I didn't want to go there or to come here, not at first, but you made me. Like your brother—my father—made you. You know, I felt like that girl in the poem 'The Lady of Shalott'—stranded, always looking out at the world but never able to go into it. Coming here, it's been the making of me—the friends I've made, learning I can step into the outside world, that I don't have to hide, after all."

I pulled her fingers to my lips and kissed them. She was so like me, like the woman I was, the girl I had been. There was nothing I could do about the tears streaming down both our faces. And then we were hugging, hugging for all we were worth, and then laughing . . . a little.

By the time we pulled apart her gown was wrinkled and our hand-kerchiefs sodden.

"But I have to know about Mr. Meyer. I've never seen him with anyone! You knew him from before, didn't you?"

I pressed my lips together, trying not to smile wider than the sun. "I did."

"Tell me—everything!"

"I will, but you need to eat something. It's a long while until dinner. I need to change my clothing."

"I'm so nervous about tonight I only want a half sandwich and tea."

"That suits me perfectly." With my own nerves aflutter, I couldn't imagine eating anything.

"All right. I'll get something from the dining room while you change. And then I want to know everything. Promise!"

I touched up my makeup and hair. By the time I'd changed into the formal wear Ruth had insisted I buy—a sleek and silken gown of deep red wine—Bernadette had returned with a plate of finger sandwiches. She fastened the tiny buttons up my back, ones I could not have hoped to reach.

"This is stunning, Mother. You're stunning." Bernadette spoke wonderingly, as if the moment might disappear.

"Ruth helped me choose." I tried to make light, but to wear something so beautiful, to feel any amount of beautiful once more was almost more than I could bear.

"I like her better all the time." She finished, stood back, and placed her hands on her hips. "Now, tell me. Wait, let's get comfortable. I think this is going to be quite a tale."

Bernadette sat cross-legged on the bed, completely out of character for my graduating daughter in her long gown. "So, how do you know Mr. Meyer?"

I pulled off my shoes and sat on the opposite side of the bed, leaning back against the bedframe, careful not to muss my hair. We'd been there before. I prayed this part of my tale would bring Bernadette happiness.

"Wait—is Mr. Meyer the man you were supposed to meet in the gardens? The man who never showed?"

Bernadette had always been perceptive, but I hadn't expected her to jump years ahead of me. At last I nodded. "I've learned, in the last few hours, that he had a very good reason for not showing up that day. I should never have doubted him, or his love."

Bernadette was silent a long time. I didn't fill the space. The details were mine. The shame that Dot and I both shared in all that had happened was our private story. Bernadette did not need to know.

"You gave up your life with Mr. Meyer to raise me. Are you sorry?"

"Never! Never for a moment. And I didn't give up my life with Stephen to raise you; I wanted you. You were all the family I had, and I loved you from the moment I saw you. Your mother had asked me to care for you and your brother if anything ever happened to her and your father. They were going to name me your godmother."

"But you didn't come back to Mr. Meyer. If it wasn't for me, you could have—"

"No. I wouldn't have returned to Lakeside. When he didn't meet me and didn't telephone or telegraph, I thought he didn't love me. I learned today that was not true. He was prevented from coming and tried to get word to me but . . . then the explosion came—something he didn't learn of for quite some time because he was away in the war. When he did learn of it, he believed me dead, as did everyone here.

"No, it was my own fault. I went into hiding. I didn't want any of my friends to see me as I was then, and that was wrong of me—to let them think I'd died, to not give them the opportunity to love me through it all. I've missed so much of life and I've denied you so much because of my fear, because of my hiding. I'm sorry, Bernadette."

Bernadette shook her head. "Stop apologizing to me, Mother. It's not right. You've nothing to be sorry about on my account. What about Mr. Meyer now? He's still in love with you, that's plain to see."

I sighed, unable to believe all that had happened in an afternoon. "I don't know. We're not the same people as we were all those years ago."

Bernadette sat up straighter. "But you are—only older and wiser. He's a good man. All the girls are wild about him. Sounds like girls have been wild about him forever. And, when you were younger you—wait. You said my family's name was MacNeill. You're a MacNeill. You're—are you Adelaide MacNeill? The one killed in the blast that they're dedicating the gymnasium to?"

I covered my face with my hands. "That's why they can't do that."

"That's why you wouldn't help them with the fundraising for the gymnasium—because you're not dead." She sat back against the bedframe. "Whoa! What a hoot. Adelaide MacNeill."

"It's not a hoot, it's a tragedy. I can't let them dedicate a building in memorial to a woman who's not dead. I can't pretend that—"

"Well, it won't matter if the school closes." Bernadette wrapped her arms around herself. "It just can't close, Mother. This can't be the end here."

"I'll do everything I can to see that Lakeside remains open, if it's possible."

"It's got to be possible. Mrs. Meyer invited me to teach here, at least before she knew about the school maybe closing. I know Portia told you so don't pretend to be surprised. I'll come home for the summer, but I can't stay there. You understand, don't you? If I don't step out into the world now, when I'm at my strongest, I may not. And there's someone I'd like you to meet, someone who's become very special to me."

Yes, Portia told me about the offer to teach, but who is this someone? She's making plans, which I knew would come. She still calls me Mother. Thank You, God! Thank You! "Yes, my darling girl, I do understand. I'll miss you, but I understand. I want you to live as full and as joyful a life as possible, as exists anywhere in this world."

"You'll be lonely there, especially when Portia marries her greengrocer."

"I will." I swallowed the lump in my throat. *Yes, I will.*

"You'll need someone to keep you occupied while I'm working here, or when I'm married, and you must realize that could happen.

After a suitable but short courtship, I suppose you'll marry Mr. Meyer. You've wasted too much time already."

"Slow down, Daughter!" It felt so good to call her that. "You, working and married, and you'd have me married, too? Besides, Stephen and I hardly know one another anymore. We've lived—still live separate lives in separate countries."

"But you'll get to know him again, won't you? We don't need to go home right away. There's no need as long as we're here together. You won't push him away or run and hide again, will you?"

When did she get to be the parent in this relationship? "I'd like to think . . . But what about you? Would you like to get to know him? Can you imagine him as a part of our lives?"

Bernadette smiled, her full, engaging smile, and wrapped her arms around me in a bear hug. She scooted off the bed, stood with one hip out and one finger on her chin, gazing toward the ceiling in consideration. "Hmm. Let me think. Handsome, gallant, war hero Mr. Meyer as my father? Would I like to see the romance of the century unfold before my eyes? Could I entertain the notion of your permanent move to Connecticut? Well—" she winked—"I suppose I could get used to the idea of you and Mr. Meyer living just down the road, as long as you don't embarrass me half to death by cuddling in public."

I gasped and we both laughed aloud until I threw a pillow at her, and she threw it back.

We made the baccalaureate dinner in time . . . barely.

Chapter Fifty

JULY 1935

The bittersweet morning of graduation Dorothy smoothed her makeup, combed her hair in place, and applied a light brush of lipstick. This would be Lakeside Ladies Academy's last graduating class. She wanted to look her best for the girls, to think only of the girls— the young ladies—waltzing their daisy chain over the hill, receiving diplomas, earned in every respect—and to imagine their futures, how they would walk into the world, heads held high, and make a positive impact, a difference.

She glanced at her husband in the mirror, watching as he struggled with cuff links, turning his wrists first one way and then another. Finally, she rose from her dressing table and nestled her back into his chest, lifting his wrist to do the job for him. He wrapped his other arm around her waist and nuzzled her neck from behind. She smiled, taking longer than necessary to work the cuff links through their buttonholes.

She'd confided to Addie that she'd not fully loved Jonas when they first married. That was true, but long past. She marveled at how their love had grown through the years. Only the secrets she'd kept hidden had created a veil between them. Her confession the day before to Stephen and to Jonas about the letter not mailed and her jealousy in those long-ago years had ripped that veil away. Jonas's forgiveness, and his understanding after wrestling with his own soul, were gifts she'd not dared hope for.

His late-night confession that he'd urged their marriage out of desperation, loneliness, and grief when he knew she was smitten with Stephen and grieving Addie came as a revelation. If anything, their mutual confessions drew them closer, enabling them to live and hope in a new way, to move as an extension of one another.

Had Dorothy not been headmistress of Lakeside Ladies Academy, she would have in that moment forgone graduation and locked their door. But she was headmistress, at least for this day.

"Duty calls, my love." She finished working the cuff links through their holes and kissed his hand.

He turned her to face him, kissed her fully on the mouth, and stood back. "May I escort the esteemed Mrs. Meyer to the podium?"

"You may. For one last time."

"Don't give up hope, my love. I haven't. Stephen hasn't. He's still working on it with the board and the bank. No matter what happens, when this long and momentous day is done, I will escort you home."

"You will." She smiled. "And I will gladly take your arm."

Tents had been erected across the lawns of the academy to shade refreshment tables. By ten thirty a small orchestra had assembled on one side, busily unpacking and tuning their instruments. Each year Dorothy worried about the weather for their outdoor ceremony, but this July morning had dawned perfect: comfortably warm and sunny with a gentle breeze off the lake—a day to remember.

Dorothy counted the chairs that had been set up earlier. Graduates would sit in the front rows, their parents and families in the section behind. Ancients, students, and visitors who'd snagged an invitation sat in the general seating areas. Members of the board of governors and visiting dignitaries sat either on the platform or with their spouses throughout the audience, depending on their role in the event. Few seats were reserved, but Dorothy had always made certain there was a particular row for the Ladies of the Lake in the years they met. Each year of her tenure Dorothy had kept one seat empty by placing a program on it in tribute to Addie. This year, that seat would be filled, and no doubt Stephen would claim the one beside her, as he should, as it should have been all along.

Dorothy placed her speech on the shelf beneath the podium, tweaked the floral arrangements on either side of the platform, and drew a deep breath. Everything looked ready. Once the audience had assembled, teachers would escort the graduating class to their seats as the orchestra played; then she and the morning's speakers would march up the center aisle to take their positions. She walked down the outside aisle to the back. It was time to greet and welcome the speakers.

"Good morning, Mrs. Meyer." The head of the board of governors, the last person Dorothy wished to see at this moment, blocked her path.

"Mr. Blankenship," she responded, forcing a smile.

"A perfect day, don't you agree?" He smiled smugly.

"It is a lovely day. I'm glad for our graduates and their families. It marks a fitting end." *The last graduating class.* She didn't want to ask, but she must know before the ceremony began. She couldn't risk being taken by surprise. "Will you announce the closing of the academy when you speak?"

His smile grew broader. "About that. Last night, after the baccalaureate service, I had the opportunity to meet with Mr. Hardinger, president of the bank. His new wife is an alumna, you know."

"I did know."

"He has agreed to delay the calling of our note."

"He has?"

"Yes. It's a messy business, really, but might save us. When the truth of the case was revealed and Mr. Shockley absconded, the bank intended to foreclose on his house, a rather palatial estate that he'd been making payments on with the school's tuition funds. Apparently the charlatan had the good grace to retitle the house to Lakeside before leaving for parts unknown. I imagine he hopes we'll drop charges. Mr. Hardinger believes that its sale should cover a fair percentage of our loan. In addition to your fundraiser, it may prove enough to make up for missed payments and reinstate our payment schedule.

"This doesn't mean we're home free, as they say, but it should move us well into next school year before we need to make more payments . . . assuming, of course, that the sale of the house goes through quickly."

Dorothy's heart fluttered, then fell. "Who can afford such a house in these times?"

"Apparently Mr. Hardinger has taken an interest. I believe he'll make us a reasonably fair offer."

"He wants to live there himself?" It sounded too good to be true.

Mr. Blankenship shrugged slightly. "He was widowed some years ago and recently remarried. His new wife is eager to move out of the first wife's house and begin entertaining, intending, I believe, to move up in local society. I think we can all afford to think well of Cupid's arrows."

Cupid's arrows . . . You've no idea! "That really is the best news possible."

"It's not a foregone conclusion, mind you, but likely enough that I believe we can safely welcome next year's class to Lakeside Ladies Academy."

"Thank you, Mr. Blankenship. Thank you!" Dorothy shook his hand.

"I might add that your fundraising efforts, Mrs. Meyer, yours and Mrs. Whitmore's, have proven most beneficial. The board won't look askance at such future endeavors—after a suitable time, tastefully and discreetly directed."

"I understand. I'll speak with Mrs. Whitmore."

"Very good. Well then, shall we welcome our speakers and prepare to graduate these young ladies for the year of our Lord nineteen hundred and thirty-five?" He offered his arm, which Dorothy took gladly, her smile outshining the sun.

"With pleasure, Mr. Blankenship."

Chapter Fifty-One

The baccalaureate service the night before had been beyond lovely by candlelight, inspiring through the choruses sung by the graduating class and the sermon delivered by Reverend Melrose, pastor of the church long attended by students and staff of Lakeside Ladies Academy. My heart had thrilled to sit with Stephen as we watched Bernadette. The moment brought to mind Lucy Maud Montgomery's words through Anne: *"Dear old world . . . you are very lovely and I am glad to be alive in you."* It was a night to remember, perhaps a new beginning for all I'd once hoped.

But I knew so well that the morning of graduation marked the true beginning of Bernadette's new life—not only achievements that I must congratulate but a life all her own that I must accept.

When I'd graduated there was no one to leave behind. I'd had no experience with leaving parents to an empty nest. Now, with Bernadette about to fly, I would be more alone than ever before.

340

Bernadette was right; Portia would marry Silas, her beloved greengrocer, next month—and she should. What of me? Did I love Stephen now as much as I loved my memories of him as a young man? Were we jumping headlong into a relationship when we both needed time to court, to get to know one another—not as the young and passionate people we'd been, but as the middle-aged man and woman we'd become? Were we running ahead of the Lord or walking in joyful acceptance of His blessing? I wanted to look at it all objectively, dispassionately, logically, but I didn't feel objective, dispassionate, or logical. I loved him. I'd always loved him, and I didn't want to miss another moment of life. Moments were all too few, each one uncertain of the next.

Bernadette was right on another score: there was no reason to rush back to Canada and every reason to stay in Connecticut for a time, for us both to get to know Stephen. There was so much I wanted to learn about his life, about the practice he and Jonas had set up together, and about the state of the academy and what I might do to help in its solvency.

Last night's service had run so late that Ruth and I'd agreed to breakfast in our rooms, then meet in the hotel lobby, where Stephen planned to join us and drive together to the academy.

I smiled as I buttoned the cuffs of the final dress Ruth had helped me select—a soft rose chiffon with billowing sleeves, heeled pumps, and a wide-brimmed hat to match, the ruffled collar just high enough to cover the worst of my scars. I took the stairs to the lobby, thinking never would I have selected a dress so showy or feminine on my own. I'd doubted Ruth's choice, but the moment I made the final turn on the stairs and saw Stephen waiting at the foot, saw his eyes alight in pleasure and eager approval, I knew Ruth had known exactly what she was doing.

"Good morning, Mrs. Murray." He smiled as slyly as a cat who'd swallowed a canary. "Beautiful. You're beautiful. You look good enough to eat."

I tried not to laugh and failed miserably. "Good morning, Mr. Meyer. You cut a dashing figure yourself today." And he did, in his trim gray suit. He took my arm and my breath at the same time. I was ashamed to realize I'd barely noticed Ruth by his side. Behind his head she gave me a wink, and I knew all was forgiven.

~

What I'd not expected, what she hadn't prepared me for in any way, was Bernadette's solo that morning. Following Mr. Blankenship's speech, Bernadette's valedictorian address, a classmate's salutatorian address, and the awarding of diplomas, her solo marked a fitting end to the day's ceremony.

In her second soprano voice, full and rich, each tone clear as the bells that rang over Halifax Harbor, Bernadette sang "Ah! Sweet Mystery of Life," a song popular when the Ladies of the Lake were young—when Stephen and I were young and full of dreams. When we were Bernadette's age.

> *Ah! Sweet mystery of life*
> *At last I've found thee*
> *Ah! I know at last the secret of it all;*
> *All the longing, seeking, striving, waiting, yearning*
> *The burning hopes, the joy and idle tears that fall!*
> *For 'tis love, and love alone, the world is seeking,*
> *And 'tis love, and love alone, that can repay!*
> *'Tis the answer, 'tis the end and all of living*
> *For it is love alone that rules for aye!*

Stephen reached for my hand as she sang. We knew the words, had lived the burning hopes, the longing, seeking, striving, waiting, yearning, even the joy and idle tears that fell. Had Bernadette chosen the song for us? No, that was impossible. Stephen and I had not been reunited until yesterday. Bernadette had not known of his existence in my life or of our thwarted romance until last evening, and her selection, with the approval of Dot, as the program testified, must have been made weeks ago.

Thank You, Father, for allowing me to hear her, that I didn't allow fear to keep me away as it's kept me hidden so many years. Thank You that Bernadette understands the supreme importance of love, of love You created, love You are, love You allow each of us, created in Your image, to share with one another.

I don't know if there were dry eyes when she finished. Mine weren't. I saw through her smile that as she sang the last note, Bernadette locked eyes with someone, but it wasn't me. I turned ever so slightly and saw the returned adoring gaze from a young man who was first on his feet to give her a standing ovation. We all stood, we all clapped, but I realized that this young man, whoever he was, held a special enthusiasm for my daughter and perhaps a significant portion of her heart.

As the class and dignitaries exited the aisle, Bernadette gave a victory wave to her young man, who brazenly winked in return.

Stephen brushed a tendril and a wayward tear from my cheek and whispered, "Does that bring back memories?"

"Blessed memories. It appears my daughter may be about to embark on ships to new horizons to create memories of her own, ships that don't include me."

Stephen tucked my hand in his. "I believe that's Charles James, a graduate last year from Dartmore."

After a flurry of congratulations for Bernadette and her friends and introduction to the dashing Charles James, now a distinguished university student, Bernadette had no eyes or ears for me.

Smiling, Stephen drew me away, offered his arm, which I happily took, and led me through the grounds and down the hill toward our gazebo. "I believe it's time we consider making some of our own memories, Mrs. Murray—Rosaline. New ones."

"Sweet ones, Mr. Meyer—Stephen. Yes, I agree."

His smile broadened as he led me up the steps and to a seat far from sight or sound of the departing guests. He brushed that pesky tendril from my cheek, then turned very serious. "I love you. I've always loved you. Every minute of every day, even when I thought you were gone forever."

I brushed the lock of breeze-swept hair from his forehead, allowing my fingers to linger at his temple before he reached for my hand. "I never stopped loving you, even when I thought I should, even when I tried."

"I hope you won't try too hard in future." His forehead creased. He looked so nervous I pitied him. "I'm wondering now what you think." He drew a rattled breath, tightening his grip on my fingers, then let them go in fear he might have squeezed too hard. He took my hand again, gently this time. "I'm settled comfortably in my practice here with Jonas, but I don't consider a move impossible. I know you're very successful in Canada. I don't know what a move to Connecticut might mean to you, so I don't want to presume. But I wonder how you'd feel, what you'd think . . . Are you married to the name Murray? I mean, do you think—in time—that a change to Rosaline Meyer might gain appeal, if only for legal purposes? Of course, you'd want to keep your professional name. Do you think we—do I have another chance?"

I smiled, placing my hands on either side of his beloved face, savoring our nearness—nearness I'd longed for most of my life—my heart too full to speak, wishing only that Stephen would stop talking. He opened his mouth to speak again, and I placed my fingers over his lips, but it did no good.

"Rosaline? Tell me, please. How does that sound to you?"

"Like music." And I laughed for joy.

If anything more was thought or spoken in those loveliest of moments, I don't remember.

Epilogue

OCTOBER 1943

When Ruth called a mandatory, unscheduled meeting of the Ladies of the Lake in the fall of 1943, we gladly and eagerly complied, assuming it was to celebrate our mutual fiftieth birthday year.

We were all ready for a celebration. The year found the United States and Canada among the Allies firmly entrenched in WWII with no clear end in sight. My dear friend and lifetime writing mentor, Lucy Maud Montgomery, to whom I'd confessed all and with whom I'd found new growth through letters, had died at home in her bed the year before. Her letters in those last years of life revealed something of my friend's struggles with depression and surely would have revealed more had I been better able to read between the lines. Her death left a decided hole in my life, and yet I believe Stephen was the only one who knew, who fully understood my loss.

Stephen and I had not waited one month after our reunion to marry. I was never sorry for the rush—not for one minute.

We lived but half a mile from Bernadette and Charles. Bernadette taught English Literature at Lakeside until the birth of their first child. From then on, she—and we—were consumed with the joys of young Addie's infancy, and later, that of young Marcus.

Growing older with my husband was like living in a secret garden. Our scars and Stephen's missing limb were visible, but each morning we opened our eyes in thanksgiving to a new world, one of hope, of quiet joy and contentment.

Together we'd created a peaceful home and carved a sanctuary in our backyard garden, a place where Bernadette and Charles weekly joined us, a welcome retreat from their busy world and one where their young children experienced the wonder and discovery of growing things, of life unfolding.

Our lives were not perfect. There were times, especially within the last couple of years, that Stephen struggled more to breathe, evidently long-term effects of the mustard gas poisoning he'd received during the Great War. I worried over him, but he refused to entertain worry. We'd learned the value of not wasting a moment of today for fear of what tomorrow might bring.

At fifty, Dorothy was still the grande dame of Lakeside Ladies Academy with no plan to terminate her tenure. The school ran like clockwork under her direction, Jonas always at her back or by her side. New programs flourished and the school's reputation ranked second to none.

Dot saw that the intended Adelaide MacNeill Memorial Gymnasium was completed in 1937, though it was only ever known to the Ancients and the public as the Ladies of the Lake Auditorium.

Between 1939 and 1943, Dot and Jonas took in seven refugee youngsters from London, sheltering them from incessant German bombing, providing their young charges with every ounce of love and opportunity any child forced far from home could possibly wish for. Unanimously, and to Dot's delight, the children dubbed them

Mother and Father Meyer. I'd never seen my friend busier, or more fulfilled, except in those moments when she doted on Bernadette's little ones as if they were her own grandniece and grandnephew.

At forty-three Susannah had become a grandmother for the first time. For years she'd rolled her eyes and disparaged women who talked nonstop about their grandchildren, doting over every picture. She became just like them, queen among them. Through the years we'd all received annual professional sepia-toned portraits of her growing brood of darlings and frequent black-and-white photographs taken with her Brownie box camera. By the time Susannah turned fifty, each of the Ladies of the Lake possessed three full albums of her sweethearts.

Despite those joys and all the outward trappings of success, Susannah's life at home was lonely. Politics and travel had all but stolen her husband, ever the social and political climber. Our friend was more than glad to escape her North Carolina home and political wifely duties to spend a week in our company.

To say we were proud of our Ruth was an understatement. At the height of her career and on her fiftieth birthday, she'd retired, much to our surprise, for she loved her work. The year before, she'd been awarded the Lifetime Achievement Award for Social Work from the Canadian School of Medicine, a regal ceremony Stephen and I had proudly attended along with Portia and Silas. It had been pure bliss to spend time with Portia again, to see her happy and reigning supreme in her own home with her husband who loved her.

Susannah had sent a request to Her Majesty, the Queen of England, Buckingham Palace, London, asking that she send a signed congratulatory card to Ruth. She sent the same request to Prime Minister William Lyon Mackenzie King at Laurier House in Sandy Hill. To the surprise of everyone but Susannah, congratulatory letters on official engraved letterhead arrived for Miss Ruth Hennessey. Our glowing Ruth had them matted and framed.

Before our meeting, I fully anticipated Ruth's revelation of some new and exciting globe-trotting adventure—or her intention once the war ended, whenever that might be. I was only glad she was too old for nursing at the front. *Caution* was not a word our friend seemed well acquainted with.

October 2 finally arrived. A chilly, gray morning gave way to brilliant blue skies and warm sunshine, a perfect fall day for which New England was famous. It was easy for Dot and me to arrange a special tea for our gazebo meeting, both of us living within a few miles of Lakeside.

Susannah and I had wanted to meet Ruth at the station, but she insisted that she would make her own arrangements—she'd learned to drive and was renting a car and would meet us at the lake at precisely three o'clock on October 2, before the first red maple leaf fell. That was our Ruth, ever our leader, and we fell into line.

Susannah fussed over the tea table and chairs, which she'd ordered Dot to have hauled down from the academy. "We're too old to sit on the floor or hard benches now, and I'm so excited we'll be together that without a table I'm likely to spill my tea." Susannah had turned into an anxious woman. But she was right. We'd reached the table-and-chairs stage of life; no more sitting cross-legged on the floor or straddling the railings.

I set out the cherry almond scones Susannah had ordered, ones Bernadette had kindly offered to bake for us. It was dear old Mrs. Potts's recipe from when we were girls. Dot arranged a platter of cucumber sandwiches and the last of the season's small tomatoes stuffed with chicken salad. We'd brewed tea at home, kept piping hot in a thermos, and poured just enough to warm a dainty pot. We'd wait to pour until Ruth arrived.

The academy's clock bonged 3:00.

"Well?" Susannah raised her eyebrows.

"She'll be along, you know that," Dot admonished. "Ruth is never late."

"Unless something's happened."

"Don't start, Susannah. You know how the trains are these days. Troop movements take precedence. She could have been delayed. Let's just enjoy the day."

The clock bonged 3:15. Susannah heaved a deep breath.

"Patience," Dot ordered.

A bright red motorcar pulled to a stop at the top of the hill. "There."

But we all stared. Bright red was not a color any of us could imagine conservative, professional Ruth Hennessey driving.

A woman stepped out of the car—a woman with Ruth's height but not her girth. A woman with a cane . . . and wearing a white turban. We stared. I squinted, uncertain. Sometimes my one eye deceived me, and I needed to look again.

Dot was first up the hill, meeting Ruth, taking her arm, as if nothing stood amiss. Susannah was on her other side in less than a moment more. I met them halfway, unable to take in what I was seeing. "Ruth?"

"Addie. Rosaline." She smiled, a little breathless.

"Addie is fine, my friend. My dear and precious friend." I took her in my arms and hugged her long and gently. She'd wasted so thin, so very thin and frail. I felt the bones of her spine, the blades of her shoulders.

"Why didn't you tell us?" Susannah scolded.

"I'm telling you now . . . showing you now." Ruth spoke evenly. "Help me to the gazebo. I need to sit down."

We did as she bid, but the walk downhill was exhausting for her, even with our help. I didn't want to think about the walk uphill.

We gave Ruth the best chair, the one with the view of the lake, surrounded by mature red maple trees, their scarlet leaves set aflame in the afternoon sun.

"I've dreamed of this . . . this place, this day, of being here with you—all of you." Ruth drew a deep breath, a sigh of contentment, a note of achievement.

"Tell us," Dot said. "What's being done?"

"We tried some experimental treatments, based on the very best research available."

"And?"

"They didn't work." She hesitated. "So little is really known, you see." Ruth smoothed the lines of her fashionable skirt.

I didn't see. I wanted to rail at the heavens. *No! We've all come so far, Lord. Give us time—time with one another. Don't take Ruth—not like this!*

Ruth looked me in the eye, as if she could read my thoughts. "'Naked came I out of my mother's womb, and naked shall I return thither: the Lord gave, and the Lord hath taken away; blessed be the name of the Lord.'"

Please, God. Not like this!

"How long?" Susannah asked the question no one else dared to ask.

"Two months. Possibly three. Or less."

"Stay with me, with Stephen and me. You will have your own room. Our garden is just outside glass doors. There's a scarlet maple there, too—one you'd love—and a holly tree, with bright red berries." I would have babbled on, but Ruth shook her head.

"I've already made my arrangements. I'm registered for home care when I return."

"But you need to be with people who love you, who know and care about you. You need to be with us—with me," I all but pleaded.

"I'm with you now. This is how I want to remember you . . . how I want you to remember me. This is what makes me happy, what I'll take with me." Ruth raised her head, her voice, and brooked no dissent.

Finally, Susannah whispered, "'Strength and honour are her clothing; and she shall rejoice in time to come.'"

We held our breath, a collective willingness not to cry, until Dot took up the Scripture we'd learned as girls: "'She openeth her mouth with wisdom; and in her tongue is the law of kindness.'"

I could not keep the tremor from my voice, but I spoke with a full heart. "'Many daughters have done virtuously, but thou excellest them all.'"

Together, Dot, Susannah, and I quoted, "'Favour is deceitful, and beauty is vain: but a woman that feareth the Lord, she shall be praised.'"

We formed a circle of hands around the table, the four of us finishing together, "'Give her the fruit of her hands; and let her own works praise her in the gates.'"

Our hands still clasped, still clinging to one another, Ruth prayed, "Forgive us our faults and failings, Lord, the things we've done or said that have brought hurt to one another or to anyone else in this life. Raise us up to be voices for You, for Your honor and glory. Until we meet again in Your Kingdom, Father, give me courage for the days ahead, and keep my sisters safe within the hollow of Your hand. Through Jesus Christ our Lord, amen."

"Amen."

Susannah poured tea. The artfully arranged scones and sandwiches lay beautiful but forgotten on our platters. We talked, chattering with the strength God gave us in the moment, for Ruth.

Ruth wanted to know everything about our lives, every detail, and we offered all we could, but fatigue clearly took its toll on our friend. I glanced at Dot and saw that she shared my concern. We'd need a wheeled chair to take Ruth up the hill. We'd need Stephen or Jonas to drive her to our home or the hotel or wherever she insisted on going.

By four the light had begun to fade and a chill set in the air.

Dot stood. "I'm just going to nip up the hill for a wheeled chair. I won't be a minute."

Ruth didn't object but laid a hand on Dot's wrist. "Before you go, let's give our pledge. Help me stand, Addie."

Once we were on our feet, Ruth said, "I want you to all promise me—not in blood this time—" she tried to smile and failed—"but with all your heart and soul."

"Anything," Susannah swore.

"You'll continue meeting together, supporting one another."

"How can we—?"

"You'll still be Ladies of the Lake. You'll need each other, and I need to know you are there for one another. Promise me. Swear it!"

I set my hand in the middle of our circle. Years ago, I'd been the first to pull back; it was only fitting that I should be the first to pledge now. One by one my sisters added their hands and their pledge, until Ruth topped us all.

"All for one and one for all!" we vowed, and raising our hands to the sky, this time in prayer and pleading for Ruth and thanksgiving for all we'd known and shared, joined for eternity, we shouted, "We are the Ladies of the Lake!"

A NOTE FROM THE AUTHOR

Women need the friendship, mentoring, companionship, and sisterhood of other women. Relationships between women are beautifully painted in the Bible and in literature.

Consider the close-knit bonds between Ruth and her mother-in-law, Naomi; between Mary, the mother of Jesus, and her older cousin, Elisabeth; between Mary and Martha of Bethany and between the women who stood at the foot of the cross as they watched their Savior die, and as they prepared to minister to His body.

Think of the women characters we've loved through literature, women who stood in the gap for one another or helped each other grow—Diana Barry and Anne Shirley in *Anne of Green Gables*; Meg, Jo, Beth, and Amy—sisters in *Little Women*; Jane Eyre and her mentor Helen Burns in *Jane Eyre*; Addie and Portia in this story, as well as our Ladies of the Lake, Addie, Dot, Ruth, and Susannah.

Such bonds are precious and can prove life-sustaining through hard times. Who, besides your sister or best friend—your sister of the heart—will tell you the truth, even when it hurts, will rejoice with you over the smallest victory, will stand with you through hard times when all others desert, and is ready to take your phone call even in the dead of night?

Friendships require honesty, trust, nurturing, investments of time and means, and sometimes sacrifice. Often deep friendships are formed during our growing years, as were those of Addie, Dot, Ruth, and Susannah.

Proverbs tells us that "iron sharpeneth iron." The best friendships don't try to conform to the pattern of one, but each encourages strengths in the other while helping to soften rough edges. We are better together than alone.

Especially blessed are those able to maintain close friendships even when time, distance, family, work, or life circumstances draw them far from each other.

But as the Ladies of the Lake learn, even the closest of friendships can be sorely tested. Jealousy, misunderstandings, competition, bullying, secrets, lies, shame, arguments—any number of things can fray relationships or completely tear them apart. It takes great humility and great love to say, "I'm sorry. I was wrong. Can we begin anew?" In the case of Addie, Dot, Ruth, and Susannah, it takes many years and requires that each of them confess the role they played in the destruction of their friendship.

Most fallings-out are not pitted against a backdrop as dramatic as WWI and the prejudice Ruth feels against the Meyer family for the death of her brother when the *Lusitania* is bombed by a German torpedo. Rarely does one friend simply disappear, as does Addie in allowing her friends to believe that she died in the Halifax Explosion. More often disagreements or vindictiveness come because of something more common, like jealousy, as in Dot's anger and secret spite when Stephen's affections turn toward Addie rather than herself. Friendships can simply slide to the back burner of neglect when life, work, family, or distance intervene, as in the case of Susannah caught up in her climb up the social ladder and in the raising of her family.

Despite their good intentions to remain close, each young woman plays a part in the failure of their friendship pact, and each middle-aged woman plays a needed part in seeking forgiveness, reconciliation, and in taking steps to tangibly demonstrate a path forward that they might travel together.

The gem is that although each one needs to step out of her comfort zone and confess things she would prefer to forget, each one knows that in the long run, her discomfort will be worth it, for herself, for her sister friends, for those who observe their relationships, and for the generations that will follow. Thankfully, for Bernadette's sake as well as her own, Addie realizes that our roles in life are not solitary but are intertwined.

At one time or another we have all been blessed with mentors or role models, and we are or will be blessed with the privilege of providing that gift to others.

I'm still learning from friendship lessons I observed in my mother and her relationships with other women over many years. My mother always made friends easily by being a friend and friendly. That may sound cliché, but she lived out the scriptural admonition to treat others as she wanted to be treated, and to love our neighbor as ourselves—even when the other person is nonresponsive.

My mother turned ninety-five years young during the editing of this book. During her long life she has blessed me with many gifts, among the most precious being her example in living graciously through adversity and in sharing family stories. Some of those stories wove their way into the heart of *Night Bird Calling* and *A Hundred Crickets Singing*. Two more family stories inspired characters in *Ladies of the Lake*.

Like Bernadette, my mother suffered terrible burns as a small child. Barely two years old, she was playing with a new comb—a treasured gift in a poor family—dancing near an open fire when the comb caught fire and burst into flame. Reluctant to let go of her new comb, the fire quickly consumed her hair and clothes, engulfing her in flames.

Doctors didn't know if she'd survive. They believed, if by some miracle she did, she would be blind and never walk. After surgeries, skin grafts, and a hospital stay of three months, my mother proved those doctors wrong on all counts. She walked, saw, went to school, grew up, worked, married, birthed four children, and lived a full life, one marked by strength, dignity, sacrificial love, and service. Like Bernadette, as a child my mother asked if she'd been named Bernice because of her burns. Of course, the answer was no. Her own mother's name was Bertha—like Bertha in this book—so it's safe to assume her name came as a connecting link to her mother.

Throughout her life my mother has done her best to hide her burns through clothing selection and careful makeup, as did Addie/Rosaline. Growing up she was self-conscious but, like Bernadette, did not allow her scars to define her. Sadly, in her nineties, my mother suffered a stroke which left her blind, the one thing she'd feared most in life. Even so, confined to a wheelchair and ultimately to bed, and suffering various degress of forgetfulness and dementia, Mom has remained a stalwart soldier whose faith inspires and whose prayers and occasional wit keep us all going, even in her final days.

Another family story my mother gave me inspired the bullying and suicide of Cal Salley. My grandaunt, May, birthed two sons. The younger son was considered simpleminded. A teen during WWII, other teens ridiculed, bullied, and teased him into believing he would be drafted and sent to war like his older brother and that he'd be forced to face German gunfire, igniting terrible fear in his childlike mind. His mother came home from work one day to find her son dead and hanging in their basement.

Ridicule, hurtful words, and bullying all have consequences, sometimes consequences beyond our imagination, as the girls handing out white feathers learned, as even the Ladies of the Lake learned when they played their prank on Mildred.

Sadly, bullying and vehemence have become unwelcome invaders of our current culture. Political divides in America have spawned anger and unfiltered speech through social media and media outlets—all in the name of individual freedom, freedom of speech, and sometimes righteousness. Words and condemnations are spoken and written for public consumption that previously would have been thought unimaginable to voice. It is as if the words of Jesus to love our neighbor as ourselves have been forgotten.

Lakeside Ladies Academy and some of its activities and rituals are modeled after the history of Miss Porter's School in Farmington, Connecticut. Miss Porter's School was established for girls in 1843 and has been attended by many notable personalities, including Jacqueline Bouvier (Jackie Kennedy Onassis), Dorothy Walker Bush (mother of President George H. W. Bush), and her granddaughter, Dorothy Bush Koch.

As for the Halifax Explosion of December 6, 1917, it occurred in the manner described. Two ships, the Norwegian *Imo*, exiting the harbor while bound for New York to pick up relief supplies before returning to Europe, and the *Mont-Blanc*, a French freighter entering the harbor, loaded to the hilt with munitions and ultimately bound for the war effort in Bordeaux, France, collided in the harbor.

Had there been no munitions aboard the *Mont-Blanc* it might have been considered a routine accident and faded into the pages of history. However, the explosion the two ships created was the most destructive man-made explosion in history prior to the dropping of the atomic bomb on Hiroshima. Many initially believed the Germans had invaded and bombed Halifax, a harbor vital in the war effort.

The Richmond district of Halifax was devastated; nearly all buildings within a half mile were destroyed; to the north, roofs were ripped off and homes destroyed in Africville, where Portia and her family lived; windows fifty miles away were blown out. The blast created a tsunami, swamping Richmond in a thirty-five-foot wave and sending people who had no idea what had just happened flying in all directions—some swept down to the harbor and drowned. On the Dartmouth side of the harbor the tsunami wiped out the homes and community of the Mi'kmaq First Nation, who had lived there for generations.

Between the blast, flying debris, fires, and destroyed buildings, 25,000 people were left without homes or shelter and 9,000 were wounded—many resulting in permanent injuries, including nearly 200 blinded. Nearly 2,000 people were killed, many upon impact. To give an idea of the force of the blast, the anchor shaft belonging to the *Mont-Blanc*, weighing 1,140 pounds, was blown two and a half miles away.

Because so many records were lost, because some bodies were never found or able to be identified, it took a great deal of time to unravel and rethread connections. During that murky time some were said to take advantage of the confusion and reinvent themselves, allowing people to believe they had died in the explosion, while exchanging their identity for a new name. That tidbit of history inspired the idea for Addie to hide away from her friends, take on a new name, and grow into a new identity.

Help from across Nova Scotia, the rest of Canada, and the United States rushed to aid Halifax that very day and from Britain and other countries for a long time to come. So immediate and generous was the medical aid and donation of supplies from Boston that to this day the people of Nova Scotia annually have their Department of Natural Resources scout the province to find the most beautiful evergreen tree and truck it 660 miles to the people of Boston. With ceremony and celebration, Bostonians proudly accept and display the tree in the Boston Common, where it remains lit throughout the Christmas season.

Adversity often seems to bring out the best in people. That was certainly true after the Halifax Explosion. Reading of the outpouring of compassion and generosity at that time reminded me of the generosity, great human kindness, and camaraderie I saw and experienced between Americans and from sympathetic leaders and citizens of other countries to the US after the attacks on 9/11. With all my heart I wish that we could again experience that kind of immediate compassion, friendship, and understanding—without waiting for a devastating event to unite us.

I hope you've enjoyed reading this story of the Ladies of the Lake. I hope it's brought back happy memories of your own growing years and of the gift of dear friendships formed through life. I hope most of all you've found renewed appreciation for your own life and health, for the precious gift we're given each morning when we wake and thank our heavenly Father for another day, for breath, for ears to hear, for eyes to see, and for those we love.

May God bless and keep you.

Until next time, by God's amazing grace,
Cathy Gohlke

I'd love to hear from you. Readers can subscribe to my newsletter and find me at my website, cathygohlke.com, on Facebook at CathyGohlkeBooks, on Goodreads, follow me on Bookbub, and subscribe to my YouTube channel, Book Gems with Cathy Gohlke: Books I Love and Love to Share. Through my website I'm glad to schedule virtual visits with book clubs, schools, churches, or reading groups.

IN GRATITUDE

Books are products of their time and of the gifts of stories received from experience, from research, from those we know and encounter, from those whose knowledge and expertise we seek. They are, most especially, gifts from the inspiration of our heavenly Father, those causes and stories He presses on our hearts that will not let us go.

Special thanks to my husband, Dan Gohlke, for whisking me away for the anniversary dream of a lifetime to the Maritimes of Nova Scotia and particularly to Lucy Maud Montgomery's Prince Edward Island, the setting and home for her fictional heroine Anne Shirley of *Anne of Green Gables*. While there I renewed my love of Montgomery's many books, gained new insights into her life, and developed greater compassion for her struggles with depression and family issues.

In Halifax we toured the Maritime Museum of the Atlantic and learned details of the Halifax Explosion of 1917, its aftermath, and how a grieving town picked up and moved forward, many of them burned, blinded, or injured. The museum bookshop provided a wealth of reading and research material about the explosion, as did the book and gift shop at the Canadian Museum of Immigration at Pier 21. Fairview Lawn Cemetery, where the remains of those unidentified after the explosion are interred (as well as victims of the *Titanic*), was a source of sadness and inspiration, as was the site of Africville, which was destroyed in the explosion, the Halifax Explosion Memorial Bell Tower that sits high atop a hill, the face of the town clock arrested at the moment of impact and left as a memorial, and the beautiful, well-kept Halifax Public Gardens. I am grateful for all these resources and especially for the book that initiated my fascination with the explosion, *The Great Halifax Explosion* by John U. Bacon.

I'm especially grateful to my mother, Bernice Lemons, who has demonstrated throughout her lifetime that our scars do not define us, nor do they keep us from living a full, rich life or from giving unreservedly to others. She inspired the character of Bernadette and so much more.

Many thanks to Natasha Kern, dear friend and wonderful literary agent, who saw beauty in this story from its beginning, and to Stephanie Broene and Sarah Rische, sisters in Christ and Tyndale editors extraordinaire, for championing and helping to shape this process to create a book that speaks my heart. Special thanks to Jackie Nuñez for the brilliant cover design that captures the characters of my story so well and to all the Tyndale Fiction Team for bringing this book to life and readers. I am so blessed to work with each of you!

Thanks to Gayle Roper, wonderful author and dear friend, whose lakeside experiences in Canada with friends gave me the idea for the title of this book, and who has long inspired me through her writing, her wisdom and faithful Christian service, and mentoring of many, including me.

Thanks to my dear family, to the sisters of my heart to whom this book is dedicated for their inspiration, faithful friendship, help, prayers, and constant care, and to dear sisters everywhere who walk beside and encourage me day by day.

I will always be grateful to my uncle, Wilbur Goforth, for reminding me that a sure way to know I am working in the will of God is to ask, "Do I have joy? Is this yoke easy? Is this burden light?" Writing continues to give me joy. Yoked with our Lord Jesus—who guides my steps—I find that writing allows my mind to breathe in fresh ways. Is writing a burden? Sometimes, yes, when I struggle to find the words to convey my heart, but it is a burden I love and one that shines as light in my soul.

Beyond all measure I thank my heavenly Father and Lord Jesus Christ for gifts of hope, life, love, family, and unmerited salvation. Life is precious because of Your love and constant, tender care. Life is joyful in Your presence. May this book become an instrument of hope and healing of relationships that points only to You, for You are the hope we crave, and You are the healing and salvation we all so desperately need.

DISCUSSION QUESTIONS

1. Addie MacNeill, an orphan from Prince Edward Island, finds connection with author Lucy Maud Montgomery and her beloved *Anne of Green Gables* heroine, Anne Shirley. Discuss the similarities and differences in the lives of these PEI girls, how those characteristics influenced their writing as they grew, and what that meant to Addie.

2. Addie is sent away to school while grieving the loss of her parents and faces a new life in a new country. Yet, on the ship bound for Boston, kindly Mrs. Simmons befriends her, focusing on her physical needs of food and companionship, on her emotional needs through inviting Addie to pour out her heart, and on her spiritual needs by reminding her that the Lord loves her and she will never be alone. Have you ever been on the receiving end of such a gift in time of need? Have you ever given such a gift, as Mrs. Simmons did? Please share your experience.

3. As a New Girl, Addie has every reason to hope Mildred Hammond, the Old Girl assigned to mentor her, will be kind and help her assimilate into life at Lakeside. Why does Mildred treat Addie as she does? What do you think of Addie's and her friends' responses to Mildred's treatment? Do any of their responses go too far?

4. When the Great War began, many German American families were treated with distrust and in some cases enmity, like the Meyer family, who had not only lived in and contributed to the community, but believed themselves well liked. Do you see any similarities in the treatment of immigrants today?

5. Augusta and Emma, the girls who distribute white feathers to men and teen boys not yet enlisted, believe they are in the right, proving their patriotism in time of war. What do you think of their actions? Were the headmistress or others in any way responsible for the girls' actions? Was there anything Dorothy or Addie might have done to prevent the tragic outcome for Cal Salley?

6. Grieving the loss of her brother, Ruth insists that Addie and Dorothy terminate their relationship with the Meyer family. Do you understand why she felt as she did? Considering the war and the pledge of the girls to stick by one another, were her demands justified?

7. Addie falls in love with Stephen Meyer even as she knows Dot has always harbored dreams of a life with him. Do you think Stephen and Addie were considerate of Dot's feelings? Could they have done anything differently in that regard? Should they have?

8. For many years, Dot guards her shame over her interference in Stephen and Addie's relationship, even keeping the secret from her husband. How does that secret impact her life and her marriage? Do you agree or disagree with her decisions? Why?

9. After the Halifax Explosion, Addie makes a life-altering decision to change her identity and completely sever herself from her past. Do you understand her reasons for doing so? How do you imagine her life might've unfolded differently if she'd remained Adelaide MacNeill?

10. In her new life, Rosaline loses the friendship of the Ladies of the Lake but finds a friend and sister in Portia, who also suffered deep loss in the explosion. How do the two women support each other? How do they differ in processing their grief? What role does faith play in their relationship?

11. At the moment when the world is opening for Bernadette, she learns the truth of her identity and her relationship to Rosaline. How do you think that knowledge will affect their relationship in years to come?

12. The enduring friendships between the Ladies of the Lake— sisters of the heart—make up the core of this story. Do you have any such deep or long-term friendships of your own? Take a moment to share who they are and what they have meant in your life.

ABOUT THE AUTHOR

Bestselling, Christy Hall of Fame, and Carol and INSPY Award–winning author Cathy Gohlke writes novels steeped with inspirational lessons, speaking of world and life events through the lens of history. She champions the battle against oppression, celebrating the freedom found only in Christ. Cathy has worked as a school librarian, drama director, and director of children's and education ministries. When not traveling to historic sites for research, she and her husband, Dan, divide their time between northern Virginia and the Jersey Shore, enjoying time with their grown children and grandchildren. Visit her website at cathygohlke.com and find her on Facebook at CathyGohlkeBooks; on Bookbub (@CathyGohlke); and on YouTube, where you can subscribe to Book Gems with Cathy Gohlke for short videos of book recommendations. Cathy welcomes invitations to virtual book club meetings through the Contact page of her website.

TYNDALE HOUSE PUBLISHERS
IS CRAZY4FICTION!

Fiction that entertains and inspires

Get to know us! Become a member of the Crazy4Fiction community. Whether you read our blog, like us on Facebook, follow us on Twitter, or receive our e-newsletter, you're sure to get the latest news on the best in Christian fiction. You might even win something along the way!

JOIN IN THE FUN TODAY.

 crazy4fiction.com

 Crazy4Fiction

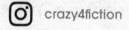 crazy4fiction

 @Crazy4Fiction

CP0021

By purchasing this book from Tyndale, you have

helped us meet the spiritual and physical needs of

people all around the world.